ALSO BY CHRIS CULVER

The Abbey
The Outsider

By
Any
Means

Chris Culver

GRAND CENTRAL
PUBLISHING

NEW YORK   BOSTON

Copyright © 2014 by Chris Culver

Grand Central Publishing
Hachette Book Group
237 Park Avenue
New York, NY 10017

www.HachetteBookGroup.com

Printed in the United States of America

RRD-C

First Edition: insert May 2014
10 9 8 7 6 5 4 3 2 1

Grand Central Publishing is a division of Hachette Book Group, Inc. The Grand Central Publishing name and logo is a trademark of Hachette Book Group, Inc.

The Hachette Speakers Bureau provides a wide range of authors for speaking events. To find out more, go to www.hachettespeakersbureau.com or call (866) 376-6591.

The publisher is not responsible for websites (or their content) that are not owned by the publisher.

ISBN: 978-1-4555-2598-0

LCCN: 2014930521

Even eight months after the Indianapolis Metropolitan Police Department transferred him to the community relations "team," Detective Sergeant Ash Rashid still resented his blue polyester uniform, but even more than the uniform, he resented the lack of a weapon. Going without it felt like driving to work without pants; it was fun at first, but it grew old quickly. He understood the reasoning behind the prohibition—few school assemblies or neighborhood watch meetings ended in gunfire—but he still would have liked to carry one if for no other reason than to compare his firearm to the ones carried by the students in some of the rougher school districts he visited. But as he drove home from a particularly long Q&A session at a meeting on the city's east side, it wasn't a disgruntled community member or an angry student who ruined his day; instead, it was a careless driver who had forcefully introduced the front end of his Mercedes to a telephone pole.

Ash pulled his gray cruiser to a stop approximately fifty feet from the vehicle, groaning as he flicked on the light bar hidden in his car's grill and rear window. With the sun still high and soft in the late afternoon sky, few people would be able to see his lights, but regulations required them for offi-

1

cer safety. They required all sorts of things for officer safety that made little sense. He pulled out a pad of paper from his utility belt and began jotting down the conditions of the scene upon his arrival. The city hadn't received any appreciable rainfall in at least a week, which meant the driver hadn't slipped on water. He must not have been going very fast, either, because the vehicle's airbags hadn't deployed on impact. If nothing else, that would save him a couple grand in repair bills at the expense of some bruising. It was a minor fender bender; unless he was too drunk to stand, he'd walk away from it without issue.

Ash slouched and closed his eyes. Having handled at least half a dozen homicides in the surrounding blocks, he knew the area fairly well even if he hadn't been there for a while. A beat cop had found a corpse stashed amid the weeds on a lot to his left just a couple of weeks ago, and the city's narcotics unit frequently conducted buy-busts in the area. He didn't want to stay there any longer than he had to, so he punched the TALK button on his radio, already dreading the response he would likely receive.

"Control, this is Charlie-thirteen. Please respond."

Charlie designated his unit—community relations—while thirteen indicated his rank, sergeant. The dispatcher wouldn't be able to individuate him by his radio call sign, but she'd have a pretty good idea if she looked him up.

"Charlie-thirteen, this is Dispatch-seventeen. Go ahead."

"Yeah, Seventeen. I've got a single-car collision on Forty-Second near the fairgrounds. It doesn't look serious, so I'd be very grateful if you could send someone by to redirect traffic. I'm on my way home."

"Negative, Charlie-thirteen. All of our officers are tied up right now in an emergency call. Please remain on site until you receive further word."

Ash closed his eyes and pinched the bridge of his nose, hoping to stave off a headache.

"Seventeen, please reevaluate deployment."

"Sorry, Charlie. The swing shift is short tonight. I'll get someone out there as soon as I can."

Ash shook his head and readjusted himself on the seat, feeling his back stick to the warm vinyl.

"You want to tell that to my wife, Seventeen?"

"Negative, Charlie-thirteen. You're on your own."

"That's what I thought."

Ash hung up the microphone and turned the radio to low before fishing his cell phone from his pocket. He called his wife far more often than he did anyone else, so her number occupied the first slot in his address book. It only took a couple of button presses to get her on the phone.

"Hey, honey. Guess whose favorite person is going to be late tonight?"

Hannah paused. "I wouldn't know. My two favorite people are in the living room with me."

She meant their two kids. Ash glanced at a colored-pencil drawing of a police officer on his dashboard that his daughter, Megan, had given to him that morning before he left for work. Now that he wore a uniform every day instead of a detective's suit, she told everybody—stranger or friend—about her police officer father.

"I suppose your third-favorite person is going to be late. Sorry."

"How late? Your sister and Nassir are coming over for *iftar* in a few hours."

Ash's stomach rumbled, reminding him that he hadn't eaten since before sunrise that morning. *Iftar* is the evening meal that breaks a Muslim's fast during Ramadan, and he had been looking forward to it all day. He glanced out his window and noticed a line of cars that had begun to queue on the street, their drivers likely thinking he would open the road and wave them through eventually. Pedestrians, meanwhile, had begun to gather on the porches and stoops of houses nearby.

"I'm not sure. I'll head out as soon as another supervisory officer gets here. Shouldn't be too long."

"Are you close? We're out of dates, so I wanted to go to the grocery store. I'd rather not lug the kids around if I can help it. You know how Megan gets."

Ash knew what she meant; the last time he had taken his daughter to the grocery store, she made beeping noises when an overweight woman backed her cart up in a crowded aisle. Megan laughed, but the overweight woman didn't find it quite that funny. Ash looked around him again, confirming his location with street signs.

"I'm about a block north of the fairgrounds. Once I get moving, it should only take me ten or fifteen minutes to get home."

"Are you sure you're not in a bar?"

Ash didn't like admitting it aloud, but the question had merit. God forbade Muslims from drinking alcohol, and Ash usually managed to avoid it. He had more difficulty on some days than others, though.

"I haven't had a drink in eight months."

"That's what you keep telling me," said Hannah, her voice a little sharp. "Are you sure you're not in a bar?"

"Positive."

"Good," she said, her voice softening to its usual tone. "What are you doing by the fairgrounds? That's a pretty rough neighborhood."

It was a good question, but maybe not for the reason Hannah expected. Off the top of his head, Ash could think of three unsolved homicides and half a dozen assaults that had occurred within five blocks of his present location. That usually kept the tourists away. Moreover, the Mercedes probably cost more than what the average resident of that neighborhood made in five years. The driver might have just been lost, but Ash's curiosity had been piqued.

"Can I call you back?" he asked. "I'm going to check something out."

"Yeah. Give me a call when you figure out when you can come home."

Ash told her that he would before hanging up. As soon as he opened his door, he coughed hard. Indiana didn't have yearly vehicle emission tests like neighboring states, so many of the cars on its streets spewed air so toxic and thick that breathing their exhaust almost hurt. In the middle of summer with its heat and humidity, hell just barely edges out a busy Indianapolis street for most uncomfortable spot in the universe.

He walked toward the Mercedes with his shirtsleeve covering his mouth and nose. The vehicle was a relatively new S550, and its black paint gleamed in the afternoon sun as if it had been freshly waxed. The rear end had neither dents nor dings, so the driver likely hadn't been hit from behind; he went into the pole on his own. No one inside moved. Ash leaned his head to the side and activated the radio on his shoulder.

"Control, this is Charlie-thirteen. Please put Emergency Services on standby. I'm not seeing movement in my car accident."

"Understood, Charlie-thirteen."

Ash walked the rest of the way to the vehicle but paused once he reached the driver-side door. As a veteran police officer and former homicide detective, he had seen things that he'd never stop seeing no matter how long he lived or how hard he tried to forget them. Grisly murders, horrific accidents, truly awful domestic abuse. Weighed against those, the scene inside the Mercedes seemed almost benign, but it still made his stomach turn.

As soon as he looked in the vehicle, two sets of cold, dead eyes greeted his own.

He swallowed the bile that threatened to rise from his gut. The driver had a full head of silver hair, a ruddy complexion, and crow's feet beside his eyes. Blood stained the back of his white Oxford shirt and stippled the vehicle's seats and headliner. His passenger appeared ten to fifteen years younger, but she was equally well dressed. She had platinum-blond hair, and she wore a silk blouse and black pencil skirt. They wore matching wedding rings, and they held hands over the center console. Some of Ash's more crass colleagues would call her a trophy wife, but the fact that they had been holding hands when they died told him she was more than that.

He took a step back from the car and coughed, clearing his throat before engaging the microphone on his shoulder.

"Dispatcher, this is Charlie-thirteen. Cancel my request for EMS. I've got bodies."

* * *

Issues of right notwithstanding, anyone who could afford that Mercedes had little business being in that neighborhood. The owner didn't work there, he didn't live there, and he probably didn't have friends who worked or lived there. Hell, he wouldn't have even had to go there to buy drugs; people who could afford hundred-thousand-dollar cars had dealers who wore suits and ties and made sales calls at work. Those two corpses were there because someone wanted them there.

Within five minutes of his radio request, a pair of patrol vehicles rolled up. Even though he had already completed his shift for the day, Ash controlled the crime scene until a superior officer or detective relieved him, and he intended to hand it off with the evidence still intact. He ordered the two freshly arrived officers to park on either end of the block and reroute traffic to secondary streets. That would piss off the commuters, but it'd protect the integrity of the scene, which, at the moment, came first.

A crowd had begun forming on the sidewalk about half a block north of the police barricade. Most of the bystanders simply talked to each other, but others pointed and stared at the crashed vehicle. Even though Ash doubted he'd get anything out of them, he'd be remiss in his duties if he didn't at least try talking to them, so he grabbed a notebook from his pocket and started walking, counting his steps to see how long it would take for the crowd to disperse. He only got to two, a new record for him. Given the neighborhood, he had anticipated that most of his potential witnesses would shy away from him, but he had expected more of a shuffle than a sprint.

Out of an original crowd of a dozen people, Ash convinced four women to talk. All four wanted to help, but none had seen the Mercedes before or heard about anyone in the neighborhood owning it. Moreover, none claimed to know anyone matching the bodies' descriptions. They couldn't tell him much, but at least they had been cooperative, which was oftentimes all he could ask for. He wrote down their names, phone numbers, and addresses in case the detective who picked up the case wanted to talk to them, but he doubted it would come to that. They didn't know anything.

When Ash arrived at his car again, a green Chevy had parked beside him. Detective Eddie Alvarez sat on the hood, talking excitedly into a cell phone. As soon as he saw Ash, he smiled and nodded a quick greeting. The two detectives were roughly the same age, but Alvarez had joined the Peace Corps after college, delaying his entry to the department until his late twenties. He didn't have a lot of experience yet, but from what Ash had heard, he worked hard to learn the nuances of the job. If he kept it up, he'd be a good detective one day.

"It's good to still see you with a badge," said Alvarez, shaking Ash's hand and taking in the scene with an extended glance. "I thought you might quit after Susan Mercer transferred you."

Ash grunted. Before joining the Community Relations team, he had been an investigator assigned to the prosecutor's office, and Susan had been his boss. Their relationship had become strained over the years, but he still considered her a damn good supervisor and the best prosecutor the city ever had. Unfortunately, barring divine intervention in the county election cycle, she'd be gone in another six months and a morally retarded gasbag would take her place. Democracy sucks sometimes.

"You didn't take into account my aversion to being homeless and my complete lack of real job skills."

"I guess I didn't," said Alvarez, motioning toward the Mercedes with his chin. "So what do you have for me?"

Ash flipped through his notebook to the correct page.

"I pulled up to the scene at a little after four and found two bodies, one male and one female, in the Mercedes. I didn't open the door because both victims were clearly gone when I arrived, but I saw a significant quantity of blood on both victims' clothes as well as throughout the vehicle's interior. I've closed off the streets and kept everyone away from the car, so you should have a fresh scene."

Alvarez shot his eyes to the remnants of the crowd Ash had just visited.

"Any witnesses?"

"None helpful. Four young women talked to me, but none saw anything. I've got their names and contact info if you want to follow up."

"You think they're solid citizens?"

He wanted to know if they were part of the drug trade, and honestly Ash couldn't say. He doubted it, though; drug dealers rarely talk to the police except when forced.

"Probably. They just didn't know anything."

Alvarez nodded and stepped toward the Mercedes. When

he saw the bodies through the front window, he made the sign of the cross over his chest and closed his eyes. Ash turned away, giving the detective a moment of privacy. A lot of newbies to the homicide squad go quiet and stay that way for a long time when they see their first few victims. Ash drank; Alvarez prayed. Outward signs of religiosity probably violated some esoteric department rule, but Ash didn't plan to report him. Besides, Alvarez wouldn't have changed even with a formal complaint against him. When Eddie and his wife found out that Ash was a Muslim, she sent him a copy of the Bible with every word in the New Testament highlighted. Someone willing to do that wouldn't change because a rule required him to. As long as his faith didn't affect his work, Ash didn't care. It wasn't his business.

"You got any thoughts on this?" Alvarez asked upon opening his eyes.

Ash hesitated to voice his opinion. Alvarez needed to develop the ability to take in the crime scene himself and form his own opinions. Only then should he compare those opinions with those of other investigators. Still, he hadn't worked that many homicides solo yet; maybe he needed a jump start.

"We don't have a lot yet. First, your victims don't belong in the neighborhood, obviously, so you'll have to figure out why they're here. Second, you'll have to deal with the locals, which isn't easy because they don't really like us here. Third, you can't see the backseat well, but I think there's going to be some blood—"

"Detective!" It was one of the uniformed patrol officers rerouting traffic at the end of the street. He waved his arms at them frantically. "You need to hear this."

"Can it wait?" shouted Alvarez.

"No."

Alvarez shook his head and scowled. "We'll continue this conversation in a minute," he said, already walking toward the officer. Ash followed a few steps behind. The patrolman's face had whitened several shades since Ash had last seen him, and his breath came low and slow.

"What's wrong?" asked Alvarez.

"The dispatcher just played me a nine-one-one call about a car accident that you need to hear."

"We're here, so roll it."

The patrolman leaned into his car and requested that the dispatcher replay the recording. Even though the volume had been turned high, Ash had to strain his ears to hear. The recording sounded distant and scratchy, making the voices difficult to understand. The caller sounded like a woman, though, and from what Ash could piece together, she had just come across a car that had run into a light pole. Assuming she had called about the Mercedes, they could use the time of her phone call to establish a timeline if nothing else. Ash almost stepped back, but then the woman's voice changed pitch and quickened.

"Someone just got out of the back. He has blood on his shirt and he's bleeding from his leg. We need an ambulance." Ash held his breath. The dispatcher warned the caller to remain in her vehicle until a patrol officer could arrive, but she didn't listen. She unbuckled her seat belt with an audible click and then bobbled her phone as she opened the door.

Don't do this. Get back in your car.

Ash felt his heart rate increase as the pitch changed in

the caller's voice. The world around him seemed to disappear.

"The police are on their way. Do you need my help? I'm a nurse."

Her voice sounded tinny and distant. She must have been holding her phone away from her face.

"Get in the car."

"I'm just trying to—"

Something, a body part likely, thumped against the car, and the caller grunted. Her phone clattered to the ground.

"I said get in the car."

Ash couldn't decipher what happened next, but it sounded like someone might have kicked the phone. He then heard shoes shuffling across the asphalt and a series of high-pitched gasps followed by a few heavy thuds. The gasps shifted into guttural but still feminine grunts, and Ash found his hand covering his mouth before he realized it had moved. The scuffle ceased after that, and the car's door opened again, beeping intermittently. The dispatcher said something, but Ash couldn't understand the words over the roar of the car's engine.

Silence momentarily hung around the patrol vehicle as the recording finished. When Ash's breath caught up with him, he brought his hand to the top of the cruiser's door to keep from falling. He spoke before anyone else.

"Damn."

2

Twenty minutes. The phone call had come in twenty minutes ago. As soon as the initial shock faded, Ash pictured a map of the area in his head and mentally drew a ring around their search zone. The major roadways would have been clogged, minimizing the chance the shooter had left town. If the department moved fast and got lucky, they could find him before he killed their Good Samaritan. He glanced at Alvarez, expecting the detective to start barking orders, but he hadn't moved. Ash decided to give him a moment to think.

"Why didn't we have this earlier?" he asked, glancing at the patrol officer.

"The dispatcher only had the location of the cell tower the call came from. She mobilized as many officers as she could to search, but she didn't know where to send people. By the time I found the phone—"

"Wait a minute," said Ash, holding up his hand. "You have the victim's phone?"

"Uh, yeah," he said, reaching into his vehicle and picking up a scuffed cell phone with a cracked screen. "I found it on the sidewalk."

Ash closed his eyes and counted to five to keep from snapping at him.

"When the team from the forensics lab arrives, give them the phone and tell them exactly where you picked it up. Our victim fought with her attacker, so the phone might have his prints on it. After that, call the dispatcher and request that she send someone to relieve you because you're going back to your precinct and writing a report about why you picked up evidence barehanded at a crime scene."

The officer straightened. "I didn't know what it was. It was just there, so I picked it—"

"I don't care," said Ash, interrupting him again. "Write it down and put it in a report. The prosecutor's office will want to know why your prints are on evidence collected at the scene, and I don't want to see you right now. Got it?"

"Yes, sir."

"Good."

For most of his career, Ash had been on the receiving end of reprimands like that, so it felt strange to give one. Despite the momentary reprieve, Alvarez's mouth still hung open and his face appeared gray. He almost looked like a statue.

"We need help, and we need it right now," said Ash.

Alvarez shook his head and took a step back, running his fingers through his wavy black hair.

"I don't know... I..."

Ash remained silent for another moment, hoping Alvarez would get himself together. He stood there with his mouth agape, continuing to shake his head in disbelief.

"Fine," said Ash. "Call your lieutenant and tell him that we need as many people down here as we can get. Use cadets in the police academy if you have to, but I want checkpoints on every road leading out of town, I want officers knocking on every door in the neighborhood, and I want more detectives down here now."

Ash motioned two uniformed officers near the crime scene's perimeter toward them. They jogged over, and he pointed at the first to arrive. "I need you to find out who our nine-one-one caller is and what she drives." He looked at the second uniform. "And I need you to call every hospital and clinic in the area and tell them to be on the lookout for someone with a puncture or gunshot wound to his leg. Our victim said the man who abducted her was bleeding from his leg. If our suspect comes by, I want him taken into custody. Got it?"

The patrol officers nodded and then ran back to their cruisers, but Alvarez remained stationary.

"Move."

Alvarez flinched and then started making calls. Ash's heart thudded against his breastbone, so he closed his eyes and counted to ten, hoping to calm it. His instincts screamed at him to run, as if doing so would somehow help the situation, so he had to force his mind to focus. With the entire patrol division on the lookout, they'd have a fair chance of finding their victim as soon as they got the make, model, and color of her car, but none of that would help if their perp ditched his car for another. In that case, they'd need to be able to track him down, and to do that they needed to discover everything they could about him, starting with the identity of his first victims.

While Alvarez called his boss, Ash called IMPD's dispatcher and read the Mercedes's license plate number. After some typing, the dispatcher informed him that the vehicle had been registered to Commonwealth Financial Services of Carmel, Indiana. A name would have been better, but they could work with a company; when backup arrived, Ash planned to send someone over there to roust information from their office.

To minimize the risk of contaminating evidence, department regulations forbade anyone but the coroner from touching a body at a crime scene, and as much as Ash wanted to dig through his victims' pockets for ID, it wouldn't be worth it. It also wouldn't be fair. Alvarez's lieutenant would assign a more senior detective to the case and send Ash packing for the evening; he had no right to make someone else's job harder just to satisfy his own curiosity. He paced near the Mercedes, trying and failing to see anything new through its windows. If there was something to find, they'd have to wait.

Given the circumstances, Ash expected a senior officer to arrive and relieve Alvarez, so it didn't surprise him when Captain Mike Bowers drove up. Bowers, the recently promoted supervisor of the entire Crimes Against Persons division, immediately began talking to Alvarez near the detective's cruiser, but he stopped and looked at Ash twice during the conversation. Eventually, he flagged him over.

"Eddie says you're calling the shots."

Ash glanced at Alvarez but couldn't get a read on him. They didn't need a fight over control of the case; their Good Samaritan didn't have time for internal police politics.

"I was the first on the scene, but it's Detective Alvarez's case. I stepped in, but I shouldn't have. I apologize."

"That's not—" began Alvarez.

"You probably shouldn't have, but you did," Bowers interrupted, his expression dour. "You also kept things moving. What would you do next?"

"It's not my place to make those calls."

"Forget your fake humility, Rashid," said Bowers. "If this were your case, what would you do next?"

He glanced at Alvarez again. The detective nodded slightly for him to continue.

"We need information more than anything else. I've already asked an officer to find out who our nine-one-one caller was and what she was driving. If we get that information to patrol quickly enough, someone might get lucky and spot our perp before he ditches his car or kills our victim. In addition, I'd send somebody to Carmel to talk to the company who owns that Mercedes. They might be able to tell us who our shooter is."

Bowers considered for a moment. "I can't help with the Mercedes, but the nine-one-one caller's name is Rebecca Cook, and she drives a red Toyota Camry that she bought new last year. I've already notified patrol."

Why ask for my opinion, then?

"It sounds like you've got things in hand."

"So far. Greg Doran and Tim Smith are coming in from the Aggravated Assault unit, but I need someone who knows what's going on to take point. Is your CO still Aleda Tovar?"

Ash hadn't expected the question, so he paused to think before answering. "Lieutenant Tovar, yeah."

"You have anything pressing going on in Community Relations?"

"I'm scheduled to visit second-grade classrooms all week. It's part of the DARE program."

"Anybody else who can do that in your unit?"

Ash shrugged. "Probably."

"Good," said Bowers. "I'll call Aleda and ask that she temporarily transfer you to my command."

"Why?"

Bowers scowled and crossed his arms. "I hope you're not fishing for a compliment, Rashid."

"I'm not," said Ash. "I'm just not sure what you expect me to do. I give presentations in elementary schools and coordinate neighborhood watch programs now."

"I don't care what unit you're in. You're a good detective, you've got a face the media knows, and you've got sergeant's stripes," said Bowers. "You're taking point with this investigation. No arguments. I'm going to notify Rebecca's family about what's going on before it hits the news."

Bowers started toward his car, but Ash put a hand on his shoulder before he could leave.

"I'll do it, but if I'm in charge, I should be the one to notify the Cooks."

"You sure?"

"If I'm running this investigation, the victim's family needs to know me. I don't want them going on the news later because they think we're keeping them out of the loop," said Ash, looking at Alvarez. "Alvarez can run the scene here. He knows what to do."

Bowers looked from Alvarez to Ash and back before nodding.

"Let's go."

It felt as if every neuron in Ash's brain had fired at once, compelling him to run in fifty different directions simultaneously. He needed someone from the forensics lab to check the Mercedes for blood or fiber evidence that might individuate the shooter, he needed someone from the coroner's office to check the victims, he needed officers from patrol to start knocking on doors, and he needed a media liaison for the inevitable onslaught of reporters. Already he felt a weight pressing down on his chest. It was probably nothing compared to what Rebecca, their victim, felt.

As soon as Ash strapped himself into Bowers's car, the captain floored the accelerator.

"Do Doran and Smith know I'm in charge of the case?"

Bowers shook his head. That would make things difficult. About a year and a half ago, Doran and Smith investigated one of Ash's former partners, Olivia Rhodes, for corruption. They were right about her, but things got messy before her arrest and Ash did some things he probably shouldn't have. The situation hadn't endeared him to either man.

While Bowers drove, Ash called both detectives. He ordered Smith to work the scene with Alvarez, pound on doors, and roust the neighbors. Doran, meanwhile, would coordinate the search for Rebecca's car with the Indiana State Police and IMPD's patrol division. Within fifteen minutes, every sworn officer within a sixty-mile radius would be on the lookout. Hopefully that'd be enough.

Ash leaned back in his seat, watching as the scenery changed around them and feeling the unease build in his stomach.

"You look tired," said Bowers, pulling his vehicle to a stop at a light.

"It's Ramadan. I've been up since five this morning."

"Are you going to be tired every day, then?"

"I can handle it."

Bowers nodded as the light shifted to green.

"What does Ramadan entail?"

"I fast during the day and eat and drink only before sunrise and after sunset. If I'm on a case, though, I can do what I need to do and make it up later."

He had left out the most important aspects of Ramadan, but Bowers didn't want to hear about the spiritual side of the month. He wanted to make sure Ash could still do the job, which wouldn't be a problem. God grants dispensations to the elderly and infirm, travelers, pregnant women, and children, allowing them to avoid fasting during Ramadan. God also grants a dispensation to those who are exhausted and can no longer continue without eating or drinking. If he absolutely needed a drink or something to eat, he could have something and then fast an additional day at the end of the month. It wouldn't be a problem.

The answer must have satisfied Bowers because he didn't ask any more questions, giving Ash a moment to call his wife and tell her that he had caught a case. She wished him luck and said she'd pray for everybody involved. About ten silent minutes after the phone call, Bowers stopped the car in front of a two-story craftsman home a couple of blocks from Butler University. The leaves from several nearby trees rustled in a warm breeze as Ash opened his door. A small, pink bike leaned against a light post in the front lawn and chalk drawings of flowers and houses adorned the sidewalks. Rebecca had at least one daughter, evidently.

"As far as we know, she's still alive," said Bowers. "That's the story we need to stick to until we hear otherwise."

"I agree."

Despite the reassurances, Ash couldn't shake the feeling that Rebecca was already dead. Both officers started for the house, but before they even made it halfway, the home's front door opened and a little girl emerged. She wore a pink shirt, blue jeans, and tennis shoes. As soon as she saw the two men on her front walkway, she ran back into the house. Within moments, an older man with fluffy white hair, big meaty jowls, and a smile walked through the door.

"Can I help you?"

"Do you know Rebecca Cook?" asked Bowers.

"I'm her father," he said, his eyebrows arched. "What's going on?"

"Can we come inside, sir?" asked Bowers. "We need to talk."

The man took a step back and started to hold up his hands as if he were going to resist, but then the smile slipped from his face and the humor left his eyes. Ash saw the same look nearly every time he did a next-of-kin notification. He took a step forward and gestured toward the house, trying to make his voice as soothing and calm as he could.

"Please, sir, Captain Bowers is right. We need to talk inside."

The man's shoulders hunched and the color ran from his face. He looked like a balloon that had just popped.

"Come in."

He turned toward the house, his eyes never leaving the ground. Once they were inside, Rebecca's husband, her father, and her mother gathered around a table in the kitchen. Ash and Bowers sat across from them, their backs to an unadorned beige wall. Rebecca's family had hung drawings and art projects on the fridge, while photographs of vacations and framed portraits of two little girls in matching plaid jumpers adorned the walls. It looked like a loving, stable home; even after well over a decade in uniform, that never ceased to bother Ash. Out of everyone in the world, the worst tragedies always seemed to befall the people least deserving of it.

Bowers introduced himself and Ash, after which Rebecca's father, Jonathan Reid, introduced Rebecca's mother, Francis, and her husband, Scott. Scott put the kids in the basement so the adults could talk without interruption; the family would tell the kids what happened later, hopefully with a counselor or other professional present who could help explain things in language understandable to children.

"Before we say anything, we need to ask you a couple of questions to make sure we're at the right house," said Bowers. "Can you tell me what Rebecca does for a living?"

"She is a school nurse with IPS," said her husband. He looked at his father-in-law and then at the table. "I'm, uh...I'm in college."

That helped explain the living arrangements at least. With her husband in school, money was probably pretty tight. Rebecca was lucky to have parents who could still take her family in.

"Your wife carried a red cell phone, correct?"

"Yeah," he said, clearing his throat. "I got it for her last year so we could stay in touch. It wasn't fancy—just a cell phone."

"Did she ever loan it out to anyone?" asked Ash.

Scott shook his head. "Never."

Ash looked at Bowers knowingly.

"I'm deeply sorry to tell you this," said Bowers. "But Mrs. Cook has been involved with an incident."

Bowers led them through the story as they knew it. The family took it stoically until the end. Then Rebecca's mother buried her face in her hands and sobbed. Jonathan put his arm across his wife's shoulder and reached for his son-in-law. They hugged at the table, while Jonathan whispered that it would be okay.

Ash couldn't remember wanting a drink that badly in a long time.

* * *

The two police officers left the house fifteen minutes later, Rebecca having become more than a name on a police report for both of them. She had two children, a loving mother and father, and a devoted spouse. Despite the relatively low salary, she worked as a school nurse in the Indianapolis Public School system and volunteered twice a week at an after-school program for impoverished children. With decent, benefits-paying jobs scarce and an economy yet to recover for many working-class families, Rebecca and a volunteer physician provided what might have been the only non-emergency care children in the program received.

Ash knew what it felt like to struggle to pay the bills, to miss his kids because he had to work overtime just to make ends meet, to work himself ragged so his family could have the things they deserved. Not only had Rebecca done all that, but she had also volunteered to help others who badly needed it. No one deserved to be the victim of a crime, but it seemed especially wrong when it happened to someone like her.

Ash checked his messages as Bowers drove them back to the crime scene. A patrol officer had found Rebecca's Toyota abandoned in the parking lot of a shuttered strip mall on the city's east side, but, despite having every squad car in the neighborhood on alert, no one had found her yet. Meanwhile, Detective Doran had called a van from the forensics lab to check out the car, but they hadn't been there long enough to find anything. Ash made a mental note to call him back for another update in a few minutes.

In addition to his message from Doran, Ash had two messages from Kristen Tanaka, a reporter with one of the local television stations. She had an uncanny ability to scoop every other news organization in the city on crime stories, mostly because she'd do anything with anyone if it enabled her to get a story. Someone had told her about Rebecca's abduction, and she wanted to know if Ash had any comment before she went live with it on the six o'clock news.

The message galled him for a number of reasons, not the least of which was the sheer fact that someone was irresponsible enough to leak the story. Their hostage taker had already killed two people, so he had shown himself capable of violence. For all anybody knew, putting his story on TV might push him over the edge again and cause him to kill Rebecca.

He called Tanaka back. He had known she had high-placed sources, but he hadn't known how good they were until that moment. She knew everything he did, and a little more. He pleaded with her to sit on her story until they found more information, but she refused even when he offered her an exclusive interview. She said she didn't need an exclusive interview, which made sense considering she could find out everything she wanted on her own. If he couldn't change her mind, he'd just have to deal with the situation as it came to him.

Bowers dropped Ash off near his cruiser about fifteen minutes after leaving Rebecca's house. The sun had dropped a couple of degrees, lengthening the shadows cast by nearby houses and trees and lowering the temperature. Despite the minor reprieve from the heat, the air still felt sticky and tasted acidic. Normally, that would have made Ash perspire through his uniform, but no sweat formed on his brow. His head pounded as well. Dehydration wouldn't be enjoyable, but he could fight through it. The other officers on the scene, though, shouldn't have to. He signed the log sheet maintained by a uniformed officer on the scene's periphery and gave twenty bucks to another uniformed officer so he could buy a couple cases of bottled water from a nearby convenience store.

The investigative team had made fair progress in Ash's absence but had yet to remove the Mercedes. He found out why upon walking toward it and finding Assistant Coroner Hector Rodriguez leaning inside the backseat. Dr. Rodriguez had black hair that had only recently begun graying and a skin tone somewhere between olive and brown. Ash had seen a lot of women—and a few men—from the police department and prosecutor's office try to flirt with him, but Rodriguez barely seemed to notice. At work, he had eyes only for the dead.

"It's good to see you, Detective Rashid," he said upon noticing Ash's arrival. "I couldn't find an ID on either of them, so don't bother asking."

"What do you have?" asked Ash, crouching beside him.

"Couple of things, maybe," said Rodriguez. "Were the doors and windows all closed when you arrived?" Ash nodded. "It looks like our shooter blasted them from the backseat, then. At that range, we'd usually see the victim's brain on the front window. Since we don't have anything, our perp used something with a pretty low muzzle velocity, like a twenty-two." He made a gun motion with his hand and pointed it at the female victim on the front seat. "If he held his gun to her head and fired, it would have enough power to penetrate the back of her skull but not enough to break through the bones in front. Instead, the round would ricochet like a steel ball inside a pinball machine. Dead almost on contact; she wouldn't have felt a thing."

Ash felt a little better after hearing that. No matter who she was or what she had done, he never liked hearing that a murder victim had suffered before dying.

"Anything else?"

"A significant quantity of blood on the backseat," he said. "I can't determine the injury that would have caused it without more information, but this quantity of blood loss necessitates our victim going to the hospital."

That added a wrinkle to things. It also explained the scene somewhat. The shooter probably hadn't intended to execute the driver with the vehicle still in motion, but something had happened and it became kill or be killed.

"Would it be a life-threatening injury?"

Rodriguez hesitated but then nodded. "Potentially, but any serious injury is life-threatening given the right circumstances and a lack of proper treatment. If he could staunch the bleeding, our shooter's primary worry would be infection."

That could slow him down, but it would also make him desperate.

"Is there any way we can make these bodies your priority at the morgue? The shooter took a hostage, so we need to find out everything we can about them."

"I've got cases we have to get to tonight, but we'll move some other people around. We'll start cutting first thing tomorrow morning."

Ash preferred earlier, but he'd take whatever he could get. "Good. Take a marked escort with you so you can get through traffic."

"Sure. Thanks, Ash."

"*Thank you.*"

Ash stood up from the Mercedes, his head feeling light and his mouth dry. He took a breath, steadying himself on his feet. The sun would go down in a couple more hours, and he'd get a drink. Hopefully he could avoid anything strenuous until then. As he took a step away from the Mercedes, he noticed a forensic technician named Haley Fox dusting one of the front doors for prints. The last time Ash saw Haley, she had been a college intern at the scene of a methamphetamine bust. She smiled, blushed, and stood upon catching his glance, reminding him of the awkward young woman he had met eight months earlier.

"Hi, Detective Rashid. It's nice to see you. I heard you talking to Dr. Rodriguez, but I didn't want to interrupt."

Ash forced himself to smile to make her a little more at ease. He had difficulty, though; given the situation, he didn't have a lot to smile about.

"You too. Tell me you have something good."

Haley looked at her feet. "Somebody wiped down the car. I couldn't even find prints on the interior side of the door handles."

Ash grimaced. A lot of criminals tried to hide their prints, but few had the technical knowledge to accomplish it. The fact that this guy did didn't bode well for their investigation. At least they had his blood on the backseat. They might be able to get a match from that.

"Thank you for looking. If you find anything, let me know."

Haley held his gaze for a moment, but then her eyes lost their focus.

"This is the first homicide I've worked. It's a little scary."

"I puked on my partner's shoes on my first homicide, so as long as you didn't do that, you're one up on me."

A flicker of a smile touched her lips, but it disappeared before reaching the rest of her face.

"Yeah, at least I didn't puke on anyone."

Ash nodded and let her go back to work before walking toward Detective Alvarez's parked cruiser, which, from the looks of things, he had turned into a makeshift command center.

"We've got nothing," he said, flattening an oversized map against his car's stamped metal hood. He circled three intersections with a blue ballpoint pen. "We've got roadblocks at all three of these intersections, but nobody's found anything. We've also talked to everybody who's walked by the scene, but no one admits to seeing anything. Meanwhile, I've got every officer who's ever patrolled this neighborhood pounding on doors. To a man, they're telling me the same thing: nobody's talking to us."

Ash flattened an edge of the map that threatened to blow away. Most of the houses had large black Xs on them, but Alvarez had circled others and even left some blank.

"You can drop the roadblocks. Greg Doran found Rebecca's car near Shadeland Avenue."

Alvarez shook his head and exhaled hard, flexing his fingers.

"Nice of somebody to tell me I've been wasting my time."
Ash caught the detective's gaze and held it.

"I'm telling you now. I just found out myself. Is that a problem?"

"No," said Alvarez, his shoulders dropping and his voice softening. "Of course not. Sorry. I'm just a little on edge."

"Everybody is," said Ash, flattening the edge of the map again. "Why are some of these houses crossed off?"

Alvarez leaned against the car and pointed at the map again.

"They're dead ends. The houses are empty or the residents are openly hostile. I circled the ones where my guys thought we made progress. I don't know if the homeowners saw anything, but at least they didn't swear at us."

Ash counted almost three times as many Xs as Os. He ground his teeth, frustrated.

"Our victims weren't here to go sightseeing. Someone in this neighborhood knows something, and I want to find out what. Get some men, get some tactical vests, and get some shotguns. I want you to go back to every house that's been crossed off and start checking for outstanding warrants against the residents. Get some cuffs on people, and get some leverage. They'll talk."

Alvarez raised his eyebrows. "If we start rounding up the residents en masse, someone will notice. We might get some TV time, and it's probably not going to be too flattering. You okay with that?"

Ash looked up from the map and nodded. "If it happens, blame me. I'll deal with the push-back."

"If that's how you want to handle it, I'm on it," said Alvarez, already reaching for a police radio. He called his officers back to the scene while Ash walked to his cruiser. He wanted to drive to Shadeland Avenue, but the case had become too big to micromanage. Detective Doran could handle an abandoned vehicle without help. More important than that, Ash needed to visit the finance company that leased John and Jane Doe's Mercedes before it closed for the day, and the longer he lingered, the more time he wasted.

He put the address into his cruiser's GPS and followed its directions northwest of town to a stucco-covered strip mall with a large organic grocery on one end and a high-end appliance dealership on the other. Retail shops spanned the length from one end to the other; none, unfortunately, looked like a finance company. Ash turned in anyway and swore to himself when he found the address the Mercedes had been registered to. It was a copy shop and mailbox center called QwikMail. Hopefully the shop's proprietor knew something.

Ash parked and got out of his car. QwikMail occupied a narrow space packed with commercial copy machines and heavy metal racks of postal supplies. A long, wooden counter at the rear of the store separated the public space from the private, and a curtained archway led into a back room. A doorbell rang as Ash opened the door, and a college-age kid stepped up to the counter, his eyes bleary and red. The entire store reeked of marijuana.

"I thought the front door was locked," said the kid, turning his head to the archway as someone in back giggled. "What can I do for you, Officer?"

The stoner emphasized the word *Officer*, which shut up the giggler quickly. Ash hadn't driven all the way out there for a drug bust, but the smell gave him cause to secure a search warrant if he wanted. Even if the stoners turned out to be uncooperative, they had given him leverage. He liked when people did that.

"I'm looking for a company called Commonwealth Financial Services. They list this as their address."

The stoner's shoulders dropped, and he took a step back, nodding, probably relieved that Ash hadn't searched him for drugs yet.

"They rent a mailbox from us. It's one of the services we provide."

"Great. Where's their actual office located?"

The stoner shrugged and looked around. "Not here. That's all I know."

"Where's their mailbox? I want to see if they have anything."

"We don't have boxes like other stores. People have their mail sent here, and we sort it into baskets in the back. That way we catch junk mail before our clients see it."

"And your clients get a street address that looks like a physical address rather than a mailbox at a strip mall."

The stoner nodded, a smile building on his face. "That's right," he said, making circular motions with his hands. "It's all part of our full-service package." The stoner in the back giggled again, presumably at the word *package*. Ash leaned his elbows against the counter and glowered. The stoner dropped his hands and took another step back, moving just enough air that Ash caught a fresh whiff of marijuana.

"How much does a mailbox cost?"

"Five hundred a month, but we take care of everything. We sign for packages, call you when they come in, sort your junk mail. It's a good deal when you consider everything."

Full service or not, it was well over three times what the post office charged for even their largest box.

"What else do your clients get for that kind of money?"

The stoner smiled broadly. "Our award-winning customer service." Ash raised his eyebrows, incredulous, causing the stoner's smile to shift into a frown. "Listen, man, I wish you had come by earlier, but I'm about to close for the night and get some food. Maybe you can come back tomorrow and talk about a box when my boss is here. If you say you're a cop, he'll even give you the policeman's discount."

"You're not closing. You're going to talk to me about Commonwealth Financial Services and the business you conduct with them."

The stoner sneered. "You can't tell us what to do just because you're a cop. I've got rights. I've read the First Amendment."

Ash didn't know how to respond to the stoner's unorthodox legal analysis of the First Amendment, so he didn't say anything for a good fifteen or twenty seconds. The stoner crossed his arms in a self-satisfied manner.

"Keep your hands where I can see them, but come around the corner. I'm going to pat you down for drugs or weapons, so if you've got anything in your pockets that can hurt me, tell me now. If you've got a knife in your pocket and don't tell me, I might get pissed off and accidentally stab you with it."

"That doesn't sound like it'd be an accident."

"You figured that out all on your own. Good for you."

The stoner took a step back and raised his hands as if trying to show that he had nothing to hide.

"You can't touch me."

Ash motioned him forward. "Yes, I can. It's called a *Terry* frisk. I have reasonable suspicion that you're in the process of or about to commit a crime and a reasonable belief that you're armed. I'm worried about my safety."

The stoner held his hands even higher. "We're just a shipping center, man. If there are drugs here, they're not mine."

"I'm sure you wouldn't mind turning out your pockets for me, then. I've got this sneaking suspicion that you're carrying something you shouldn't be."

The stoner seemed to think for a moment before putting his hands down and looking left and right. He leaned forward. "I've got some ganja in my pocket, but it's not mine. It's my friend's. He asked me to carry it for him."

The stoner tilted his head toward the archway. Ash thought about calling IMPD's dispatcher and requesting backup, but he was more interested in information than a bust. If he started making arrests now, he'd waste time he didn't have.

"Here's the deal," said Ash, taking a notepad from a pouch on his utility belt and dropping it on the counter. "Tell your friend that I'll help him out if he helps me out. I need to see the records you have on Commonwealth Financial Services. You show them to me, and I'll forget about the drugs."

The stoner narrowed his eyes and furrowed his brow, apparently thinking. After a moment of silence, he nodded.

"You're all right, dude," he said, walking toward a computer on the other end of the counter. "I'll print out their file. But after that, you've got to go. I've got work to do."

Ash agreed, and his new stoner friend turned to the computer. Within two minutes, he handed Ash a printout with fields for a mailbox user's name, home address, phone number, and e-mail address. It would have been helpful had it been filled out. The only field with information on it noted that a representative from Commonwealth had paid in cash for a six-month lease and that he didn't want to receive co-branded offers from QwikMail's partners. Ash dropped the paper on the counter.

"You're messing with me, right? This better be a joke."

"No man," said the stoner, shaking his head. "This is all we have in the system. If a customer pays cash, that's all we ask for. That's the whole point of this place. If you don't have a regular address, you can get your mail here."

Despite the stoner's profession of innocence, Ash had a pretty good idea of what the "whole point" of QwikMail was. A couple of months back, David Lee, a detective in the narcotics squad, joked that with some recent crackdowns in the local drug supply chain, the postal service had become the biggest drug dealer in town. Shipping drugs had one big problem, though: You need a safe place to ship them to. If a user ships them to his own house, he'll eventually be caught and the police will know who to arrest. If he ships them to a friend's house, chances are that his friend will smoke his weed. If he ships them to a place like QwikMail, though, he's got anonymity and security, at least for a time.

"Who picked up the mail?"

The stoner shrugged. "Some woman. I think her name was Kate. Or maybe it was Kim. I don't know. It was one of those K names."

"Was she blond, about thirty years old?"

"That's right," he said, grinning and nodding. "She had a nice pair of snuggle puppies." Ash scrunched his eyebrows, not understanding. The stoner cupped his hands above his chest. "Her boobs. They were nice. I don't think they were real, though."

Ash wrote down the name but omitted any facts about her anatomy.

"Did Kate have a last name?"

"Probably," said the stoner. "Most people do, unless they're like Bono or Madonna."

Ash forced himself to smile. "To clarify, you're telling me that you don't know her last name?"

"I asked, but she wouldn't tell me."

Had Ash known Kate before she passed, he would have congratulated her for her common sense, something found in an increasingly small portion of the population.

"Do you know anything else about her?"

"Other than the fake boob thing? Because I don't really know that. I'm just speculating."

"Yes, other than the fake boob speculation."

The stoner seemed to think for a moment. "Nope. That's it, man."

"Are you keeping any mail for the company right now? If so, I'd like to see it."

"I'd have to see a warrant before I show you anything."

Ash lowered his gaze, growing tired of the conversation. Time for a new tact. He pointed to the front entrance.

"I can get a warrant, but I'll do you one better. Do you see that door?" The stoner nodded. "Do you see those cars in the parking lot?" He nodded again. "One of those cars is mine. If you don't get me Commonwealth Financial Services' mail, I'm going to arrest you for possession of marijuana and throw you in the back of my car. I'm then going to take a drug dog through here and have it find whatever it can. If we find any other drugs, I'll charge you with trafficking. Do you know what the penalty is for that?"

"Dude, man, I can't show you her mail. It's against company policy—"

"Twenty years." The stoner stuttered something, but he didn't relent. "Kate is dead, and so is her husband. The man who killed them abducted another woman. Do you want her death on your hands?"

The stoner didn't say anything, so Ash started walking around the counter.

"All right, all right. I'll check to see if they have anything."

"Good," said Ash. The stoner walked through the archway in back. Ash heard him whisper to the giggler, but he couldn't understand what either of the men said. A moment later he came back empty-handed, but apparently sensing Ash's annoyance, he stopped walking while he was still well out of arm's reach.

"According to my coworker, Kate came by yesterday and picked everything up. Her basket is empty."

"Are you sure?" The stoner shuffled back a step and nodded. Ash didn't trust him, but the kid didn't seem to be lying. He grabbed a business card from his wallet. "You'll call me if you find anything?"

The stoner nodded again, so Ash put the card on the counter and slid it toward him before walking out. He hadn't spent much time inside, but with the drive over, he had wasted half an hour to find out that Jane Doe was in fact named Kate Doe. Or Katie Doe. Or something like that. Hopefully Eddie Alvarez and the rest of the team had made better progress.

3

Konstantin Bukoholov felt his eyes droop as the young man in front of the conference room droned on about the company he and his siblings were trying to sell. Ostensibly, Kostya had yet to make a decision about the purchase, but in reality, his accountants had already made it for him. According to them, he had far more cash than the receipts of his various companies allowed. Thirty years ago, it wouldn't have been a concern. He knew the presidents of at least three regional banks who would allow him to drop off bundles of cash for deposit without asking a single question. Now, with everyone looking for terrorists, every dollar he deposited to every bank with which he did business had to be explained. Even basic bookkeeping had become a nightmare.

Kostya glanced at the city's skyline through the window to keep himself awake. Business deals used to be easy. He'd shake a partner's hand, exchange some money, and it'd be done. Now he had to spend several hundred dollars an hour to hire lawyers who only told him whatever he wanted to hear anyway. It seemed like such a waste.

"Are you all right, Mr. Bukoholov?"

He snapped his head forward and glared at the speaker.

James Cooper. He buried his father two weeks ago and already had the family business on the market. In another decade, Kostya knew it might be his kids up there selling off assets he'd spent his entire life developing.

"My welfare is not your concern, Mr. Cooper," he said. "Your total receipts for the past three years have averaged fourteen million dollars per year. How much of that is cash?"

"The exact figure depends on the location, but company wide, forty percent of our sales are cash. Before he died, Dad considered lowering the price of gasoline by a couple of cents per gallon for cash sales, but we haven't implemented it yet. Our accountants forecast—"

Cooper kept talking, but Kostya ignored him as he felt his cell phone vibrate against his chest. Very few people, most of whom waited for him in the building, knew his personal cell phone number. He fished the phone out of his pocket and glanced at the screen. He didn't recognize the number, but he knew its owner. For a moment, his breath caught in his throat.

"That's fine," said Kostya, interrupting Cooper's sales pitch. "I'll pay your asking price." He looked at the lawyer to his left. "Mr. Evans and his firm will complete the sale on my behalf. Thank you for your time. I'm sure we'll be in touch."

Cooper startled and stared at him, but the lawyers quickly stood.

"You don't want to hear—" began Cooper.

"No," said Kostya. "Good day."

Cooper didn't move at first, but then he gathered his briefcase and pranced out of the room along with the attorneys.

Kostya hated paying off a rich man's children for assets they didn't earn or deserve, but he took solace in knowing they'd probably lose everything he gave them within a few years and die penniless. The sale would cost six million dollars, but the stations would allow him to move three or four million of otherwise-unaccounted-for cash a year into legitimate, interest-earning bank accounts. He'd earn his investment back in two years; hopefully he'd live long enough to see it.

Kostya answered his phone. "Kara?"

"Afraid not." The voice belonged to a man, one Kostya didn't recognize. That didn't surprise him, though; he rarely knew the men in Kara's life. "Who am I speaking to?"

"That's none of your concern," said Kostya. "How did you get Kara's phone?"

"I took it from her after I blew her head off and killed her husband."

It took a moment for that to register, but once it did, Kostya's heart seized in his chest like an old piece of machinery, and he coughed hard. When he spoke again, his voice possessed little strength.

"You killed her?"

"That's how I got her phone. It was an awful waste of a fine piece of ass if you ask me. I'm calling you because I wanted to find out what kind of a man she'd take orders from."

Kostya's hand shook. He tried to force strength back into his voice but found he had little.

"I don't give orders to anyone, least of all to her."

"Sure you don't. Kara was a real piece of work. She and her husband didn't make too many friends in my line of business, and I'm willing to bet you don't want too many people knowing she worked for you. Give me some money, and no one will."

Kostya swallowed and then took one breath followed by another. That helped some.

"Do you know who I am?" he asked.

"I don't need to. I've got Kara's phone, and you're the fourth number listed in her address book. She labeled you 'boss.' That's all my people are going to need."

Boss. Kara had never worked for him, but it didn't surprise him that she would call him that. They had never gotten along well.

"How much money do you want?"

"A hundred thousand dollars. Cash. We'll call that a start."

Given the nature of the request, Kostya thought it reasonable. A smart man wouldn't pay blackmail, though; if he did it once, he'd do it for the rest of his life.

"Let's meet in person to discuss this."

"I don't think so. You've got twenty-four hours, and you've got my number."

"I'll think about it."

Kostya hung up the phone before the caller did. He didn't know what to feel. He hadn't seen Kara in almost a decade, but he kept a picture of her in his desk at home and thought about her almost every day. She called him once a few years ago but hung up within a minute of placing the call. He missed her. Kostya kept his eyes on the table, processing the conversation. Eventually, his brother-in-law, Lev, stepped into the room and shut the door behind him. A detective Bukoholov knew referred to Lev as "the Hulk"; the appellation fit.

"Cooper said you agreed to his asking price. What's wrong?"

Kostya took a deep breath, drawing on a well of internal strength before looking at his brother-in-law. The ice around his heart began to melt as rage built inside him.

"Someone claims to have murdered my daughter. We have work to do."

4

As soon as Ash got back in his car, his stomach rumbled. He ignored it and took out his cell phone. Eddie Alvarez answered before the phone finished ringing once.

"It's Ash. In your interviews, has anyone mentioned the name Kate or Katie?"

Alvarez clucked his tongue twice, thinking. "Not to me. Why?"

"I talked to the guy who handles John and Jane Doe's mail. He thought our female vic was named Kate."

"We picked up four felons on our warrant sweep. I could run the name by them and see if it's familiar."

Try as he might, Ash couldn't help but feel disappointed; they were no further along than they had been when he first arrived at the scene.

"Yeah, talk to them and then grab Tim Smith and recanvas the neighborhood. If someone says he's heard rumors about a Kate or Katie, I want him brought in. Our vics were into something, and I want to know what."

Alvarez paused. "That's a lot of work for a long shot."

Ash had been in Alvarez's shoes on cases before, so he understood the detective's reluctance. Alvarez wasn't trying to weasel his way out of work; he was looking for work worth doing. Ash doubted they'd turn up anything new, but a name could possibly jog someone's memory. They didn't have enough leads to be choosy yet.

"I know it's a lot of work, but we won't have anything until we can ID our victims. I told an officer to call the local hospitals. Did he find anything?"

"A couple of stabbings and a shooting, but nothing that seems plausible for our case."

"How about Doran? He say anything about the car?"

"Just that he popped the trunk and didn't find Rebecca inside. I think he plans to have the car towed back to the lab."

"At least he didn't find a body. Good luck out there."

Ash expected Alvarez to hang up, but he didn't.

"You ever handled a case like this before?" Alvarez asked.

"Not quite. We'll get her back, though. Just get out there and do what you need to do."

"I said a prayer for her. I think it'll help."

"It can't hurt. Good luck."

Alvarez hung up the phone, and Ash stayed still to think. He liked Alvarez, and he had heard good things about him. That phone call proved he shouldn't have been in Homicide, though. The assignment would wear on him, break him down over time. No matter how many cases he solved or murderers he locked up, he'd just find more the next day. He could probably forget most of those cases; other cases, though, would stick with him long after he went home. Some guys could handle that, but a guy who said prayers for the dead would only end up bitter and angry. Ash knew that firsthand. Unfortunately, he didn't have time to sit down with him and deal with it at the moment.

He put his car in gear and called Greg Doran for directions to Rebecca's abandoned car. During the drive, he kept replaying his conversation with the stoner at QwikMail in his head. John and Kate Doe spent five hundred bucks a month on an anonymous mail service. They were hiding something, obviously, but Ash didn't know what. Hopefully that ignorance wouldn't keep him from finding out who killed them.

While still two miles from Shadeland Avenue, Ash called Detective Sergeant David Lee of the narcotics squad. He picked up his cell phone before it finished ringing once.

"Hey, buddy," said Lee. "I don't get to talk to a celebrity every day. You've been on the news. Kristen Tanaka said you picked up a double by the fairgrounds."

Ash grunted. "It's more than that. Our perp carjacked a woman who happened to be in the area. As far as we know, they're still together."

"No shit?"

"No shit."

Lee exhaled softly. "What do you need?"

"Information right now. I think my homicide victims were involved with something they shouldn't have been. Are you guys looking at anyone named Kate or Katie?"

David was silent for a moment. "What else do you have on her?"

"She's blond, maybe thirty years old, attractive. Found her in a Mercedes with her husband. He's still a John Doe. He looks like he's in his forties or early fifties."

David grunted. "Description's not ringing any bells."

Ash strained his eyes and peered at the changing scenery around him. The sun had very nearly set, leaving a world shrouded in shadows. Shadeland Avenue ran north and south on the east side of town. If a resident drove long enough, he'd find grocery stores, hotels, drugstores, used car lots—really whatever he could want—along its four lanes. If he knew the right signs, he'd also find prostitutes, drug dealers, and even a pawnshop that wasn't too particular about the ownership of the goods it sold.

"If you haven't heard of Kate, how about Katherine or Kara or some other name that starts with K?"

"I need more than a first name if you want me to find something. Does she have a street name?"

"I don't know yet. Maybe you can answer this: If there were fights in the drug supply chain, would any of your confidential informants hear about them?"

"They would have heard rumors at least. It's pretty quiet right now, though. We've still got drugs moving into the city, obviously, but a lot of players have left town. I guess IMPD was too much for them."

Ash had heard about that exodus, but he doubted the department had much to do with it. The dealers didn't leave; a politically savvy gangster named Konstantin Bukoholov forced them out, with Ash's inadvertent help. Bukoholov had even indirectly offered him a job in the prosecutor's office as payment for his services. One day Ash would have to deal with him, but for the moment, Bukoholov wasn't his concern.

"If you keep an ear out for me, I'd appreciate it."

"Will do. Oh, and hey, *Ramadan Kareem*."

The phrase loses something in the translation, but David had just wished him a generous Ramadan. It took a moment for Ash to get over his initial surprise.

"*Allahu akram*. Did you convert and not tell anyone?"

"No, but my sister just married a Muslim man in Jersey. What does *Allahu akram* mean?"

"'God is most generous.' It's a polite response."

"Cool. Sorry to hear about your case, but I'll ask around and see what I can find. If I hear anything, I'll give you a call back."

"Thanks."

Ash hung up and drove the rest of the way to the scene. When he pulled into the strip mall, he immediately hit a pothole big enough that his car shuddered. Greg Doran leaned against an unmarked cruiser about a hundred yards away, while two forensic technicians photographed a red Toyota Camry. An IMPD tow truck stood idle in the mall's fire lane. Aside from Rebecca's Toyota, every car in the lot belonged to the city, and as he neared the building, he could see why. The strip mall had room for a dozen stores, but only two storefronts had signs over their doors, and neither looked as if paying customers had crossed their thresholds in years.

Ash parked beside Doran's Crown Vic and stepped out. The evening had yet to overcome the day's heat, but Ash didn't sweat. His head hurt as well and he felt tired, three telltales signs of dehydration. Thankfully, the sun would go down soon. If he didn't pass out, he could make it. Detective Doran nodded and exhaled a lungful of smoke as soon as he saw Ash.

"You found anything?"

"Not really," said Doran, throwing his cigarette down and grinding it under his heel. Ash walked toward Rebecca's car. Doran had left the trunk propped open, but the windows and doors were still closed. "We dusted the exterior for prints and pulled seven distinct sets. Most are probably going to be from Rebecca's family, but we might get lucky. I wanted to have the car towed to the lab before we touched the interior in case there's fiber evidence that might blow away out here."

Ash nodded and walked around the vehicle. The remnants of the graphite powder the forensic team had used to check for prints clung to the door panels.

"Anything in the trunk?" asked Ash upon reaching the back of the car.

"Just jumper cables," said Doran, joining Ash. "The lab vacuumed for fibers, but it'll take them a while to analyze things."

Even though Doran hadn't found anything in the trunk, Ash knelt down to get a look at the interior anyway. He didn't find anything new, but he did find something missing.

"Did you guys find a bright yellow handle anywhere?"

"No," said Doran, his voice uncertain. "Why?"

Ash pointed to an indention in the lid of the trunk.

"This is missing the internal trunk release," he said, already taking out his cell phone and dialing Eddie Alvarez's number. The detective picked up quickly. "The scene by the fairgrounds still secure?"

"For now. The Mercedes has been towed, but I've still got guys down there."

"Good. I need them to start searching for a bright yellow lever. It probably glows in the dark."

"What kind of lever is it?"

"It's the internal trunk release from Rebecca's car. It's a safety feature in case you get locked inside. The guy who kidnapped Rebecca might have ripped it out, and if he did, it might have his prints on it."

Alvarez didn't say anything for a few seconds. "I'll call it in and tell them to be on the lookout."

"Good. And if you find it, don't bother calling me. Just get it printed. I want to find out who this guy is."

"Will do."

Ash hung up, and Detective Doran cleared his throat and shuffled back a step. He looked uncomfortable.

"I should have seen that earlier."

"Don't worry about it," said Ash, slipping his phone back in his pocket. "My wife's thinking about buying the same car. It's the only reason I knew to look. Did you find any witnesses?"

Doran panned his gaze over the strip mall before shaking his head. "None of the stores here have been open for at least two or three years."

Ash pointed to a pawnshop and a liquor store across the street. "How about those two?"

Doran removed a notebook from his pocket. "The guy who runs the pawnshop didn't see anything." He looked up and pointed toward the empty parking spots near Shadeland. "He did mention that someone parked a green Pontiac Grand Am near the street for a couple of weeks. The guy in the pawnshop thinks it was for sale, but he doesn't know if someone bought it or the guy trying to sell it finally decided to quit."

Ash nodded. "Did you follow up with auto theft?"

"Yeah, but they didn't have anything. I already called patrol and told them to be on the lookout for a suspicious green Pontiac. Nothing so far."

"How about the liquor store?"

Doran shook his head. "Waste of time. The guy who runs

it didn't stop smoking the entire time I was there. Literally lit a new cigarette on the tip of each one he finished. The front windows are so covered in film that you can't see anything through them."

Ash nodded and stared at the street. Even well after rush hour, dozens of cars still lined up at every stoplight on Shadeland. That number would probably double during busy times of day. With that many people around, someone must have seen their perp drag Rebecca out of her car and throw her in another. It would have been nice if they could be bothered to make a two-minute call to 911 to save her life. He took another quick look around the parking lot but didn't find anything.

"Wrap it up here when you can, and then head downtown. We'll release some information to the press tonight, but I want to meet with everyone first for status updates. Meet me around eight-thirty. I'll reserve a conference room."

"Sure. I'll be there."

Ash got back in his car and buckled in before heading into traffic. In elementary school, he used to read comic books and adventure stories beneath his desk when he should have been listening to the teacher. He liked Batman the best; he lost his parents just like Ash lost his father. For much of his childhood, Ash had dreamed about being a hero and going back in time to save his father. Most boys in his position probably had the same fantasy. In the comic books, the hero almost always saved the day—at the last moment, he'd sweep in and save the girl or rescue the kids or win the race. In real life, the hero rarely wins, a lesson Ash had learned when he became a police officer. He hoped and prayed that this case would be an exception.

5

When Ash reached the interstate, he called Mike Bowers and asked him to set up a press conference for nine that night. They couldn't stop the TV stations around town from reporting the story, but they could at least share real information rather than rumors and speculation. That would go a long way to consoling the nerves of a city rubbed raw by a sensational news story. As soon as he hung up, Ash glanced at his watch. The sun hadn't even set yet, but he had already worn the same uniform for over thirteen hours. As much as he disliked admitting it, appearances mattered, which meant he needed fresh clothes and a shower if he wanted people to take him seriously. He also wouldn't mind grabbing some food.

When he got home, lights illuminated the front room of the house but the rest were mired in shadow. He and Hannah had planned to have his sister and her husband over for dinner, but the family must have gone out in his absence. Ash parked in the driveway and went through the side door to the kitchen. His daughter had strewn coloring books and drawings on the breakfast table, and his son had left his roll-along rocking horse beside the door that led to their backyard. He found a note beside the mi-

50

crowave; Hannah had taken the kids and met Ash's sister and brother-in-law at their mosque for a potluck *iftar* meal. Over the years, Ash had missed a lot of family gatherings because of work, but all the practice didn't make things easier. When he worked long, odd hours, his kids missed him and he missed them. He made a mental note to call before everybody went to bed.

Ash rinsed off the day's grime in the shower before changing into a suit and tie in his bedroom. He also grabbed his department-issued, forty-caliber Glock 22 from a lockbox in his closet. As a community relations officer who spent most of his days in elementary school auditoriums or providing security advice to worried city residents, Ash rarely carried a firearm and hadn't worn a holster since qualifying on the shooting range a few months ago. The nylon felt stiff and unfamiliar to his shoulders after such a long absence, but the feeling faded quickly. He hadn't always worn a shoulder holster; he began by wearing a holster attached to his belt and only switched eight years ago when he was still a homicide detective. He and a partner—the best one Ash ever had—came under fire while trying to execute an arrest warrant on a man suspected of killing his wife and her boyfriend. Ash took a round to the shoulder, but their suspect shot Ash's partner in his neck. The round nicked a major artery, and he died on the sidewalk. Ever since then, Ash had worn a shoulder holster. It caused a dull ache to spread across his chest whenever he put it on, a constant reminder of the friend he lost and the life he could have lost had he been just a little less lucky.

Once dressed, he called the detectives in his hodgepodge task force and requested that they meet him downtown in about half an hour. The sun had set while he was in the shower, so Ash had a glass of water and then *salat al-Maghrib*, evening prayer, before making himself two chicken sandwiches. Traditionally, he would have broken the Ramadan fast with a date, but they didn't have any. A chicken sandwich would do. He wolfed both down, feeling better almost instantly, then headed to his car.

A layer of clouds stretched across the evening sky. Early onset arthritis had few advantages, but it did have one: He rarely had to consult a meteorologist to know when he should bring an umbrella to work. The throbbing in his shoulder let him know that they'd receive rain soon. The city needed it, but it'd make outdoor crime scenes difficult.

When he arrived at the homicide squad's floor downtown, Eddie Alvarez, Greg Doran, and Tim Smith had already set up camp in the conference room. Someone had evidently ordered pizza because he found three boxes from a local place and a roll of paper towels on the table.

"The bottom is cheese," said Alvarez, pointing to an unopened box. "The other two have sausage or pepperoni on them."

"Thanks," said Ash, shuffling the tower of pizza boxes around so he could open the bottom one. He had already eaten two sandwiches, but a day without food had left him famished. "Have you guys eaten yet?"

Tim Smith burped an affirmative and leaned back in his chair. Their conference room had built-in sound and video systems for presentations and space for eight comfortable leather chairs around its center table. Unknown to most, the department had also installed pinhole cameras in the walls and microphones behind acoustically transparent panels in the ceiling, making the room an effective spot for inter-rogations as well as interviews. With the flick of a switch beside the door, a computer would record everything said and done in the room for playback in court.

"Captain Bowers had us order you a cheese pizza," said Smith, digging between his front teeth with a fingernail. He flicked something out before wiping his hands on his pants. "Why is that?"

Smith already knew the answer, so Ash stared at him, trying to figure out why he had asked the question.

"I'm a Muslim, so I don't eat pork. You know that."

"But you drink."

Eddie Alvarez started to say something, but Ash held up a hand to stop him. He didn't keep his faith a secret, but he didn't try to flaunt it, either. Over the years, he had become accustomed to the questions, though, some of which were hostile.

"If you're worried about my ability to handle this case, I haven't had a drink in over eight months. If you genuinely have questions about Islam, I'll give you the name of the Imam at my mosque. If you're wasting my time, please stop."

Smith crossed his arms. "I just have one question, and I'd like you to answer it. About a year and a half ago, you broke my window. Were you drunk then?"

Ash lowered his eyebrows, confused. "I don't know what you're talking about, and even if I did, we've got other mat-ters to focus on."

"I'm not taking orders from you until you answer my question. Do you remember when Rachel Haddad died?"

"That's enough, Tim," growled Doran.

Ash should have let Doran stop it there, but his mouth and his common sense didn't always communicate well.

"Rachel was my niece. Of course I remember."

"Captain Bowers ordered us to follow you after she died. When we did, you broke a window on my wife's car and stuck a gun in my face. I want to know if you were drunk."

The story jogged a memory, causing Ash to grip the end of the table hard enough that his fingers hurt.

"For the record, I never stuck a gun in your face. I pressed it to the back of your head. If you had been even halfway decent at your job, that wouldn't have happened."

"And if you had been—" began Smith.

"Shut up," growled Doran again, drowning out his partner. "This isn't the time or the place."

"No," said Smith. "This is exactly the time and place. This guy's a washed-out drunk. You can't tell me you're okay taking orders from him."

"Yes, I can," said Doran. "That's what we've been ordered to do, so that's our job."

Doran stared at his partner with hard, green eyes. Eventually, Smith shook his head and muttered that Ash was guilty of doing something quite inappropriate with his mother. Ash counted to five, breathing deeply, before speaking.

"Would you like to be reassigned, Detective?"

Smith looked at Doran and then Alvarez, both of whom glared at him.

"No. I'm fine."

"Good," said Ash. "And I suppose for your own edification, Detective, I was sober." Smith scowled but didn't say anything. Ash panned his gaze to the other men in the room. "With that out of the way, let's try to focus on Rebecca Cook. Do we have anything on her car yet?"

Doran leaned forward and opened his notebook.

"Forensic services had it towed back to their garage, and they're working on it now. Like I told you earlier, we found seven sets of prints on the car's exterior. At least three of those sets were so small that they probably came from kids. The techs are cataloging everything now. Do we have prints from the vic's family to eliminate them?"

"Not yet," said Ash. "But I'll have someone swing by tonight to get them. How's the inside look?"

"Hair, fibers, fingernail clippings. It's a family car, so un-til we get samples from Rebecca's family, we're not going to know if something's from our perp or from one of her kids."

"And still no witnesses, right?"

"None that have come forward."

Ash wrote the pertinent facts in his notebook before turn-ing to Eddie Alvarez. "How about the scene by the fair-grounds?"

Alvarez shifted on his seat and cleared his throat. "After you called about the trunk release, I had my men look around. They found it in the grass beside the road. We didn't see it earlier because it blended into the weeds. We've got a smudge and a partial on it. The lab is running it through our databases right now."

It wasn't much, but he'd take any good news he could get. Maybe they'd get lucky and find their perp in the system.

"How about the victim's phone? A patrolman picked it up."

Alvarez's nostrils flared as he exhaled. "Nothing. We

might have had a print on it at one time, but when Ryan picked it up, he smudged the whole thing. It's useless."

Ash threw his pencil on the table and sighed.

"Okay. Here's the plan so far. Mike Bowers and I are going to hold a news conference at nine, and we're going to ask the public for help. We should be able to make the ten o'clock newscast. When that happens, I want one guy on the phone at all times, two guys following up on leads, and one guy sleeping. We'll rotate every two hours, and nobody will go home until we find Rebecca. Questions?"

Smith raised his hand. Ash wanted to ignore him, but he nodded in the detective's direction.

"We going to get overtime on this?" asked Smith, looking at Doran and then Alvarez. "I don't know about these guys, but I've already worked my shift today. If I'm not getting overtime, I'm going home."

Ash nodded toward the door, feeling his temper start to rise.

"I'm sure Captain Bowers will authorize overtime, but why don't you go home anyway? I can find someone who actually wants to be here."

Smith shifted under the stares of the men around him.

"If we're getting paid, I'll stay. That's all I was asking. I just wanted to know."

"I'm glad you're so cooperative," said Ash. "Any other questions?"

"We got anyone else on our team?" asked Alvarez.

"If we need help, I'll call David Lee from Narcotics or Paul Murphy from Auto Theft. Both of them know the east side of town well, so they ought to be able to help us there."

Lee and Murphy both had enough seniority within the

department to put Smith in his place if he became mouthy. Since the guys didn't have any more questions, he dismissed them for the next half hour so they could call their wives and tuck their kids into bed. He also took a moment to call his family. Kaden, his youngest, babbled for a few seconds, while Megan, his daughter, told him a story about her day. Hannah, his wife, wished him luck, which he likely needed.

At just before nine, he met Mike Bowers in the lobby of the building for the press conference. Every station in town, save for Kristen Tanaka's, had a reporter in attendance. She knew everything they planned to report anyway, so that didn't surprise anyone. For the next twenty minutes, they candidly answered questions about the case and asked the public for help. Hopefully it would get them somewhere.

6

Indianapolis, 2002. Despite the manicured lawns, the land-scaped flowerbeds, the expensive suburban homes, and the numerous people he saw, Kostya had never driven on a lonelier road in his life. He supposed he would have felt that way driving from any gravesite, though. His daughter Kara sat in the passenger's seat of his Jaguar, staring out the window. She appeared thinner and paler than he remembered, but she still had her mother's rounded cheeks and naturally straw-colored hair. Storm gray and cold, her eyes seemed to be the only physical characteristic he had passed on to her.

"It was a dignified service," he said, pulling the car into traffic and away from the cemetery. "Your mother would have liked it."

"You have no idea what my mother would have liked. You weren't around enough to find out."

"I wasn't around very much because she asked me to stay away. Believe it or not, I cared about Alicia enough to respect her wishes."

He glanced over, catching Kara's gaze. She quickly withdrew and turned to face the window again.

"What makes you think my wishes would be any different from hers?"

"It was just a hope."

Kara didn't even look at him that time. He glanced in his rearview mirror. A navy blue Ford followed two car lengths back. He didn't know what agency its occupants worked for, but it didn't really matter. They followed him wherever he went and had since he relocated to the state four years prior. They hadn't even bothered trying to hide during his ex-wife's funeral.

"I'm going to get a cup of coffee," he said, braking suddenly. The vehicle behind him came to within two feet of hitting him. Kara either didn't notice or pretended not to. "Would you like something?"

"It doesn't look like I have much of a choice."

"You always have a choice. I've worked too hard for you not to have that."

She ignored him, and he turned into a coffee shop with a covered concrete patio and a bright red awning over the front door. Several people sat on wrought-iron chairs outside; most looked happy. Kostya parked in the first open spot he came to and checked to see if his escort had followed him in. They continued driving, though, giving him a welcome moment of privacy with his daughter.

"I can take you home if you'd like."

"We're here," she said, opening her door. "We might as well get something."

Kostya followed her, noticing several men stare at his daughter. As soon as they saw him, most of those stares turned away quickly; those who kept eyeing his daughter turned after receiving an extended glance from him. Kara had her mother's good looks and had likely become inured to the attention over the years, but Kostya didn't like people looking at her, not like that at least.

"I'll get coffee if you sit down."

"Black, no cream," said Kara, slowly lowering herself into a plush armchair big enough to accommodate two of her. Kostya ordered and paid for two small black coffees before sitting across from his daughter on an identical plush chair. A young man read the paper on a love seat nearby, but Kostya ignored him and said nothing until a barista arrived with their coffee.

"Thank you," he said, smiling slightly as the young woman walked away. The coffee tasted good, but he hadn't stopped for a drink. After his first sip, he settled the cup on the table and looked at his daughter, trying to draw her glance. "How are you?"

She turned toward him, her eyes indifferent.

"Why are you interested? After Mom kicked you out, I saw you, what, twice a year? You didn't seem interested in me then."

He looked at his cup. "It was complicated."

"No, it wasn't. If you really cared, you would have been there. We needed help, and you just...I don't even know what to say to you. Mom's dead, and you think you can waltz back into my life? It doesn't work like that."

The man reading the paper folded it slowly and left. Kostya grimaced.

"I may not have been a very good father, but I don't want to lose you like I lost your mother."

"You already have," said Kara, reaching into her purse and pulling out a thin, white roll of paper. Kostya recognized the smell when she lit it and exhaled in his direction. He stood and looked at their growing audience.

"It's time to go," he said, motioning her forward. "This isn't the place for this."

Kara removed the joint from her mouth and looked at it, her eyebrows raised.

"This bothers you? A little dope?" She looked him up and down before standing. "You probably sold this to my dealer."

He nodded apologies to the shop's other patrons before escorting his daughter back to their car. She threw the remnants of her joint out the window as they drove away, but the smell lingered in his vehicle.

"I lost my mother and father when I was young," said Kostya, adjusting the vents on his car to rid it of the smell. "I know what it's like."

"That sucks. I never had a father, so I didn't lose much."

As much as he tried to restrain himself, the barbs hurt, and Kostya felt his temper rise.

"I tried to be there for you both. I truly did."

"Great. I feel better now," said Kara. "You killed my mom, but that's okay because you were always there for us."

"I didn't kill your mother. She died because she was sick. I sent her to clinics, to doctors, to retreats. I drove her to therapy. I sat up with her at night when she cried herself to sleep. I loved your mother, and I did everything I could for her. I will not tolerate you saying otherwise."

"You can't even say it, can you?" said Kara. "She killed herself, and it's your fault."

Kostya felt his heart ache, but something deep inside him refused to let that show.

"I loved your mother very much. I would have given anything for her. She knew that."

"Mom never loved you. She was scared of you," said Kara, shifting on her seat so she could face him. "She went to those clinics to get away from you, and I can see why."

"She had no reason to be scared of me. No one does."

Kara scoffed. "Do you think I'm stupid?"

"Of course not," said Kostya, straightening. "You're my daughter. I'd never think you were stupid."

"I know what you do for a living."

He didn't say anything for a moment. "And what do you think that is?"

She looked forward and started to say something, but quickly shut her mouth. Finally she asked, "What do you want from me? You want me to sit on your lap and call you Daddy? It's too late for that. It's too late for a lot of things."

"I'm sorry."

"I'm not."

Kostya drove for another twenty minutes in silence before pulling to a stop in front of a two-story brick home near Butler University. Alicia had planted yellow mums beside the door; she loved flowers. Kostya didn't say anything, not knowing what to say.

"Don't worry," said Kara, opening her door. "I'll be out of here in a month so you can sell the place. You won't ever have to see me again."

"The house is yours. It's part of the trust fund I started for you. You can stay in it while you finish college, or you can sell it. Mr. Evans, the lawyer we met with yesterday, will assist you with whatever you want."

Kara's back stiffened, but she didn't get out of the car. "What do I have to do for it?"

"Nothing. Just please try to be happy."

She put one leg out of the car but didn't try to leave. "I don't think we need to see each other again."

"If that's what you want," said Kostya.

"It is," she said, standing. Kostya watched his daughter walk into her house. She lived up to her word. He never saw her again.

*   *   *

Despite having written its address on letters twice a year, Kostya hadn't set foot in front of the small, redbrick home in well over ten years. Little had changed. The yellow mums in the front lawn had been swapped with azaleas, and someone had painted the trim around the windows gray. A hose snaked across the front lawn to a crab apple tree. Somewhere along the way, it appeared her mother's house had become Kara's home. He wished he had been part of it.

"Park out front instead of the drive. I want to be able to leave quickly."

Kostya's nephew Michael nodded and slowed their paneled van. Kostya owned two such vehicles, and both had magnetic panels that could be affixed to the sides to disguise the vehicle's ownership. Tonight, they had attached panels with the logo of a local HVAC company on the outside; that should keep them from arousing the attention of the neighbors.

As soon as Michael brought their van to a stop, Kostya stepped out and walked toward the home, stopping only to bend and pick up a decorative rock from a flowerbed to the right of the door. His knees and back creaked with the strain of the motion as he bent farther to retrieve the tarnished brass key underneath. Alicia had placed that rock on the porch to hide a house key fifteen years ago when

Kara went to high school. Seeing it again made Kostya smile.

Within thirty seconds of arriving, four men stood in what had once been Kara's entryway. Lev and his two sons, James and Michael, immediately began searching the home for information about Kara's life, while Kostya stayed in the entryway and looked around. He saw his daughter in every corner of the room and wished he had seen it while she was still alive.

The entryway opened into an open-concept living room with attached kitchen and stairway to the second floor. When he bought the home for Alicia, cheap oak paneling had covered the walls, but Kara had pulled all that down and replaced it with drywall painted a cheery yellow. The hardwood floor creaked as he walked around. She had dusted the wooden coffee table, end tables, and fireplace mantel. Vacuum lines crisscrossed the rug in the center of the floor. When he knew her, Kara didn't even seem to understand how a vacuum worked. He missed watching her grow up.

While his nephews searched the bedrooms, Kostya walked toward the mantel above the fireplace and picked up a black-and-white picture of a wedding. Kara smiled as her new husband fed her a piece of cake at the reception. She looked happy. He hadn't planned to take anything from the house, but he tucked the picture beneath his arm and walked to the kitchen, feeling a dull hollowness build inside him.If Kara had kept the home's original layout, the upstairs had three bedrooms and two bathrooms; he doubted anyone would find anything there, though. Assuming it still existed, he wanted to find the home office.

He passed a small powder room beside the kitchen before stopping at the last door on the left. The office had been a large corner bedroom at one time, but upon buying the house, Alicia had hired a contractor to refinish the hardwood floors and install built-in bookshelves along two of the walls. Kara hadn't changed it much except to fill those bookshelves with legal textbooks. Her diploma hung on the wall. His daughter had become a lawyer apparently, one more major event he had missed in her life.

Lev looked up from his search of the desk when Kostya walked in.

"Have you found anything?"

"Kara changed her name. Her last name is Elliot now, like her husband. She saved your letters," he said, sliding a thick stack of opened envelopes across the desk. Kostya added them to the portrait under his arm. Twice a year— on her birthday and Christmas—he wrote her a letter asking for her forgiveness, and twice a year he told her that he would be at a park near the White River downtown if she'd be willing to see him. She never showed, but he kept going year after year in the hopes that one day she'd change her mind.

"Anything else?" he asked.

"Maybe," said Lev, reaching down to a drawer and picking up a stack of folded color pamphlets. He slid them across the desk and took a step back. "Tell me what you think of these."

The pamphlets had been written in half a dozen languages and contained pictures of smiling men and women carrying backpacks and walking through a bucolic college campus. Kostya flipped through the pamphlets until he found one written in Russian, a language he understood. They advertised a student exchange program that would allow young women to come to the United States from abroad and study and work part-time to pay their way. The pictures looked innocuous, but the pamphlet read like a sales pitch.

"What does this company get out of its exchange students?" asked Kostya.

"Nothing according to their literature. They're a charity."

Lev sounded suspicious and rightfully so. Everybody had an angle, even supposed do-gooders out to save the world.

"See what else we can find."

They searched for another ten minutes. Kara kept a copy of her taxes in her desk; in addition to dispersals from her trust fund, she had made just over a hundred thousand dollars each year for the past three years from a company called Commonwealth Financial Services. As they left the room, Lev bumped into a wooden filing cabinet beside the desk, causing it to slide across the floor on wheels hidden in the base, revealing a safe built into the wall. Lev immediately bent and tried to open it, but its handle wouldn't budge.

"We can remove this, but we'll make some noise," said Lev, standing. "It's your call."

"Let me try something," said Kostya, kneeling before the safe and feeling his knees creak. Kara's safe had a keypad like a telephone instead of a spinning dial, making it easy to use. He typed in her birthday, but that didn't work. He then tried Alicia's, but that didn't work either. He didn't bother trying his own; she wouldn't have used that. As a last resort, he typed 05-22-02, the date Alicia passed away.

The lock clicked, and the door swung open, exposing the interior.

"Anything?" asked Lev. Kostya nodded and reached inside. He found four envelopes; the first two held cash, probably emergency money. The third envelope held her birth certificate, her wedding certificate, and other important documents. Kostya slipped that one into his jacket's pocket. The fourth envelope felt heavier than the others. He slipped the top flap from the interior and pulled out eight passports from various countries. They all belonged to young women, mostly teenagers. He also found a black address book.

"What is this?" asked Lev.

"I don't know," said Kostya, holding out a hand. Lev pulled him to his feet. "We'll find out. I know someone at the—"

Heavy footsteps interrupted him. James walked into the room, his face drawn and his breath shallow.

"We found something in the basement."

"What is it?" asked Kostya.

"A girl."

Kostya fingered the passports. "Is she alive?"

"Oh yeah. She ambushed us and hit Michael with a lamp. He's still trying to calm her down."

Kostya glanced at Lev. "Come on."

When they arrived in the kitchen, Michael stood at the top of the basement stairs, repeatedly calling for the girl at the bottom to calm down. It didn't work, possibly because they didn't speak the same language. Every time Michael spoke, the girl would respond in Russian so quickly that even Kostya, a native Russian speaker, had trouble understanding it. He put his hand on his nephew's shoulder and asked him to take a step back.

"Why can't you leave me alone?" The girl's voice was high pitched and breathless.

Kostya answered in Russian. "We're not here to hurt you. I'm an old man. I couldn't hurt you if I tried. Can I come down and talk?"

She hesitated. "No. I'll hit you if you come. Stay up there."

"I understand," said Kostya, speaking as he had to his own children when they were young. "Do you know Kara?"

"Yes. She's my friend."

"She was my daughter. She and her husband passed away this afternoon, and I'm trying to find out what happened to her. Can I come down now?"

The girl didn't say anything.

"Please," said Kostya. "I need to find out why my daughter is dead. Will you talk to me?"

"Kara's dead?"

"Yes," said Kostya. "I loved her very much. I don't know what happened."

The girl remained silent for a moment. "You can come down. Just you, though."

Kostya looked over his shoulder at his brother-in-law. They had worked with each other for so long that they didn't need to communicate plans verbally anymore. Lev would stay at the top, but he and his boys would come down if they heard a scuffle.

When he reached the bottom of the stairs, Kostya visually searched the basement for threats, an old habit he had picked up as a young man in a Soviet prison. Kara hadn't finished the room, but it looked and smelled clean and dry. Someone had painted the cinder block walls white, while the floor was bare concrete. He found a couch, bookshelf, and bed in one corner and a washing machine and dryer on the other side. He looked at the girl last. She was exceedingly pretty. Fear, hope, and pain merged in her eyes to form a gaze that was simultaneously pitying and pitiful. At one glance, Kostya knew she didn't pose a threat. She tried to hold his eyes for a moment, but then she looked at her feet.

"What do you want?" she asked.

"I'm not here to hurt you," said Kostya. "So please don't be scared."

"Okay."

She didn't seem convinced. Kostya smiled, hoping to put her at ease. He had only looked at the passports briefly, but he hadn't seen her before. He didn't know what, if anything, that meant.

"Do you live here?" he asked.

She looked at the bed and nodded but didn't try to make eye contact.

"For two weeks. Kara and Daniel took care of me. They were very good people."

"Daniel was her husband?"

She nodded. "Kara talked about her father some. She said you might be able to help me, but Daniel said it was too risky to call you."

He wanted to ask what else Kara had said about him, but he refrained. They didn't have time for that.

"How did you meet my daughter?"

She hesitated at first. "She and Daniel saved me."

"Tell me about it."

She choked up. "I don't know if I can."

Kostya knew what a frightened child looked like. He spoke softly.

"Try to take it one word at a time. I need to know. As long as I'm here, no one will ever hurt you."

She stared at him, apparently trying to gauge his sincerity before walking to the bed and sitting down. Kostya sat nearby on the couch, his hands folded on his lap. The girl introduced herself as Iskra Konev and said she grew up in a small town in the Ukraine, an area which was, coincidentally, not far from a farm owned by Kostya's aunt and uncle. She stumbled over her sentences at first, but she picked up speed quickly once she began talking. A woman named Ann had brought her to the United States with the promise that she'd be able to go to college and work in an office to pay her way. When she arrived, she found Ann had a quite different future in mind for her. Iskra never said exactly what Ann forced her to do, but Kostya knew. From the way Iskra shied away from him, from the way she held her hands across her chest, from the way she wouldn't make eye contact. She said that after a week of her new life, she wanted to kill herself; after six months, she already felt dead. Had she been his child, he would have lied to her and said that everything would be okay. It wouldn't, though, not for her or anyone in her circumstances. She was beyond comfort any human could give.

"Did Kara say why she didn't take you to the police?"

Iskra shook her head. "No."

Kostya stayed still, trying to think that through. His daughter was playing a game he didn't understand yet, which meant he would need to step carefully. Kostya rocked his weight forward and stood, his knees smarting from the movement.

"I'm going to send you home."

Iskra shook her head. "I can't pay you."

"You don't need to," said Kostya. "I'm sending you home. My daughter would have wanted that. "

"I...I don't...," she began.

Kostya shushed her. "It's done. I'm sending you home."

"I don't have a passport yet."

"Let me worry about that," said Kostya, trying not to grimace as he took his first few stiff-legged steps toward the stairway. Apparently sensing that he wasn't a threat, Iskra followed him a few steps back, but as soon as she saw Lev and his boys in the kitchen, she started shaking and pressing her back against the nearest wall.

"It's all right," said Kostya, his voice soft. "These men are my family. They're Kara's family." He pointed to Lev. "This is her uncle, and his sons are her cousins. They won't hurt you."

She bit her lower lip and nodded. Her eyes looked like those of a wild animal caught in a snare.

Kostya put his hand on Lev's shoulder. "My brother-in-law and his son Michael will drive you to people who can take care of you. Lev is my oldest and best friend. You'll be as safe with him as you would be with me. We'll get you home as soon as we can."

She nodded and put her arms across her chest. Kostya smiled at her and held her gaze. She dropped her eyes from his.

"Thank you."

"Of course," he said, keeping his hand on Lev's shoulder. "If you'll excuse us for a moment, we need to make arrangements."

He took Michael and Lev to the living room and spoke in low, hushed tones.

"This young lady has been through more pain in her life than anyone deserves. Bury her deep enough that her body is undisturbed by animals."

"Of course," said Lev. Kostya looked at his nephew. Michael swallowed hard and nodded.

"Good boy," said Kostya, squeezing his nephew's shoulder. "Your brother and I will take care of the house." Kostya walked back to the kitchen and smiled at Iskra. "They will take you to Chicago, which is four hours from here. Take all the time you need to get ready. I'll make arrangements while Lev and Michael drive."

"Thank you," she said. "I can never repay you for this."

"You don't need to. I'm truly sorry for what's happened to you."

Iskra used the restroom and gathered a small bag of clothes. As soon as she was packed, Lev and Michael escorted her to one of the vans out front and James grabbed a red four-gallon container of gasoline from the garage. He doused the furniture and floors with the liquid while Kostya turned on the gas stove to high. The air in the kitchen quickly became toxic, so they went to the front porch. Kara may have saved Iskra's life for a time, but Kostya doubted her hands were completely clean. With what happened to Iskra, there'd be more bodies to bury before they were through.

"We're done here. Light it up."

7

A technician from the station's IT department rerouted the tip line to three phones in the conference room. As soon as their story aired, they'd get calls from just about every nut job, paranoid schizophrenic, and crazy asshole within a hundred-mile radius, and they'd be fed lines of bullshit so thick it'd be hard to tell the truth from the fecal matter. It'd be a lot like watching a presidential debate. Someone out there knew something, though. No one can disappear completely, least of all someone with a hostage and an injury.

Ash stood and paced the room, his stomach twisting the way it did when he and his family huddled in the basement after hearing tornado sirens. All five detectives on the task force knew their jobs, four homicide detectives stood on call if needed, and the rest of the department stood ready to back him up in case of an emergency. He shouldn't have felt nervous, but he did.

"Kristen Tanaka didn't attend the press conference tonight," he said.

"She was probably out boffing somebody for tipping her off to the case," said Smith, leaning back in his chair and sticking his legs on the table. "I don't know how you get invited to the party, but I hear she does that sort of thing."

Ash shook his head but didn't say anything. Kristen might fail a journalistic ethics class, but he didn't think she'd skip a press conference with the lead detective on a major case to thank a source. She might, though, if she had a meeting with someone more pressing.

"Does anybody know how to use this thing?" he asked, grabbing one of the room's three remote controls from the table.

"I've got it," said Alvarez. Ash threw him the remote, and the detective hit half a dozen buttons, causing the lights to dim, a screen to roll down, and the projector to spontaneously turn on. "What channel you want?"

"Whatever channel Kristen Tanaka is on."

Alvarez flipped through the lineup until coming to the local channels. Rebecca's abduction led the newscast at Tanaka's station, but the lead anchor covered the story, not her. He even showed an edited clip of Captain Bowers speaking at the press conference; the station must have purchased the video from one of the other broadcasters. They stuck to the department's narrative: a still unknown suspect abducted Rebecca, and they needed help finding him. Almost as soon as the station flashed the number for the Crime Stoppers tip line, the phone banks lit up and the detectives went to work.

Even with that story aired, the unease didn't leave Ash's stomach. Tanaka should have handled it. She had something else going on. He found out what when the anchor introduced the second story of the night and the video shifted to a live report from the parking lot of the state fairgrounds, roughly a block from the corner where Rebecca had been abducted. The camera panned to Kristen and a heavyset woman in sweatpants and a purple tank top. The woman shifted her weight from foot to foot, shaking her head slightly. The camera probably made her nervous, but her weight shifting made it look as if she had to go to the bathroom. That probably wasn't her intent.

"Unfortunately, as tragic as Rebecca Cook's case is, she wasn't the only victim tonight," said Kristen. "At approximately six this evening, three police officers carrying shotguns came to Lynette Rogers's near-north-side home and dragged her unarmed son to the front lawn where they Tasered him repeatedly after he reported not knowing anything about Ms. Cook's disappearance..."

Ash swore aloud, causing Alvarez to stop speaking mid-sentence and look up, his eyebrows raised quizzically. Ash pointed to the screen and swore again.

"He resisted arrest," said Smith, resting a phone against his chest so the caller he had been speaking to couldn't hear him. "What should we have done? The asshole had an outstanding warrant against him for assaulting his parole officer with a lead pipe. He came at us, and we Tasered him because we didn't know if he was armed. It was him or us."

If true, Detective Smith had acted correctly to protect the other officers in his detail, but that probably wouldn't help matters much. The situation had been ugly all night, but now Detective Smith had just set foot in front of a giant fan in the midst of a shit-throwing contest.

"Make sure to detail it in your report," he said, leaning against the table and glancing at the screen again. Tanaka's witness claimed that the police tried to kill her son and make it look like an accident. Ash could only shake his head; the assertion made little sense, but lots of people would still believe it. Finding cooperative witnesses was always a challenge, but now it would become damn near impossible. He swore under his breath and looked at his fellow officers. "Tanaka got this from someone. Who was at the arrest?"

Alvarez hung up the phone but ignored the next blinking light.

"Smith, me, and Dion Butler from patrol. I've been with Smith the entire night, and neither of us called anybody. Butler just finished her probationary period, so I doubt too many reporters have been grooming her for stories."

Ash rubbed his forehead, feeling a headache growing. Life seemed so much simpler as a detective. He didn't have to deal with things like this.

"Someone talked to her, so we need to find..." Ash stopped himself before finishing the remark. Kristen had completed her interview with Lynette Rogers and moved on to an interview with Sylvia Lombardo, the deputy chief. The headache he had been hoping to stave off started throbbing. Lombardo had ambitions well beyond IMPD and made little secret of it. Normally, that didn't matter; she did her job well, and then she went home at the end of the day. About a week ago, though, she gave thirty days notice, ostensibly so she could spend more time with her family, but in actuality, everyone knew she had her eye on the vacant director's position in the Department of Public Safety, the civilian agency that oversaw the law enforcement community in Indianapolis. If the mayor appointed her to it, IMPD would become her plaything. Ash fervently hoped it didn't come to that.

"I wondered if you could comment on these allegations, Sylvia," said Kristen.

"Let me first say that my heart goes out to the Cook family. IMPD is doing everything we possibly can to find Rebecca, and I'm confident we will. As to these specific allegations, I can't comment except to say that if my officers acted improperly or illegally, I will personally ensure that they face a suitable punishment, including criminal prosecution if warranted."

She'd have a difficult time doing that as a civilian, but the point probably scored well with the public and the mayor's office.

"So where does Ms. Cook's case go from here?"

Lombardo took a deep breath. "As with every case we work, our investigation into Ms. Cook's abduction is fluid and dynamic. In situations like this, we will bring as much manpower to bear on the issue as we can and will consult with our federal partners as well."

"So, the FBI?"

"Our department maintains a strong working relationship with the Bureau, so yes."

"Why didn't you bring in the FBI immediately?"

"We give wide latitude, within procedure of course, to our officers in the field. In this case, those officers did not feel bringing in the Bureau was warranted."

"As a law enforcement official, what do you believe?"

Lombardo held her hand to her chest. "Personally? As a mother and a thirty-year veteran of the Indianapolis Police Department, I'd want everything possible done.

Beyond that, I don't feel it's appropriate for me to comment."

"Would that include—"

"Turn this off and get to work." The voice belonged to Mike Bowers. Ash turned and saw him standing in the doorway, pointing an index finger at him. "I want to see you out here for a moment."

Ash didn't know how much Bowers had seen of the broadcast, but he assumed he had at least heard about the incident with the Taser. As Alvarez's and Smith's supervisor on the case, he deserved the ass-chewing he was about to receive, but he didn't have to like it. Bowers didn't have a private office on that floor, so their conversation took place in front of the entire homicide squad. Most of the detectives had enough tact to turn away.

"Whatever happened with the Taser is on me," said Ash. "I told Alvarez and Smith to be aggressive, and they were."

"Make sure they get their reports squared away. As long as they followed procedure, they'll clear a board of inquiry. We can't keep Chief Lombardo off the news, but I'll try to keep her out of the loop as much as I can. There are going to be leaks, though."

Ash felt his shoulders relax. "I get the feeling she doesn't like me very much."

"This isn't about you or Rebecca Cook. She's capitalizing on a tragedy to get her face on TV in a positive light. Don't give her any more excuses to talk about you or this investigation, and you'll be fine. Are you set for the night?"

"I've got three teams rotating between the phones, the streets, and Pamela's."

Pamela's was a room in the basement with a couple of

cots in it. At one time, it had an old poster of Pamela An-
derson in a red string bikini on the ceiling, but someone
from HR took it down about a year ago. She said female
officers had complained. Since then, Pamela's received far
fewer visitors.

"Good. Get to it."

He clapped Ash on the shoulder and then turned around.
Alvarez and Smith had resumed their duties on the phone
when Ash stepped back into the conference room.

"Anything?"

"Nothing promising yet," said Doran. "We'll get there,
though."

"I hope you're right."

*　　*　　*

The calls came in pretty steady from about ten to midnight.
A number of people said they had information they'd share
for a reward, but they would only talk if they had money in
their pockets. When pressed for information, those callers
invariably hung up or lied in the hopes that they'd manage
to get a detail correct by sheer chance. They wasted everyone's time, including their own. The rest of the callers
seemed sincere, but they knew little more than the liars and
nut jobs. Two calls in the first shift merited a follow-up, so
Doran and Smith drove out. The first came from an elderly
woman who thought she saw a woman being forced into a
car. As it turned out, she witnessed her neighbor, a design
student at a local art school, putting a mannequin on her
backseat for a fashion show. The second call involved a couple of guys in a fraternity stuffing a blow-up doll in the back

of their hippy philosophy professor's car. That call amused everyone at least, even while it wasted their time.

Since Ash had been up since five that morning, he took the first shift in Pamela's at midnight. It felt like he had barely closed his eyes by the time Alvarez woke him up at a little before two.

"We got another one."

Ash blinked several times trying to wake up. The basement air tasted and smelled musty.

"We've got another what?" he asked, rubbing sleep out of his eyes.

Alvarez turned on the light, illuminating the room. Once his eyes adjusted, Ash saw, in addition to a pair of cots, half a dozen filing cabinets, four metal desks, and two bronze desk lamps so old he could have taken them on *Antiques Roadshow*. He had been so tired on his way in that he hadn't noticed anything but the beds.

"We just got a call from a woman about two blocks from Shadeland Avenue. She claims to have seen a Caucasian man carrying a small Caucasian woman from a green Pontiac Grand Am."

Ash sat up straighter. The pawnshop owner on Shadeland had mentioned a green Grand Am, but they hadn't released that information to anyone. It might have been a good lead.

"What else do we have?"

Alvarez shook his head. "Not a lot. According to our caller, the man carried the woman over his shoulder and broke into a foreclosed home about fifteen minutes ago. The caller is watching the house now, but no one's come out yet."

"If it's Rebecca, where have they been for the past few

hours?" asked Ash, standing, but almost instantly stagger-
ing back as blood rushed through his system, momentarily
making his head light.

"Maybe just driving around until they found somewhere
to lie low," said Alvarez. "I don't know. Your guess is as
good as mine."

"It's the right part of town, but it's not enough for a search
warrant. She said the house is a foreclosure?" Alvarez nodded. "No one should be in that this time of night. We'll
check it out. If we can find signs of a break-in, that'll give
us probable cause to call in the violent crime unit and detain
everyone. You have everything you need?"

"Of course."

"Let's go."

Alvarez left the room first. Ash swayed on his feet. Two
hours of sleep helped, but he needed at least four hours
more to overcome the heavy, drunken feeling in his limbs.
At least he had experience being drunk, so he knew how
to conduct himself. He steadied himself and jogged up the
stairs. The temperature outside had dropped about fifteen
degrees since his last outing, and water puddled on low
points on the sidewalks. His shoulder spoke the truth earlier: It had rained. Thankfully, they had finished clearing
their outdoor crime scenes already.

Ash pulled his jacket tight around him and looked left
and right before walking to the parking lot across the street.
He felt a cold, nervous chill travel up and down his spine.
Just eight months ago, a trio of misguided police officers
had ambushed him on his way to the building from which
he just exited, leaving him battered and bruised. He remembered that night vividly, not because of the beating but

because of what happened afterward. His wife confronted him about his drinking for the first time, and he realized what a serious problem he had. He still had a hard time staying out of bars or away from liquor stores, but it had become easier now; he no longer felt alone.

Ash wanted more officers with them, but he couldn't justify the resources without further evidence of a crime. He considered taking Doran and Smith, but he needed at least one of them on the phones and the other on standby in case another credible call came in. Backup was always a phone call away, so their absence shouldn't be a problem.

That late in the evening, there were few cars on the street, so Ash didn't bother turning on the light bar or siren as he pulled out of the parking lot. Even without them, the few drivers he encountered had enough common sense to get out of the way of the speeding police cruiser. Both he and Alvarez understood the situation, so neither of them spoke. The guy who abducted Rebecca had already killed two people. If they found him, he probably wouldn't go quietly.

"You okay with what we're about to do?" asked Ash.

Alvarez adjusted himself on the seat and slipped a hand to the holster on his belt. "We're about to investigate a lead in a kidnapping. Of course I'm okay with that."

Ash glanced over. Alvarez stared straight ahead, his gaze intense, focused and ready. After his hesitation at the crime scene that afternoon, Ash was glad to see the detective's newfound poise. Maybe he just needed a little direction after all. He turned his attention back to the road. Unlike his visit to Shadeland Avenue earlier that afternoon, few cars lined up at the stoplights and most of the shops were closed. With the house still a couple of blocks away, Alvarez closed his eyes and made the sign of the cross over his chest, his lips moving as he prayed.

Ash killed the lights on his cruiser before turning into the neighborhood their caller had alerted them to. Single-story ranch homes lined the street with the occasional two-story popping up for good measure. Their caller had given them the address of a two-story Colonial with a brick chimney and white siding. Ash drove past without slowing. It looked like a nice family home; save the late-model green Pontiac in the driveway, it also looked abandoned. He parked at the end of the block and turned off the engine, but didn't say anything until Alvarez finished praying.

"Until we learn otherwise, we're here for information," said Ash. "But if Rebecca's in there and in trouble, we might have to go in. Will you be okay with that?"

Alvarez's chest rose and fell, but he nodded.

"Do you understand what I'm really asking?" asked Ash. "More than likely, our caller is a neighborhood busybody who saw a couple of kids screwing around. If she isn't and this is an emergency, we'll have to act on our own. Do you understand what I'm getting at? You can't hesitate like you did at the fairgrounds today."

Alvarez didn't turn to look at him. "You heard I was in the Peace Corps, didn't you?" he asked.

"Yeah," said Ash.

"Because I grew up speaking Spanish, they sent me to Juarez, Mexico, to teach English. I started dating the crime reporter for the local newspaper. I was going to marry her when my tour ended."

"Okay," said Ash, unsure why Alvarez thought it appropriate to tell him about the history of his love life right now.

"About two months before my tour was over, I took Marisol out to lunch at a café by my school. Two guys with guns came in and grabbed her. I tried to stop them, but one of them hit me on the head with the butt of his rifle and knocked me out cold. A day later, a police officer showed me a video a local cartel boss sent him. A fifteen-year-old kid from one of my classes slit Marisol's throat with a butcher knife so dull he had to use it like a saw. The cop said that's what happens to people who talk about things they shouldn't talk about."

"Wow," said Ash, exhaling slowly. "I'm sorry."

"Don't be sorry. Back then, I couldn't have done anything, but now I can. If Rebecca is in there, I'm getting her back. I don't care what I have to do."

Ash took a moment to respond. Before being hired, Alvarez would have gone through a mental health evaluation, an evaluation he should have flunked with something like that in his past. The admission changed the situation, made Ash realize for the first time how volatile it could become. He drummed his fingers on the steering wheel, thinking. For all they knew, it could be a couple of teenagers who snuck in looking for somewhere to fool around without their parents' watchful eyes; they'd be in enough trouble as it was. They didn't need a detective with something to prove and a score to settle chasing after them.

"Unless we hear someone screaming or another indication of imminent danger to a bystander, we're staying out of the house," said Ash. "We go in only as an absolute last resort. Are you okay with that?"

"If this guy's got Rebecca in there, I say we charge in before he knows we're coming."

Ash shook his head. "This can't work like that. If we charge in there, he's going to shoot her and us. We have to be smart. Are you okay with that? If not, I will get someone who is."

"Then what do you want to do?"

"I want to walk around the house and find out how the people inside got there. As soon as we find a broken window or a door that's been kicked down, we'll call for backup. They'll handle the extraction."

Alvarez took a deep breath. "What if we don't find anything?"

"If there are people inside, we'll find something."

"But what—"

"That's enough," said Ash, interrupting him. "I understand your frustration. If I could, I'd kick down that door and drag our suspect out by his hair. We're not bulletproof, though, and neither is Rebecca. If she's in there, we need to get her out safely. I'm not going to hear any arguments on this."

"All right, then."

Ash watched his partner for the next few seconds, trying to get a read on him.

"What?" asked Alvarez.

"Nothing," said Ash, turning his eyes to the front. "Let's just be careful."

Alvarez opened his door first, but Ash followed shortly thereafter. The evening air was cool and thick, and a slick sheen of moisture reflected off the grass beside their vehicle. Ash had parked three houses away from their target. Between them and it stood two hundred yards of grass and shrubbery. Even with a partially clouded sky, enough light reflected from the moon to silhouette them both against the sidewalk. If someone happened to look out the window of their target home, they'd be easy to spot.

Ash pointed to the side yard between two of the nearest houses and ran forward with Alvarez a few feet behind him. The rain earlier had left the ground spongy and wet. Trees filtered the moonlight in the home's backyard, casting long shadows on the grass. Ash stayed in those shadows and ran west, toward the partially fenced backyard of their target house, but stopped on the edge of the property and knelt in darkness beside a tree.

"You hear anything?" asked Ash.

"Just crickets."

The house had two rear doors and half a dozen windows, none of which were open or broken. Whoever had broken in hadn't come that way.

"There's nothing here. What do you want to do?" asked Alvarez.

"We just got here, okay?" asked Ash. "We'll check out the property and report back to Captain Bowers once we find something. If we can't find anything, we'll wake up the neighbors. They might have seen something."

"If Rebecca's in there, I'm not walking away from this," said Alvarez, raising his voice and shaking his head. "We need to get in there ourselves. We can go through the back door."

Ash tried not to grind his teeth. "We've already gone over this. We have no idea what's in that house. Even if Rebecca is in there, we don't know what the guy who kidnapped her is carrying. Are you comfortable going in there if our suspect has an assault rifle and body armor? I'm not.

And if it's not Rebecca, I don't want some stupid kid to get hurt."

Alvarez shook his head and looked at the house. "From the stories I've heard about you, I thought you'd be the first one through the door."

"Don't believe everything you hear."

"I don't like this."

"You're not supposed to," said Ash. "If this is our guy, he murdered two people and kidnapped a third. You're supposed to be pissed, but you can't be stupid."

Alvarez looked away but finally nodded. "All right. We'll do it your way. I don't want this to go bad."

It's already bad.

"Good. Let's move."

Both men crouched low and crept toward the front of the house. Their target home had a long, narrow lot, so only about ten feet of shadows and grass stood between it and the home next door. It hid them well. Just like the windows on the rear of the house, the windows overlooking the side yard were securely fastened. Ash crept toward the home's front corner but stopped when he caught sight of an overgrown evergreen bush in the front yard. He had told countless homeowner associations to have residents trim their evergreen bushes well for just this reason: Someone had broken into the house and used the thick, needlelike leaves of a Yew to cover his entrance point. Ash put a finger to his lips and then pointed it out.

"Slowly move to the backyard and call Captain Bowers. Tell him we need backup immediately."

Alvarez licked his lips and then nodded. He slipped into the night. Ash heard his voice, but he couldn't make out the words. If someone in the house heard, hopefully he'd think it was the wind. When Alvarez came back again, he was breathing hard.

"We've got SWAT coming in."

"ETA?" asked Ash.

"They've been on standby all night, so ten to fifteen minutes. We'll have patrol officers here in five."

Normally it'd take at least half an hour to get the entire SWAT team together, so ten to fifteen minutes was a great response time. Even still, a lot could happen in ten to fifteen minutes, much more than he cared to think about.

"All right. Call the dispatcher and tell the patrol units to maintain their distance from the house. We don't want to spook our suspect."

"I already did."

Ash glanced at him and nodded. "Good. Thank you."

He settled his back against the house. The night air was thick from the storm earlier, and it didn't fill his lungs the way it should have. He couldn't get a deep enough breath to relax. That wasn't such a bad thing, though; he didn't need to relax given their situation. Ash glanced at his watch, noting the time before leaning his back against the house and planting his feet in the grass. Silence descended upon them.

In that quiet stillness, he heard it for the first time, faint, like a branch rubbing against his window on a cold winter night. A voice. Ash closed his eyes and held his breath. He heard it again, fainter this time.

"Don't say a word."

Ash glanced at Alvarez and motioned toward the window with his head.

"Did you hear that?" he whispered.

Alvarez nodded. "Yeah. What do we do?"

"We wait for our team. Meantime, send Bowers a text message with an update. Tell him we might have a hostage situation."

Alvarez's index finger flashed across the screen on his phone. Ash could have done it himself, but he wasn't nearly as fast. Within thirty seconds, he glanced up at Ash.

"It's done."

At that time of night, their backup wouldn't run into much traffic. Ash nodded and glanced at the house. *Hold on, honey.*

Time rarely played by the rules out in the field. A single moment could feel like a year or it could pass so fast you barely had time to register that it was gone. Ash didn't know how long he waited outside for the first patrol officers to hurry toward the house—it could have been a minute, or it could have been five. However long it took, the patrol officers parked far enough away from the house he couldn't see their car. Unfortunately, they didn't try to hide; they simply walked to a neighbor's yard and stood still. As soon as he saw them, Ash heard a familiar noise from inside the house, a muffled thud followed by a sliding, scraping sound. The home evidently had wooden windows. Like the wooden windows on his own house, they contracted and expanded with changes in humidity, meaning they didn't fit tight in the frame like a more modern, vinyl window. Their suspect had just opened one.

"Who's there?"

One of the patrol officers started to walk forward, but Ash stepped into the front yard, his hand held in front of him, stopping the officer. The front of the house had a neatly trimmed lawn and freshly mulched flowerbeds. A FOR SALE sign hung beside the driveway with a black bar along the bottom announcing it as a foreclosure. Their suspect had opened a window on the second floor, but Ash couldn't see him in the evening light. Alvarez followed a step back, his firearm held at his side.

"We're police officers. We're just here to talk."

"I don't have anything to talk about."

"I think you do," said Ash, crossing toward the sidewalk where the patrol officers stood. They needed cover in case their suspect had a rifle, so he told one of the officers to get his car before turning his attention back to their suspect. "I know you've got someone in there with you. Who is it?"

"That's none of your business."

"It is my business," said Ash. "Is it Rebecca Cook?"

Ash counted to five, waiting. "No, it's my daughter."

Ash's heart sank at the admission, but it didn't change the job in front of him. Like many of the officers in his department, he had sat through seminars on hostage negotiation before, so he knew the basic dos and don'ts. Hopefully they could get a professional quickly. "I've got a little girl of my own. What's your little girl's name?"

The man's voice wavered. "Madison."

"Madison. That's a pretty name. Is Madison okay?"

"She's fine."

The patrol vehicle rolled forward, and all four officers stepped behind it, putting it between them and the house and giving them some cover. There was no sign of Bowers or the SWAT team yet.

"We'd really like it if you and Madison would come out and talk to us face-to-face. Can you do that for me?"

"No. We're staying here."

"Okay," said Ash. "Can I talk to Madison?"

"Why?"

"I want to make sure that she's doing okay."

"She's fine. I already told you."

Hopefully he was being honest because Ash didn't want to push him more than he already had.

"I'm glad. Here's what's going on. I'm Sergeant Ash Rashid with the Indianapolis Metropolitan Police Department. I'm here to talk to you and make sure everybody stays safe. We're going to get through this, and everybody's going to be fine. I want you to know that. What's your name?"

The guy in the house didn't answer for a moment. "Jonathan."

"Do you mind if I call you that?"

"Go ahead."

"Good," said Ash, nodding and glancing at Alvarez. "Get the plate number from the Pontiac in the drive and see if it's registered to anyone named Jonathan. Find out what we can about him." He looked back at the house. "First of all, Jonathan, are you okay? If you or anyone else in there needs medical attention, I can call an ambulance."

"We're fine."

"Good deal. I want to thank you for keeping your cool. Nobody's hurt, and we want to keep it that way. That counts a lot, and we all appreciate that. Right now, this is just a trespassing situation, and we can all walk away from this. My goal is to make that happen. Do you believe me?"

He didn't respond.

"Do you believe me, Jonathan? I want to end this before anyone gets hurt. Only you can make that happen."

"Just leave us alone."

"That's the one thing I can't do," said Ash. "Can you tell me what's going on?"

Again, Jonathan didn't respond. Alvarez leaned close. "The Pontiac is registered to Jonathan Hartley at this address."

"So this is his house," said Ash, nodding. That potentially told them a lot about their hostage taker's mind-set. It also told them how dangerous he was. Losing a house to foreclosure would depress even the most cheerful person. And if he was depressed, he might not think he had much to live for, giving him little reason to hesitate to kill himself, his daughter, or others. Ash lowered his voice and looked at Alvarez. "How far out is the SWAT team?"

"Should be here any minute now."

Ash looked at the house again. "A lot of police officers are on their way. Is that okay?"

"I didn't ask for this," said Jonathan, his voice high. "Just leave us alone."

"I know you didn't ask for this, but the police officers are coming. They won't do anything without my say, so you don't have anything to be afraid of. And if you want, I can call them and tell them to stay away. I can do that, but only if you do something for me. Let Madison go."

"She's staying here."

Ash hadn't expected that to work, but it was worth trying. "If you don't let her go, the SWAT team will come. There's nothing I can do to stop that. Do you understand?"

"I didn't want any of this to happen."

Ash thought he could hear an engine somewhere in the distance, so he looked at one of the patrol officers. "Get on the radio and tell the SWAT team to roll in slowly. I don't want to spook this guy." He looked at the house again. "I know you didn't. This is just a misunderstanding. I don't think you intended to hurt anyone. I still don't think you intend to hurt anyone. Can you tell me what's going on? Is this your house?"

"The bank took it." Ash grimaced as Jonathan spat the words out. That was obviously a touchy subject. As Jonathan spoke, the SWAT team's black armored van crept toward the scene with a row of patrol vehicles behind it. A hostage negotiation could take hours or even days, but certain times during the negotiation were more dangerous than others. The chaos of the first few minutes were usually the worst, but any change in the environment could precipitate a violent response from a hostage taker. Ash held his breath as the truck pulled to a stop. Thankfully, the men inside didn't pop the doors and spring out. Instead, they opened them slowly and stepped out like a bunch of kids testing the thickness of the ice covering a pond before going skating. Ash nodded toward Captain Bowers as he strode toward him. The captain leaned close.

"We've got a negotiator coming in. Is the hostage taker talking?"

"Yeah. I don't know if he's armed, but he's got his daughter with him. I think he's depressed, but I don't know if he's violent."

One of the SWAT team members came to the cruiser, carrying a briefcase. He set it on the hood and removed a thermal imaging camera. Its attached video screen showed the hot spots in the house, including the position of their hostage taker and his daughter. Jonathan paced a room in the center of the home while Madison huddled in one corner. They were alone in the house.

"Keep talking to him."

Ash nodded again. "The SWAT team is here, Jonathan, but we can all still walk away from this. You haven't hurt anybody, and we appreciate that. Did you come here because the bank took your house?"

"It's my house. I bought it. I raised my kids in it," shouted Jonathan, his voice almost hoarse. "They had no right to take it."

"I'm sorry they took your house," said Ash, forcing his voice to remain even. "I can't help you if you're upset, though. Okay? If you're calm, we can talk our way through this."

Ash waited and watched the thermal imaging monitor. Jonathan had stopped pacing and stood near his daughter with his arm outstretched. Ash couldn't see a firearm, but Jonathan very well could have been pointing one at Madison at that moment. His heartbeat increased in tempo, and he glanced at Alvarez and Bowers.

"Is anybody looking for this girl's mom?"

"Her name's Amy Hartley, and she lives in an apartment a couple of blocks away," said Bowers. "I've got uniforms picking her up."

"How'd you find her?"

Bowers's eyes flicked to the house. "BMV records. She's listed as his next of kin, and she updated her driver's license information."

"Where's our negotiator? We need somebody who actually knows what he's doing."

Bowers shrugged. "He's coming from Mooresville, so it's a half-hour drive. That's all I know."

Ash swore under his breath and then wiped sweat off his forehead. "Can I get some water?"

Bowers looked at Alvarez. The detective nodded and jogged off. The SWAT team had positioned themselves around the front of the house, but everyone remained behind a vehicle for cover. If Jonathan started shooting at them, they'd probably be fine. Madison had no such protection. Ash watched the thermal monitor. Jonathan still stood over his daughter. She hugged her knees to her chest, forming a ball. Aside from their names, he didn't know the first thing about either of them. If he was going to talk him down, he needed more information than he had.

Alvarez jogged back to the cruiser carrying a half-empty bottle of water.

"This was Carmichael's. It's all I could find," he said, handing the bottle to Ash. "I sent her to a convenience store to get some more."

Ash unscrewed the top and took a long gulp. Jonathan didn't seem to be in the talking mood, so Ash didn't say anything. He didn't know if that silence was a good sign or not. His hands shook, so as soon as he finished the water, he threw the empty bottle inside the nearest cruiser and put them in his pockets, hoping no one else had seen. Within five minutes, a gray Crown Vic joined the procession of vehicles in front of the house. A uniformed officer stepped out and opened the rear door for a petite blonde in jeans and a T-shirt. Her brown eyes were wide and her brow furrowed. The officer directed her toward Ash and Captain Bowers.

"Are you Amy?" asked Ash. She nodded. "And you're Jonathan's wife, right?"

She nodded, but then caught herself and shook her head.

"We're getting a divorce. I served him papers this after-noon."

That both complicated and helped explain the situation. Ash nodded. "Does he own any firearms?"

She nodded. "A couple. He has a pistol for home protection and a couple of hunting rifles."

"Okay," said Ash. "We have a professional hostage negotiator coming in. I'm sure he'll talk to you in a little bit. In the meantime—"

"Who is that?" It was the first time Jonathan had spoken in several minutes. The thermal monitor showed him near the window. "Is that Amy?"

Ash waved her down and then pointed toward the SWAT team's armored transport. He waved over a patrol officer. "Get her somewhere safe."

The patrol officer put his arm around Amy's shoulders and led her to the rear of the SWAT team's truck. Ash stopped watching at that point and turned toward the house. "That is Amy. She's worried about Madison and you. She doesn't want anyone hurt."

Jonathan didn't say anything for a moment, but Ash watched him cross the room to stand over his daughter again. He extended his arm and time seemed to slow. Ash stood up straighter. His heart thudded against his breast-bone.

Don't do this.

"Tell Amy this is on her."

"Don't do—"

The gunshot cut Ash's scream short. The entire scene erupted. The SWAT members sprinted forward, tactical rifles bared in front of them.

"Call it in. We need ambulances right now," said Ash, shouting at the nearest patrol officer. She practically dove into her vehicle and grabbed the radio. Ash held his breath, powerless to do anything else. Jim Price, the SWAT team's point man, reached the front door first. He blew the dead bolt with a breaching shotgun and took a step back. The next man in line kicked the door forward, his rifle held in front of him like a shield. Each team member then sprinted single file into the house after him, their heads swiveling left and right. Even from outside, Ash could hear their boots pound against doors as they cleared the rooms.

Come on, come on, come on.

Jonathan had only fired one shot. Over and over, Ash found himself praying that Jonathan had shot himself, but over and over, he found an image of a dead little girl clawing its way into his consciousness. He heard more thuds and more shouts as the officers moved through the house. Moments seemed to take days.

"Gun. Gun."

"Drop it."

The cacophony of voices stopped only with the report of a firearm. Ash held his breath and found himself counting the seconds.

"House is clear."

The announcement had taken a four count. Ash didn't know what that meant, but he sprinted toward the house anyway. It was a center-hall Colonial with a staircase immediately in front of the door. Most of the action seemed to be happening on the second floor, so Ash ran up and followed a line of officers to a small, auxiliary bedroom near the center of the house. The room held a mattress and blanket, but no other furniture to hide behind. A middle-aged man lay sprawled out near the window, most of his face gone. A blond girl—she couldn't have been more than twelve—lay on the ground near the door. Her blood had begun to puddle beneath her and froth formed around her lips. She cried even as she struggled to breathe.

One of the SWAT team members knelt beside her and held his hand a few inches from her mouth.

"She's breathing, but it's irregular. Get the kit and get me an ambulance right now."

Ash jumped back into the hallway to let them work.

Please let her be okay, God.

Eventually, Jim Price ran toward them, carrying a red and white box. He tossed it to one of the officers inside the room, while another tilted Madison on her side. Blood ran onto the carpet, probably draining from her lungs. Price tore pieces of duct tape off a spool and handed them to another officer who wrapped them around her chest, over her wound. Whether the compression was supposed to hold her blood in or whether the tape was supposed to help her gaping chest wound, Ash didn't know. He ran back to his car and motioned for Eddie Alvarez.

"Get in."

Ash waited for the ambulance to arrive. Two paramedics ran into the house and carried the girl out within a minute. As soon as that happened, Ash turned on the cruiser, as well as its lights and sirens. Being nearly three in the morning, the roads were mostly empty, but he cleared a path to the hospital anyway. Aside from prayer, it was the only constructive thing he could do.

8

Ash parked in the garage beside the children's hospital and watched from across the street while paramedics wheeled Madison inside. Several more police cars followed, including one holding Amy Hartley, Madison's mother. She cried hysterically. Neither Ash nor Alvarez had any real connection to the Hartley family, but they went in the emergency room's waiting area anyway. Both men knew they had paperwork to fill out and statements to give, but at the moment, neither seemed to care. Ash didn't, at least. His focus remained on Madison.

About half an hour after they arrived, Mike Bowers walked into the waiting room and sat down beside them.

"Any news on her father?" asked Alvarez.

"Dead. Single self-inflicted gunshot wound," said Bowers. He sighed. "Why the son of a bitch had to take his daughter with him, I don't know."

They waited an hour and then another before a nurse came out. She had bloodstains on her smock and her face was white.

"Are you the officers who brought Madison Hartley in?"

Bowers nodded.

"She's lost a lot of blood, but she's stable."

"She's going to make it?" asked Ash.

"We think so. The occlusive dressing put on her before she arrived here prevented her lung from collapsing. It probably saved her life."

The tension Ash had been carrying in his gut rushed out of him and he slumped over in his chair. Bowers furrowed his brow, so Ash filled him in. "Somebody from the SWAT team covered her wound with duct tape."

"I'll make sure the officer gets a letter of commendation for that," said Bowers, nodding toward the nurse. "Thank you." The nurse nodded before leaving the waiting room and Bowers looked at them. "It's time for us to get out of here. We've still got work to do."

"You want us to give statements?" asked Ash.

"You'll need to eventually, but now I want you to go home and get changed. We've still got to find Rebecca."

The reminder put things back into prospective. Ash drove Alvarez back to the station for his car and then drove home with the sun threatening to rise on the horizon. Normally, his family would sleep in for another hour in the summer, but during Ramadan everybody woke up early. He met Megan, Kaden, and Hannah in the kitchen.

"Hey, Bob." Megan waved at him from their breakfast table while eating a piece of toast. Jam had dripped onto one of the fluffy cartoon cows printed on her pajamas, and her hair flew in every direction at once. She smiled at him, happy despite the early hour.

He walked to the table and kissed her forehead. "It's *Baba*, sweetheart. If you don't want to call me *Baba*, you can call me Dad. You can't call me Bob, though. It's inappropriate."

"Kaden does."

Ash smiled. "Yes, but he can't say *Baba*. You can."

Megan stuck out her bottom lip and dropped her toast in protest, but Hannah intervened before she could say anything else.

"Finish your breakfast," she said. "*Baba* and I need to talk."

Megan's eyes opened wide as if she had suddenly realized something. She motioned Ash forward and lowered her voice. Her secret-telling ability had improved from the days when she shouted them at the top of her lungs.

"*Ummi's* mad at you for missing *iftar* last night. I forgot to tell you earlier."

Ash glanced at his wife; she didn't glare at him, but his daughter's assessment didn't seem too far off.

"Thanks for the tip."

He kissed her forehead again and started to walk toward his wife, but Megan grabbed the arm of his sweatshirt before he could step away.

"Is Kaden going to Hell?"

"No, of course not. Why are you asking that?"

"Because he doesn't fast. I fasted half a day yesterday, so I'm not going to Hell. I'm worried about him, though."

Ash patted her back. "He's a baby, so he's excused. We can talk about this later if you want."

"Okay," she said, stuffing a piece of toast in her mouth.

Ash joined his wife at the stove. She stirred a small pot of oatmeal far more vigorously than required.

"I saw the shooting on the news when I got up this morning," she said. "Who was hurt?"

Ash grimaced. "A young girl named Madison. Her dad

took her hostage and shot her before killing himself. I meant to call you, but I got wrapped up in things."

Hannah inhaled through her nose. "Like what?"

"Eddie Alvarez and I cleared traffic in front of the ambulance on the way to the hospital. We didn't think Madison had a lot of time."

"Did she survive?"

"Yeah."

Hannah put the spoon down. "I'm very glad she's alive. I'm also very upset that you didn't call me and tell me you were okay."

"I'm sorry. I—"

"I even tried to call you," she said, interrupting him. "You didn't pick up the phone."

"I had to turn it off in the hospital."

"The news didn't say who was shot, but I recognized the people at the scene. I knew you were there, but I didn't know if you were dead. I didn't know if you had been hurt. I didn't know if you were in the hospital." She took a deep breath. "That was mean. Turning off your phone without calling me wasn't just inconsiderate—it was mean. I want you to know that."

When she finally took her eyes off the oatmeal to look at him, Ash saw red streaks in the whites of her eyes. That didn't happen when she lost her temper; that happened when he hurt her.

"I screwed up. I'm sorry."

"You could have called me before you went into the hospital. I don't think that's too much to ask. A two-minute phone call to tell me that our kids still have a father. Or if you couldn't call me, ask someone else to.

I don't care who it comes from. I just want to know if you're okay."

No matter how hard they worked at it, many police officers had a hard time staying married. Ash knew at least three guys who had gone home after a day at work to find their spouses had cleared out their houses and left without leaving so much as a note. The hours sucked, the pay rarely kept up with inflation, and the stress followed everyone home. Ash loved his family more than anything in the world. They gave him purpose and a reason to get up in the morning, but he had a hard time balancing their needs against a job that continually demanded more and more of him.

"You're right, and I'm sorry. I should have called. I got wrapped up in the moment, and I didn't even think."

"I know, and that hurts most of all. You don't think about us." Ash started to protest, but she put her hand on his chest. "Don't say anything. I just need some time alone. Can you take care of the kids?"

He nodded, and she pushed past him and hurried to their bedroom before he could respond. Ash stayed at the stove at first, but then he took the oatmeal off the heat and sat beside his daughter at the table.

"Are you in trouble, *Baba*?"

"Yeah, kiddo, I'm in big trouble."

*   *   *

Hannah came out of the bedroom about half an hour later. By that time, Ash had fed the kids and done the dishes. Helping out around the house didn't make up for being an ass, but hopefully it showed that he was trying. The two of them talked for a few minutes, but it would take a lot more than a conversation to resolve things. He had *suhoor*, the predawn meal during Ramadan, and then said dawn prayers right before the sun rose.

Given Madison's shooting the night before, Ash didn't know how his day would go. He hadn't fired a shot, but the department's brass still could put him on leave until he saw a psychiatrist. Ash didn't want that or think it necessary, but there wasn't much he could do to fight it. On the other hand, a visit to a psychiatrist would do Eddie Alvarez some good. Ash left his house at a quarter to eight and drove into work. When he got there, he found the homicide squad's conference room empty, so he took a seat at the head of the table and called Eddie Alvarez on his cell phone.

"Hey, Eddie, it's Ash Rashid. How you doing?"

Alvarez yawned. "Fine, all considered. You?"

"I'm good, thanks. I'm calling this morning because I need to talk to you about what you said last night."

"Yeah, I thought you might. It's not going to happen again. You're a superior officer, and you made the right call. I see that now. I won't question your judgment again."

"That's not why I'm calling," said Ash. "Tell me again about Marisol, your girl when you were in the Peace Corps."

Alvarez grunted. "I'd rather not. I don't even know why I told you about her last night."

"You told me about her because you were stressed out. How often do you think about her when you're at work?"

"Are you asking me as my superior officer or as a friend?"

"Both."

"Well, I don't think she's any of your business either way."

Ash hadn't wanted the conversation to go like this, but he had come in mentally prepared for it. "If she's on your mind a lot, then your mind isn't on work. That's dangerous. You understand what I'm saying?"

"I get it. It won't happen again. I already said that."

"Aside from me, who knows about her?"

"Nobody, not even my wife."

Ash nodded. "I need you to tell your CO. I also think you need to talk to somebody. I can make you an appointment with the station psychiatrist if you want."

Alvarez chuckled. "Are you serious?"

"Yeah."

"Why?"

"Because if your mind is on her, you're a liability to everyone around you. Last night, you wanted to charge into a home, not knowing who was there, if he was armed, or even who he was with. You could have gotten us and the hostage killed. It was reckless."

Alvarez chuckled again, but Ash couldn't detect merriment in the sound. "You're seriously lecturing me? Mr. One-Eighty-Seven is calling me reckless?"

"I'm not lecturing you. I'm saying you need some help. That's it." Ash paused. "And who's Mr. One-Eighty-Seven?"

"You. One-Eighty-Seven, it's the section in the California penal code about murder."

Ash didn't respond for a moment, trying to understand the reference. "First of all, we live in Indiana, so whoever calls me that watches too much TV. Second, I haven't worked homicide in several years."

"People don't call you that because you worked homicide. They call you that because you're involved in so many."

Ash blinked and shook his head. "I don't even know what to say to that."

"I told you something in confidence. I didn't expect you to throw it back at me. Besides, I'm not the only man on this job with a past. I know what you did when your niece died. Don't tell me that didn't change you."

"I investigated drug traffickers when my niece died."

"When you investigate somebody, you put him in jail. You tracked down the people who sold your niece drugs and put every single one of them in the ground. You know how many people look up to you because of that?"

"Hopefully nobody."

"A lot of people. If you do this to me, this is going to hurt you more than it's going to hurt me. You think people will trust you after this?"

"If this makes people distrust me, that's their fault. This is my job. End of discussion," said Ash. "You tell your CO today, or I will. Is that clear?"

"Piss off."

Alvarez hung up, and Ash felt himself slump into his seat before he slipped his phone back into his pocket. As he did that, someone near the door cleared his throat, and Ash looked up to see Captain Bowers in the doorway, his arms crossed.

"Something you want to tell me, Ash?"

"How much did you hear?"

"A bit. Was that Eddie Alvarez's voice?"

Ash nodded. "Minor personal issue. Can we drop it for now? I can talk to you about it later if needed."

Bowers smiled. "If it's something I need to hear, I'd like you to tell me now."

"If you order me, I'll talk. I'd like to give Alvarez some time to do the right thing first, though."

Bowers cocked his head to the side and raised his eyebrows. "All right. But Alvarez is off the case until one of you talks to me."

"I agree."

Bowers stood up straighter. "You wouldn't have given in that easily unless there was a problem. What'd he do?"

"If Alvarez hasn't contacted you by the end of the day, I'll sit down with you. Can we drop it until then?"

"Until the end of the day," said Bowers, crossing the room. He pulled out a chair and sat down. "I asked Greg Doran to attend John and Kate Doe's autopsies this morning and sent Smith home a couple of hours ago. If you're not up for this investigation after last night, now's the time to tell me. I can get a replacement."

"I'm fine."

"Good. I thought you would be. You need anything?"

"I don't know just yet. I'll call Doran and Smith and see how they're progressing. If we do need anything, I'll let you know. You going to send me somebody to replace Alvarez?"

"I'll find someone if you need help. Anything else?"

"Have you ever heard of Mr. One-Eighty-Seven?"

Bowers blinked. "I've heard the nickname, but I wouldn't look too much into it. Every time you've been involved in a shooting, you've been cleared."

"So you know that's me."

"I didn't think it was a secret," said Bowers.

"It was to me."

"Now you know," said Bowers. "Does that change anything?"

"I don't know," said Ash. He squinted. "Have I really been involved in that many shootings?"

Bowers stood up. "Just work the case. Once we get Rebecca back, you can take a long vacation to think about your life."

Perhaps he was right; introspection could wait. Rebecca couldn't. "I'll do that."

Bowers left, and Ash glanced at his watch. It was half past eight in the morning. If John and Kate Doe received the first cut of the morning, Doran should have been out. Ash dialed the detective's phone and waited through three rings for him to pick up.

"Doran, it's Ash."

"Hey. I heard what happened last night. You okay?"

"I'm fine. Where are you?"

"Coroner's office. We just finished John Doe's autopsy. We've got Kate Doe up next."

Rodriguez must have been running behind. "You learn anything new?"

"Our shooter tapped John twice in the head with a twenty-two. Entry wounds were so close together it looked like one shot. The rounds broke up in his skull, so we don't have anything for ballistics matching. I'm guessing we'll see the same thing with Kate."

Ash allowed himself to sink deep in his seat.

"Sounds like our shooter's had some practice."

"Yeah," said Doran. "Seems that way. Did you see Chief Lombardo on TV this morning?"

Ash rubbed sleep out of his eyes and stifled a yawn.

"No, but I can guess what she said. We're undisciplined barbarians rampaging across the countryside. We don't know what we're doing. I should be in jail for murder. Things like that."

"She was a little more subtle than that, but you got the gist. Rebecca's family made an appearance, too."

"What'd they say?"

"About what you'd expect after last night. They're concerned about the direction of the case. They also pleaded with whoever has Rebecca. They want her home. They also asked us to bring in the Bureau."

Ash sighed. The FBI had great investigators, so he wouldn't have hesitated to bring them in if he thought it appropriate. They didn't need them for Rebecca's abduction, though. The man who took her didn't know who she was, which meant he probably wouldn't be making any ransom demands. Without those, they wouldn't need the Bureau's technical support or their operational expertise. To find Rebecca, they'd just have to kick down every door covering every shit-hole apartment, tenement building, and abandoned warehouse in the county. The Feds would just get in their way.

"What are you doing the rest of the day?" asked Ash. He pulled his phone away from his ear as it beeped, signaling another call. He didn't recognize the number, so he ignored it and continued his conversation.

"I'll witness Kate Doe's autopsy next and then type up some notes. You got other plans for me?"

"No, but I need you to do me a favor. Call Tim Smith and tell him to get the vehicle identification number from John and Kate Doe's Mercedes. We couldn't find who they were through the BMV, so we'll think outside the box. Tell him to buy a vehicle history report on their car from the Internet. That should at least give him the name of the dealership that sold it. Even though they registered the car to a corporation, someone drove it off the lot. The dealership should know who that is, so he should be able to get a name. If the dealership doesn't want to work with him, tell him to get a warrant."

"All right. I'm on it. I'll call you as soon as I get anything."

"Good."

Ash hung up the phone and glanced at the screen. In addition to the call he had ignored, someone had sent him several text messages requesting a call back. He had to thumb through three of them before finding one with a name. Detective Joan Pace, and she needed to see him as soon as possible. That couldn't be good.

9

Near Voroshilovsk, Ukraine, 1948.

The temperature had dropped well below the freezing point, and a thick pad of snow blanketed the hills surrounding the farmhouse. Kostya's aunt and uncle used to own the farm outright, but now they shared it as part of a collective and sent most of what they grew far away. At least they had been able to keep a plot of land for themselves. Kostya held his hands near his aunt and uncle's coal-fired stove, trying to warm himself. He was eleven, and the Great Patriotic War had been over for three years, long enough for many wounds to heal but not nearly long enough for others. His younger sister, Anastasiya, huddled beside him. Their clothes fit only just, but the small farmhouse kept out most of the chill, and its garden provided an adequate supply of food, something few of their neighbors could boast.

A figure scrambled to Kostya's left, running toward them at full speed before tapping both Anastasiya and Kostya on the shoulder.

"Go to jail, robbers."

Kostya's cousin Fedor had taught them Cossacks and Robbers a year earlier, but neither Kostya nor Anastasiya had mastered it. They had grown up during the Siege of Leningrad and, until recently, had very little time or energy for games. Immediately Kostya sprang to his feet.

"That's not fair. We weren't hiding."

"Too bad," shouted Fedor, already running out of the house. Kostya slipped on a pair of shoes and followed, his feet crunching in the snow. It still felt strange to stretch his legs and run for the enjoyment of it. During the war, if he had seen anyone running, Kostya would have dived into the nearest shelter for fear of a bombing run. Now he ran knowing that the worst that would happen was a wrestling match with his cousin. He smiled and laughed without realizing it.

"I'll get you."

Fedor looked over his shoulder and mocked his cousin as he rounded the corner of the family's old barn. He didn't see the man standing there and slammed directly into the lower body of Vladimir Orlesky, the area's representative from the Ministry of State Security. Many had hoped that life would improve after the Patriotic War, that the state would become more liberal in its dealings with the people. In fact, the opposite had occurred. Those considered a threat to the state were arrested and sent to forced labor camps or executed. All the MGB needed was a name whispered by an informant, a suspicion of anti-Soviet sympathies, or evidence of a conversation with the wrong person.

Kostya hurried to reach his cousin. Along with Vladimir, three men carrying machine guns stood by the barn, their faces impassive.

"He's sorry," said Kostya, pulling his cousin back. "He didn't mean to hit you."

Vladimir knelt down. "Of course he didn't," he said, putting a hand on Kostya's and Fedor's shoulders. "You're good boys.

We need more strong boys like you two." He squeezed hard and looked at Fedor. "Is your father home?"

Fedor shook his head.

"Then get your mother."

"I'll get her," said Fedor, looking down at the ground, his breath shallow and weak. Everyone knew to fear Vladimir, but never had he bothered the Abramoffs before; they had never given him reason. Kostya followed his cousin back to the house, trembling. Myra stood at the stove when they arrived, stirring a pot of cabbage and potato soup. She was his mother's younger sister, and every day that passed, she looked more and more like Kostya's mother. He had begun to see her more and more like that as well. His sister, Anastasiya, stood beside her aunt.

"Vladimir is here for you," said Fedor.

Myra immediately handed the spoon she had been holding to Anastasiya and turned to the boys, her face drained of color.

"Then why is he outside? Invite him in."

Fedor scurried off, but Kostya stayed in the kitchen. Myra turned to him.

"Go find something better to do outside. Take Fedor and Anastasiya, too."

Anastasiya and Kostya both ran after their cousin and met him near the front door. The soldiers stayed outside, but Vladimir walked through the home as if he owned it. The state had no private property—no private means of production—but its citizens still had personal property, including their homes. Vladimir had no right to be in there, but no one had the power to stop him. Even though Myra had tried to send the kids outside, they stayed in the front room and watched while the adults spoke in the kitchen.

"Your son ran into me and nearly knocked me down," said Vladimir. "He's a strong boy. You should be proud."

"I'm sorry he hit you," said Myra. "I'll punish him for that."

Vladimir made a shushing noise. "No need. He meant nothing by it. Boys will be boys."

"Thank you."

Kostya crept around the corner so he could see the adults speaking. Vladimir put a hand on Myra's shoulder.

"I've heard rumors that there are men in the area stirring up trouble."

Myra tried to take a step back, but Vladimir kept his hold on her shoulder.

"I haven't heard that," she said.

"Of course you haven't," he said, his eyes passing up and down her. "Where's your husband been lately?"

"He works in a steel mill in Zaporozhye."

"Ahh," said Vladimir, nodding. "It must get lonely without him."

Myra twisted her shoulder out of his grasp and went back to the stove. "He was asked to go, and we're happy to do what's needed."

"Still, these are dangerous times, especially without a man in the house. With your permission, I would like my men to search your home in case there are things here that might be dangerous for you or your family."

Myra hesitated. Even Kostya knew he could search without permission. He wanted something else.

"We have nothing to hide."

"I certainly hope not," said Vladimir, running a finger along Myra's cheek. He barked an order for his men to come inside and search. The house had few rooms, but the soldiers took their time anyway. They started in the sleeping loft and uncovered a trove of books that belonged to Kostya's uncle Piotr, a former history professor. Most of the books were benign—Marx, Engels, and Lenin—but others provided grounds for an arrest. One—*The Wealth of Nations* by Adam Smith—had Kostya's bookmark in it, a piece of fabric torn from his mother's favorite dress before she died during the siege of Leningrad. Kostya kept the fabric in it so he wouldn't lose it.

Vladimir conferred with his men outside while Kostya and his family stayed in the kitchen. No one spoke, but Myra prayed. Kostya had never heard his aunt pray before, but it seemed right. He closed his eyes and joined in. Eventually, he heard Vladimir's footsteps traipse through the home again.

"This isn't good, Myra," he said, palming Piotr's book. "We found sacks of wheat in the basement. Whole sacks. What are we going to do about this?"

Myra pushed ahead of the children. "We grew the wheat in our garden. I've paid the taxes. We have every right to it."

Vladimir shook his head. "I'm not here about taxes. Where's your son?"

She pointed to Fedor, and Vladimir slapped her hard across the cheek. Myra gasped, and Fedor surged forward, but Kostya held him back.

"I don't want to do this," he said, looking at the two boys. "I'm not interested in Fedor. I'm interested in Vanya, your eldest. Where is he?"

"He left three or four months ago. I haven't seen him since."

Vladimir slapped her again, knocking her back. When she straightened, blood trickled from the side of her mouth. Kostya felt his shoulders rise as anger built in him. Myra had taken him in when no one else would. She'd cared for him. She'd protected his sister. Every fiber of his being wanted to lash out at the man hurting her, but he couldn't move. He couldn't do anything, even stop his cousin. Fedor had his father's wide shoulders and powerful legs. He writhed against Kostya's grip before breaking free and charging across the room. He didn't even make it halfway before one of Vladimir's soldiers struck him on the temple with the butt of his rifle. The boy went down hard, unmoving. Frustrated, helpless rage coursed through Kostya, and he squeezed his hands into fists.

"I don't want to be here, Myra. My men don't want to be here," said Vladimir, looking at Fedor. "And none of us want to hurt you or your family, but you're not letting us do our jobs. I have reports of your son conspiring with traitors, and now I find you stockpiling food. Is it for you, or is it for him? I don't know, and that troubles me. If you were in my position, what would you do?"

Myra looked down at Fedor, who still hadn't stirred. She started toward him, ignoring Vladimir, but before she could reach him, the MGB officer grabbed her by the hair and slammed her against the wall beside the stove, rattling a row of teacups resting on a shelf beside her. Dust flew into the air, and Myra gasped in pain. Kostya wanted to rush forward and attack Vladimir, but he'd just get hurt like his cousin.

"Look at me when I speak to you. What would you do if you were in my position?"

"I don't know."

Vladimir's grip seemed to relax some. He sighed disgustedly. "Tend to Fedor."

She immediately knelt down at Fedor's side and cradled his head in her lap. She shed no tears, but it wasn't because of a lack of empathy or love; Myra had already lost two children during the Great Patriotic War, and like most women in Eastern Europe at that time, she had cried enough to last a lifetime. She rolled him onto his back and checked his chest for breath.

"If you're going to arrest me, then arrest me. Just leave my children alone."

Vladimir knelt down and took her hand. "I don't think it will come to an arrest," he said, sliding his arm up her shoulder and then to her cheek. Myra's back stiffened at the intimate, tender gesture. "With your husband gone, I think we can come to an arrangement."'

Myra's breath momentarily stopped. At the time, Kostya didn't understand what Vladimir had proposed, what his aunt had sacrificed, but he did later.

"Kostya, take your sister and get out."

"But Fedor—"

"Do as your aunt says," said Vladimir. "This isn't your business."

Kostya looked at Myra and then at the soldiers Vladimir had brought with him. They leered at his aunt.

"Please, don't hurt her," said Kostya.

Vladimir stood and smiled. "I promise that I'll be gentle."

Kostya took his sister's hand and led her to the barn. The soldiers followed a few steps back, laughing. Time lost meaning as they shivered outside. When Vladimir emerged from the house, he carried Fedor's still unmoving body. They took him to the hospital, where a surgeon said his skull had been fractured and his brain had begun swelling uncontrollably. He died a couple of days later, and Kostya saw his aunt cry for the first time. The soldier who struck him lost a week's pay for his excessive use of force. Vladimir visited the farm once a week from then on out, always when Uncle Piotr was gone. Neither Myra nor

Kostya nor Anastasiya ever discussed those visits, and unlike their neighbors, they never went to bed hungry.

Kostya never forgot the look his aunt had when she welcomed Vladimir into the house and asked the children to go to the barn. Fear, pain, emptiness. He loved his aunt and his family; Myra protected them as best she could. Kostya vowed that one day, he'd protect her as well.

10

When Kostya looked out of his windows, he saw corn-fields amid subdivisions stretching for miles. He and Lev were headed to New Palestine, a largely rural bedroom community on the city's east side. Iskra Konev, the young woman he had met at his daughter's home, gave him the general location, while Leonard Wilson, a local politician and soon-to-be prosecutor, gave him the specific address. As he gazed out his window, he saw a community on the precipice. New roads stretched through once-pristine fields, while road crews hurried to complete projects designed to accommodate the expected deluge of new residents.

Almost an hour after leaving his downtown house, the road narrowed and forests once again surrounded the street. They had reached the east side of the suburb, well past the area the developers had touched. Lev slowed the car, and Kostya peered left and right, looking for a break in the tree line that would indicate their turn. He pointed at a carved, wooden sign for the Dandelion Inn about half a mile up the road.

"That's it."

Lev grunted and turned onto the gravel road Kostya had pointed out. A thick copse of trees shielded the inn from prying eyes, but in the center of the glade stood a two-story farmhouse with a slate roof and a porch running the entire length of the first floor. Two young women in bathing suits sunned themselves on the front lawn. They looked up when Lev parked but quickly went back to their lounging when he didn't acknowledge them.

"Women," he said.

"I see," said Kostya. "Let's try not to disturb them."

The Dandelion Inn occupied a historic Greek revival mansion that looked very much like the White House. Kostya walked through an unlocked wooden front door that was twice as tall as him and into a formal oval-shaped entryway. A gently curving staircase on the right side of the room led to a second-floor landing, while hallways branched left and right into additional rooms. It smelled like cinnamon potpourri.

Kostya cleared his throat, hoping to get someone's attention. Almost immediately, a woman with shoulder-length straw-colored hair, softly tanned skin, and a set of very full lips stepped out of the hallway on the right side of the room. Fashionable wire-rimmed glasses covered emerald green eyes and a white blouse that accentuated rather than concealed curves covered her torso. Under other circumstances, Kostya would have thought she looked like a very attractive librarian. Her eyes told a different story, though. They moved quickly from him to Lev and then back, probing and evaluating both men in a glance.

"Can I help you gentlemen?" she asked, smiling and slipping her glasses into the front pocket of her shirt. "I'm Ann."

"I hope so, Ann," said Kostya, mimicking her smile. "My

youngest daughter is getting married in a few months, so we're looking for a place to house my family when they arrive."

Her smile quickly turned into a polite frown.

"Oh, bad luck. We're one of the few bed-and-breakfasts in the region to offer the full line of services that we do, so we're booked pretty tight this summer. I'm not sure if we can accommodate a wedding party until this winter."

He didn't bother forcing any emotion into his face; he hadn't expected to be offered a room.

"That is truly bad luck," said Kostya. "Perhaps we can take a tour anyway. I occasionally bring potential business associates into the area, and I'd very much like for them to have somewhere nice to stay."

"I'd be happy to give you a tour," she said, smiling again. "Let me grab the phone in case someone calls. Just this way."

She led them down the hallway from which she had emerged to a simple, square room with a wide oak desk and two comfortable, brown leather chairs in front. A picture window overlooking the front yard allowed in light and gave them a view of the lawn, including the sunbathers. Kostya looked at Ann again and smiled.

"What sort of business are you in?" she asked. "If you don't mind my asking, of course."

Kostya glanced at Lev. The big man shut the door.

"No, I don't mind you asking," he said, slowly lowering himself into one of the chairs in front of her desk. She took the hint and sat down. "I'm in the entertainment industry, and I've heard good things about the services your staff provides. Everyone I've spoken to who has stayed here has left well satisfied."

A quizzical look passed over Ann's face, and she tilted her head to the side before speaking.

"We do strive to provide an excellent guest experience." She batted her eyes, but not in an overt attempt to be provocative. It looked like a nervous twitch; in her line of work, she had much to be nervous about. "Would you mind telling me who referred you to our establishment so I can thank him personally?"

"Leonard Wilson."

The name relaxed her. "Mr. Wilson is one of our favorite customers. What is your name, sir? So I can confirm the referral."

"Konstantin Ivanovich Bukoholov. Leonard, like all my friends, calls me Kostya." Ann nodded and started dialing. "I've heard about a girl who works here. Russian, I think, probably eighteen or nineteen years old. Very pretty with sandy blond hair. Is she here? I'd like to say hello."

Ann covered the mouthpiece of the phone with a hand and narrowed her eyes, thinking. "It sounds like you're talking about Iskra, but she recently quit and went home."

Kostya glanced at Lev; they had come to the right place.

"How unfortunate," he said. "Tell me, how many security guards do you have? Some of the guests I'd bring are very security conscious."

"We have two full-time guards on staff," she said quickly. "If it's an issue, we can bring more on temporarily for your guests."

Kostya started to ask something else, but Ann pressed a finger to her lips and smiled. "Just another minute, and I'll be with you."

"I think I'd like to talk now," said Kostya, glancing at Lev. "Please end her call."

Without ceremony, Lev stood and pulled the cord from the phone's base. Ann opened her mouth in surprise but quickly regained her composure and leaned forward.

"Excuse me," she said, putting the phone back on its cradle. "I don't know who you gentlemen are, but if this is how you treat people, I'm going to ask you to leave."

"Oh, we won't be leaving," said Kostya, watching as Lev positioned himself in front of the room's only door. He turned his attention back to their host. "We have quite a few things to talk about."

Ann folded her hands on the desk and smirked. "I do not know what you've heard about this establishment, but I can assure you that our management will not tolerate this sort of behavior. If you leave now, we might be able to avoid an unpleasant altercation."

Kostya leaned forward. "We're already in the midst of an unpleasant altercation. Stand up and come along with us."

Ann stayed still as her eyes passed from Lev to Kostya and back. She started to push her chair back from the desk as if she had acquiesced, but then her hand shot forward. Before she could pull anything out of the desk's center drawer, Lev stepped across the room and slammed it shut, catching her fingers inside. She gasped, and he backhanded her across the jaw hard enough to send her rolling chair against the wall.

"She was reaching for this," said Lev, removing a chrome revolver from the desk. Kostya leaned forward and picked up the firearm from Lev's outstretched hand. Each slot in its revolving chamber held a round, and it looked to be in working order. Kostya slipped it into his pocket.

"You should be careful with a loaded firearm," he said. "You never know who will find it."

Ann wiped blood from her mouth. "Why are you doing this?"

Kostya's eyes never wavered from hers.

"Because you've hurt people I care about."

Her shoulders heaved as her breath increased in tempo. "What are you going to do to me?"

"Not what you probably expect," said Kostya. "You'll take a ride with us, answer some questions, and that will be it."

Ann wiped blood from the corner of her mouth. "Who are you?"

"Someone you don't want to upset. That's all you need to know," said Kostya. Blood dripped down Ann's chin and onto her blouse. Kostya leaned forward and wiped the streak with a handkerchief. She flinched but otherwise didn't move. "Do you have an ice maker in your freezer?"

She didn't answer at first, so Kostya repeated the question.

"Yes, we have an ice maker."

"Good. We'll stop by the kitchen on the way out so you can get something for your hand. We're not cruel. We don't hurt people if we don't have to. This will be much easier if you do as we ask. You have my promise."

Even defenseless, Ann paused before standing and allowing Kostya and Lev to escort her from the office. Maybe she thought someone would save her, or maybe she suspected she had seen her last sunrise. It didn't matter as long as she answered his questions. As he promised, they stopped by the kitchen before leaving. Stainless steel lined the walls behind the cabinets and food preparation areas, while white marble countertops gleamed in the morning sunlight. Kostya smelled bread baking but saw nothing in the ovens. That smell dissipated once Lev blew out the scented candle beside the stove. Two doors led out of the room; one—the door through which they had just passed—led deeper into the house, while the other led to the parking lot behind the inn.

Kostya wrapped a handful of ice in a linen towel and handed it to Ann while Lev stood by the door to the hallway.

"I'm sorry about your hand," said Kostya. "I just came here for information. I did not intend to hurt you."

She nodded and wrapped the ice around her fist.

"I didn't—"

She stopped speaking mid-sentence as the exterior door opened and closed. A young man stepped inside, his brow furrowed as he took in the scene. Lev likely had thirty to forty pounds on him, but while Lev had grown softer with age, the young man had cords of muscles visible through his T-shirt. Elaborate tattoos wrapped around his forearms and biceps. Iskra had mentioned him. Kostya pulled the revolver from his pocket and fired twice before the newcomer could react. The rounds caught him on both sides of the chest, dropping him in place but not killing him. In the silence that followed the shots, Kostya heard a gurgling noise as the young man struggled to breathe with fluid-filled lungs. Kostya walked over and held the firearm at his waist, pointed at the man's forehead.

"Enjoy Hell."

He fired once more, this time into his skull. Fresh blood

and gray brain matter painted the tile. Ann shrieked loudly, so Lev grabbed a dishtowel and held it over her mouth, muffling the sound.

"Gun works," said Lev, struggling to hold Ann in place.

"Trigger pull's light," said Kostya, slipping the still hot firearm into his pocket. Once his hands were free, he massaged his wrists, feeling shooting pains run into his forearms from the exertion of holding the weapon steady. It had been several years since he fired a gun, and he had forgotten how much it exasperated the dull pain of his carpal tunnel. "I want this place shut down. Do we still have the passports from Kara's safe?" Lev nodded. "Take them to Detective Ashraf Rashid's house along with a note listing this address. He'll take care of things for us."

Lev looked down to the woman he held captive. She clawed at his forearm to little effect.

"What about her?"

"Keep her alive, but shut her up. She has a long afternoon ahead of her."

11

As soon as he could, Ash called Detective Pace, who immediately directed him to an executive-level conference room several stories up and told him to hurry. He didn't bother waiting for the elevator; instead, he sprinted up a concrete and steel stairway to the appropriate floor. The executive-level conference room typically held policy meetings among the department's decision-makers and civilian overseers, so Ash didn't know what to expect. When he reached the floor, a uniformed lieutenant escorted him down a wood-paneled hallway to the room, where he met Captain Bowers and Daniel Reddington, the chief of detectives.

Ash knew Chief Reddington only in passing, having had few opportunities to meet with someone so high in the department's hierarchy. From what he had gathered, Reddington, unlike most of the department's powerful elite who had been appointed after years of sycophantic ass-kissing, earned his position by moving up through the ranks and making cases. He understood firsthand the challenges a detective faced on the job and fought hard for sometimes scarce resources. Most people who knew him liked him.

"You didn't answer your phone," said Bowers. "We really needed to get in touch with you."

"I was getting my team together," said Ash, pulling out a chair across the table from Reddington and Bowers. "I saw that I received a phone call, but I didn't recognize the number. What's going on?"

Reddington removed a cell phone from his pocket and laid it on the table.

"Detective Pace covered the Crime Stoppers tip line this morning and received this call approximately five minutes ago."

Reddington flicked his finger across his phone's touch screen and then sat down as a recording played over the speakerphone. A phone rang twice before a woman cleared her throat and answered.

"Crime Stopper's tip line. What can I do for you?"

"I've got a tip for Detective Ash Rashid. I saw him on TV. It's about the girl that was kidnapped yesterday."

Something about the voice sounded familiar, but Ash couldn't figure out what. The accent was a slow, Southern drawl, but certain words seemed almost clipped. It sounded forced and fake.

"Detective Rashid isn't available right now, but I'm Detective Joan Pace. If need be, I can call Detective Rashid and bring him into the conversation."

The voice paused. "That ain't going to work, Detective Pace. I'm only going to talk to Detective Rashid. If you want to hear what I have to say, get him on the phone."

Ash realized then when he had heard the voice before. He leaned forward and tapped a button on the phone, pausing the recording.

"That's the guy who kidnapped Rebecca. I recognize him from her nine-one-one call. Did we get a trace on this?"

"We tried," said Reddington. "He called us with a satellite phone leased from a company in the Middle East. Not even his carrier knows where he is."

Ash blinked, trying to think through that. "What kind of person carries a satellite phone?"

"Is that really important?" asked Reddington.

"I don't carry one, and I doubt anyone else here does, either. If we can figure out why our suspect has one, it could tell us something important about him," said Ash. Before Reddington could respond, Ash hit the PLAY button on the phone again, continuing the conversation.

"Detective Rashid isn't available. If you tell me what you have to report, I'll call him on your behalf."

"Hold on just a moment."

Ash heard silence for another second or two, and then he thought he heard a phone being put down. Faintly, he heard panting and then a muffled cry.

"Please help me. I'm in a white barn—"

Ash held his breath. He recognized that voice, too. Rebecca. She stopped speaking abruptly after a hollow thud.

"What just happened?" asked Pace, her voice suddenly strident.

"I believe you have reason to call Detective Rashid now. If not, I can hit her again, but I can't guarantee her safety if I do. She's been through a lot."

"Is that Rebecca Cook with you?"

"So the TV tells me. I never thought to ask last night."

Pace took a breath. "You need to let her go. You can drop her off somewhere and we'll pick her up. We don't even have to see each other. It's in your best interest that we get her back safely."

The caller laughed. "Somehow I get the impression that you don't really care too much about my interests."

"You're right. Our primary interest is Rebecca, but we can help you, too. We found the Mercedes in Indianapolis. I know that accidents happen. Maybe you got into a fight with your friends and shot them by mistake. Maybe they fired at you first. I don't know. If you were defending yourself, you probably didn't even do anything wrong. If Rebecca gets hurt, though, that could be serious. You need to let her go so I can help you."

"They teach you to slather on the bullshit this thick in the police academy, or is that something you learn from other detectives?"

"Can you let me talk to her so I can see if she's okay?"

"She's not in the talking mood right now."

"How can I verify that you're holding Rebecca and this isn't a prank?"

The caller paused, apparently thinking. "You have my solemn word that this isn't a prank. Aside from that, though, maybe you can ask her husband or her boyfriend about the birthmark she's got on her hip. Probably wouldn't even see it if she wore a bathing suit."

Pace inhaled sharply. "If you hurt her, it's going to be much harder to help you."

"And if you keep talking to me and not getting Detective Rashid, Rebecca's going to have a difficult time breathing."

"I understand. I'm trying to get in touch with him. If we call you back on this number, will you be able to answer?"

"I'll be waiting."

The recording ended, plunging the room into silence. Ash took a breath, his first since hearing Rebecca speak.

"What did Tech Services say about the call?" he asked.

"The conversation lasted a minute and seventeen seconds," said Bowers.

"They couldn't get anything about his location?"

"Satellite phones are exempt from the FCC requirements that allow us to track cell phones," said Bowers. "We don't even know what continent he's on."

Ash took that in with a heavy breath. "So what's the plan?"

"You're going to call him back," said Reddington. "We'll get whatever information we can out of him. If you can keep him talking long enough, he might slip. Anything you can get out of him helps."

"Okay," said Ash, nodding. His head almost felt light. "When do you want to start?"

"Five minutes ago would have been nice," said Reddington. "Since you were otherwise occupied, we'll do it as soon as we can."

Ash stayed in the conference room as Tech Services set up the call. Nobody spoke; they just worked. The technicians brought in a new phone with an integrated recording device and a laptop that would monitor the signal. Five minutes after setting it up, they made the call.

"Is this Detective Rashid?"

"Yeah. Who's this?"

The conference room now had six people in it, and everyone focused on the phone. Reddington had proposed manipulating Ash's voice so other detectives could pretend to be him in case he became unavailable for later calls, but Bowers nixed that idea. Even if they could make two detectives sound exactly alike, there'd be obvious differences in their word choices and speech cadence. If their perp caught them trying to trick him, he might kill Rebecca.

"I don't think we're on a first-name basis just yet, so why don't you call me Mr. Palmer."

"Sure," said Ash. "Before we discuss anything, I need to talk to Rebecca."

"No, let's talk about what I want first."

Ash felt his heart rate rise. "I appreciate that you want something, but before I can give you anything, I've got to talk to Rebecca. If this is going to work, this has to be a two-way street. We both have to give—"

The phone went dead in his hand. Ash sighed and looked up at the technician on the laptop.

"That didn't give you anything, did it?"

The tech shook his head and closed his eyes. "I don't even know what I'm doing. I've never had to work with a satellite phone before."

"Just do your best," said Reddington. "We'll bring in additional staff with more expertise when we can. In the meantime, you're what we've got."

The technician flexed his fingers. "I'll do what I can."

"When you're ready, call him back."

They waited in silence for a few minutes as the technician typed. Eventually, he sat straighter. "I think he's in North America. I think that's what the information I've received so far says."

That didn't narrow it down much, but it was a start. "That's good," said Ash. "Are we ready to place that call?"

The tech typed again and then nodded. "I'm calling now."

Ash leaned forward and waited as the phone rang and only took a breath once someone picked up.

"You there, Mr. Palmer?"

"Is this Detective Rashid?"

Rebecca's voice was soft. He could practically feel her trembling through the phone.

"Yeah. Call me Ash. Are you hurt?"

"Yes," she said, crying. "He hit me, and I passed out. There were two men....When I woke up..." Her voice trailed to nothingness. "Please help me."

"We're doing everything we can," he said, speaking quickly. "Our entire department is looking for you. We'll find you."

Rebecca started to say something else, but before she could, Ash heard a noise akin to meat being smacked against a countertop. Rebecca didn't make any other sound after that.

"Is that good enough for you, Detective Rashid?" asked Palmer.

More than anything in the world, Ash wanted to reach through the phone and grab his throat and squeeze. He forced his voice to remain calm.

"Please don't hurt her again."

"I didn't do anything to her she hasn't had done to her before."

Ash exhaled through his nose.

"For the good of our relationship, please don't hurt her again. We can't work with you if you hurt her."

"Oh, you don't want to work with me? So should I just go ahead and kill her now to save us all some time?"

"No, don't kill her. Tell me what you want, and I'll see if I can get it."

Ash knew he had broken a primary rule of hostage nego-
tiating, acquiescing to demands before even hearing them,
but he blurted it out without thinking.

"I like that attitude."

"I'm glad," said Ash. "We want Rebecca back safely, and
we're willing to work with you to get that. What do you
want?"

"What everybody wants. Money. Let's say you give me
twenty thousand dollars. As soon as I get my money, you'll
get the girl."

"We'll have to talk to her family about that. IMPD
doesn't have the money to pay ransom."

"Then get on the horn with her family and call me back
in an hour."

Ash glanced at Bowers and Reddington. They had already started talking to themselves, presumably trying to
figure out their options.

"I'll go to their house and talk to them," said Ash. "But I
need something from you first. Who were the people in the
Mercedes?"

Reddington and Bowers stopped talking and stared at
him. Palmer's voice went flat, his accent gone.

"I fail to see how that's germane to our discussion."

"We haven't been able to identify them yet, so their families don't know what's going on. If you know their names,
it would help us a lot. And if you help us, we'll help you.
That's how this works."

Palmer paused for a moment. "Do you think I'm an
idiot?"

"Of course not."

"Then don't treat me like one. Get my money and

try not to be too distracted by details that don't pertain to you."

"If you tell me who—"

Palmer hung up before Ash could finish another question. He stared at the laptop for a moment, his hands shaking, before looking at the technician from the services division.

"Anything?"

The tech put up his hands and shrugged. "I don't know. I'm way out of my depth here."

"You did your best. That's all we can ask for," said Reddington. He looked at the rest of the people in the room. "We've got one hour, and I expect us to be better prepared next time. I'm going to call Kevin Havelock at the local FBI field office. Hopefully he'll have a few technicians he can spare." He looked at the befuddled tech. "I want you to work with them and show them our system." He looked at Bowers. "Mike, you're going to coordinate with the state police. If we get a location on Palmer, we'll probably need their help. Someone needs to talk to the Cook family as well, so we'll get the chaplain."

"Just send Rashid," said Bowers. "He talked to the Cooks before, and he knows the case."

Reddington looked at Ash from his chest to his head as if appraising him. "I'd rather he stay here."

Ash knew Reddington had said something about him, but his brain didn't process it.

"Ash," said Bowers, his voice sharp. "You with us?"

Ash blinked and cleared his mind. "Yeah, but we shouldn't go to the Cooks yet. Palmer's setting us up."

12

Before Ash could say anything further, Mike Bowers held up a hand, stopping him.

"Everybody clear out of the room," he said, shooing the technical support staff and other detectives out. Ash stayed put by the conference table while Reddington closed the door and glanced at Captain Bowers.

"Are you worried about any staff member in particular?" asked Reddington.

"No," said Bowers. "But our people have talked to the media enough. I don't want to give anyone else temptation. Ash occasionally has lucid moments, and I'd rather keep his idea off the TV for a while."

Occasionally lucid. Ash's stock had moved up in the world. Reddington nodded and leaned against the conference table.

"What do you think, Detective?"

Ash took a deep breath, forcing his disparate thoughts into some semblance of order.

"Palmer's not interested in the ransom money. He's trying to tie us up and waste our time."

"Why do you think that?" asked Bowers.

"Because he only asked for twenty thousand dollars.

136

That's nothing. More than that, he doesn't even know if Rebecca's family can afford it. I don't have twenty grand sitting around, and I have a decent job, my own house, and a retirement fund. Rebecca lives with her parents. If this guy was after money, he'd go to the Geist reservoir and kidnap one of those rich guys who lives on the waterfront."

Reddington blinked and glanced at Bowers before looking at Ash again.

"Even if you're right, our plans stay the same. I'll raise your concerns with Agent Havelock and make sure he takes them into advisement. We're going to get this guy. There's no doubt about it in my mind."

Ash had more than a few doubts of his own, but he decided against raising them. "I can talk to the Cooks. They know me."

Reddington hesitated. "I appreciate that, Detective, but if Mr. Palmer calls back, I need you by the phone, not twenty minutes away."

Ash wanted to protest, but Reddington was right. "Who's going to talk to the family, then?"

"We'll get the chaplain," said Bowers. "It's not ideal, but they'll be fine."

"We're settled," said Reddington. "Everybody get to work."

"So my job is to just sit around?" asked Ash. Reddington looked at him for a moment but then picked up a notepad and pen from the conference room table. He scribbled something down quickly, tore the page out, and handed it to Ash.

"You want a job, that's a drink order. Get me some coffee."

Before Ash could protest, Bowers escorted him from the conference room and shut the door behind him. Ash crumbled the note and threw it into the nearest trash can.

"Asshole."

With nothing to do but wait, Ash went to the floor's break room and turned on the television. It took almost an hour for Bowers to call him again, and by that time, a dozen people stood outside the conference room conversing. Reddington and Bowers stood next to a tall, thin man with graying hair and a black suit. Bowers waved Ash over, but Reddington hardly looked at him.

"The Cooks are on board," said Bowers. "They'll get the money together if we think that'll get Rebecca back."

"Great," said Ash. He nodded toward the thin man. "And who is this?"

"Kevin Havelock," he said, extending his hand. "I'm the special agent in charge of the local FBI field office. You must be Detective Rashid." Ash nodded, and they shook hands. "I'm glad you're here. In our experience, continuity of communication is important in cases like this."

"Have you handled many kidnappings?"

"Four, and we got three of our victims back safely. If we need him, we have an agent in Chicago who handles two or three kidnappings a year."

"And in those cases you've investigated, how many involved ransom demands of less than twenty thousand dollars?"

Havelock furrowed his brow. "None, but my cases involved fairly wealthy individuals. Why?"

Reddington answered before Ash could. "Detective Rashid believes the ransom demand is some kind of ruse."

"And why do you think that?" asked Havelock.

"It just doesn't feel right," said Ash. "Twenty grand doesn't feel like enough money."

Havelock straightened and nodded, resuming his commanding posture. "In the scheme of things, it's not. Twenty grand might be all our subject needs, though. When dealing with street thugs, you can't assume they think like you do."

"I've worked with bad guys a few times, so I realize that," said Ash. "I don't think Palmer is just some jerk off the street. He seems to know what he's doing."

Havelock flashed a weak but still patronizing smile. "I think you're overestimating his ability."

Ash glanced at Bowers for support, but the captain shook his head slightly.

"What's the risk if I am? I'm suggesting that we be cautious. Maybe we should start questioning why he's making such low demands instead of acquiescing to them."

Havelock took a deep breath. "I appreciate your concern. We will proceed with the utmost caution."

Chief Reddington glanced at Havelock and then at Ash again. "Does that satisfy you, Detective?"

"No. Does it satisfy you?"

Reddington started to say something, but Havelock held up a hand, stopping him.

"I appreciate your point of view," he said, folding his hands. "This is a partnership between my people and yours. We need to work together, and I need you to understand that I will keep your concerns in mind."

A representative from the Public Employee's Retirement Fund, the government agency that oversaw IMPD's pension, gave Ash a similar answer when he asked about some questionable investment decisions the fund had made. It had sounded like paternalistic bullshit then, too.

"Whatever," said Ash, pushing his way through the throng of people around the conference table. "Let's just get to it."

Reddington and Bowers exchanged glances before joining Ash around the phone. Ash had told Palmer that he'd call back in an hour, but they had blown past that timeline.

"Are we ready?" asked Ash. Havelock glanced up, and one of the technicians he brought nodded.

"Go ahead, Detective," said Havelock. "We've rerouted the phone through our equipment so our techs can remotely activate the GPS chip on his phone and get his coordinates. If he had a standard cell phone, we'd be able to do it without an issue. Since he's got a satellite phone, we're going to have to do some work."

Ash hesitated. "I'm a little fuzzy on what we're doing. What do you mean we're going to remotely activate the GPS chip on Palmer's phone?"

Havelock looked at his technician. "We'll piggyback a signal through the satellite and crack his phone's security," said the technician. "That should allow us to access the phone's functions, including its GPS chip."

"I see," said Ash, nodding. "So you're going to break in. And you guys are sure this is legal?"

Havelock glanced at him but then looked back at his technician. "It's the position of the federal government that an individual's location is not information subject to Fourth Amendment protection. We won't access other parts of his phone."

"Okay," said Ash, still nodding. "But let me just get this

straight. You're going to break into Palmer's phone and electronically trespass on his private property in order to track his location. That kind of sounds like we should get a warrant."

Havelock narrowed his eyes at Ash. "Are you a legal expert as well as a detective now?"

"That's what my law school diploma says. That and *cum laude* and a bunch of other Latin words."

"If you have a concern," said Havelock, "you can take it up with my boss. He's the president of the United States, and he lives in Washington, D.C. Make sure to make an appointment. In the meantime, can we get to work?"

"I'm just looking out for this case. Once we catch Palmer, I want him to go to jail. I don't want the case thrown out because we cheated."

"Why don't you let the Department of Justice handle that?" asked Havelock. "We have some pretty good lawyers."

"You'd better."

Havelock looked at his technician. "Dial."

The phone rang twice before Palmer picked up. "For a while there, I didn't think you would call me back, Detective. I'm glad to hear you're still cooperating."

Havelock mouthed something, and all but one of the technicians crept out, making the room feel better almost instantly.

"We are cooperating, and the Cook family has agreed to your request. Twenty thousand dollars for Rebecca. That's what we talked about, right?"

"I'm glad to hear they're open to my reasonable request."

"And we're glad to hear that you're so reasonable," said

Ash. "Most men in your situation would have asked for more money."

Palmer chuckled. "You want me to ask for more? I can, you know."

"No. I didn't say that," said Ash. "The Cooks don't have a lot of money. Twenty thousand is all they could get together in such a short amount of time. Thank you for not asking for more."

"You're a funny man, Detective Rashid. I didn't expect to receive your thanks."

"What are you going to do with the money?"

"I was thinking about blowing some on cheap booze and fast women. Beyond that, I don't think it's any of your business."

"I respect that," said Ash. "Didn't mean to offend you. Let's talk about Rebecca. How am I going to get her back?"

"Under the auspices that you're telling the truth, I'll be honest with you. Put the cash in a backpack and take it to the northeast side of the park in front of the Central Library downtown at eleven tonight. And just to keep you honest, if I see anybody other than you, Rebecca's brain is going to get intimate with a forty-five auto."

A computer recorded the call, but Ash wrote the information down anyway.

"That's a pretty big firearm. I thought you were more into small weapons after the twenty-two you used on the people in the Mercedes."

Palmer chuckled. "You use different tools for different projects."

"I guess so. Where will I get Rebecca?"

"You'll receive further instructions at the park, and if you cooperate, everything will be fine. One of my partners will drop her off near the Scottish Rite Cathedral. If you want, I'll even put a nice, pretty bow around her neck. How's that sound to you?"

"It sounded fine until you mentioned your partners. How do I know I can trust them?"

"Probably can't, but you don't need to. They won't screw you as long as you cooperate with me."

"You trust them that much?"

Palmer chuckled again. "No, but I know where their families live. In my business, that's usually all it takes to ensure compliance. You have any more questions?"

"What guarantees will you give me for my own safety?"

"Other than my solemn pledge that you won't come to any harm?"

"Yeah," said Ash. "Other than that."

"I suppose you can pray."

"Great, thank you."

Palmer hung up, but Ash stayed still, his heart rate elevated. Palmer's assurances to the contrary, Ash couldn't shake the feeling that no matter how careful they were, this wasn't going to end well for anyone.

*   *   *

"We've got him," said Havelock once Ash exited the conference room. "We tracked his phone to the Eagle Creek Airpark. Our officers are en route."

It took a second for that to register. Eagle Creek Airpark was a small municipal airport with one runway on the far northwestern quadrant of Indianapolis. It mainly serviced private aircraft and the occasional charter flight, so it didn't get a lot of traffic. Ash had been there only once because someone thought he spotted a body in the Eagle Creek Reservoir nearby; it turned out to be a log. Aside from a plane or a boat, the airport had few exits, making it a poor spot for a hideout. It did have hiding places, though; maybe they had just gotten lucky.

Ash didn't like admitting it, but they should have brought in the FBI earlier. Havelock's crew was able to find Palmer with one phone call. If he had called them the night before, maybe they wouldn't have had to go to the home off Shadeland, and maybe Madison wouldn't have been shot. The realization came like a punch to the gut.

"Rashid." Ash looked up to see Mike Bowers waving at him. "Let's go."

The drive to the airpark didn't take long. Ash rode in the back of an FBI SUV with Havelock and Bowers while a long stream of patrol vehicles followed. Members of IMPD's SWAT team planned to breach the hangar first and subdue everyone they found inside while uniformed officers surrounded the building to prevent suspects from running. Ash, Bowers, and Havelock would remain outside as part of the command structure.

Their driver parked on the street several blocks from the target. The airpark had been built on an open field bounded by a lake and marina on one side and middle-class housing developments and apartments on the other three. According to the FBI's technicians, Palmer had called from a hangar east of the runway. They had him cornered even before he moved. It didn't seem right.

Ash climbed out of the SUV and immediately smelled

the nearby lake. No one with half a brain would pick such a bad hiding spot. Ash could spot five planes from where he stood, which meant there were likely at least an equal number of mechanics, FAA administrators, pilots, and security guards in the area. What's more, he stood on the only road out of the area. He couldn't shake the feeling that they had made a misstep somewhere.

"How much surveillance have we done on this place?" he asked.

"Enough," said Havelock, barely glancing at him. He took a two-way radio from the car. "Are all units in place?"

"Give us five."

Ash didn't recognize the voice, so he didn't know if IMPD or the FBI had taken the lead. It didn't matter either way; they both would know what to do. Bowers came around from the other side of the car carrying a pair of field glasses. He looked around the complex and then handed them to Ash. The hangar had metal walls painted white and a roof reddened with rust. Three men wearing tactical vests and carrying assault rifles stood on each of the two corners that he could see, while another eight stood in front of a windowless metal door near the street. Assuming Havelock had positioned an equal number of men behind the hangar as he had the front, Palmer would have to get past twenty men to escape.

"We're ready."

The voice came on the radio again. Havelock looked to Bowers for confirmation before speaking.

"Go on your mark."

Bowers didn't ask for the binoculars back, so Ash watched the events unfold. Two of the men in front of the hangar door picked up a portable battering ram while a third man counted down from three with his fingers. As soon as the man counting reached one, the men on the battering ram slammed it into the door hard enough that the sound carried all the way to their SUV. Those two men then got out of the way and the man who counted down lobbed a pair of flash bangs into the building. They went off like a firecracker, and the men rushed inside. Ash held his breath, preparing himself for gunfire that never came.

"Building's clear. They're not here."

Havelock put the radio to his mouth. "Check again. Look for lockers, closets, or anywhere big enough to hide. All units outside, stay in position. We're on our way."

As soon as he finished speaking, Havelock climbed into the SUV and pounded on the dashboard. The driver took off, leaving Bowers and Ash where they stood. Neither officer said anything for a moment.

"I love interagency cooperation," said Ash.

"Shut up, Ash," said Bowers, already walking toward the hangar. Ash caught up in a few steps but didn't say anything. When they reached the hangar, Havelock had already walked inside. The interior was big enough that it could have housed two or three dozen full-sized busses. It was also empty and dark, the windows near the ceiling having been painted over.

"See if we can get some lights on in here," said Havelock. A couple of IMPD officers pulled open the hangar's main door, spilling sunlight inside and illuminating the interior. Exposed metal beams supported the ceiling and walls but left few hiding places. There was no sign of Rebecca Cook or Palmer. In fact, only one thing in the entire building stood out: a wooden desk in the middle of the room.

Ash walked without saying a word and found Bowers and Havelock beside him. The desk appeared ordinary in all respects save a handwritten note taped to the top.

Twenty grand. Tonight. I don't want to hurt anyone if I don't have to. 213 Parkview.

"What's at 213 Parkview?" asked Havelock.

Ash glanced at Bowers before speaking. "It's Rebecca's home address. He's threatening her family."

13

Havelock stepped away from the desk and called in a forensic team to check out the warehouse. Bowers and Ash stayed where they were.

"You think this Palmer guy would be stupid enough to take his phone with him?" asked Bowers.

"Not if he knows we can track it. I doubt it's here, though. Even if he just used it for this job, it'd have call histories, maybe text messages from his employer, possibly fingerprints. If it were me, I'd burn it."

"I'll tell our guys to look for burn marks. I'm also going to get some divers for the lake."

Bowers walked back to their portable command post at the SUV. Palmer had done a lot of work so far, and none of it made sense yet. The Cooks seemed like nice people, but they also seemed average in almost every way. Ash had met a lot of criminals, and Palmer was anything but average. When he murdered John and Kate Doe, he used a round that disintegrated in their skulls, negating the possibility of a ballistics match to his firearm. When he left their car, he wiped away his fingerprints and took the victims' wallets. After that, he called IMPD but used a phone they couldn't track. Ash rarely found that degree of professionalism and forethought among ordinary criminals, so it boggled the mind that Palmer would get away with a double homicide only to abduct the first woman he came across and demand a twenty-thousand-dollar ransom. It didn't make sense unless there was something else going on.

Once the forensic teams started working on the desk and warehouse, Ash, Bowers, and Havelock drove back to the station downtown. The two administrators went upstairs to the deputy chief's office, while Ash went to the conference room their task force had been assigned to. Reddington may not have wanted him there, but as long as Palmer wanted a familiar voice to talk to, he'd have a part of the case. So far, his department's investigation had focused almost entirely on Rebecca and Palmer. It had another side, too, though, and they would be foolish to ignore it. They needed to start looking at John and Kate Doe.

Ash took out his cell phone and called Greg Doran's desk phone. Instead of Doran, he got Detective Tim Smith.

"Hey," said Ash, surprised. "I thought I called Greg's desk."

"You did, but he's taking a piss. What do you want, Rashid?"

Ash paused for a second. "I wanted to talk to Greg. That's why I called his desk."

"Don't you have something better to do than to bother us?"

"Not really."

"We're working, okay? Don't call this number again unless it's important."

Smith hung up the phone. Their relationship remained consistent at least. Ash gave Doran a few minutes to get out of the bathroom before dialing his personal cell phone. The detective picked up on the first ring.

"Hey, Doran, it's Ash. If you ever consider beating your partner with a rubber hose behind the building, let me know. I'll pay to watch."

Doran grunted. "You were the prank caller he talked to, huh?"

"Yeah," said Ash. "I'm calling to see if you found anything about the Mercedes."

"We got lucky. Dealership gave us his name without a fight. Daniel E. Elliot. He bought the car two years ago."

Ash slumped into his seat, glad to hear some good news.

"That's great. Were you able to ID John Doe?"

"Not officially," said Doran. "But I looked up his driver's license. The picture and our corpse are a match."

"Good. We'll see if we can track down his next of kin for an official ID. You find anything else about him?"

"A couple of things. He's a lawyer with a license to practice in Indiana and in the federal court system. No arrest record."

"Are you near a computer?"

"Yeah, I just got back to my desk. Tim's with me."

Ash wanted to ask him to give Tim the finger, but he decided that wouldn't help their working relationship.

"Look up Elliot on the marriage license database. He was with his wife when he died. If we're lucky, they got married in Indiana."

"I'm on it," said Doran, already typing. Ash took his notebook from his pocket and flipped through its pages until he came to a clean one and waited. "We've got four potential records. Do you have anything to narrow it down?"

"The woman's name may be Kate."

"I don't have a record with a Kate, but I've got a Kara," he said. "Give me a minute or two. I'll look her up and see if I can get a picture." He paused again and Ash heard typing. "That's our vic. Karen Konstantinovna Elliot. Bet that was a pain in the ass to spell in elementary school."

Ash didn't recognize the name, but after taking a Russian literature course in college, he recognized the type.

"It's a patronymic. It means her father was named Konstantin. Does the marriage license list her maiden name?"

"Bukoholov."

It took a second for that to sink in, but when it did, it felt like Ash had been slapped.

"Kara Elliot's father was Konstantin Bukoholov."

"Should that mean something to me?" asked Doran.

"It means I need to talk to Captain Bowers."

"When you talk to him, can you ask him if Tim and I are still part of this case? Other than my trip to the morgue and Tim's trip to the Mercedes dealership, we've been sitting around all morning while you guys work. As much as I like goofing off at work, I like earning my paycheck even more."

"I'll talk to him. In the meantime, we need to get into Kara and Daniel Elliot's house. Have Tim secure the scene, and while he's doing that, I want you putting together an affidavit for a search warrant. I'll ask Bowers to send some men your way."

"Sounds good. As soon as you get me a team, we'll hit the house."

"Good. I'll talk to you later."

Ash hung up and jogged to the elevator. Reddington's office was just a couple of floors up, but it felt far removed from the rest of the department. The lobby outside the elevator had wood-paneled walls and a uniformed sergeant behind an oversized wooden desk. Ash introduced himself to the sergeant, who made a phone call to the chief before leading him back. Chief Reddington, Agent Havelock, and Captain Bowers met him inside Reddington's palatial office.

"I'm glad you're here, Rashid," said Reddington. "I just got off the phone with the Cook family. Their bank has agreed to loan them twenty thousand dollars cash. Are you comfortable making the exchange?"

Ash hadn't thought about the actual exchange yet, but even without serious thought, he didn't like it. The Central Library had a concrete slab in front of it big enough to host a circus. Buildings surrounded it on all sides. A shooter could hide near any of those buildings and take potshots at him. Worse, he wouldn't even have cover.

"If I do, what's the plan?"

"It'll be a straight-up swap. We'll drop off the money where he wants it, we'll get the girl, and then we'll follow Palmer until we can safely apprehend him."

Ash inhaled deeply. "What if Rebecca isn't there? I highly doubt it's going to be that easy."

"Whatever we do will depend on the situation. Our first priority will be your safety. We'll suit you up in a bullet-resistant vest, and we'll have officers in full tactical gear near the cathedral ready to pull you out if need be. We'll also have shooters placed on top of buildings nearby. If your life is in imminent danger, they will shoot. The key here will be overwhelming force. We will bring enough men to overcome whatever he does."

Ash didn't like the ambiguity of the plan any more than he liked the location of the swap; unfortunately, it sounded like the best they could do without more information.

"I guess I don't have anything better to do tonight."

"I'm glad you're so enthusiastic," said Bowers.

Chief Reddington glanced at him before looking back at Ash. "I assume you came up here for a reason. What do you need?"

"I do have a reason," said Ash, thinking back to why he actually came up. "Greg Doran and Tim Smith found out who our victims in the Mercedes were."

"Good," said Reddington. "Tell them to follow up. We'll give them whatever resources they need. Until we get Rebecca back, though, she's our focus up here."

"One of the victims was named Kara Elliot," said Ash, glancing at Bowers. "Her father is Konstantin Bukoholov."

Bowers tilted his head back and exhaled heavily through his mouth. He swore while Reddington's eyes shot to Havelock.

"That's interesting," said Havelock. "We'll have to look into it."

"Bukoholov is the biggest drug trafficker in the region, and I just told you that his daughter has been murdered," said Ash. "I'd say that's more than interesting."

"Bukoholov may have ties to criminal groups, but our sources say he's a bit player at most," said Havelock, shaking his head. "We had him under surveillance, but we dropped it when we didn't find anything."

Ash narrowed his gaze. Bukoholov wasn't a bit player, and anyone who had done even a little research would know that.

"When did you cut your surveillance on him?"

"About a year and a half ago. It was right after we arrested Karen Rea for trafficking cocaine from South America. If I recall, you were involved in that investigation, weren't you?"

"Yeah. She abducted my wife and daughter. Captain Bowers helped me get them back."

"Then you know about the drug trade in this city. We don't have organized groups. We've got thugs, and Bukoholov happens to be one of them."

Ash crossed his arms. "About the time we arrested Karen Rea, an FBI agent I worked with told me that the Agency no longer considers drugs a priority. You seem pretty well informed."

Before Havelock could say anything, Bowers put his arm around Ash's shoulders.

"I think you've said enough, Ash," he said, steering him toward the door. He looked over his shoulder. "I'm going to escort Sergeant Rashid to the elevator. I'll be right back."

Once they exited the room, Bowers dropped his arm and pulled the door shut behind him. "Whatever you were going to say to Havelock, drop it," he said. "This isn't a fight you want."

"Maybe I spoke out of turn, but Havelock is either lying or he's an idiot. Bukoholov isn't a bit player, and you know it as well as I do."

Bowers glanced at Reddington's door. "If the FBI had Bukoholov under surveillance, would they have ever seen you together?"

Ash felt his shoulders dip. "Yeah, but—"

"Thank you for being honest," Bowers interrupted. "If

you had surveillance video of a gangster visiting the home of a detective as well as video of that same detective visiting that same gangster at Military Park a couple of weeks later, would you trust him?"

Ash blinked several times. "They have video of that?"

Bowers nodded. "Yeah, and Havelock showed Reddington and me the video this morning."

"It's not what it looks like."

"I should hope not because it looks like a police officer and a gangster are colluding."

"Bukoholov has come to me with information in the past. A couple of months back, he came to my house and told me about a hit-and-run accident involving a woman I knew. After that investigation, I met him in Military Park to tell him not to contact me again. That's all it was. It's no different than meeting with a confidential informant."

"Except that in this case, your confidential informant isn't just some kid caught buying weed from an undercover police officer. He's a drug trafficker with his fingers in city government. Let me ask you this: What did Bukoholov get out of that hit-and-run investigation he tipped you off to?"

A solidified power base.

"I don't know."

Bowers crossed his arms and stared. "After showing me the video, Havelock told me something else. Bukoholov is funding a political action committee supporting Leonard Wilson's campaign for prosecutor. Didn't you do some campaigning for Wilson?"

Ash ground his teeth. "Not intentionally."

"But I bet you'll get something out of it," said Bowers, raising his eyebrows.

"Wilson has offered me a position in the prosecutors office if he's elected. I haven't accepted."

Bowers swore under his breath and started walking down the hall. He pulled Ash into the executive conference room and shut the door, giving them a bit of privacy.

"You're climbing a mountain without a lot of safety gear, Ash. Reddington wanted to turn this over to Internal Affairs. He already thought you were reckless for what you did during the Thomas Rahal trial last year, and now he's questioning if he can trust you. That's not good."

Susan Mercer, Ash's old boss, tried Thomas Rahal for murder eight months ago. It had looked like a simple case. She even had a confession. During an investigation into a related crime, Ash found out Susan's case was anything but simple; by the time he finished, he had sent a well-respected detective to prison for the rest of his life and a number of other officers to their graves. Nobody came out a winner.

"I've done nothing wrong."

"You've done plenty wrong," said Bowers. "You're working today because Palmer wants you, and I vouched for you."

"What would you have me do? Ignore information because I don't like the source?"

Bowers sighed and looked out the window. "I'm not telling you to ignore anything. I'm just telling you to consider what your source gets out of talking to you. Did you know Wilson used to be a cop?"

Ash's posture softened. "Somebody told me. He left the department to go to law school, though."

"That's the official story. You want to hear the real one?"

"Sure," said Ash, feeling disquiet build within him.

"Understand that I don't have firsthand knowledge of this because it was before my time. My dad was a cop for forty years. He sat on a committee that investigated complaints against officers. It's what the department had before the Internal Affairs unit was created. Wilson was a detective in vice back then, did lots of prostitution cases. Dad says he got close to some of the girls he arrested. *Real* close. Some of them were fifteen, sixteen years old."

"I'm sure if your dad could prove Wilson was involved in wrongdoing, he would have."

"Right," Bowers snorted. "You know how often the prostitutes vice detectives bring in claim the arresting officer offered to let them go for a freebie?"

"I've never worked vice."

"Well, I'll fill you in. Every other time, I'd say. Dad couldn't ever bring a case against him, but Wilson was dirty, even back then."

"I've never seen him break the law."

"That's not the point. Wilson was a cop," said Bowers. "He swore an oath to uphold the law, but then he used his position to break it. Even if you just get information from him, that's the sort of man you work with when you talk to people like Konstantin Bukoholov. You think you can trust somebody like that? You can't. He and his friends are using you and our department to do their work for them. That's why we're concerned when we see you two together. Keep that in mind next time you see him."

Bowers turned to go back to Reddington's office.

"If Wilson was picking up prostitutes on the job or letting them go for sex, why haven't I heard about it before now?"

"Maybe you haven't been listening to the right people."

He stopped. "And I'll see you tonight. Try to stay out of trouble in the meantime. I've put myself on the line for you."

Bowers left the conference room, and Ash felt his shoulders slump. He didn't want to work with Leonard Wilson any more than he wanted to work with Konstantin Bukoholov, but sometimes it was necessary. Maybe in a perfect world, he could afford to be idealistic, but not in this one. In this one, he had to get his hands dirty, and if that meant a gangster got something he wanted, so be it. Bukoholov and Wilson would get their comeuppance eventually. They all did. As he walked toward the elevator, Ash took out his cell phone and called home. Hannah picked up.

"Hey, hon, I've got to go out tonight, but I'm going to head home early. You want me to pick up anything on the way?"

"No, but somebody just came by with an envelope for you. It was really weird. It has a bunch of passports in it and a note with an address on it."

"You know who it's from?"

"No, but the guy who brought it by was huge. You'd know him if you had seen him before."

"Did he say anything?"

"He just asked me to give you the envelope. He was very nice, but he was hard to understand. He had an accent. Who was he?"

Ash hoped he was wrong, but he could only think of one man who fit the description.

"Someone who shouldn't have been there. I'm on my way right now."

Ash slipped his phone in his pocket and pounded the

DOWN button on the elevator. One of Bukoholov's henchmen had just come calling.

*   *   *

Megan met him at the back door with a juice box in hand when he got home, having already finished fasting for the day. Children, even during *Ramadan*, aren't required to fast, although some try. Hannah and Ash let Megan go half a day; in practical terms, that meant she skipped a morning snack. It allowed her to feel included in the events without hurting herself, and it had the added benefit of teaching her a little bit about patience and delayed gratification, lessons a lot of the people he arrested had missed when they were children. Ash gave her a hug and pushed her on the swing to get her started before joining his wife and son inside the living room.

Kaden, Ash's youngest, had just had his first birthday and his favorite pastime had become stacking things up and then knocking them over. In his more destructive moments, he also seemed to enjoy removing the petals from flowers and pulling heavy pots out of the kitchen cabinets. When Ash walked into the room, Kaden dropped a plastic container full of blocks and waddled toward him, grinning. Ash couldn't help but grin back and pick him up.

"I'm glad you're home," said Hannah, closing the laptop she had been working on before standing up. Ash shifted Kaden to his other side and kissed his wife hello. Unlike in previous months, she didn't linger to smell his breath. After eight hard-fought months of sobriety, he had earned some of her trust back. It felt good. "The envelope I told you about is in the kitchen."

"I'll look at it in a moment," said Ash, making a face at Kaden. The baby smiled. "I want to spend some time with you guys first. You up to anything?"

"Just hanging out," said Hannah. "Hamid Aziz called this morning. He said you don't need to take Nour and Jake out again."

Dating among devout Muslims is a little different than it is for most Americans. The Prophet said that whenever a man is alone with a woman, the devil makes a third. Some Muslims take that very seriously and, aside from a spouse or close relative, never allow themselves to be alone in a room with someone of the opposite sex. Others are more lackadaisical. Nour Aziz fell somewhere in the middle of the spectrum. Her aunt and uncle introduced her to a man at their mosque, and the two seemed to get along well. They didn't feel comfortable on dates alone, though, so Nour asked her father if he knew anyone who'd be willing to chaperone a date or two. He called Ash, the only police officer he knew.

"That's too bad," said Ash. "I really thought they hit it off well."

Hannah cocked her head at him. "What did you guys do?"

"Jake suggested some kind of hike, but the way I see it, dating is like a job interview. I thought Nour would want to know if Jake could protect her, so I called in a favor from a friend of mine and took them to the gun range at work."

Hannah nodded. "Jake and Nour still plan to see each other, but your sister is going to chaperone them. They think she'll be more compatible with them."

"Oh," said Ash. He paused. "I took you to the gun range before we were married. You had fun, didn't you?"

"No, but I still married you. And I've felt safe around paper targets ever since."

"I'm glad to hear it."

He hung out with them for only about fifteen minutes, but it was the best part of his day. Hannah showed him pictures of a used minivan she thought they should consider. She originally thought they'd just buy another regular-sized car, but between diaper bags, strollers, and backpacks, they needed more room. The van cost more than most of the cars they had looked at, but it had a lot of safety features. They could make it work if she really wanted it. Ash had never expected his wife to become a suburban soccer mom, but she had become content with the role, and because of that, so was he.

At about two in the afternoon, he put Kaden back on the ground near a pile of blocks and went to the kitchen, where he found a manila envelope on the counter beside the back door. Ash unfolded the clasp and dumped out the contents. Eight passports, a couple of brochures—one of which had been written in Arabic—and a note. He opened a passport from the Republic of Uzbekistan. It belonged to a nineteen-year-old Uzbek girl named Sabina; she had a one-year student visa. He quickly opened two other passports and found similar information. One belonged to a young woman from the Czech Republic and another belonged to a girl from India. Both had student visas. He flipped through the rest and found a similar pattern. All belonged to young women, and all had one- to two-year student visas. What Bukoholov wanted him to make out of that, Ash didn't know.

Next he muddled through the brochure, which advertised a student-exchange program. If the passports belonged to program participants, he at least had an idea of why they all had student visas. The note simply contained the address of a bed-and-breakfast in New Palestine.

Bukoholov didn't act without reason. The last time he suggested Ash look into something, he got some very bad men off the street and saved the lives of several innocent people. He also ended up in the middle of an interdepartmental mess that forced a very strong candidate out of the primary race for county prosecutor, ensuring that Leonard Wilson, a man amenable to Bukoholov's agenda, won. Bukoholov would reap the benefits of that tip for years.

Ash had little doubt that Bukoholov would get something from this tip, too, but equally, he had little doubt that someone needed to check it out. Just not him, not with Agent Havelock and his own department already suspicious of him. Ash took out his phone and looked up the number of the Hancock County Sheriff's Department and called them up. As soon as he introduced himself, the civilian receptionist transferred his call to Craig Davis, the deputy sheriff.

"What can we do for you, Detective Rashid?"

"I've got some information for you. A confidential informant I run contacted me and said that something illegal might be going on in a business in your jurisdiction."

"And which business would that be?"

"The Dandelion Inn. It's in New Palestine."

Davis didn't respond for a moment, presumably as he wrote the information down. "Your CI give you any details?"

Ash looked at the brochures and passports on his table. "Not really, but it might involve some college kids."

"Okaaay," said Davis, drawing the word out. "You think drugs?"

"Possibly, but I don't know. My CI hears a lot of things. If he gives me a tip, it's usually pretty important. I've made a couple of big cases because of him."

"And this place, the Dandelion Inn, is in New Pal?"

"That's the address I've been given."

"All right," said Davis. "It's just that we don't get a lot of problems in New Pal. It's families and farmers, not a whole lot there."

"I understand that," said Ash. "I'd consider it a personal favor if you checked it out. I'll owe you one."

"Yes, you will," said Davis. He yawned. "I'll have somebody swing by this afternoon."

"I'd strongly suggest you send at least two officers and warn them that the people in the inn might be armed."

Davis clucked his tongue. "Are you holding information back on me, Detective Rashid?"

"No, I'm telling you everything I know. My CI has given me extremely reliable tips about high-level criminal activity in the past. I've brought down a lot of violent suspects because of him. I don't know what's at the inn, but judging by my CI's track record, you might run into some dangerous characters."

"I'll tell my guys. Can I reach you at this number if I need to get in touch with you?"

"Sure. It's my cell."

Davis said he'd call if he found anything and then hung up the phone. Hopefully that'd be the end of that. Ash repackaged the contents of his envelope and took it back to the living room. Hannah had resumed typing whatever document she had been working on when he arrived. She had a blog on which she reviewed bad movies and had started developing quite a following. She said they might even be able to get some money out of it one day; now, though, payment came in the form of free movies from studios Ash had never heard of. Most were worth about what she paid for them.

"I'm going to take a nap," said Ash. "If somebody calls my cell, can you wake me up? It might be important."

"Sure, sweetheart," said Hannah. Ash thanked her and then went to the bedroom. When he put his head on the pillow, it felt as if no sooner had he closed his eyes than Megan came to wake him up. Two hours had passed according to the clock on his nightstand. He opened his eyes wide, yawned, and sat up. Megan thrust a cell phone toward him.

"Here you go."

The phone buzzed, so Ash answered and mouthed *Thank you* to his daughter. She ran out of the room, presumably to wherever Hannah was.

"Ash Rashid. What's going on?" he asked, blinking sleep from his eyes.

"Detective Rashid, this is Craig Davis from the Hancock County Sheriff's Department. I need you to come out to the location you gave me earlier."

"Did you find something?"

"Yeah. And I think you should come out here to see it."

"All right," said Ash, glancing at his watch. He had work that night, but not for several more hours. He had time. "I'll be there as soon as I can."

"See you then."

Ash hung up the phone and put his work clothes back on before heading to the living room. Hannah sat on the floor with Kaden while Megan lay on the couch.

"I'm going to head back to work for a little while," said Ash. "I'll try to be back for *iftar*, but I can't make any promises. I might be late."

Hannah smiled at Kaden and then looked up at him. "Late like last night?"

"We're going to try to get Rebecca Cook back tonight. The guy who took her asked for me. I don't know why."

"What does that mean?"

"It means I'm dropping off the ransom money and hopefully getting Rebecca. I'll be wearing a bullet-resistant vest, and I'll have half our department watching my back."

Hannah sighed and closed her eyes. "Why does this never happen to anybody but you?"

"I didn't ask for this. It just happened."

Hannah nodded and looked at Megan.

"Hug your father, Megan. He's got to go to work."

Megan sprung up immediately and latched on to Ash's waist. "Bye, Bob."

"Bye, sweetheart. Stay out of trouble."

"I will."

Ash looked up at Hannah again. "I'll call you before anything happens."

"Sure."

Ash hugged Kaden on his way out of the house and then entered the bed-and-breakfast's address on the GPS in his cruiser. Time to see what Bukoholov had found.

14

The Dandelion Inn stood in the center of a roughly ten-acre clearing in a wooded area east of New Palestine. It had a gravel lot and a four-car garage to the west of the main building and a storage shed in the distance, near the tree line. Two uniformed Hancock County sheriff's deputies stood watch beside the inn's front door, while a big man with tattoos on his forearms sat in handcuffs on the steps. Ash parked beside one of the five police cruisers in the lot and stepped out to get a look at the building. Aside from some thick black bars over the casement windows in the basement, it looked like a high-end bed-and-breakfast, exactly what it purported to be.

Ash waved to the deputies on the front porch and walked toward them. He unclipped his badge from his belt and slipped it into the front pocket of his jacket.

"I'm Detective Ash Rashid. I'm looking for Craig Davis. He's expecting me."

One of the deputies nodded to the other and then disappeared into the house. The second deputy took a step forward and thrust a clipboard in front of him.

"Can I get you to sign the log sheet, Detective Rashid?" said the deputy. Ash looked at the deputy's nametag. Andy

Maitlin. Evidently, Bukoholov had come through again; Hancock County had found something if they needed a log sheet. Ash scribbled his name in the correct box of the form and then nodded.

"What'd you guys find?"

Maitlin raised his eyebrows and shook his head. "We're still trying to figure that out."

Ash looked down at the handcuffed man. "Who's our friend?"

"Marvin Spencer," said Maitlin. "He had a firearm on his hip when we pulled up, so we sat him down and ran a warrant check on him. Turns out he's wanted in Cincinnati for passing bad checks. We arrested him and then ran a protective sweep inside."

Ash raised his eyebrows. "I assume you didn't call me in to see Mr. Spencer."

"No, we didn't," said Maitlin, nodding. "I'll let Craig fill you in."

Ash only had to wait for another minute for Deputy Sheriff Craig Davis to walk through the front door. He had thinning black hair, a trim figure, and a mustache. Ash shook his hand and nodded to Marvin Spencer.

"I see you guys are already making arrests."

"Yeah, Mr. Spencer greeted my officers on arrival. I think we'll be holding him for a while."

"He say anything?" asked Ash, glancing at the prisoner.

"Fuck you," said Spencer.

Ash looked back at Davis. "He say anything other than that?"

"That's it."

"He's not very friendly, is he?"

"Nope. No, he's not."

Ash nodded toward the house. "What have you got?"

"I think you should see it first."

"Sure."

The porch creaked as Ash followed Davis. The entryway had obviously been built to impress, but Ash had little time to take stock of his surroundings before Sheriff Davis darted to a hallway on the right side of the room. They passed an empty office and walked straight toward a modern, commercial kitchen with stainless steel countertops and appliances. Ash covered his nose with the sleeve of his shirt, hoping to block out an almost overpowering odor of bleach. His shoes stuck to the porcelain tile and came off with a lurching noise. The inn's janitorial staff probably hadn't rinsed off their cleanser properly.

Davis ignored both the smell and the sticky floor as he walked toward a door near the opposite side of the room. Ash found his eyes drawn to grease stains along one exterior wall. He would have dismissed them as the result of cooking spatter had they been closer to the stove, but grease wouldn't fly all the way across the room, not in that quantity. Moreover, he found a brown splotch in the crevice of an otherwise white window frame near the back door. It may have been paint, but it looked an awful lot like clotted blood.

"Did you guys see this yet?" he asked.

"See what?" asked Davis.

"I think it's blood."

He nodded. "I'll put somebody on it, but that doesn't surprise me. The real surprise is downstairs. Come on."

Ash hesitated and then walked toward the door Davis

had stopped near. It had a barrel latch screwed into the frame, allowing someone in the kitchen to lock someone else in the basement. First bars on the windows and now a lock on the door. That's not something you find on too many hotels. The sheriff walked down a carpeted set of stairs, and Ash followed. The basement ran the entire length of the house and had welded metal cots spaced every few feet from one end to the other. It looked like a dormitory.

Ash walked toward a group of police officers on the far side of the room, counting sixteen cots—nine of which had bedding—as he went. The air smelled sweet, almost flowery. It was perfume, and since none of the officers in the house were women, Ash doubted it came from one of them. As he walked closer to the group, he noticed that most of them were staring at a poster on the blank exterior wall of a bathroom. The perfume smell became stronger.

"Is this it?"

"Yep," said Davis, walking past his officers. He pulled the poster back like a door, exposing a cavity in the wall. Ash heard whispers coming from inside.

"What's going on?" he asked.

"Take a look, Detective."

Ash stepped around the sheriff and hesitated before putting his head past the poster. The cavity opened into a small room with a bare bulb light fixture and thin carpet. A number of young women in pajamas huddled in the corner.

"Hi, ladies," he said, unsure what else to say. A couple of the girls closest to the door pressed back on those behind them, trying to get away from him. Ash took the hint and backed off himself. Davis nodded at him when he emerged.

"Tell me that's why you called me here and that you didn't find anything worse."

"That's why we called you."

"Did you try coaxing them out yet?"

"We tried speaking to them in Spanish, English, and German. They didn't respond, and nobody here speaks anything else. I've got a couple of female officers on the way. We're hoping they might have more success than we've had."

Ash nodded. "Can I try something first?"

"Go right ahead."

Ash stuck his head back in the room and cast his gaze over the women again.

They huddled and trembled together like a pack of frightened animals.

"*As-salamu alaykum.*"

Peace be upon you. It was the standard greeting given by Muslims around the world. Given that there were a billion and a half Muslims worldwide, Ash thought it was worth a shot. Two girls stepped forward, clinging to each other. The oldest could have been in college, but the other girl was probably fifteen or sixteen. Both wore pajamas, and both cried against the other's chest so their words came out distorted.

"*Walaikum salam.*"

And peace be upon you. Ash looked over his shoulder at the officers outside.

"We're going to need some backup."

15

Voroshilovsk, Ukraine, 1954.

The cell stunk of sweat, excrement, and mildew. Most men stayed for a day or two before being tried or executed, but Kostya had already been there for a full week. The men he had been arrested with had already come and gone, having been able to afford the necessary bribes to the appropriate guards. They had probably returned to work, peddling illegal wares to those men and women fortunate enough to be able to afford a few luxury items.

Kostya, meanwhile, sat on the ground with his back against a brick wall, watching as guards patrolled the hallway outside. He had been arrested for purchasing strawberries, a birthday present for his sister, from a black market dealer in Voroshilovsk. Most likely they had been split among the men who arrested him and eaten on the spot.

Two men sat across from him in the cell, but he didn't bother trying to talk to them. Dirt and sweat caked their faces so thoroughly that he couldn't even determine their ethnicity. He had seen several men like them come during the past week; by now, those men had been executed or sent to a forced labor camp in Siberia. Kostya felt a little surprised that hadn't happened to him yet. It happened to prisoners unable to pay, and

171

he saw little point in fighting a system meant to degrade, humiliate, and dehumanize him at every step.

He leaned his head against the wall and closed his eyes, knowing he might get few chances for real rest in the future. Before sleep could overtake him, though, someone inserted a key into the cell door's lock and swung the door open.

"Get up, Kostya."

He recognized the voice before opening his eyes, having heard it at least once a week for the better part of ten years. Vladimir Orlesky. In one way or another, Vladimir had been part of the state security apparatus for all of Kostya's life. When Kostya moved to his aunt and uncle's farm when he was eleven, Vladimir had been a part of the MGB. Since Stalin's death, though, that ministry had been merged with another to form the Ministry of Internal Affairs, the MVD. Though the names changed, the mission didn't: protect the dictatorship of the Communist Party through any means necessary. Vladimir may have been following orders, but that didn't make him any less repugnant.

Kostya's eyes fluttered open to take in his captor.

"Congratulations on surviving the great purge so far," he said. "I thought you of all people would be exterminated in the first wave."

A grimace formed on Vladimir's face. Although little had happened in the Ukraine yet, newspapers sponsored by the Communist Party reported on the trials of several former secret police officers who had been arrested in Moscow for putting the interests of their organization and themselves above the party and government. Once the party finished parading them about the country as an example, they'd be shot. Everyone knew it, including them.

"You're very talkative for someone in a cell."

Kostya shrugged. "I have nowhere to go. I've accepted my fate. Nothing I can do will change that."

"At least you know your place."

Kostya closed his eyes again. "What do you want?"

"You're a smart boy, I'm told. Your aunt speaks highly of you. She says you want to be a doctor."

"As long as I'm in your cell, it doesn't matter what I want. Is that what you wanted to hear?"

"If you were released right now, what would you do?"

Kostya opened his eyes and crossed his arms. "Why are you wasting my time? We both know what's going to happen. I'll have a trial, and men whose crimes are blacker than any I've ever even contemplated will pronounce me guilty of buying my sister a birthday present. They'll send me to prison, and you'll go on doing whatever you want. I'm tired of it, and I'm tired of playing along."

"You're free to go."

Kostya scoffed. "You want to shoot me in the back and call it an escape attempt?"

"If I wanted you dead, I wouldn't need the excuse. I'd shoot you in the head here. Now stand up and go."

Kostya eyed him for a moment, but then pushed himself off the wall and stood. "What is this?"

"A pardon in lieu of your family's extraordinary services to the state."

Kostya felt his shoulders fall. He didn't have any famous leaders or soldiers in his family, just an aunt who cared enough about him to sacrifice herself for his safety.

"Myra did this?"

Vladimir shook his head and reached into his pocket for a

173

strip of tattered cloth. Kostya recognized the fabric immediately; he used to have an identical bit before Vladimir confiscated it several years earlier. It had come from the dress his mother wore before she died. Anastasiya had the only other strip in existence, and she wouldn't have let it out of her sight if she could help it.

"Your aunt was unavailable. Return this to your sister and apologize on behalf of my men. Some of them can be...demanding."

Kostya's hands shook, but he tried to keep the revulsion from his voice. "What did you do to her?"

"We gave her a birthday present."

For a moment, Kostya couldn't speak. He wanted to hit him, to strike back with everything he had. Vladimir wanted that, though; he would have sent an underling if he didn't. Kostya's vision clouded as moisture sprang to his eyes. He blinked it away and held his breath to choke the emotion from his voice.

"My family has never done anything to you. I won't forget this."

Vladimir shook his head, the outline of a smile on his lips.

"It doesn't matter. You're going to go to school and become a doctor, just like your family wants. You're weak, like your uncle. That's all you have in you. Your tears betray that as much as anything you could say."

Kostya wiped his cheek. "Whatever I am, whatever I have in me, you've put there. I will kill you for this."

"I sincerely hope to see you try. Now get out. I have real work to do."

* * *

The warehouse had stood in that spot for so long its elaborate exterior brickwork and leaded glass windows had become pieces of history. As Kostya stepped inside, the sterile, white paint that covered every surface in the building reflected and magnified the artificially bright light from the overhead lamps. Just five years ago, two hundred workers in that plant pumped out fifty thousand meals ready to eat for the U.S. military every day, but with the wars in Iraq and Afghanistan more or less over, the factory's output had slowed and then stopped completely. The U.S. military still paid for the space, but one of Kostya's companies owned the building. Other, active industrial sites surrounded them, but no workers had stepped into Kostya's building in several months; they wouldn't have guests anytime soon.

Lev opened a metal folding chair for Kostya beside a drain in the concrete floor.

"Thank you. Please bring her in."

Lev nodded and directed his boys to follow him back to their van. Kostya didn't relish committing violence, but he understood its utility when applied judiciously. He needed information that Ann had, and while she may not be receptive to his entreaties yet, she would be with the right motivation. When Lev returned, he carried an unconscious Ann over his shoulder while his son Michael wheeled in a sturdy wooden swivel chair. Lev put her in the chair and Michael secured her arms and legs to the frame with white zip ties, ensuring that she couldn't move. James, meanwhile, wheeled in a pressurized gas cylinder with attached tubing and bright yellow mask. Once his son had the apparatus set up, Lev broke a packet of smelling salts open and held it beneath Ann's nose. She jerked awake immediately as the aroma of ammonia permeated the surroundings. Her eyes shot around the room, wide and terrified.

"Where am I?"

"Nowhere you've ever been before, I'm sure," said Kostya. "I thought we could talk here uninterrupted."

Ann's nostrils flared as she exhaled, but the fear in her eyes subsided somewhat, as did her heavy breathing.

"What do you want?"

"Information."

"I don't know anything."

Kostya frowned. "That's what you said earlier. I had hoped you would reconsider."

Ann used her feet to inch the chair toward Kostya, but stopped when one of the wheels hit the drain embedded into the floor.

"I have money in a safe at the inn. If you let me go, it's yours. Almost two hundred thousand dollars."

Kostya shook his head. "I'm not interested in your money."

"My employers can give you more. A million dollars. Cash. It's yours if you let me go."

Kostya pretended to consider before shaking his head. "No. I appreciate the offer, but I've already got enough money. Who are your employers?"

Ann straightened. "If you kill me, you'll find out when they come after your family."

Kostya looked at his brother-in-law. "Considering my family, I'll take my chances."

She flinched and tried to back off. "What do you want with me?"

"Just information, as I said."

"Then ask me a question."

"I'm glad you're agreeable. This is normally so much more difficult. Tell me," said Kostya, leaning so close to Ann that he could smell the remnants of her perfume. "What did Kara Bukoholov do for you?"

"I don't know Kara Bukoholov."

"Kara Elliot."

Ann didn't say anything. Kostya leaned back and stood up slowly, his knees hurting.

"When I was nineteen, my little sister and I were sent to a forced labor camp in Siberia. MVD officers took me from college." Kostya looked at Lev. "It's where I met my future brother-in-law, actually."

"Charming family history," said Ann.

Kostya chuckled. "I was a janitor when I was there, so I cleaned the interrogation rooms. I saw guards beat prisoners with sticks, shock them with electrodes, inject them with drugs. They were cruel men."

"Are you telling me this to scare me?"

"No," said Kostya. "I don't have the stomach to do those sorts of things. Besides, those weren't designed to get someone to talk. There were limited recreation opportunities, so the guards took whatever they could get."

"They sound lovely."

Kostya smiled. "To break someone, they were more methodical. One guard in particular was smarter than the others. He recognized that psychological pain was, in many ways, even worse than physical pain. I remember one morning in particular. He ordered me to help him strap a man to a table and then force him to swallow a long rag. While I watched, the guard then put the other end of the rag in a bucket of water suspended from the ceiling. Every time the prisoner took a breath, water would slide down that rag and into his lungs, drowning him over the course of hours. The prisoner knew he was killing himself and couldn't do anything about it. You do that to a man and then revive him enough times, he'll tell you anything you want to know."

Ann looked around.

"I don't see a bucket of water here."

"No, of course not," said Kostya, motioning his nephew James forward. "I don't have that kind of time."

James wheeled the canister forward and stopped behind Ann. She flinched as he secured the rubber mask over her mouth and nose. She held her breath for about a minute after he turned on the gas, but when she inhaled, she shuddered and Kostya could hear the chair creak as she fought the restraints.

"It's just carbon dioxide. If you talk, it won't hurt you permanently."

Kostya nodded to his nephew after thirty more seconds. James killed the gas and removed the mask from her face. She slumped forward, gasping.

"You know why I use the gas?" Ann tilted her head back and spit at him. Kostya took a handkerchief from his pocket and wiped his shoulder. "We used to use a pillow, but people would bite their lips, thrash their heads around and bite us. It was too much work. This is much more humane, don't you think?"

She spit at him again. "I told you. I don't know Kara Elliot."

"I think you do, and I had hoped this would be easier," said Kostya, nodding toward his nephew. James put the mask on again. Instead of releasing her thirty seconds after she took her first breath, though, he kept the mask on for a full minute. She fought even harder, but the chair and restraints held. As she gasped and panted afterward, Kostya had James put the air on again. She didn't last long before passing out, so Lev had to use the smelling salts on her again to wake her up. When she woke, red tinged the whites of her eyes, her capillaries having burst.

"My partners are going to find you and kill you," she said between gasps.

"Threats without the possibility of action are pointless. I don't want to do this to you, but I need to find out what happened to my daughter. Tell me and this will end."

Ann narrowed her eyes. "No."

"So be it," said Kostya, nodding toward his nephew. They continued gassing her and then reviving her for about half an hour. Unlike earlier, though, Kostya didn't give her the opportunity to talk. Eventually, she started crying and shaking even with the gas off.

"Talk to me. Tell me what I want to know, and this will be over. Nod if you agree."

She shuddered and then nodded, so James took the mask off her face. She breathed deeply, tears streaming freely down her cheeks. None of the men said anything, but Kostya leaned forward and wiped her tears away with a handkerchief.

"I didn't want to do that. Please understand, this isn't personal. I don't like to hurt people."

Ann's lips moved, but no sound emerged. Kostya glanced at one of his nephews.

"Give her some water."

Michael cut the zip tie from one of Ann's arms and handed her a bottle of water. She drank and held it against her forehead.

"How did you know my daughter?"

Ann didn't say anything. Kostya looked over his shoulder at his nephew.

"Put the mask on her again."

"Kara worked for us," said Ann quickly. "She and her husband took care of our money."

Kostya blinked and took a deep breath. "How did she take care of your money?"

"Our business is mostly cash. She worked with investment banks and other companies so we could put it in the bank."

"So she laundered it."

Ann didn't respond. At least that explained why Kara didn't go to the police with Iskra.

"Did she know how you earned your money?" asked Kostya.

"Not at first, but her husband found out, and then papers and documents started going missing. When they stopped working with us, we didn't know what to do. We thought they were working with the government. When Daniel, Kara's husband, took Iskra, we knew we had to do something."

"You decided to kill them."

"Not us. My boss did."

"What's his name?"

Ann shook her head. "I don't know. I've never met him. He tells me where to go to find new girls and arranges for me to bring them back to the U.S."

"What about the money?"

"We send half of everything we earn via wire transfer to an account in the Cayman Islands."

"Surely you know something about your employer, a name at least."

She started to say something, but then stopped. "His name is Lukas. He's from Chicago. That's all I know."

"Are you sure that's all you know?"

She paused.

"He has an accent. I think he's German."

"What else?"

"That's it. I've never met him in person or seen a picture, and I don't know anything else. I work with the girls and manage the bed-and-breakfast. I don't deal with security."

Kostya had always found it curious when he ran across people who went into business with strangers. You couldn't trust someone you didn't know.

"Thank you for your help," said Kostya, standing.

Ann inched forward on her chair, her face drawn. "I told you what I know," she said. "Please let me go."

Kostya took a step back and glanced at Lev. "Get rid of her."

While Lev removed a firearm from his pocket, Kostya walked toward the warehouse's exit. The shot that silenced Ann echoed in the warehouse but would be muffled by the building's thick walls, ensuring none of the neighbors heard. Kostya had bought it for that very feature. He may not have been able to get much out of Ann, but he could at least be assured that she wouldn't be running a bed-and-breakfast again anytime soon.

16

One of the girls who answered Ash's greeting spoke a few words of Arabic, enabling him to determine that she came from Pakistan. Indianapolis wasn't replete with Urdu speakers, but Ash knew a few from his mosque. He called one family up; unfortunately, none of the adults in the Tahir household were home, but Sadia, the family's eldest daughter, was. She didn't have native Urdu fluency like her mother and father, but she spoke it better than anyone the Hancock County Sheriff's Department could bring in. With Sadia still on the line, Ash handed his cell phone to one of the Pakistani girls. The conversation was halting, but after a few minutes, the Pakistani girl started crying and then shouting to the other Pakistani girl. They hugged each other and then gestured for the rest of the girls to follow them out of their secret room.

There were nine of them in all, one for each of the cots with sheets on it. One of the girls had a yellow bruise on her cheek, but none looked malnourished. They huddled together, leaning against each other for support.

"We need some paramedics to check them out," said Ash, looking at Sheriff Davis.

"They're already on the way."

"Good," said Ash, nodding. "I say we all put our firearms where they can't be seen and slowly leave. Hopefully they'll follow, but they seem pretty spooked."

"They seem *terrified*," said Davis, correcting him. "What the hell went on in here?"

Ash took a quick look around the room and shook his head. "I don't know if I want to know."

The officers did as Ash suggested and backed off. As Ash had hoped, the Pakistani girls led the rest of the girls to the porch, but even with almost a dozen officers outside, no one quite knew what to do. Without knowing what went on, Ash guessed that it'd be a big investigation, probably too big for a rural sheriff's department to handle on its own. Likely, Sheriff Davis would call in the state police for assistance; they had good detectives, so Ash had little worry that they'd figure things out given time.

Until help arrived, though, the local officers had their hands full trying to communicate with their new guests. As it turned out, most of the girls spoke enough English to take direction but not nearly enough for an effective interview. A couple of them, from their conversations with each other, sounded as if they spoke Russian, but Ash couldn't differentiate between Russian and any number of other Slavic languages. He didn't even have a guess about some of the other girls' languages. Indianapolis had a couple of universities and colleges; maybe someone from one of their linguistic departments could help.

Ash left the girls on the front porch and went back into the house. Sheriff Davis stood in the entryway, his eyes panning over the interior.

"Have you guys secured search warrants yet?" asked Ash.

"Not yet, so we're waiting before we begin a real search," he said. "We've detained Mr. Spencer."

"If you need help, I'm sure my department will be happy to oblige."

"Thank you, Sergeant," said Davis. "But I'm going to request the FBI come in on this. Those girls aren't local."

"It sounds like you guys will be in good hands," said Ash, reaching into his pocket. He took out a business card and handed it to the sheriff. "If you need anything from me, please give me a call. That has my cell phone number and office number. I'm on another case right now, so I'm going to head out."

The sheriff slipped the card into a pocket on the front of his uniform and nodded. "I'll call you if I need you. And if anyone in the media asks, I'll give credit where it's due. We wouldn't have found this without you."

"I'd prefer if you kept my involvement quiet. I've been on TV enough."

Davis narrowed his eyes before nodding. "All right. We'll do that."

"Thank you."

Ash left the building and headed to his cruiser. The interior had turned into an oven in the summer sun, but at least his air conditioner worked well, something few cruisers in the department's aging fleet could boast. As he drove to the city, his mind kept coming back to the envelope Bukoholov had given him. When he stopped and thought about it for a moment, that tip bothered him just as much as the young women he had found. For all he knew, Bukoholov could have been sitting on that information for weeks or even months, waiting for the most opportune moment to turn it to the police, when doing so would provide the most benefit for him. Because that, above all else, was how he operated. Having the Dandelion Inn closed and its proprietors arrested furthered some end Ash didn't know about, gave Bukoholov something he wanted.

The old man had used him, plain and simple; he had known that going in. The part that rankled Ash the most, though, the part that would likely keep him awake at night if he let it, was that he couldn't do anything about it. As long as Bukoholov's tips allowed him to save someone's life, he had to follow up on them. The cost to his career didn't matter. At the end of his days, maybe Ash would be called to account for that, but now he did what he had to. In a world full of sinners, the good guys couldn't all be saints.

He took the interstate back to town but stopped at a gas station near I-465 when his cell phone started to ring. It was Mike Bowers. They didn't talk long, nor did Bowers mention the Dandelion Inn, which was good. Hopefully Sheriff Davis would do as Ash asked and keep his involvement anonymous. Bowers said the FBI's tactical team needed him to come in so they could go over the logistics of that night's swap, so Ash skipped going home and drove downtown. When he arrived, he found five people in the conference room waiting for him: Agent Havelock, Captain Bowers, Chief Reddington, and two other FBI agents with extensive tactical backgrounds. Someone had put an oversized backpack on the table along with a poster-sized map of the downtown area.

"We've got quite a bit to cover, so listen up," said Havelock. He pointed to the backpack and told Ash to pick it up. They hadn't even put the money in yet, and it still felt heavier than any bag Ash had ever carried. "We're waiting for funds from the Cooks' bank, but that's the bag we'll be using. The first thing you'll notice about it is the weight. There's a layer of Kevlar between the nylon layers and a ceramic plate sewn into the back, similar to the ones found in bullet-resistant jackets. It'll provide decent protection against handguns, but rifles are iffy.

"We've also sewn a GPS beacon into the bag's lining, which should allow us to track it. In the eventuality that Palmer tosses the bag, we've slipped a thin, wireless transmitter between bills in two of the stacks of cash. They're similar to the beacons cross-country skiers use in case of avalanches, and, unfortunately, they have the same range limitations. You will have a microphone and earpiece on you at all times, so we'll be able to stay in touch. Finally, we will also have a helicopter on standby a couple of minutes out. Questions?"

"Yeah," said Ash. "Can I get a watch that shoots laser beams? I've always wanted one of those."

Bowers and most of the FBI agents tittered, but Havelock's expression didn't change.

"I'm afraid we're out," he said. "Do you have any questions pertinent to this operation or your equipment?"

"I think I'm okay."

"Good."

Havelock turned it over to his two other agents to discuss the tactical setup. They planned to place three sniper teams on the roofs of three nearby buildings. That high up, they ought to have been able to cover the entire park, giving

Palmer few spots from which he could hide and shoot. The exchange itself would be the easy part. Bowers would drop off Ash a couple of blocks away, and he'd walk to the appointed spot and wait for further instructions. Another team would wait at the Scottish Rite Cathedral to pick up Rebecca. Police teams would then shadow the bag—and whoever happened to carry it—hopefully back to Palmer. On paper, it sounded easy. In the field, though, things rarely went as planned.

*   *   *

Ash spent the rest of the afternoon and evening with his family at home. Normally, he would have taken the kids out somewhere, but with the temperature near the hundred-degree mark, no one wanted to leave the house. That worked out better for him, anyway, because it allowed him to conserve energy until sundown when he could eat and drink again. They had afternoon prayers together as a family, something they rarely had the opportunity to do. Megan seemed to like that. The kids went to bed at around eight, giving Ash a few minutes alone with his wife. She pretended to like his bad jokes, and he pretended to enjoy her terrible choice in movies. It was just nice to be with her.

At the appointed time, she filled a thermos full of coffee so awful Ash could feel his own life slip away every time he drank it. She had made it for him for the first time the day after they were married, and he didn't have the heart to tell her it was the most vile liquid ever to pass between his lips. Once the sun set, he'd have a few sips and then try to find something to water it down with.

CHRIS CULVER

He drove to the station on his own, but felt a little woozy upon getting out of his car. He almost had to sit back down. He had done a lot of physical work that day without water, so his dehydration was evidently catching up with him. The sun would go down in another half hour, and he could suck it up until then. When he got to the conference room inside the homicide department, he discovered that the Cooks' bank had come through with the money. Two bricks of one-hundred-dollar bills, twenty thousand dollars total, sat on the conference room table when he walked in. It carried a much heavier weight than its mass alone.

Ash took a seat as Agent Havelock went over the security arrangements again. He probably should have listened, but Ash couldn't force himself to pay attention to the same speech he had already heard several times. Instead, he tried to see the holes in their security plan; unfortunately, it didn't take a lot of imagination to find them. He wouldn't carry a gun, so his safety rested with the FBI's shooters if Palmer or his minions started firing at him. That would work for the open spaces, but not even the best marksmen in the world could see through trees or shoot around obstacles. He doubted the exchange itself would go smoothly, either. Palmer might not even show up. So many things could go wrong that Ash had difficulty envisioning it going right.

Havelock finished the briefing at about nine. Ash tried to stand, but became dizzy and fell into his chair. He didn't think anyone had noticed, but then Bowers came behind him and knelt to speak to him.

"I saw that. Tell me you're sober, Ash."

Ash's mind felt clouded, so it took him a moment to process the comment. He eventually shook his head.

"I'm just tired and thirsty."

"You're pale. Are you sick?"

"No, I just need some water. I haven't had anything all day."

The corners of Bowers's lips inched upward.

"You're kidding me. It was a hundred degrees today, and you've been working outside."

"It's Ramadan. The heat isn't an excuse."

The beginnings of a smile slipped off Bowers's face.

"You look like you're going to pass out at any moment. I don't care if it's Ramadan. As your superior officer, I'm ordering you to drink whenever you're thirsty. Day or night, it doesn't matter."

"I'll be fine," said Ash. "People have been celebrating Ramadan by fasting since the eighth century."

"I've given you an order. Disobey it at your own peril."

"If my health is in danger, I'll have a drink, even during the day. Is that fair?"

"Yeah, good," said Bowers. "Now go get a sandwich or something. You've got a long night."

Instead of getting a sandwich, Ash took a couple of gulps of water at the nearest drinking fountain and then found a quiet spot for *Maghrib*, the fourth of five daily prayers. Only then did he go to the deli nearest the station and order enough food for three people. The other diners stared at him at first, but Ash didn't pay attention. He had begun focusing on his task that night. If everything went according to plan, Rebecca would safely be in custody in another few hours and Palmer would be wearing an orange jail-issued jumpsuit. He prayed that things would go that easily.

After dinner, Ash took a walk downtown, hoping exercise would banish his nervous jitters. A lot of very good people had given input on Agent Havelock's plan, and while no one described it as perfect, nearly everyone agreed that it could work. A lot hinged on the unknown, though, and that left Ash feeling apprehensive.

At about ten, Ash went back to his office and texted his wife to let her know that he was thinking of her. She responded immediately and said that she had been praying for him. Prayer couldn't hurt. He gingerly sipped the coffee she had given him; if nothing else, it woke him up. At about twenty to eleven, he and Mike Bowers left the building. The security teams had set up hours earlier, so their detail consisted only of Bowers's personal vehicle, a nearly new Honda Accord. Before dropping Ash off, he swung by the library where they would do the exchange. The park in front of it contained five square blocks of green space crisscrossed by sidewalks and festooned with fountains and sculptures. At that time of night, no one walked its paths or admired its decorations; Ash had rarely seen such a lonely, empty place.

In accordance with the plan they had worked out, Bowers dropped Ash off near Monument Circle two blocks away. He took a couple of breaths and swallowed the nervous pit in his stomach, then headed north. Before he could leave the Circle, a "homeless man" pulled a two-way radio from a bag of aluminum cans and said, "Good luck." Ash nodded his thanks but mostly kept his gaze in front of him. He knew the area fairly well, having visited a bar off Monument Circle at least once a week during his drinking days. As he passed, he heard jazz coming from within. The bouncer sitting outside said hello but didn't seem to recognize him. That made Ash pause for a moment. Just a year ago, he could walk down certain streets in the city and be recognized by every bartender, cocktail waitress, or bouncer he passed. He felt proud of his new anonymity.

"Can you hear me, Ash?"

Ash adjusted his earpiece and lowered his chin so he could speak into the microphone taped behind the lapel of his jacket.

"Yeah, Mike. You're loud and clear."

"Our teams are in place, and Agent Havelock is talking to them right now. We'll monitor you on your way. As of this moment, a young man is sitting on a bench near the spot you're walking toward. He's probably just waiting for the bus, but we wanted to keep you apprised. Our shooters are on him if he tries anything, so the drop-off is still a go. Good luck."

"Thank you."

The first block of the park contained a fountain in the center with sidewalks radiating from it like the spokes on a bicycle wheel. A young couple held hands on a bench overlooking the street. The man wore a pair of black slacks, a white Oxford shirt, and shiny black shoes, while his significant other wore a similarly expensive-looking black skirt. It was a little late for an evening in the park, but there were a couple of large corporate law firms in the area. They might have just gotten off work. Ash nodded and smiled hello to them but stayed on the outskirts of the park where his own people could keep an eye on him.

"I'm on North Meridian, crossing East Vermont. I don't see anybody, but I hope you're watching me."

"We are. You just passed two of Havelock's agents by the fountain. Apparently they just got married. It's very sweet."

"Newlyweds. That explains why they're still talking to each other."

Ash stayed on the west side of the park and walked past the Indiana War Memorial, a limestone neoclassic monument, before coming to a stone obelisk and fountain in the center of a field of grass.

"There's a lot of stuff down here. Are we still clear?"

"As far as we can tell," said Bowers. "You're going to run into some trees about half a block ahead of you. We have two officers waiting at a bus stop there. The Scottish Rite Cathedral will be on your left. We have several officers watching that."

"Understood."

Ash kept walking and, as Bowers had said, soon ran into a row of trees planted along the edge of the park. Their leaves allowed just enough light from the moon and stars to filter through that Ash could avoid tripping on cracks in the sidewalk. The cathedral to his left was an imposing Gothic building with coffered wooden doors inset into the stonework. Palmer hadn't specified where he'd pick up Rebecca exactly, but hopefully he'd find her soon.

He kept walking until he reached the central library. The kid Bowers had mentioned earlier still sat on the bench. He had an overgrown, unkempt hairstyle and several days' worth of facial hair on his chin. Despite a temperature in the upper seventies, he wore a pair of tight jeans and a sweater. He might have been homeless, but then again, he might have been a graduate student at one of the nearby universities. Ash always had difficulty telling them apart.

"Shaggy's still here," said Ash. "Should I wait him out?"

Bowers didn't respond for a moment. "Havelock says yes. If we need to, we'll send somebody by to pick him up."

"Good. I'm going to have a seat. This bag weighs a ton."

Ash walked to the bus stop at which the kid was sitting and removed the backpack. Whoever picked it up would notice the weight, but hopefully he wouldn't surmise that it contained as much electronic gear as it did. Ash relaxed and rotated his shoulders, feeling bone click against bone. His doctor suggested that he have the entire shoulder joint replaced with a prosthetic, but Ash refused when he found out how long the post-op recovery period was. He liked playing with his kids too much; he could grin and bear the discomfort until they grew up some.

"Put the bag on your back and come with me."

Ash cocked his head to the left to look at the speaker. Shaggy tapped his feet against the ground and darted his gaze from building to building.

"Excuse me?" asked Ash.

"Put on the backpack and come with me," he said. "I'm supposed to take you to the cathedral to get what you came for."

Shaggy looked nervous; if he had a firearm on him, the situation could get ugly fast. Ash slowly sat straighter and talked into the microphone on his lapel in case Bowers hadn't heard that.

"You want me to put on the backpack, and then we'll get Rebecca."

"Did I stutter? Put it on." Shaggy's Adam's apple bobbed as he swallowed and looked around the park.

Ash waited for Bowers to say something.

"We're watching," said Bowers. "Do as he says."

"Okay," said Ash, standing up. He slipped the backpack on, wincing as it wrenched his shoulder back. Shaggy walked toward him.

"Okay. Start walking toward the cathedral."

"I'm walking toward the cathedral now," said Ash, his heart starting to beat fast.

"Stop repeating everything I say. You're making me nervous."

"That's not my intention," said Ash, forcing his voice to be as calm as possible. "Did Palmer say where Rebecca will be?"

Shaggy shook his head quickly. "I don't know anything about anybody named Rebecca. I'm just supposed to lead you over there."

"So you're just a courier," said Ash into the microphone on his lapel. "You're not with Palmer."

"Stop talking, man. I've got a knife. You screw with me, you get stabbed."

Ash slowly put up his hands. Shaggy jerked his head around, looking around them.

"Relax, buddy," he said. "I'm cooperating. I'm just here for the girl. As long as you've got a knife, you're in charge. Nothing will happen."

Hopefully he had sent the message clear enough. Ash looked at a low-slung medical building about half a block away. Havelock had stationed a sniper team there; they ought to be able to see everything he did. He slowly shook his head at them, hoping to wave them off unless absolutely necessary. Shaggy didn't pose a threat to anyone except himself. He probably didn't even know what he had stepped into. A bead of sweat formed on Ash's forehead and slid down his brow. He blinked it out of his eye rather than move his hands.

"There's a van headed your way up Meridian," said Bowers in Ash's earpiece.

Ash nodded once in the direction of the sniper's perch, hoping they'd relay his understanding to Bowers. He heard the vehicle a moment later. The van looked like the sort he warned his kids to avoid getting into. It had white paint and windows so deeply tinted that he couldn't see inside. Rust ate at the wheel wells. It pulled to a stop in front of him, and the side door closest to him slid open, exposing an all-metal interior. There were no rear seats, but there were two men inside, one in the driver's seat and one in the rear compartment. Both wore jeans and polo shirts, one in blue and the other in yellow. Neither carried weapons, but both men wore ski masks. He felt bolstered by that. If they felt the need to protect their identities, it meant they likely planned to keep him alive. Before Ash could say anything, one of the men thrust a cell phone toward him.

"He's going to kill my kids. Please do whatever he wants."

Ash knew Rebecca's voice, and he could practically feel the tension in it. Shaggy backed off quickly, his hands up, before turning and sprinting up Meridian Street toward Monument Circle. He wouldn't make it far.

"Your family is in protective custody. They're fine. Are you okay?"

Ash heard Rebecca shout, and then someone bobbled the phone. The next voice belonged to Palmer.

"You can get in the van, or you can hear Ms. Cook's last moments. It's up to you, Detective."

The guy with the blue polo shirt ended the call and waved Ash forward.

"Do not get in the vehicle, Ash. Whatever you do, do not—"

Ash removed the earpiece before Bowers could say anything else. He had come too far to give up and let Rebecca die.

"I'm unarmed," he said, holding up his hands. "I will cooperate. Call Palmer back and tell him not to hurt Rebecca."

The guy leaned out of the van and looked left and right.

"Tell your partners not to follow us, or she dies."

Ash took a breath to give him time to think. If Palmer's men wanted him dead, they would have shot him as soon as he opened the door. Neither even seemed to have a weapon, though. Maybe this was how they intended to do the swap. Ash lowered his chin to his lapel.

"They're going to kill Rebecca if you follow us. Stay back. Let me work this." He looked at the men inside again. "Good enough?"

Blue shirt nodded and motioned Ash forward.

Please God, let this be a good idea.

He got in the van and closed the door behind him.

17

The van's driver seemed fixated on plowing into every pothole he could find, making the ride so rough Ash felt his teeth clang together at least twice in the first minute. When they were about half a block from the pickup point, Blue Shirt called Palmer to let him know Ash had gotten into the vehicle. Neither man in the car nor Palmer seemed interested in talking to Ash, which allowed him to look out the windows and memorize their route. They took Meridian Street south, past the cathedral and park. He caught sight of the newlywed couple he had seen near the fountain tackling Shaggy. That poor stupid kid didn't stand a chance, and neither did his friends in the polo shirts. Every police officer in the city likely had a description of the van. They'd never make it out of town.

Blue Shirt hung up the phone after making his call and cocked his head at Ash.

"Give me the backpack."

Ash shimmied it off his shoulders and handed it over, glad to have forty pounds off his back. Blue Shirt zipped it open, removed the money, and fanned through each bundle like a deck of cards. It only took a moment to find the transmitters and a moment longer to throw them behind him, near the rear door. Once he had the money taken care of, he transferred the bundles to a second backpack and threw the FBI-issued one near the transmitters at the back of the van. He then pulled a pair of mesh athletic shorts and a red polo shirt from his own bag and threw them near Ash's feet.

"Change. Now."

"You're not even going to buy me dinner first?"

"Tell your friends good-bye and take off your clothes."

Ash unclipped the microphone from the lapel of his jacket and whispered that he was going dark before removing the transmitter from his pocket. It felt and looked like a cell phone. Blue Shirt leaned forward and tossed it out of the driver's window, making Ash feel nervous for the first time since getting in. As long as they had the backpack, though, he'd be fine.

"I get the feeling you guys have done this before," said Ash, taking off his shoes.

"Shut up and strip."

Apparently they weren't conversationalists. Ash removed his pants, jacket, and shirt before putting on the shirt and shorts Blue Shirt handed him. The running shoes they gave him slipped on his heel, so he laced them up tight. Yellow Shirt turned south on Capital Avenue, putting the Indiana Statehouse to his right. Ash pretended to slip and looked out the van's rear window. He couldn't see a police car anywhere around him.

"Where are we going?" asked Ash.

"You'll find out soon enough."

Definitely weren't conversationalists. Ash thought he could take them out if need be. That would likely doom Rebecca, though, so he didn't want to take the chance unless he had to. From Capital Avenue, they hung a left on Maryland Street, near the center of the city. Glass pedestrian tunnels above the asphalt connected many of the buildings around him, while Circle Centre Mall and its various restaurants and bars lay directly ahead. People crowded the sidewalks at even that late hour.

Yellow Shirt slowed the van and hung a left into one of the mall's parking garages. The lights inside looked artificial and eerily bright after the black of evening. Ash's heart started thumping. His captors evidently intended to switch cars, a move simultaneously smart and stupid. Switching cars and getting rid of any transmitters Ash had brought with him would improve their chances of escape, but they had to know IMPD would wait for them as they exited onto the street.

"Are you sure this is what you guys want to do?" asked Ash. "You're going to get caught here. There aren't enough exits."

"Shut up and get out," said Blue Shirt. "Act casual and Rebecca lives. One phone call from us, she'll get a bullet in her head."

"Okay," said Ash, opening the sliding door. Before he could step out, Blue Shirt reached into his bag and handed Ash a blue Indianapolis Colts baseball cap.

"Put it on tight and keep your head down. If you make a commotion, we start making calls."

"Sure," said Ash, slipping the cap over his head. Blue Shirt and Yellow Shirt then slipped off the ski masks they had been wearing. Both men appeared roughly Ash's age, and both had very hard eyes. Blue Shirt had brown hair, blue eyes and a chin with an inch-long scar on it. Yellow

Shirt had black hair buzzed short, green eyes and olive-colored skin. Both men slipped on their caps and pulled the brims low. Ash didn't know what significance to attribute to the removal of their ski masks, but it didn't fill him with warm and fuzzy feelings. They had planned everything so far quite well, and he had the feeling this would be, too.

Blue Shirt slid open the van's sliding door and prodded Ash out. They had parked on the second floor of the parking garage. Cars, trucks and SUVs occupied most of the spots, limiting his visibility.

"Where are we headed?" asked Ash.

"Just follow my lead," said Blue Shirt. "And hurry. We're late."

The parking garage looked just like every other parking garage Ash had ever been in. Thick concrete pillars supported the ceiling above, while the poured concrete walls had been painted a stark white. The air felt sticky. There were a lot of hiding places in there and way too many civilians for his colleagues to mount an ambush; they'd be waiting at the exits.

Blue Shirt led Ash to a nearby stairwell. Instead of going down to the street level or up to additional floors, they entered the mall itself. The mezzanine stretched upwards four stories and had a rounded glass ceiling high overhead. The late movie must have just let out because people buzzed around a movie theater nearby. Ash, as requested, kept his head down and followed Blue Shirt. He wanted to leave a message for his colleagues, but he couldn't think of anything that wouldn't draw undue attention to him. He even tried looking for a police officer or mall security guard who might remember his face, but he didn't see any.

Blue Shirt led him up an escalator and down another to the far side of the building. Yellow Shirt made a call on the way, but Ash couldn't tell who, if anyone, he talked to. Eventually, they entered a glass tube that led to the second-story lobby of a nearby hotel. The valet had a black Mazda SUV with dark tinted windows waiting for them out front. Ash climbed into the back while Yellow Shirt climbed into the front. Blue Shirt sat beside him. They pulled into traffic within five minutes of ditching their previous vehicle, just another anonymous vehicle on its way home.

Ash sank into the seat. As expected, he saw uniformed officers hurrying from one street corner to the next outside the mall, shouting at each other and speaking into radios. A checkpoint stopped every car exiting from the mall's parking garages, but no one seemed to have considered the hotels. Yellow Shirt turned north onto Illinois Street, but Ash didn't have a way of telling his colleagues that. He started to breathe heavily.

"Put this on," said Blue Shirt, pulling what looked like a black pillowcase out of his bag. "Over your head."

"You first."

Blue Shirt reached into his bag again. He removed a small semiautomatic pistol. Ash turned to the side, so his chest faced his opponent. He reached behind him with his right arm, slowly reaching for the door handle. He pulled it, but nothing happened. They must have put on the child safety locks. Ash's heart started to beat faster.

"Put it on," said Blue Shirt. "I don't want to kill you, but I don't want you to get any ideas about being a hero and trying something stupid."

Blue Shirt held the gun far enough away from Ash that

he'd have to lean over to grab it. Had it been closer, he might have been able to snag it before Blue Shirt got a shot off. He took a breath to slow his racing heart and put up his hands slowly.

"I'm not a hero," said Ash. "I'm just trying to get Rebecca. I'm a police officer. If you kill me, there will be nowhere for you to hide. You will be pursued for the rest of your life."

Blue Shirt's expression didn't change.

"Put the pillowcase over your head. If you cooperate, we'll take you to Rebecca. If you don't, you're both dead. Those are the rules. Comply or I will shoot you. I kid you not."

Ash swallowed and pulled the pillowcase over his face. Some light pierced the fabric, allowing him to see the car's interior lights but not the outside world.

"Lean back and take a nap if you want," said Blue Shirt. "We've got a long ride."

Ash stayed as alert as he could. He tried to determine their route by feel, but he got confused quickly. They made too many turns for him to keep track. Eventually, they hung a wide, looping right, and he felt the car accelerate, presumably as they merged onto the interstate. Indianapolis had interstates leading out of it in nearly every cardinal direction, and they could have taken any one of them. They kept a steady pace for about an hour, but then they slowed on an exit ramp. Ash saw a few lights outside the SUV, but not many. They probably belonged to a gas station or two. Ash reached to his door again and tried the window switch. Like the door, the window didn't move. Yellow Shirt had cranked the air conditioner, but sweat beaded on Ash's forehead. He didn't have a lot of options.

The SUV accelerated past the lights and onto a dark,

smooth road. Ash tried to think his way through his situation. With two assailants, at least one of whom had a gun, the odds weren't in his favor. As soon as they got out of the car, he would need to move fast. If he could take out Blue Shirt and get his weapon, he'd have a pretty good chance. He thought he could do that, too. He could see shapes and outlines through the fabric over his head, and it looked as if Blue Shirt's hands were at his side. If he moved quick enough, Ash thought he could hit Blue Shirt's throat before he reacted. It probably wouldn't kill him, but it ought to incapacitate him long enough to secure his weapon. He needed to find the right time, though.

Yellow Shirt slowed the car as the road became rougher.

"We're almost there, Princess," said Blue Shirt. "Rebecca's just up the road. Lean back and relax. You're not nearly as good as you think you are. If you try anything, I will kill you."

Ash hadn't realized he had tensed up. He forced himself to sit back.

"I'm not going to try anything," he said. "I'm just here for Rebecca."

"Sure," said Blue Shirt. "If it's all the same, though, I'm going to keep my gun out. And seriously, please don't try anything. This car is a rental. If I shoot you in it, I'm going to lose my security deposit."

"We wouldn't want that," said Ash.

"No, we wouldn't."

Ash rode in silence for another few minutes. The road became rougher still and eventually turned to gravel. Abruptly, the car's tires bit into the ground, throwing Ash forward against his seat belt. Before he could figure out what had happened, Blue Shirt hit him on the temple hard enough that he saw lights dance in his eyes. Blue Shirt then ripped off Ash's pillowcase and stuck a flashlight in his face, temporarily blinding him and disorienting him further.

Ash blinked, trying to clear his vision when Blue Shirt punched him in the head again. Even sitting still, he felt dizzy. Blue Shirt disengaged Ash's seat belt, and someone ripped open his door. Before Ash could stop him, Yellow Shirt yanked him out of the car and then shoved him facedown into a patch of grass by the roadside. The ground felt warm after the Mazda's leather. Yellow Shirt got back in the car before Ash regained his senses. Dust and gravel struck him in the face and body as the SUV vaulted forward.

Ash stayed motionless, trying to catch his breath and process what the hell had just happened. When his eyes adjusted to the newfound darkness, he realized that he had been deposited in a dry, shallow ditch beside a gravel road. A farmer had planted soybeans in a field to his right and corn in a field on his left. Aside from the fading taillights of the men who dumped him out there, Ash couldn't see light anywhere. He did see stars, though, thousands of them, amid a backdrop of black.

He closed his eyes and silently thanked God for keeping him alive. When he opened them again, they had adjusted well enough that he saw a driveway about twenty feet up the road. Hopefully the person living at the end of it would be willing to let a stranger use his phone. Ash followed the narrow gravel road until he reached a whitewashed barn with a green asphalt roof. A safety light cast a bluish white light around the driveway. Obviously, the barn had electricity; maybe if he got lucky, it'd have a phone, too.

The gravel crunched under Ash's feet as he walked. Insects buzzed and sang around him, while mice and other nocturnal animals scurried through nearby fields. Aside from bobcats, Indiana didn't have large predators, so no animals posed a danger to him. It still felt a little eerie.

"Anybody in here?" he yelled upon reaching the structure. No one answered, so he dug his heels into the ground and strained as he pulled open the sliding door on the side facing the road. It opened on a rusted track, producing a squeal loud enough that Ash stopped before he had the door even halfway open. If anyone lived nearby, they would have heard that. He searched alongside the nearest interior wall until he found a light switch.

"I'm a police officer. If you can hear me, please don't shoot me."

The barn looked like something from a bygone era, but the farmer who owned it had retrofitted it with fluorescent overhead lights. Thick beams supported the roof structure and a hayloft to his left, while stalls for animals lined the walls to his right. It smelled musty, and dust particles floated in the air. The floor was bare dirt. Ash walked toward a worktable in the center of the room but stopped five or six feet away. A white sheet marred by brownish red stains covered the table, while a rolling stand beside it held stainless steel medical tools as well as an oversized pill bottle of something called cephalexin. It looked like an operating theater or a spot to torture someone. Either way, Ash felt vulnerable without a firearm.

He took a breath and continued searching. Two of the livestock stalls on the right side of the room stood empty. Judging by the accumulation of spiderwebs inside them, they had been for some time. Someone had enclosed the third stall with plywood. Ash walked to the enclosed stall, listening for movement from within.

Nothing.

"Anyone in here?"

When no one responded, he undid the latch and pulled the door open, exposing the interior. As soon as he did, he felt the strength go out of his legs and bile rise in the back of his throat. As promised, Palmer had taken him to Rebecca Cook. Her nude body lay huddled in the corner, her hands tied behind her back, her face locked in a visage of perpetual pain. He could see tear streaks through the dirt on her cheeks. Blood painted the boards behind her, while a thin, black pinprick of a hole adorned her forehead. Her eyes looked like those of a doll. They bore into him, and he felt himself being swallowed whole by the blackness. He fell against the door.

Palmer got everything he wanted and still shot her in the head. He could have just left her there and never seen her again. She wouldn't have chased him; she wouldn't have gone after him. Instead, he murdered her and left her alone in a stall built for animals. Ash stayed at the edge of the stall long enough for the scene to etch onto whatever remained of his soul.

"I'm sorry."

The internal reservoir of strength Ash believed he carried disappeared quickly, leaving something dull and empty in its place. He left the barn and, as soon as he was far enough away that he wouldn't contaminate the crime scene, vomited on the grass. His stomach roiled, but no matter how many times he blinked, he couldn't stop seeing her. Ash had left so many parts of himself blackened and dead at

crime scenes that he hadn't thought they could bother him anymore, but this one did. Rebecca had a family; she had kids, parents, a husband. He retched again until nothing remained in his stomach.

A breeze blew across his skin, chilling him. He stayed there until his legs felt strong enough to support him. As far from civilization as he was, he doubted any passerby would stumble upon the scene and contaminate it, but animals might. He needed help. He went back to the barn and stared at the stall in which Rebecca rested.

"I'll be back," he said, shutting and latching the door. He left the barn and shut the light off behind him. He had seen lights on the drive over, so Ash walked roughly in their direction, carefully placing each foot directly in front of the other. Keeping his mind busy on even such a banal, stupid task kept him from thinking about Rebecca's body.

After about a mile, the road transitioned from gravel to asphalt, and he saw buildings in the distance. He walked for another two miles or so before those buildings became identifiable businesses. Ash recognized the area, having stopped there on a recent trip to a Purdue University football game. Yellow Shirt had dropped him off near I-65, a north-south running interstate that connected Chicago with the Gulf of Mexico. Ash walked to the nearest building, a five-story hotel, and pulled open the front door.

The hotel's lobby hadn't been built to impress anyone. It was perhaps twenty feet square and had a coffeemaker on top of a folding table, newspaper racks, and a couple of chairs. A chest-high piece of oak built into a pass-through in the wall served as the front desk. A young man sat up and put a sociology textbook on the counter as soon as Ash walked in.

CHRIS CULVER

"Can I help you?"

"I need to use your phone."

The sociology student frowned. "Sorry, but it's for guests only. I think there's a pay phone at the—"

Ash held up a hand before the student could respond. He took a couple of breaths. "I'm a police officer, and I just found a woman's body. Give me your goddamn phone so I can call nine-one-one and get some help."

He opened his mouth. "Is the body in the hotel?"

Ash breathed out of his nose. The clerk hadn't done anything wrong, so Ash had no right to snap at him. His insides felt twisted. Something violent seemed to be building inside him.

"It's not in the hotel. Just call nine-one-one and tell them to get a supervisory officer out here as soon as possible."

"All right," the clerk said, already picking up the phone and dialing.

"Do you have a bathroom?"

The clerk looked up from the phone. "What?"

"Do you have a bathroom?" asked Ash, his voice sharp and loud. "I want to wash off my face."

The kid flinched. "Sorry. It's for guests only, too."

Ash took a step back from the desk, not wanting to start a fight. He tried to force the anger from his voice and face.

"I'm going to wait outside."

The kid nodded, so Ash left the building and sat at a wood and wrought-iron bench out front. A breeze blew from the surrounding fields, and Ash could hear the interstate in the distance. He buried his face in his hands.

God, let this day just end.

18

Within fifteen minutes, two deputies from the Tippecanoe County Sheriff's Department arrived at the hotel. They listened to Ash's story and then retraced his steps to the barn, where he showed them the body. While one deputy called Mike Bowers to confirm Ash's identity, the other called Lafayette, the nearest city, and requested assistance. Eventually, one of the deputies let Ash borrow his cell phone to call Hannah. Bowers had picked her up when the exchange went wrong, so she was downtown. She cried a lot, and he told her that he loved her and would come home as soon as he could.

The detectives from Lafayette arrived next. They'd probably end up working the case alongside detectives from Indianapolis, but from all appearances, Rebecca had died in their jurisdiction. They'd receive the blame if the case went awry, so they deserved to know everything he knew. Ash gave them an official statement and then sat on the grass outside the barn as more people arrived. He felt completely hollow, like his emotions had shut down for the day. Captain Bowers and two Indianapolis homicide detectives arrived within an hour, their lights flashing. Detectives Lupo and Pace would stay and work with the locals, but Bowers had come to give Ash a ride home. Thankfully, he didn't ask Ash what he had seen; he wasn't ready for that yet. They drove for about half an hour before either man said anything at all.

"Are you going to be okay to drive if I drop you off at your car, or do you want me to take you home?"

The outskirts of the city lay twenty miles ahead of them, but homes and businesses had already begun dotting the cornfields as the suburbs encroached on what had perennially been farmland. Ash rubbed his eyes.

"Just take me home. Hannah will take me to pick up the car tomorrow."

"Sure."

Ash looked out the window but didn't say anything for a few moments. "I used to tell myself that this job would get easier the longer I stayed in it."

Bowers looked at him for a moment. "It doesn't. The memories accumulate," he said. "They ought to put that in the training manuals they hand out at the academy."

"Honesty probably wouldn't be good for recruitment," said Ash. He paused before speaking again. "Those assholes in the van took my wallet. Before we get to my house, can you loan me a few bucks and take me by a drugstore along the way?"

"Of course. What do you need to get?"

"Something that'll help me sleep."

"Sure."

Ash directed Bowers to a twenty-four-hour pharmacy about two blocks from his house where he bought a pint of cheap bourbon in a plastic bottle. He felt dirty doing it, but he knew that without it, he'd break down. He didn't want to see Rebecca when he closed his eyes that night. He didn't want that pain or that memory. He wanted to feel numb. Bowers drove him back to the house, where Hannah sat on the front porch, waiting for them. As soon as Ash got out of the car, she ran toward him and squeezed her arms right around his chest, whispering the same phrase over and over again.

Thank you, God.

Bowers drove off without saying a word, leaving Ash alone with his wife. Her hair smelled like lilacs; he missed that when she wasn't around. Hannah and the kids were the glue that kept him from falling apart. Whenever he had a bad day, they waited for him at the end of it. They saw past his faults and accepted him, bruises and baggage included. His cheeks burned, and the bottle in his hand felt heavier than the liquor inside ought.

"Sorry I disappeared."

Hannah nodded and took a step back. "What happened to that woman?"

Ash swallowed a lump in his throat. "She didn't make it."

"I'm sorry."

"Me too," he said, looking at his feet. "We should go inside. I need to throw something away."

For the first time, Hannah noticed his paper sack from the drugstore. "What is it?"

"It's a mistake."

She nodded and followed him in, not saying anything even when he pulled the bottle from the bag. He tried to put it in the trash, but she wouldn't let him. She knew he'd just take it out later. Instead, she put her hand on his and led him to the sink. They poured it down together and then watched as the liquid drained away. Ash's hands shook.

"Thank you," he whispered. "I've had a bad day."

*　*　*

Ash didn't go to work the next day. Instead, he got up early with Hannah. The kids were still at their aunt Yasmina and uncle Jack's, so Ash and Hannah had the home to themselves. They had *suhoor* and dawn prayer before the sun rose and then went back to bed. Neither of them said anything; they just spent the morning together.

At a little before eight, they drove downtown to pick up his car, and then he drove to his sister-in-law's house to pick up the kids. Kaden slept for most of the ride home, but Megan squirmed beside her little brother on the backseat, her eyes wide.

"Uncle Jack and Aunt Yasmina don't pray in the morning," she said.

"They're not Muslims, honey," said Ash, glancing in his rearview mirror. "They go to a Christian church."

"Oh," she said. "Does that mean they're going to Hell?"

He looked in the rearview mirror again, trying to catch her eye. She had asked him about whether Kaden would go to Hell just a day earlier.

"Why are you asking me that, honey?"

Megan shrugged. "I don't know. Uncle Nassir said something about it. I was just asking."

That explained it. Nassir was the only Muslim man Ash knew who actually used the word *infidel*; his beliefs tended toward the intolerant. Ash focused on the road ahead of him again.

"God gave the Christians a message just like He gave us a message. He'll figure it out; that's not our job." Ash glanced in the mirror again. Megan started to say something, so he spoke before she could. "That means you don't need to worry about it. And don't listen to Uncle Nassir. He's not as smart as he thinks he is."

"Okay," said Megan, leaning her head against the seat behind her. Megan had apparently exhausted her theological questions because she remained silent for the rest of the ride. She ran into the house as soon as Ash helped her out of her seat. Kaden's eyes opened and closed as Ash picked him up, but he didn't seem ready to wake. He did manage to drool on Ash's shirt, though. He rarely slept well in unfamiliar settings, so he had probably stayed up later than usual.

Ash took him to the living room and sat down still holding him. Eventually, the phone rang and Hannah traded him it for the baby. Ash glanced at the caller ID before answering. Captain Bowers. Ash allowed himself to sink into the seat before answering.

"Mike, what's up?"

"I'm calling to see how you're doing. This has been a tough case."

"Yeah," said Ash, sighing. "This one's going to stay with me."

"I know, and that's why I don't like asking. I'm going to request that you're given a week off with pay, but before I do that, I need you to come in this afternoon and give an official statement about the operation last night. The administration's in cover-their-ass mode and wants to move. You know how that is."

With Rebecca's death, the case was over. Some time off could do him good.

"Yeah, I do know how that is," he said. "They're not gunning for me, are they?"

"No, but even if they were, I wouldn't let them. If anybody goes down for this, it's going to be me. I've got enough years on the job to retire with a full pension."

"I appreciate that," said Ash, genuinely surprised.

"You might want to put your union lawyer on standby just in case."

"I'll give her a call," said Ash, rubbing sleep out of his eyes.

"Before you go, Ash, you did the right thing with Eddie Alvarez. His lieutenant told me about his girl in Mexico." Bowers sighed. "That was messed up."

It took Ash a moment to remember the story about Alvarez's murdered girlfriend and what it had made him want to do at the home off Shadeland Avenue.

"It affected his judgment, so I thought somebody needed to hear it."

"Yeah, I can imagine. We put him on administrative leave, but I doubt he's going to be back."

"You think he's going to quit?" asked Ash.

Bowers paused. "He didn't mention the story during his psych evaluation when we hired him."

"So?"

"Aside from the very real questions about his fitness for duty, lying during the hiring process gives us grounds for termination."

"He didn't lie. He just didn't mention it."

"It's a lie by omission. Any way you look at it, he should have told us."

"If you're worried about his mental health, move him to a less stressful beat. Hell, put him in Community Relations. We don't even carry guns. He'd fit in better than me."

"I appreciate that you're looking out for him, but I've already sent in my recommendation to the Disciplinary Board of Captains."

"Don't you sit on the board?" asked Ash.

"I've recused myself. And that's the end of the discussion. I didn't like making the decision any more than you liked forcing Alvarez to turn himself in. You did the right thing, though, and so did I. Got it?"

"Yeah."

"Good. Then get some rest and come by at two this afternoon for our meeting."

"I'll be there."

Bowers hung up the phone, and Ash looked at Megan. She cocked her head to the side and squinted at him.

"What were you and that man talking about?"

"It's nothing you need to worry about, honey."

"You sounded mad."

"I'm a little upset, but I'm fine. You don't need to worry about me."

"Can I play on the swing?"

"Sure."

Ash watched her disappear into the backyard before picking up his phone again. He didn't know what to say to Eddie Alvarez, but he felt like he needed to say something.

He dialed the detective's number, but it immediately went to voice mail.

"Eddie, it's Ash Rashid. I need to talk to you. Give me a call back." He paused. "It's about work. Just call me." He tried to think of something else to say, but little sprang to mind. "I'm, uh, sorry. Okay? Just call me. We'll talk, and maybe we can figure something out."

As if he had any pull with his department at all. He felt like a schmuck. Ash slipped his phone into his pocket and stood up. As soon as he saw Megan in the backyard, he remembered someone else he needed to call. The Hancock County Sheriff's Department and the FBI would take care of the girls he found in the Dandelion Inn, but Sadia Tahir deserved a personal thank-you for her help with the Urdu-speaking girl.

Ash searched through his phone's memory for the Tahirs' number. Leena Tahir, Sadia's mother, picked up. A TV blared in the background. Ash didn't talk to her long, but she sounded upset. He couldn't figure out what had upset her, though, because she kept slipping into Urdu, her native tongue. Eventually, she put Sadia on the phone.

"Hi, Sadia, I'm Detective Ashraf Rashid with the Indianapolis Metropolitan Police Department. Is your mother okay?"

"No, she's mad. I am, too."

Ash inhaled. He hadn't meant to step into the middle of a family fight.

"I'm sorry to hear that. I'm calling to thank you for your help yesterday. I'm sure you made it a lot easier for that Pakistani girl."

"Did they tell you to call, Mr. Rashid?"

"Did who tell me to call?"

"Those men who kicked us out of the hospital. My mom and I went to the hospital this morning so we could have *Fajr* with Amina. They wouldn't even let us in to see her."

Salat al-Fajr, dawn prayer, is performed between dawn and sunrise. Sadia and her mom had probably been turned away because they came before regular visitation hours.

"I'm sure they didn't mean anything. They were probably afraid you'd wake up the neighbors or something."

"That wasn't it. We made arrangements with the head nurse the night before, and she said we could come in for prayers if we were quiet. As soon as we got on Amina's floor, though, an FBI agent told us to go away."

Amina must have been the Pakistani girl. Unfortunately, the story made sense. The Hancock County sheriff had told Ash he planned to bring in the FBI. If they took over the case, they probably brought in their own Urdu speaker to translate for Amina. It sounded like they had tightened security, too. Ash rubbed his eyebrow.

"Sorry that happened to you. The FBI can be a little strict about security. I'll tell you what, though. I'll make some calls and see if I can get you put on the visitor's list so you can have prayers with her. Would that be okay?"

Sadia sighed. "That'd be better than nothing. Amina is scared, Mr. Rashid, and I don't think they're helping."

"I'll see what I can do. I can't guarantee that I'll get you in to see her, but I'll do my best."

"Thank you."

She hung up the phone and Ash sighed. Hannah resumed folding laundry and looked at him.

"Everything okay?"

"Yeah," said Ash, already punching in Mike Bowers's number on his phone. "Sadia and Leena weren't allowed to visit a girl at the hospital this morning. I'm going to see what I can do for them."

Hannah nodded and turned her attention away from him. Ash sat on the bed and waited for Bowers to pick up.

"Hey, Mike. It's Ash Rashid, and I need a favor. Do you have a phone number for Special Agent Havelock at the Bureau?"

"Why would you need to talk to Havelock?"

"It's a personal request. A family from my mosque wants to see a girl I found in the Dandelion Inn yesterday. They wanted to have prayers with her, but an FBI agent turned them away."

"What's the family's name?"

"Sadia and Leena Tahir. They want to visit a girl named Amina."

"Okay," said Bowers. "I'll call him."

"Thanks."

Ash hung up the phone and helped Hannah fold the rest of the laundry. The load contained mostly towels, so it went quickly. After that, he met Megan outside and pushed her on the swing for a while. They both had fun until Megan jumped out and went flying across the lawn in mock imitation of Superman. A friend of hers had done something similar and broke her arm, so Megan knew what could happen to her. She also knew her parents didn't like her doing it, but she did it anyway. Ash took her inside immediately and made her sit in the naughty chair in the kitchen. Most kids didn't start a rebellious streak until they become teenagers, but Megan had started early. He dreaded the years to come.

As Megan glared at him from the corner of the room, he felt his phone buzz. Ash took it from his pocket and put it to his ear.

"Sergeant Rashid, I'm glad I got you on the phone. Do you have a few minutes to talk?"

It was Havelock. Ash looked directly at his daughter. She crossed her arms and screwed up her face. He would have thought it cute had she not been in trouble.

"I can give you six minutes. Maybe twelve if my daughter's attitude doesn't improve." Megan stuck out her bottom lip, clearly pouting. "Twelve it is."

"Thank you," said Havelock hesitantly. "I just received a phone call from Captain Bowers with your request, and I've put Sadia and Leena Tahir on our approved visitor list. They will be allowed full access to Amina during regular visitation hours or whatever hours they can set up with the nursing staff."

"That's great. Thank you. I'll give them a call and tell them."

"Before you do," said Havelock, speaking quickly, "I need to talk to you for a few minutes. I'm in Wishard Hospital right now. Would you be willing to come down here for a conversation?"

Ash raised his eyebrows. "After last night, I'm exhausted. Can we do this some other time?"

"If you're too tired to drive, I'll have a car pick you up."

Ash paused for a moment. "What's happened?"

"We'll talk about that when you get here."

He didn't make it sound as if Ash had a choice in the matter.

"I'll head out in a few minutes."

"Good. See you then."

Havelock hung up, and Ash leaned against his kitchen counter, thinking and wondering what the FBI agent wanted.

"Can I get up now?"

It took Ash a moment to respond to his daughter's question.

"No. You stay there. I've got to talk to *Ummi*."

"Fine," said Megan, sounding exasperated. If she kept doing that, he'd increase her time on the chair. She'd learn eventually, but even at six years old, she displayed a stubbornness that rivaled his own. Sometimes lessons took a little while to sink into her head. Ash went back to the bedroom he and Hannah shared and found his wife putting sheets into the linen closet in their en suite bathroom.

"Hey, honey, I've got to go into work."

"I was looking forward to you being here for a while," she said.

"So was I," said Ash. "But they said they would send a car for me if I didn't go in. It wasn't a request."

"What's wrong?" she asked, her back straighter than it had been a moment earlier.

"I don't know. If I'm back early enough, I'll make dinner. How's that sound?"

Hannah began refolding a pillowcase. "Sounds like you're threatening me. I've had your food."

"I'll be back as soon as I can. Okay?"

"Okay," she said.

He kissed her and then walked to the hallway. Megan peered around the corner near the kitchen, but as soon as she saw him, she ran, presumably back to her chair. Ash followed her back.

"That's three more minutes," he said, opening the door to the driveway. "I've got to go to work, but *Ummi*'s watching."

She stamped her feet twice. Ash stayed in the doorway, his eyebrows raised.

"Fine."

"I love you and I'll see you tonight. Okay, sweetheart?"

Megan turned her head away and stared out the window. She'd get over that soon enough. Ash got into his cruiser and started driving. He had gone to law school about a mile from Wishard Hospital, so he knew exactly where to go. When he got to the lobby, a uniformed IMPD officer stood watch beside the information desk. Even for a busy hospital like Wishard, that was unusual. Ash nodded to the officer and then showed his badge to the receptionist. She wore hospital scrubs and had black hair pulled back from her face.

"I'm looking for Special Agent Havelock from the FBI, and I've been told that he's here. Do you know where he is?"

Instead of answering, the receptionist looked at the officer beside the desk.

"Are you Sergeant Rashid?" he asked. Ash nodded. "Agent Havelock asked me to take you upstairs."

"Sure," said Ash, smiling at the receptionist. She half-smiled back, but she seemed nervous. He looked back at the officer. "Security's tight today, isn't it?"

"We've had an incident," he said, walking toward a row of elevators. "If you could please follow me, sir."

Ash followed, trepidation growing in his gut. *Incidents* worried him. Despite a crowd in the lobby, few people followed them into the elevator. They made two stops before reaching the fourth floor where two men in suits stood outside waiting for them. Their eyes took in everyone in the elevator at a glance but lingered on Ash.

"Agent Havelock is at the nurses' station," said the officer, holding the elevator door open. Clearly he didn't plan to leave, so Ash stepped forward. The door closed behind him. Ash saw a couple of nurses and doctors in the hallway, but he didn't hear the chattering or footsteps he had heard on earlier floors.

"This way, Sergeant Rashid," said one of the men in suits, gesturing down the hallway.

"What kind of incident did you have last night?" asked Ash, trying to keep his voice nonchalant. "I assume it wasn't just that the hospital ran out of ice cream."

"Kevin Havelock will be able to fill you in better than I can."

Ash clipped his badge to his belt and nodded, following the FBI agent. None of the nurses or doctors that they passed gave him more than a glance. With whatever having happened the night before still fresh in people's minds, a police officer walking around the floor must not have been much of a surprise. When they got about halfway down the hall, Havelock and a woman in a gray pantsuit stepped out of a private room. The woman had brunette hair, lightly tanned skin, and striking blue eyes. Wrinkles had just begun forming around her lips and a few gray strands sprung from her scalp.

"Sorry to interrupt a day off," said Havelock, nodding to the woman beside him. "This is Clair Eckert. She's an assistant U.S. attorney."

Clair's eyes passed over him quickly, but she made no move to shake his hand.

"It's very nice to finally meet you, Mr. Rashid," she said. "Did Konstantin Bukoholov tip you off to the Dandelion Inn?"

Ash considered Clair for a moment and then slipped his hands into the pockets of his pants.

"That's your opening? You're not even going to try to sweet-talk me first?"

Havelock held up a hand and stepped forward. "We've had a long night, Sergeant," he said. He took a breath and closed his eyes. "Let's start over. Thank you for coming in on a day off. Can I get you a cup of coffee?"

"It's Ramadan. I can't drink until sunset."

"Would it offend you if we had some?" asked Havelock. Ash took a closer look at him. His eyelids drooped and red streaks tinged the whites of his eyes.

"No. What happened?"

"We'll talk in a moment," he said, motioning toward the agents near the elevator. The man who had escorted Ash jogged toward them. "James, can you get two coffees from the cafeteria? Black."

"Sure," said James, nodding.

Havelock turned his attention back to Ash.

"The nurses are letting us use their break room. Come on."

Ash followed Havelock and Clair to an employee break room beside the floor's nursing station. Oak cabinets hung on two of the walls, and a refrigerator opposite the door hummed loudly. Someone had scattered pictures across a table in the center of the floor. They looked like still images from a surveillance camera, at least one of which hung just a few feet from where they stood.

"This was taken by the elevator," said Ash, reaching toward the table and picking up a picture of two men in suits. "I just passed the camera on my way here. What happened?"

Clair and Havelock walked to the far side of the table. Clair glared at him, but Havelock's features looked softer. He took a breath.

"Seven of the girls you found in the Dandelion Inn yesterday were removed from the hospital last night."

"What do you mean 'removed'?"

"Those men in that picture you just picked up came to the hospital last night and somehow convinced the girls to leave. They brought clothes and makeup. By the time the girls were in the lobby, they looked like regular visitors. No one thought to stop them."

"Weren't they under guard?"

"Of course they were under guard," said Clair. "We're not stupid."

"I'm not saying you are," said Ash. "I'm just trying to get the facts."

"There should have been four officers on the floor," said Havelock. "When you disappeared, your department pulled three of those officers from their post to assist in searching for you."

Ash swore under his breath. "What about the guy who stayed? Why did he let the girls go?"

Havelock glanced at Clair. She crossed her arms.

"The two men who came claimed to be FBI agents acting under my authority. They had falsified credentials and a signed order they claimed was from a judge. They looked legit."

Ash panned his gaze to Clair. "How'd they find your name?"

A vein beneath Clair's eye twitched. His old boss's eye had done the same thing when he really pissed her off.

"Probably from my department's website. Why does it matter?"

Ash took a step back. "I'm just trying to figure out what happened and what everyone's place is here. What do you need from me?"

"We want to know how you found the Dandelion Inn," she said. "And we want to know right now."

"And your assumption is that Konstantin Bukoholov told me," said Ash.

"Are we wrong?" asked Havelock.

Ash considered his answer for a moment. "Someone delivered an envelope containing passports, brochures for a student exchange program, and the address of the Dandelion Inn to my house yesterday."

"And that made you decide to drive out there?" asked Clair. "An envelope?"

"Not by itself," said Ash. "I didn't see the man who dropped it off, but my wife's description matched Bukoholov's brother-in-law. I went to the inn because, as despicable as he is, Bukoholov is a good source of information. When he suggests I look at something, it's usually worth looking at."

Clair's lips moved, but no sound came out for the first few moments. "You do realize what he does for a living?"

"Yes," said Ash. "And one day I hope to put him in prison

for it. In the meantime, if he tells me something that might save someone's life, I'm going to act on it."

"And what does Mr. Bukoholov get out of this arrangement?"

Ash forced himself to smile. "He doesn't usually tell me."

"And yet you still do exactly what he wants," said Clair. "Not knowing the consequences at all."

"We don't get to make that choice. If I can prevent an innocent person from being hurt, I will, even if that means Bukoholov flourishes because of what I've done. That's the trade-off. It's dirty, but that's life."

Clair leaned forward. "Not anymore, it's not. Marvin Spencer's going to turn on his boss. I'm confident of that, which means that despite everything you've done for Konstantin Bukoholov, we're going to get him."

It took Ash a moment to remember that Spencer was the meathead Sheriff Davis had arrested at the Dandelion Inn the day before.

"If Marvin Spencer says Bukoholov ran the Dandelion Inn, why am I here?" Ash waited, but Clair didn't respond. "He's not talking, is he?"

"He asked to see a lawyer," said Clair. "But he will talk. We found significant quantities of blood in the kitchen. Someone died in there. He knows it, and he knows he's going to fry for it."

"Reading between the lines, you don't even know exactly what to charge him with," said Ash.

"We're still finding things out," said Clair. "That's how investigations work."

"Don't you think it's premature to consider bringing in someone like Bukoholov?"

"If we don't, he's going to come after our girls again. We've got two left, and I'm not going to lose them."

Ash looked at the table in front of him. "Tell me this. Who is Marvin Spencer's lawyer?"

Clair looked at Havelock.

"He called a firm in Chicago," said Havelock. "They're licensed in Indiana, so they're driving down now."

Ash shook his head. "Then you better start looking for a new suspect. Spencer doesn't work for Bukoholov."

Clair snorted. "And how do you know that?"

"Because Bukoholov keeps John Meyers and Associates on permanent retainer for his employees. They're local. He wouldn't seek outside counsel for a case like this."

"Do you know that?" asked Havelock. "Or are you speculating?"

"I'm pretty certain," said Ash, raising his eyebrows. "Bukoholov told me about a year and a half ago. I doubt he's changed since."

Clair shook her head. "You're unbelievable."

"That's what my wife says, too," said Ash. "What are you talking about?"

"That you're that close to a gangster and still have a badge," she said, her throat growing red.

"Don't get mad at me," said Ash. "You two made the shit sandwich and called it a hamburger. I'm just trying to keep you from wasting your time. By all means, though, do whatever you want."

Clair muttered something, and Havelock sighed.

"What else do you know about the place?" he asked.

"Nothing," said Ash. "I received a note suggesting that I check it out, so I did. End of story. You probably know more than I do." He took a breath. "What about the two girls who stayed in the hospital? What have they said?"

"We're still looking for translators," said Havelock. "Nearly every Urdu speaker the Bureau employs has been sent to D.C. to work on terrorism cases. We can't even tell what language the other girl speaks. Someone on my staff thought it might be Nepalese."

"I know a few Urdu speakers who are willing to talk to Amina. Your officers kicked them out this morning."

"The Tahir family isn't cleared for the investigation," said Clair. "I appreciate that they came down here, but I can't use them."

"Then it sure seems like you're stuck, doesn't it?" said Ash. "Have fun figuring it out. Unless I'm under arrest, I'm going home."

Ash started for the door, but Havelock cleared his throat before he got there.

"Wait a minute, Ash," he said. "Would you vouch for Leena Tahir?"

"What do you mean?"

"Is she trustworthy?"

Ash held up a hand with his palm toward Agent Havelock. "I solemnly swear that Leena Tahir is trustworthy to the best of my knowledge."

The oath didn't seem to impress Havelock, but he looked at Clair.

"It's your call. The daughter's too young, but I'm okay with the mom as long as her record is clean. This might be as good as we can get given the circumstances."

Clair stared at Ash for a moment before looking at Havelock. She nodded slightly.

"Given the circumstances, I agree," she said. She looked back at Ash. "Stay away from Konstantin Bukoholov. I'm warning you."

"Thank you for the warning," said Ash, standing straighter. "Unless there's anything else, I'm going to leave."

Clair waved him off. Apparently that passed for a dismissal in the U.S. Attorney's Office. Ash went back to the hallway, but he had no intention of driving home. Amina had information about the people who kept her in the Dandelion Inn, and she probably even knew who had abducted the other girls the night before. What the others seemed to forget was that she was a traumatized child who deserved to have someone looking out for her interests.

Neither Agent Havelock nor Clair Eckhart were bad people, and Ash had little doubt they would have helped Amina as well as they could in other circumstances. Working a case, though, it's easy to become so focused on the end result, on arresting a suspect, that everything else takes second place. Amina wasn't just a lead to explore or a detail to write off at the end of an investigation; she was a little girl. She was someone's daughter, someone's sister, someone's friend. Somewhere, someone loved her and wanted her home. As a father, Ash couldn't forget that, even if acting on it meant earning the enmity of his colleagues. He had made the mistake of sitting around too often, and he was tired of it.

He took out his cell phone and called the Tahir household. Sadia picked up.

"Sadia, it's Ash Rashid again. Someone from the local FBI field office is probably going to call your mom soon about talking to Amina. I need you to do me a favor first."

19

After his conversation with Sadia, Ash walked to a coffee shop about two blocks from the hospital and bought a newspaper. As expected, Rebecca's death made the front page. The reporter called the ransom exchange a botched operation, but he didn't go so far as to say that it directly led to her death. The story titillated enough to sell papers but remained ambiguous enough to avoid lying outright. Beyond noting that she had died, details about Rebecca remained scarce, which made Ash breathe a little easier. The public didn't need to hear about her last moments.

Ash folded the paper about half an hour after entering the coffee shop and left it on the table in front of him, wishing he had gone to a bar and ordered a shot of bourbon. Eventually, he walked outside to clear his mind. The morning was already warm, but it was bearable. He didn't have anywhere to go, so he just walked around for a little while.

About an hour after leaving the hospital, and while Ash sat on a bench in Military Park, his phone started buzzing. He looked at the caller ID before picking up. Captain Bowers. It had taken him longer than Ash expected.

"You just can't sit still, can you?" asked Bowers as soon as Ash answered the phone.

"I try to be active," said Ash. "Megan said I was getting fat a little while ago, so I've been trying to exercise as often as I can."

"Funny," said Bowers. "Kevin Havelock is pissed with you right now. He just called Dan Reddington, and Dan called me."

"Havelock was pissed at me before he even met me."

"Now he's got cause. Some girl he's trying to interview at Wishard Hospital refuses to talk to him unless you're also in the room. You care to fill me in on that?"

"Without knowing the details, I assume the girl in question is one of the victims from the Dandelion Inn."

"That's probably a safe assumption. Why does she want you in the room?"

Ash shrugged even though Bowers couldn't see him.

"She might have heard that I'm an attorney, and that I'm a Muslim, and that I'd be more than willing to make sure her rights are protected."

Bowers muttered something, but Ash couldn't understand what. Eventually, he cleared his throat. "Are you sure you've thought this through?"

"It didn't take much thought. This girl needs help, and I can provide it. End of story."

"No, it's not the end of the story, Ash," said Bowers. "Step outside yourself for a moment and imagine how this looks from our prospective. You've got ties with a gangster, that gangster has ties to this case, and now it looks like you're interfering with that case."

"I don't have ties to anyone, and I'm really getting tired of defending myself. I want Bukoholov in prison, and I will do everything in my power to put him there. I'm not willing to ignore a kid in trouble, though, just so I can play departmental politics better."

"This isn't about departmental politics. Whether you believe it or not, I'm looking out for you, and I'm warning you that you're stepping into something you shouldn't."

Ash leaned back on his bench. "We've had our differences, and I appreciate everything you've done for me. But we both know where this is going. For the past couple of years, I've been shuffled around our department like I'm some divorcée's unwanted child and I'm growing tired of it. I'm tired of wasting my time."

"You may not like your regular assignment, but you're hardly wasting your time," said Bowers. "You're a good cop. Think through what you plan to say next. This isn't the time to put in your papers."

"I know that, and I don't plan on it," said Ash. "Amina needs help. If she's by herself, Agent Havelock and Clair Eckert from the U.S. Attorney's Office are going to steamroll her. Neither of them care about her. She's just a source of information to them."

"I can't give you career advice, Ash, but think about what you're doing before you do it. You're reckless, you're frequently insubordinate, and you can be a real asshole, but you're a good detective. Don't throw that away lightly."

"I like to think people would understand why I'm doing this."

"Your friends, yeah. Dan Reddington and the rest of the administration? I don't know."

"How about you?" Ash didn't know why he asked it, but the question popped out of his mouth before he could stop himself.

Bowers didn't say anything for a few seconds. "I understand why you're doing it, but I don't think you should. You've got a law degree, but you're not a lawyer. You're a cop. Sometimes I think you forget that."

"No, Mike, I've never forgotten that. And you're right. I don't practice law. I'm a cop, but I'm also a husband and a father. I don't stop being any of those just because I wear a badge."

"I'm not saying you should."

"Then what are you saying?" asked Ash.

"You know, forget everything I said. Do whatever the hell you want. I don't care," said Bowers. "And get over to the hospital. You may not care, but our department still has to work with the Bureau occasionally, and I'd rather not have you poison that relationship."

"I'll be nothing but professional."

"I hope so."

Ash hung up and slipped the phone into his pocket. If there had been a cab or bus in sight, he would have taken it. He couldn't find one, though, so he started walking. Even at a relatively quick pace, it took him nearly twenty minutes to make it back to the hospital. He wiped sweat off his brow with paper towels in one of the restrooms on the first floor before taking the elevator to Amina's floor. Agent Havelock and Clair met him in the nurses' break room they had been in earlier and walked to Amina's room without saying a word.

Amina was thin and had a dark complexion, even for a Pakistani. She had brown eyes and thin lips. She wore a hospital gown, but someone had loosely covered her head with a pink shawl. Leena Tahir sat beside her bed, holding

Amina's hand. As soon as Agent Havelock and Ash walked in the room, Amina sat up straighter and scooted toward the far side of her bed, away from them. Both men took the hint and stopped walking. She didn't seem overly scared, but clearly they made her uncomfortable.

"Is Amina okay with us in here?" asked Havelock, his voice surprisingly gentle. "I can get a female agent to come down here instead of me." He looked at Ash. "I can also recommend a female attorney with immigration experience."

Leena leaned close and whispered something to Amina. They talked for a moment, and then Leena took a couple of breaths.

"She'll be okay," said Leena. "She doesn't like men seeing her undressed."

"If she'd like to put something else on, we can leave and come back," said Ash. Leena translated the question, and Amina nodded. Ash, Havelock, and Clair left the room for a moment. When they came back, Amina wore a thick pink robe over her gown. It didn't seem like much of a change, but it made her feel secure enough to answer questions.

Havelock started the interview slowly with questions about her background, his voice soft. The more Amina spoke, the less she hesitated before answering as she gained confidence. Havelock never pressured her to give more information than she wanted to, and his tone remained calm, measured, and patient. He was gentle enough that he could have been talking to one of his own kids.

When he finished the introductory questions, Clair handed Amina one of the brochures Ash had found in the envelope the Hulk had delivered.

"Have you seen this before?" he asked. Amina nodded after having the question translated.

"She said an American woman came to her family's farm and gave that brochure to her father. A lot of charities came through and did that, especially to help girls," said Leena. "The woman said her charity would take Amina and her sister, Faria, to the United States so they could go to school and work part-time."

"Did anyone check to make sure it was legitimate?" asked Clair. Leena didn't bother translating the question.

"Amina's father can't read," she said. "Even if he wanted to research it, he couldn't. The culture in the tribal regions is generally opposed to formal education for girls, so he probably thought this was the only opportunity his daughters would ever have to go to school."

Clair started to ask something else, but Havelock held a hand in front of her.

"How did this work?" asked Havelock. "Her family received the brochure. What happened next?"

Leena and Amina conferred for a few minutes.

"Her dad tracked down the American in a nearby village and told her that both of his daughters were interested. She interviewed them both and told them about the program. They would both go to a private American high school, but since Faria was only fifteen, she couldn't work off-campus. She'd have to sweep classrooms and things like that. She said Amina would be able to get a good job off-campus and go to school. The American helped them get visas."

"How'd they get to the U.S.?" asked Havelock.

Leena translated the question.

"The woman gave her tickets and set up the travel arrangements. She and her sister flew from Lahore, Pakistan, and they stopped in three airports along the way, but they didn't stay anywhere for long. The first city in the United States they went to was Chicago."

"Okay," said Havelock. "Did they stay in Chicago, or did they come right to Indianapolis?"

Amina and Leena conferred for a few minutes, suspending the conversation.

"She thinks they stayed in Chicago for a little while. A man and a woman met her in the airport. Including Amina and Faria, they picked up four girls in a van and drove them all to an apartment."

"Does she have an idea where this apartment was?"

Leena started to translate the question, but Amina shook her head before the older woman even finished speaking. Havelock should have expected that, though; Amina came from a village in rural Pakistan. Going to any major city would have put her so far out of her element that she could have missed even the most familiar of things right in front of her.

"Can you ask her to describe her situation in Chicago?" asked Clair. "Was she a prisoner? Did she work?"

Leena translated and then listened intently while Amina spoke.

"She and Faria lived with six other girls in a two-bedroom apartment. The first night she was brought in, they were given ledger books and were told that they owed twenty thousand dollars each for the program's administration fees and the flight from Lahore to Chicago. They owed an additional fifteen hundred dollars each every month for room and board. To pay that, they were contracted out to clean houses. They earned seventy dollars a day and worked from sunrise to sunset. None of the girls went to school."

"Was she able to go wherever she wanted, or was she locked up?" asked Ash. Having her freedom of movement restricted wasn't one of the elements of a human trafficking charge—at least according to Indiana law—but it'd be easier to prove if Amina's was. She started to say something at first, but then she caught herself.

"No one monitored them day to day," said Leena. "But one of the other girls in the apartment was in charge. If Amina was late, she was hit. If she tried to leave the apartment or the jobsite, the top girl called a lady and she'd be punished."

"What do you mean by punished?" asked Havelock.

Ash liked the question; already Havelock seemed to be building a workable case. Many people seem to think that if a girl goes willingly with her captors, the police can't do anything. That may have been true at one time, but not anymore. If Amina's captors threatened her or one of her family members with violence for noncompliance, they had already committed a major felony. That charge alone would be worth twenty years in prison. Add on ancillary charges like criminal confinement and her captors would face life without the possibility of parole. Leena looked at Amina and translated the question, but Amina shook her head. Leena repeated the question and then rubbed Amina's arm reassuringly. When Amina spoke, her voice barely qualified as a whisper.

"The lady hurt her," said Leena. "That's all Amina wants to say."

"That's good enough for now," said Ash. "She doesn't need to say anymore." He glanced at Havelock and Clair.

"If you need more detail for trial, you can get it when she's more comfortable."

"That's fine," said Havelock, nodding. "How long was she confined in the apartment?"

Leena and Amina talked again.

"Approximately four months."

Ash wrote a couple of notes. He had seen Amina's face when he and Havelock walked into the room. Men made her uncomfortable. Something else had happened to her, and he almost felt afraid to ask.

"How did you get from Chicago to Indianapolis?" asked Clair. Leena translated as Amina spoke.

"Every now and then, a woman named Ann would come to the apartment. Every time she came, she'd drop off a cake and take a girl with her. She told Amina and the other girls that the girls who were taken had paid off their debts and were sent home or moved to nicer places. Whenever Ann came, the girls had a celebration. Amina kept track of everything she earned, but she still prayed that Ann would come for her and Faria early. That had happened before, so when Ann came and called for her, she thought God had answered her prayers. At first, Ann didn't want Faria, so Amina begged. Eventually, she gave in and took them both."

"And Ann took them to Indianapolis?" asked Clair.

Leena and Amina spoke for another moment, and then Leena nodded.

"She thinks so, but she isn't sure. No one told her where they were going."

"Did she go anywhere besides the Dandelion Inn?" asked Havelock.

Amina, after hearing the translation, shook her head. She

straightened herself on the bed, and Ash thought he could see her tremble slightly. Leena put a hand on Amina's upper arm. More than most, Ash knew how painful it could be to trudge through old memories. Amina's pain was real, immediate and visceral. As a father and human being, it made his heart ache to see her in it.

"If Amina would like, we can take a break," said Ash. Leena and Amina spoke for a moment.

"She wants to finish," said Leena. "She wants to get this done."

"Can she tell us about Indianapolis?" asked Havelock. "We'll talk at whatever pace she's comfortable with."

Tears ran down Amina's cheeks as she spoke.

"It was late when they arrived at the bed-and-breakfast. There were cots in the basement and other girls there, but she and Faria were the only girls who spoke Urdu. Amina thought they were there to join the cleaning staff, but on her first night, two men who worked at the bed-and-breakfast got her out of her cot. They took her to one of the rooms upstairs and made her drink something. She said it burned her throat. Then they made her take some pills that made her tired. She couldn't move."

Ash could feel his heart thumping against his rib cage. Amina cried steadily now.

"Did they hurt her?" asked Claire.

Leena took a breath. "They raped her, yes."

He knew it was coming, but it still hurt to hear.

"Could she identify those men if she saw them again?" he asked.

Leena translated the question and then nodded when Amina spoke.

"She thinks so. She said they had paint on their arms. I think she means tattoos."

Marvin Spencer, the man they had picked up at the B&B had tattoos on his arms. Ash might not be able to prove that Spencer assaulted her yet, but that didn't matter. Many of the men in Indiana's prisons had committed crimes so awful they'd never see an open field again. Many also had children of their own, and they wouldn't take kindly to men who drugged and raped a defenseless seventeen-year-old girl. Spencer would be dead within a week if they didn't do anything. As much as that appealed to Ash, he couldn't condone his murder. They'd have to put him in protective custody.

"How about her sister, Faria? Was she hurt, too?"

Amina trembled, but then nodded. Faria was fifteen years old. The thought made Ash want to reconsider putting Spencer in protective custody. "Did those men assault her often?"

"Not them," said Leena, translating. "There were new men every night. Three or four sometimes. Ann told her that she earned fifty dollars every time she was with a client. Amina said she pretended she was married to them because it made it easier. After a big night, Ann would sometimes give her makeup and chocolate. She shared it with her sister. Some of the girls fought with her because of that. They didn't get as much."

"Did any of the girls ever try to escape?" asked Clair.

Amina didn't say anything for a moment. Leena rubbed her arm, encouraging her to speak.

"She said she didn't have anywhere to go, so she focused on the ledger. That was her only way out. Ann told her that if she ran away, they'd kill Faria and her family in Pakistan."

"What about others?" asked Havelock. "Did others try to escape?"

"Amina says a girl named Iskra did," said Leena. "A regular client walked her out. Nobody saw her again. They put locks on the doors after that."

"How long was she at the Dandelion Inn?" asked Ash.

It took Leena a few minutes to get an answer from her.

"She doesn't know. She kept track of days at first, but she stopped doing that after a month. She didn't have another way to keep track."

Havelock looked at Clair and then to Ash.

"I think this is a good start," he said. "We'll have to talk to Amina again, but I have enough to go on for now."

Amina must have sensed the conversation had come to an end because she started speaking rapidly.

"Amina wants to know if her sister is okay," said Leena, looking at Ash. "No one has told her."

Ash looked at Havelock and Clair and raised his eyebrows.

"Faria was taken again last night," said Havelock. "We're doing everything we can to find her."

Amina took the answer more stoically than Ash expected. She simply nodded, accepting the tragedy as if it were simply another, expected part of life. It was unfair. Ash cleared his throat.

"If she's okay with answering it," he said, "I have one more question. Can you ask if Amina has ever heard of someone named Kara Elliot? Or Konstantin Bukoholov?"

Amina nodded and spoke as soon as Leena translated the question.

"She didn't know Kara Elliot, but she met Daniel Elliot. He was a regular client, but he never touched anyone. He would rent a girl for the entire night and let her sleep alone on the bed while he stayed in a chair. He would leave the next morning. He did that twice with Amina. They were the only two nights she had at the bed-and-breakfast where she wasn't forced to sleep with a stranger. He was also the man who took Iskra."

At first, Ash was so appalled by the concept of renting a girl for the night that he didn't hear the rest of what Amina said. Then it hit him.

Daniel Elliot, Kara Elliot's husband, rescued a girl. Ash didn't know how much a single girl in a brothel like the Dandelion Inn could earn over her lifetime, but it likely reached well into the six figures. He had seen people murder someone over thirty bucks found in a lost wallet; a couple hundred grand provided a hell of a lot of motive, enough even to bring in a specialist like Palmer. He killed Kara and Daniel Elliot, probably while trying to recapture Iskra.

If he was right about that, he finally understood Bukoholov's connection. The old man didn't have an interest in the club; he wanted to find the people who killed his family. Ash couldn't prove anything, but the theory fit what he knew so far. That could make things ugly.

Ash looked at Leena.

"Please thank Amina from the bottom of my heart for talking to us. We'll do everything we possibly can for her and her sister," he said. He looked at Havelock and then Clair. "We need to talk outside."

20

Ash pulled the door shut behind him as he escorted Clair and Agent Havelock from the room. Aside from his own footsteps, Ash heard little in the hallway. With what happened the night before, there didn't seem to be a lot of demand for beds on that floor. Ash's hands practically shook as he scratched an itch on the back of his head.

"I held back before," he said. "Bukoholov tipped me off to the Dandelion Inn."

Clair crossed her arms. "Why the sudden bout of honesty?"

"Because the man who killed his daughter still has at least seven girls, including Amina's little sister. We need to find them before Bukoholov does."

"You think he'd kill them if he found them first?" asked Havelock.

"No," said Ash. "But if we don't find them first, they might get caught somewhere we don't want them to be."

Clair stared at him for a moment, but then broke eye contact and looked at Havelock.

"Thank you for the information," she said. "We'll try to keep your office informed about our investigation."

"That's not enough," said Ash. "What are you going to do? We need to work together."

"We don't have to do—" began Clair.

"I'll call Chief Reddington," said Havelock, interrupting her. "We will work with your department where appropriate, but our victims are likely well outside your jurisdiction right now. If we need you specifically, I'll call." He looked up and waved over one of the agents from the elevator. "Unless you need to speak with Amina further, James will escort you to your car."

Ash didn't like to admit it, but Havelock had raised a fair point. IMPD's jurisdiction extended to the city's borders but no farther. The state police could investigate anywhere in Indiana, but even their jurisdiction had limits. The FBI had the clearest mandate and was in the best position to help of any agency they could bring in. It still stung a little to admit that.

"No need for the escort," said Ash. "I'm not going to cause a problem."

Havelock smiled. "Then enjoy your vacation. We'll be in touch if we need you."

"Thank you," said Ash, turning toward the elevator. The same agent who had escorted Ash earlier followed him through the lobby and to the hospital's front door. When he arrived at his car, he took out his cell phone and sent an e-mail to one of his old law professors who taught courses in transnational crime and international law. She had written papers on human trafficking, so she knew the laws relating to it better than he did. Even though Amina had been brought to the U.S. against her will, Ash would still have to work with Pakistan's consulate and the State Department to secure an emergency visa for her. After that, he'd have to figure out how to pay for her medical care. The hospital might write off her bills, but they might not. It'd be better to find a charity now that could help her out. Help from an attorney who specialized in those sorts of cases would be very welcome.

Once he finished that e-mail, he called Mike Bowers.

"I hope you're not calling to postpone our meeting this afternoon," said Bowers upon picking up. "A lot of people have had to rearrange their schedules for it."

"No, we're still on for that," said Ash. He turned on his car and put the air conditioning to high. "I just got out of an interview with Kevin Havelock from the Bureau and Clair Eckert from the U.S. Attorney's Office. I think you should hear some of the things I found out."

"You're talking about the interview with the Pakistani girl, right?"

"Yeah," said Ash.

"If you're her lawyer, wouldn't you be violating her privacy by talking to me?"

"No. The privilege doesn't extend to attorney-client conversations if there's a third party present. There were several in the room with us."

"Okay," said Bowers. "Tell me what you found out."

Ash led him through the interview as well as he could. Even after Ash finished speaking, Bowers didn't say anything.

"So now you know everything I know," said Ash. "How do you want to handle this?"

Bowers grunted. "It sounds like our hands are tied. The Dandelion Inn is in Hancock County, so we can't touch that.

Rebecca was murdered in Tippecanoe County, so that's not ours, either. If you're right and the girls are outside Marion County, they're out of our reach, too. We don't have a lot we can do."

"Who's working Kara's and Daniel Elliot's murders? They were killed in town, so they should be ours."

"Doran and Smith know the evidence, so they're still on it."

Ash exhaled loudly. "Has either of them even worked a homicide before?"

"Yeah, Doran has. He transferred out a couple of years ago because he didn't like the hours. They'll do right by the case."

Ash blinked. "I know you told me to take a few days off, but I found Kara and Daniel, I found Rebecca, and I talked to Palmer. I know this case better than anyone in our department."

"After what you saw, I don't even think you're fit to resume your duties as a community relations officer, let alone leading a major homicide investigation."

"I'm fine. I really am."

"You're not fine, and we both know that," said Bowers. He paused for a few beats. "Even if I put you on leave, it's not going to change what you do, will it?"

"Palmer killed three people and helped abduct seven children, Mike."

"So that's a no," he said. "Fine. You can work the case, but since you're still temporarily under my command, I'll put you on limited duty as our liaison officer for this case. You'll work with the state police, the Bureau, and our detective division to keep everybody up to date. I'm also going to call

Aleda Tovar, your CO in Community Relations, and tell her what's going on. Once this case is done, you're going back to her and she'll have the ultimate authority about your status, but I'm going to recommend you see a station psychiatrist before you resume active duty."

"Chief Reddington didn't seem too happy the last time I saw him. Is he okay with this?"

Bowers took a breath. "He will be. This is an important job, so if you go AWOL, I'm going to take the fall as much as you. That won't happen, will it?"

"I'll do my best. Do Doran and Smith have anything on the Elliot murder yet?"

"I'll make sure they brief you," said Bowers. "Just to be crystal clear, you are not a field officer on this case. You've got a badge, but I don't want you doing anything stupid."

"I've got it."

"Good. I'll see you in a bit."

Bowers hung up. Almost instinctively, Ash started driving back to the station. He stopped at the end of the parking lot, though. As the liaison officer, he needed to talk to everyone involved with the case, and while Bukoholov wouldn't make any official reports, he had a better criminal intelligence apparatus than either the Bureau or IMPD. Assuming he'd give it, his help could be invaluable. Of course, if someone from his department or the FBI caught him visiting Bukoholov, he'd be off the case immediately and possibly out of a job. Normally, that would have swayed him to stay away, but given that they had multiple victims still unaccounted for, the risks seemed worth it, at least once he had given himself some protection.

Ash searched for the nearest electronics store with his cell phone and headed over. Once there, he bought a prepaid cell phone and some airtime with cash and allowed the kid behind the counter to set it up for him. Bukoholov wouldn't recognize the number, but that didn't matter as long as Ash sent the right message. He thumbed it in as he walked back to his car.

I'm the guy who shot your nephew a year and a half ago. Call me on a clean phone.

Within two minutes of sending the text, Ash had a call back from a number he didn't recognize. He answered and heard a train in the background on the other end.

"Is this you?" he asked.

"Unless you shot someone else's nephew," said Bukoholov. "What do you want?"

"I had hoped to talk to you for a few minutes."

Bukoholov paused until the train passed. "Unfortunately, I'm out of town for a few days. Come by my bar next week. We can set up an appointment to talk then."

"Where are you? I'll drive out to meet you."

"I'm out of town."

Ash looked around to make sure no one was watching his vehicle. "I know what you're doing. I know Kara Elliot was your daughter."

"My family affairs are none of your concern. Leave it be, Detective."

"Let us handle this. We're going to get the men who killed her. That's what we do, and we're very good at it."

"Not this time," said Bukoholov. He hung up the phone, and Ash stayed still for a moment. The old man had never blown him off like that before, so the abrupt end to the conversation came as something of a surprise.

That could have gone better.

Ash slipped his phone into his pocket but stayed still in the car to think. He had reached the point in his case when things usually started falling together. Instead, this case had fallen apart. Palmer had killed Rebecca and then disappeared before anyone could find him. Worse, Palmer's colleagues had abducted seven teenage girls so they could rent them by the hour as if they were cheap motel rooms.

Ash's hands shook. They hadn't done that for almost eight months, but he hadn't wanted a drink that bad in at least eight months. He could see two bars from where he stood, at least one of which served a full menu. Plenty of people had drinks with lunch, so no one would even look at him twice for ordering something. Of course, he wouldn't be able to look at himself for breaking the fast with a shot of bourbon. He needed to focus on something productive.

Ash took a deep breath and forced his mind back to his case. They needed to find Palmer, but unfortunately, they didn't know a lot about him yet. The detectives from Tippecanoe County might be able to find something in the barn where he found Rebecca, but they had a lot of ground to cover and a lot of evidence to comb through. They'd be slow, possibly too slow to be useful for him. The sheriff's department in Hancock County, likewise, would do a good job at the bed-and-breakfast, but it would take a while for their investigation to get off the ground. That didn't leave them with a lot of options.

Kara and Daniel Elliot. If Daniel was really killed for what he did at the Dandelion Inn, Marvin Spencer might know something. Talking to him beat sitting around, at least. Ash drove back to the station and took the elevator to the Aggravated Assault unit. Like the homicide unit, the Agg Assault guys had a bullpen instead of private offices. Ash spotted Tim Smith at a desk beneath the windows on the far side of the room and started over. Smith looked up before he made it even halfway.

"You here to get me fired like you got Alvarez fired?"

Ash straightened. "He's on administrative leave. No one's fired him yet."

"That help you sleep at night?" asked Smith. "Knowing a guy with three kids and a wife hasn't been fired yet?"

"Whether you believe it or not, I did the right thing. Alvarez is a good man and I don't want him fired, but if he is he'll get another job and be able to go home to tuck those kids in at night. If he stays on the street, he'll eventually go home in a coffin."

Smith leaned back and scratched his forehead with his middle finger. Ash crossed his arms.

"I appreciate your professionalism."

"Did you say something?" asked Smith, pushing his left ear forward with his still extended middle finger. "I didn't hear you."

Ash could have written him up for insubordination, but he didn't think doing so would help his reputation much.

"I'm here to work," said Ash. "What are you here for?"

"Free coffee?" asked Smith, shrugging.

"Where's Greg?"

"Who?"

Ash clenched his teeth and counted to five before answering. "Your partner."

"Oh, *Detective Doran*," said Smith. "He's at home. His

daughter's going to college in a few weeks, so he's helping her pack."

"Why isn't he here working the Elliot case?"

Smith shrugged. "Nothing to work."

"Are you telling me you have Palmer in custody?" asked Ash.

Smith didn't say anything for a few seconds, but then he crossed his arms. "Not at this time, but we'll get him."

"So you're telling me you have nothing to do at all," said Ash. "Just to be clear."

Smith shrugged. "What can you do? The sergeant supervising us on this case—that's you, by the way—has been AWOL."

"Did you ever get into Daniel and Kara's house?"

"Yep, but somebody torched it. The arson investigator found signs of an accelerant inside."

"Like gas?"

"That is an example of an accelerant, Sergeant Rashid."

Ash felt his temper rising, so he forced a measure of calmness into his voice he didn't feel. "Did the arson investigator tell you what sort of accelerant was used?"

"He's still analyzing it."

"Good," said Ash, carefully thinking through his next question to minimize Smith's ability to give him a one-word answer. "Was anyone able to tell you when this fire happened?"

"Yeah."

Ash closed his eyes. "Who told you and what time was it?"

"Old lady next door said she took her dog out for a walk at around eight, and the house was still standing. By the time she came back, someone had lit it up."

"Did the arson squad find anything salvageable in the house?"

"A safe, but it was open when they got there. Nothing but ashes inside."

Ash nodded to himself. He could only think of two people with a potential motive to burn the place: Konstantin Bukoholov or Palmer. Whoever did it had a reason, probably in an attempt to hide evidence. If the Elliots kept evidence of something criminal at home, they might have kept it elsewhere, too.

"Have you had any luck finding the Elliots' office?"

"Nope, but we went by QwikMail. You didn't mention it was run by a couple of potheads."

"I didn't think it was germane," said Ash.

"Well, I think it is, and I'm thinking about notifying Internal Affairs. One of those potheads told us you two had a deal. That's kind of... What's the word?" He put his fist to his chin in imitation of Rodin's famous sculpture and paused before looking up again. "Disconcerting. It's disconcerting when a police officer doesn't arrest a drug trafficker."

Ash closed his eyes. "He had some weed on him for personal use. I told him I wouldn't arrest him if he gave me the information I wanted."

Smith shook his head. "Detective Doran and I found two pounds of marijuana and three hundred grams of meth in that building. They weren't keeping that for personal use." Smith leaned forward and looked left and right. "Just curious here, but how much money did they give you to leave without arresting them? A couple grand?"

The fact that the stoners at QwikMail still had drugs

didn't surprise him, but the quantity did. "They didn't give me anything but information. You can file your complaint if you want, but it's completely ungrounded."

"You know, I think I will file that complaint. It'll help me sleep better at night."

"I'm glad," said Ash. "Before you do that, I've got some real work for you. I need you to find out if Kate and Daniel Elliot had a safe deposit box."

"Why?"

Ash was tempted to respond "Because I said so," but instead he took a breath. "Because they might have kept something pertinent to our investigation in one. It will help us make a case at trial."

"What do you want me to do? Just call banks and ask if Kara and Daniel were customers?"

"Yeah, and ask about Commonwealth Financial Products, too. They might have gotten one under a company name."

Smith squinted at him. "You doing this just to waste my time?"

"No. I'm ordering you to do this because it could help our case. Like me or not, I'm still your superior officer. If you keep questioning me, I'm going to write you up for insubordination. That complaint, I guarantee you, will stick."

"And while I'm wasting my time with this, what are you going to be wasting Greg's time with?"

"I'm going to call him and ask him to talk to a prisoner in Hancock County."

"Who?"

Ash was growing tired of the questions, but answering them beat arguing about them. "A guy named Marvin

Spencer. The Hancock County Sheriff's Department picked him up yesterday at a bordello full of underage girls outside New Palestine. Daniel Elliot took one of those girls out and was then shot. I think Spencer knows something. "

Smith sat up straighter.

"Then why should I waste my time on this safe deposit thing? I should interrogate him with Greg."

"Spencer's got a lawyer, so he won't talk to us anytime soon. We know Palmer killed the Elliots, but if we go after him in court without looking at other viable suspects, his lawyers will tear us apart. I'm sending Greg out there to cover all our bases. He won't be able to get anything, but we've got to go through the motions."

Smith seemed to weigh that for a moment before settling back down and turning to his computer. "At least I won't be the only one wasting my time."

Unfortunately, he was probably right.

* * *

Greg Doran sounded neither surprised nor annoyed when Ash called. The veteran detective simply thought for a moment and agreed that somebody needed to go. Ash, meanwhile, had another idea. He called the Hancock County Sheriff's Department and made arrangements for Doran's visit. While he had someone on the phone, he also asked about Spencer's personal information, ostensibly for IMPD's own records. Ash wrote the information down and hung up.

Spencer lived on the twentieth floor of a high-rise apartment building just two blocks from the Central Library.

When Ash drove to the address, he found an apartment building that appeared to have been built in the late seventies or early eighties. Balconies jutted from the structure like legs on a centipede while twin radio towers extended from the top floor like antennae. Ash parked in a private lot on North Alabama Street and looked to the west. He could see the bell tower of the Scottish Rite Cathedral a couple of blocks away. Rebecca hadn't been far from his mind since her death, but seeing the cathedral where he should have picked her up brought her to the forefront. That, in turn, made him want to get a drink.

He climbed out of his car to take his mind off things and walked into the building. The lobby had low ceilings, a marble floor, and a bank of steel mail slots on one wall. He found the elevator and took it to Spencer's floor. No one tried to stop him; with as many apartments as the building contained, its residents probably saw a lot of unfamiliar faces. Gray carpet flecked with black covered the ground of the public areas on the twentieth floor, while crown molding adorned the ceiling. That high up, each floor had four apartments, one on each corner of the building. The tenants probably had two or three thousand square feet each. Not bad for a simple man who helped out at a bed-and-breakfast.

As soon as he arrived at Spencer's door, he knocked hard, hoping to find a helpful girlfriend or roommate. That'd be the ideal situation. If Spencer had a girlfriend who stayed at the apartment and kept her stuff there, she would have common authority over the entire place and could let him search whatever he wanted. It wouldn't matter if she had signed the lease or not. A roommate, while not quite as helpful because he wouldn't have common authority over Spencer's bedroom, could at least let Ash inside the apartment to search the common areas. He waited for a moment when no one answered and knocked again.

"I'm a police officer. If anyone is inside, please open the door."

A door down the hall opened and a short young man with glasses and wavy hair stuck his head out. His eyelids drooped and his shirt appeared wrinkled. He looked as if he had been woken from a nap. Ash nodded in the young man's direction and unhooked his badge from his belt to show him the ID.

"Sorry to disturb you."

"Marvin isn't there. He was arrested yesterday."

Ash hadn't planned to talk to the neighbors, but it would seem out of place if he didn't say something. He walked toward the man's door.

"I'm Sergeant Ash Rashid with the Indianapolis Metro Police Department. Are you free to talk for a few minutes?"

"I guess. I'm Ben."

"Thank you, Ben." Ash pointed over his shoulder at Spencer's door with his thumb. "How'd you know we arrested your neighbor?"

"Because you guys knocked on the wrong door and woke my girlfriend and me up last night. It was like four in the morning. She was pissed."

A knock at the door at that time of morning would piss most people off. "By 'you guys,' you mean police officers?"

"They were with the FBI, I think."

"Really?" asked Ash. "I didn't know they had come by. Was it a big team?"

"Two guys in suits."

Ash looked over his shoulder at Spencer's door. Normally, when an officer finished searching an apartment, he'd tape a notice of entry across the door and sill. Anyone who tried to enter the apartment afterward would break that notice, informing the police that their crime scene was no longer secure and that any evidence taken from the room from that point would be inadmissible in court. Marvin's door didn't have any such notice, which didn't make sense.

"Did you get a good look at the men who came by?"

"It was late," said Ben. "They both wore suits, and they had FBI badges. They said they had a warrant."

If Ash had to guess, that was what they told the officer assigned to watch the girls at the hospital, too.

"Did your landlord let them in?" asked Ash.

"They had a key. They tried to open my door with it first. Almost scared me to death. I thought someone was trying to break into my apartment."

"Okay," said Ash, nodding as he removed his cell phone from his pocket. He dialed Agent Havelock's number but kept his eyes on Ben. "Are you going to be around today?"

"For most of the day."

"Good. I think there are going to be some people interested in talking to you."

Ben started to protest, but Havelock had picked up his phone. Ash held up his finger, silencing the younger man.

"Hey. This is Ash Rashid, and I'm following up on a few things related to Daniel and Kara Elliot's murder. Did you or anyone from your office serve a search warrant on Marvin Spencer's apartment?"

"Not yet."

Ash scratched his brow and exhaled. "That's what I thought. You're going to want to get down here. I think Palmer may have broken in."

*   *   *

In most burglary cases, a home's occupant would grant the police permission to search the building for evidence of the crime. Ash doubted Marvin Spencer would be so accommodating, so he waited in the hallway for Havelock's team to arrive. The first members, a four-person team of forensic technicians, arrived about ten minutes after Ash placed his call. They said Havelock and Clair Eckert were drawing up the warrant application and would likely arrive within half an hour. Not wanting to waste his time, Ash walked to the apartment next door and knocked. Ben, the young man Ash had talked to a few minutes earlier, answered within just a minute.

"Yeah?"

"I just wanted to give you a heads-up. We're going to search the apartment next door shortly, so you might hear some noises."

"Okay," said Ben, looking over his shoulder. "Is that it?"

"Not quite," said Ash. "I wanted to ask you a couple of general questions about Marvin. Is that okay?"

"Do I have a choice?"

"Of course you have a choice," said Ash, nodding. "But if you don't talk to me, the FBI agent I'm working this case with will be here next. Neither of us can compel you to answer questions, but he can really ruin your day. If you talk to me now, I'll share my notes with him and hopefully we won't have to disturb you again. That's the best offer you're going to get all day."

"Do we have to do this in my apartment? Because it's a mess. I don't even have anywhere for you to sit."

"We'll talk right here," said Ash, reaching into his jacket for a notepad. "Is that all right?"

"All right," said Ben.

"Great, thank you," said Ash. "So what's your full name, Ben?"

"Uh, Benjamin William Richardson."

Ben's voice almost cracked. Ash was tempted to smile at his nervousness, but he kept it off his face. "And you live here, right?"

"With my girlfriend."

Ash wrote that down. "Have you ever been interviewed by the police before?"

Ben hesitated. "I got busted for pot in college."

"Well, we're not interested in marijuana, so you don't have to be nervous. Even if you've got some on you or in your apartment, I really don't care. As long as you don't smoke up in front of me, you're not going to get in trouble."

That seemed to relax him a little. He took a breath and nodded. "Okay."

"So, did you know Marvin?"

"Not really. I saw him some, but just going in and out of his apartment. We didn't usually even say hello to each other."

"Did Marvin live alone?"

Ben started to answer, but then caught himself and leaned against the door frame, his arms loosely across his chest. "I think so. I didn't really pay that much attention, though."

"Did you ever see him bring a girl home?"

"Sometimes. I don't know if they were girlfriends or what. Like I said, we didn't really know each other."

Ash nodded. "You're doing fine. The girls you saw, how old do you think they were?"

Ben shrugged. "I don't know. Twenty-five, thirty."

Probably not girls from the Dandelion Inn. "Has he had anyone over lately?"

Ben shrugged. "He had a girl over three or four nights ago. She was a soprano." He reached into his apartment and knocked on the nearest wall. "Cheap construction. I can hear every time my neighbor farts."

"Aside from me and the guys who came in early this morning, has anyone else come by?"

"No. It's been dead."

"Is there anything you want to tell me about Marvin?"

"My girlfriend thinks he's creepy. I think it was just the tattoos, though."

Marvin trafficked young women; *vile* was probably a better descriptor than *creepy*.

"You can at least tell your girlfriend not to worry about him. He's going to be in jail for a while," said Ash. He gestured to the door across the hall with his head. "Are your other neighbors usually home during the day? I might talk to them if they are."

He shook his head. "No, everybody's at work or school. I work out of the house."

"Since you're here in the day, I'm going to ask you for another favor. It's possible someone will come back to

Marvin's apartment, and if that happens, I want you to stay inside your apartment and call the police. Can you do that?" Ben nodded, so Ash slipped his notebook into his jacket pocket and removed a business card from his wallet. "This is my card. If you have any questions for me, or if you think of anything about Marvin, give me a call or send me an e-mail. I'll get back to you as quickly as I can. That sound good?"

"That sounds fine."

"Good. Thank you."

Ben nodded and shut his door. Havelock still hadn't arrived yet, so Ash knocked on the doors of the two other apartments on the floor, but no one answered either place. He expected that in the middle of the day. On the off chance that the other neighbors had more information, Ash tore two pages out of his notebook and wrote a quick note on each requesting a call. He slipped a note and a copy of his business card beneath each door. After that, he sat down on the floor beside Marvin's door and closed his eyes to wait.

Agent Havelock, Clair Eckert, and the building's manager, a woman named Tonya, arrived about twenty minutes later, their warrant in hand. Tonya opened Spencer's door and stepped back while Agent Havelock and Ash walked in, their firearms at their sides. The apartment had a galley-style kitchen and living room combination immediately in front of the door. Picture windows overlooked the city, giving him a nearly unobstructed view of the Scottish Rite Cathedral and the park near which it stood. Palmer very well could have stood beside that window and watched with binoculars as Ash got into the van.

"This is the FBI serving a search warrant," said Havelock. "If anyone can hear my voice, please come to the living room immediately."

No one emerged, so Ash crossed the threshold that separated the marble entryway from the living room and felt his shoes sink in the plush gray carpet. The builder may have skimped on the soundproofing between apartments, but he had gone all out on the interior finishes. Crown molding ran around the entire ceiling in the living room, and the kitchen cabinets were topped with a thick slab of black granite. Havelock motioned for Ash to follow him through an open doorway on the left. It led to a bedroom that had been turned into a home office. Ash checked out the walk-in closet while Havelock threw back the shower curtain in the attached bathroom. Neither found anyone, nor did it look as if anyone had searched the room.

They went to the bedroom on the other side of the apartment next. It had a king-sized bed, a dresser, and a chest of drawers. Clothes overflowed a laundry basket on the far side of the room, but nothing appeared to have been rifled through. When burglars break into a house to search for something, they usually pull out drawers and dump their contents on the ground, overturn the furniture looking for hidden compartments, and occasionally even cut some holes in the walls. Marvin's apartment didn't have any of that. Havelock and Ash checked the few places big enough to hide someone before declaring the apartment clear and allowing the civilian forensic technicians inside. As the technicians set up to work, Havelock motioned for Ash to follow him into the hallway. He pulled the door shut slightly, leaving just a crack, and leaned close to Ash.

"I know you play fast with the rules, but tell me you actually had a report that someone broke into this apartment. It will look bad for all of us if you lied so we could get in here."

Ash motioned toward Ben's door with his head. "The neighbor told me. I wouldn't have called you if he hadn't."

Havelock stared directly into Ash's eyes, as if trying to gauge his sincerity. Eventually, he looked back toward the door. "If you're going to stay, get some gloves. I don't want you disturbing the scene."

Ash followed Havelock back inside and got a pair of purple polypropylene gloves from one of the evidence technicians. While the techs tried to fingerprint the door, Ash walked back through the bedroom and opened the drawers on the end tables. He found a package of condoms in one, but no pictures or other personal mementos that would indicate Spencer had a real relationship with anyone. After that, he went to the kitchen and flipped through a stack of mail on the counter. Bills and catalogs, mostly. He stopped when he glanced at the phone in the kitchen. A red light on the answering machine blinked over and over, indicating that someone had left a message. Ash looked up. Havelock and Clair Eckert were conferring with each other near the far window, while the evidence technicians looked busy cataloging fingerprints near the door and windows.

Ash hesitated and then waved over one of the technicians. "Can you do me a favor and take a look at this phone?"

The tech looked at Agent Havelock for permission, and only then did he start dusting the exterior for prints. That hadn't been what Ash had in mind, but he waited anyway while he lifted a set. Once that was done, he let Ash pick it up. He didn't bother checking the messages—Spencer likely kept his voice mail password protected. Instead, he looked at the phone log. Someone had called Spencer from the same number eight times in the past three days. Ash entered that number in his cell phone and noted that he should call it when he had the chance.

All in all, the apartment disappointed him. If Palmer had really broken in, he probably knew exactly what he wanted and left everything else alone. Aside from the phone log, Ash doubted they'd get anything from it. They were going to have to do better than that. He put the phone back on its cradle and then walked toward Agent Havelock.

"Spencer had some messages that might be worth checking. I don't know if your warrant will cover them, though. Unless you need me further, I'm going to head out."

Clair narrowed her eyes at Ash. "You said you talked to a neighbor. What was his name?"

Ash reached into his jacket and flipped through his notepad. He hadn't gotten much from Ben, so he just tore out the pages with his notes on them and handed them over. "The guy's name is Ben Richardson. He didn't seem to know much."

Havelock flipped through the notes and nodded. "Thank you for the call, Sergeant Rashid. I'm sure we'll be in touch."

"Good luck."

Ash took the elevator to the lobby and walked to his car. He didn't get in and drive off right away; instead, he opened the two front doors to air it out and hopefully cool it down. Since the seats felt too hot to sit on, Ash stayed outside and called the phone number of the individual who had been so intent on getting in touch with Spencer. The phone didn't even ring; it simply went to an electronic message telling him that he had just called a number that didn't receive incoming calls. The message repeated, thanking him again for calling the Pendleton Correctional Facility. Spencer had been getting calls from someone in prison.

21

Pendleton contained both maximum- and minimum-security units and famously housed John Dillinger for several years in the midtwenties. As far as prisons went, it had a surprising number of rehabilitative amenities. Inmates could learn a trade, earn a GED, or even receive college credit through a local university. Politicians derided the programs as an unnecessary waste of taxpayer dollars, but they rarely mentioned that those opportunities lowered the rate of recidivism for many crimes and kept a lot of men from going back to prison later in life, saving the state massive amounts of money. The courts around Indianapolis sent a lot of convicts out there, so Ash knew the facility fairly well. He also knew that its warden wouldn't allow an inmate to make that many phone calls that quickly. If a prisoner made them, he had a deal with somebody.

Ash called the facility's main operator, who, after he introduced himself, transferred Ash's call to the assistant warden's office. The assistant warden, a man named Tyler Addison, listened politely as Ash laid out the basics of the case and the timing of the phone calls. Addison promised to find out what he could as quickly as he could. Ash wouldn't have put much faith in that, but for one fact: Cameras filmed every exchange between guards and prisoners, every phone call, and every patrol on the floor. If someone had made calls on behalf of a prisoner, Addison would find out quickly.

Ash drove to his office. By the time he got there, Addison had already finished reviewing surveillance video that had been shot at the time of the last phone call. A female corrections officer had given a prisoner access to a phone in a restricted area. Unfortunately, that inmate never turned toward the camera, so no one at the prison could identify him yet. They would as soon as they went through enough film, but that would take a while. In the meantime, Addison had placed her in custody pending an arrest for official misconduct, a felony under Indiana law.

The drive would take at least forty minutes, but without much else going on with the case, Ash had time. As the liaison officer, he could even make a decent case that he should be the one to go. He told Addison that he'd be over as quickly as he could before hopping in his car and driving off.

Pendleton and its surrounding buildings occupied a five-hundred-acre tract of what could have been extremely productive farmland. A thirty-foot-high razor-wire and chain-link fence surrounded the maximum-security buildings, but a minimum-security dormitory sat just outside. In the distance, he could even see a juvenile facility. A good number of men spent most of their lives on those five hundred acres, going to the juvenile facility as teenagers and then graduating to the adult facility years later. Sad and frustrating didn't begin to describe it.

Ash parked in front of the administrative building of the main prison and stepped out of his car. Heat radiated from the asphalt so strongly that he felt it through the soles of his shoes. The administrative building had been built well before the rest of the jail, and it showed. It had large picture windows, ornate stone molding on the roof, and impressive ornamentation in the brickwork. Someone had been proud to build that place. Had Ash not known better, he could have mistaken it for a school. Before going inside, he pulled his jacket back, exposing the badge on his belt.

Warden Addison met Ash in the lobby and then led him to a booth where he could check his firearm for the duration of his stay at the prison. After that, they walked to an un-adorned room normally used by inmates to speak with their attorneys. Ash couldn't see cameras anywhere, but he could see a red panic button beside the door. The suspected guard walked in by herself a few moments later. She had smooth, evenly tanned skin, brown hair pulled back from her face, and smile lines beside her eyes. When Ash showed her his badge, she dropped her gaze and looked at the table.

"What agency are you with?" she asked, her voice soft. Before answering, Ash gestured at the seat across from him at the table and she sat down, being careful not to sit on the baton still at her hip. Corrections officers had signifi-cant law enforcement and crowd control training, but they didn't go to the police academy. She probably didn't know the rather nuanced rules that guided an interrogation. Ash could use that.

"I'm Ash Rashid, and I'm a detective sergeant with the Indianapolis Metropolitan Police Department. Just so I know what to call you, what's your name?"

"Rita Morehouse," she said. She started to say something else but then looked away. "Why do you want to talk to me?"

She looked at him again, her lower lip trembling. Had Rita been a regular witness, Ash would have averted his eyes and given her a moment to herself. He refused with her, though; she put on a uniform every morning, and she knew the sort of men housed in a maximum-security facility. Few of them had joined the local church choir when young, and few would have scruples about ordering a murder over the phone. Ash held her gaze and watched as the tremble passed from her lips to her shoulders.

"I think you have a pretty good idea," said Ash. "I know that you allowed an inmate to place unauthorized calls to a man named Marvin Spencer. I want to know the inmate's name."

Her hand moved from the table to her upper chest and throat. "I don't know what you're talking about."

"You don't need to make this hard on yourself. It's on video. You're not doing yourself any favors by holding back on me."

She wiped a tear from her cheek. "I've got kids," she said. "I could lose my job."

"You think I drove from Indianapolis because I'm interested in having you fired? You allowed an inmate to call a man suspected of human trafficking. You facilitated criminal acts and can therefore be prosecuted for those criminal acts. Conspiracy to commit murder, rape, promotion of prostitution, human trafficking. Take your pick. Any of those will put you in jail for the rest of your life. Cooperate with me and the prosecutor might go easier on you."

Rita started sobbing before he even finished speaking. Ash couldn't make deals with anyone, nor did he think the local prosecutor would actually charge her with anything beyond official misconduct. That would get her fired and it could even send her to prison for a year, but more than likely, she'd plea it down or receive a suspended sentence. She had done something stupid, but she hadn't ruined her life no matter what he said. He didn't want her to know that, though.

"I need a name. Who was he?" Ash waited for fifteen or so seconds, but she didn't respond. "We're going to find out anyway once we look at the film. Time matters in the case I'm working, though, so I need a name now." He waited again, but she didn't say anything. Ash decided to use a different tactic. "You said you had kids. Do you have family around who'd be willing to take care of them?"

"Why?"

"Because I don't think you'll be seeing them anytime soon. Tell me what I want to know, and make this right. I bet you're a good mom. Do the right thing here so you can see your children grow up."

She looked away, pursed her lips, and squeezed her eyes tight. Ash thought he had her, so he gave her some time to think. Eventually, she wiped tears off her cheeks with the back of one hand.

"He told me he was trying to set up a birthday party for his daughter," she said. "I didn't know what he was really doing."

"Unfortunately, he lied to you. What was his name?"

She took a deep breath and looked at the table. "Nathan Ross. He's a nonviolent offender on my block. I didn't think he'd do anything like this. He told me I was helping out his kids."

"Thank you for your honesty. You've done the right thing," said Ash, already planning his next move. He stood up and walked to the door, but stopped before opening it. "Before I go, tell me one thing. Why did you really help this guy?"

She looked at the table. "He said I was pretty. No one has told me that in a long time."

"I'll tell the local prosecutor that you helped me. In the meantime, you should call a defense lawyer because you're going to need some help."

* * *

Rita stayed in the interview room while the guard who had been outside escorted Ash to Warden Addison's corner office. The warden shared a receptionist and waiting room with the prison's chief counsel, but the guard escorting him must have been under orders to let him through quickly. He nodded to the receptionist and then knocked on his boss's door before Ash even had time to take in his surroundings. Two men greeted him inside: Addison, whom Ash had met earlier, and a major from the Department of Corrections' Internal Affairs division. The major must have been stationed nearby for him to get out there so quickly.

Ash sat on one of two brown leather chairs in front of the warden's gargantuan oak desk, while the major took the chair beside him. Addison's office had wood-framed windows on two walls, one set of which overlooked a concrete exercise yard inside the prison, while the other overlooked a field of soybean plants beyond the prison's fence. A picture of Addison shaking the previous governor's hand occupied a place of honor on the wall behind the warden's chair.

"First off, your officer admitted to me that she allowed a prisoner to place some phone calls," said Ash. "I don't know what damage, if any, her actions have caused, but she is cooperating."

Addison nodded, but his face remained impassive and unreadable. "Very good," he said. "Did she give you the prisoner's name?"

"Guy named Nathan Ross. She said he was a nonviolent offender on her block."

Addison nodded and began typing on his computer. While he did that, the major looked at Ash.

"She sleeping with him, too?"

"I didn't ask."

"She probably is," he said. "She'd be the third one this year. The last two were nurses. You think with their college degree they'd be smart enough to keep their pants on. No such luck. If I had my way, we wouldn't hire them."

Ash presumed he meant he wouldn't hire women rather than nurses. He didn't ask him to correct that minor ambiguity, though.

"You find Ross's records?" asked Ash, directing the question to Addison.

"Yeah," he said, glancing from the computer to Ash and then back. "He's in the third year of an eight-year rip for forgery and identity deception. He's up for parole in a couple of months. He's been written up for having cigarettes in his cell, but he hasn't ever gotten violent with anyone."

"You have any of his trial records?"

The warden shook his head. "We don't have those, but you're in luck. Marion County prosecuted him, lady named Susan Mercer. You know her?"

Ash grunted. He *did* know her and had even got along with her for several years. Their relationship became strained after he testified for the defense in the middle of the largest murder trial she ever prosecuted. He had done the right thing, but he couldn't help but regret the collateral damage it caused.

"I wouldn't say that makes me lucky," said Ash, standing and removing his cell phone from his jacket. "If you'll excuse me, I'm going to make a call."

The warden nodded and Ash slipped through the door and into the lobby. Susan answered quickly, and while her tone remained civil, she spoke mostly in one- or two-word answers, almost as if she were a witness under hostile examination in court. She had a nearly encyclopedic recall of cases she tried, though, so she recognized Ross's name.

A clerk caught him trying to buy booze with a stolen credit card at a liquor store almost five years ago and called the police. The first officer on the scene suspected Ross had a weapon, so he patted him down and found eight fake IDs for eight young women of various ethnicities as well as a revolver in his pockets. The IDs appeared genuine and even had many of the same security features a real, state-issued ID would have. None of the young women on them could be found in the system, though. Thinking Ross made them for illegal immigrants, detectives secured a search warrant for his home and found printmaking equipment and stacks of fraudulent birth certificates and Social Security cards. Despite being offered a generous plea deal, Ross never cooperated and he never identified the eight young women he had made documents for. If he had made those IDs for human traffickers, Ash understood his silence.

He thanked Susan for the information before going back to the warden's office, catching the tail end of a conversation about a problematic inmate in one of the blocks. Addison and the major quieted almost as soon as Ash came in.

"Did you get what you needed?" asked the warden.

"Mostly," said Ash. "Ross was arrested for making fake IDs for young women, and he's trying to get in touch with a man who traffics in young women. I need to talk to him."

"Rita Morehouse," said the major, shaking his head. "Never should have hired her."

"You've made your opinion known, Terrance," said the warden. "She's not going to be working here anymore if it makes you feel better."

Terrance held up his hands defensively. "Didn't mean any offense. I know you don't make the policy."

"I appreciate that," said the warden. "Find Mr. Ross and bring him here." He looked at Ash. "Thank you for bringing this to our attention. We will work with the Madison County prosecutor's office and your own office to ensure that Mr. Ross and Ms. Morehouse are punished appropriately."

"Does Ross have a cellmate?"

"We're at over a hundred percent capacity right now. Everybody's got a cellmate."

"Then get him, too," said Ash. "I've got an idea."

The warden looked at Terrance again. "Do it."

He left without saying another word. Ash excused himself as well and went to the prison chapel for afternoon prayers. Even just a few minutes away from the case cleared his head and made the world a little easier to take. Ross may not have been as bad as Palmer or Spencer, but he played a pivotal role in the trafficker's organization. Even the thought of being in the same room as him caused an almost primal, instinctual anger to form in Ash's gut.

By the time he got back to the assistant warden's office, Terrance had returned with sweat beading on his brow and dark patches on his uniform. Ross and his cellmate had been in the exercise yard outside, so it took several guards to find them amid the other prisoners. With that many bodies on that much concrete, the temperature must have been off the charts. Ash didn't plan to use anything the cellmate said, so he almost felt guilty for asking the guards to bring him. On the other hand, Terrance's comments about women had proven him to be an asshole, and Ash didn't have a lot of sympathy for assholes.

He asked the guards to put both men in separate interview rooms but he didn't go immediately to either one. Instead, he let them stew and wait alone for about twenty minutes. When he went into the room with the cellmate, the guy had his head on the table and looked to be asleep. Like a lot of prisoners, he had several visible tattoos, one of which was a crude drawing of a red bird sitting atop a baseball bat; the lines were blotchy and the ink looked faded, but Ash recognized the logo. Ross's cellmate liked the St. Louis Cardinals. Ash gently woke him up and introduced himself. He didn't have to say much to get the prisoner talking. As soon as Ash asked if the prisoner had seen the Cardinals and Astros game, he opened his mouth and only stopped talking to take a breath.

Unbeknownst to the prisoner, Ash wasn't the only person watching him talk. If Terrance had gotten the timing right, he would have "accidently" led Ross to the wrong room, thereby allowing him to see through the one-way mirror built into the door. To him, it would have looked like a detective and his cellmate were having an animated discussion. The technique may have been old and clichéd, but turning people against each other and playing them for information worked well. Ross probably didn't tell his cellmate everything, but everybody talks in prison and that creates opportunities.

About five minutes after starting his baseball discussion, Ash ended the conversation and pounded on the door for the guard to let him out. He then crossed the hallway to peer through the one-way mirror on the door of the other interview room. Ross had thin shoulders and a scar on an otherwise unadorned chin. Unlike the other men Ash had run into on the case, no tattoos covered his arms and little malice glinted in his eye. He paced the room, his arms at his side. He never stopped moving his fingers. Had he been on the outside, Ross could have passed for an accountant who had just blown a meeting with his most important client. Ash let him pace for another moment, letting his nervousness build before walking inside.

"Hey," said Ross, taking a seat and leaning against the table. "I wondered when someone would come to talk to me."

Ash sat across from him at the table and rested his elbows on top. Ross crossed his arms and put his hands on top of his biceps. He tried to keep his nervousness under wraps, but his hands trembled and his breath came shallow and quick.

"Sorry about the delay. I was in the bathroom."

Ross's eyes darted to the door and then back to Ash.

"Fine, sure. Who are you and what do you want?"

Ash pulled back his jacket so Ross could see his badge.

"I'm Sergeant Ashraf Rashid with the Indianapolis Metropolitan Police Department. I'm here to give you an opportunity to come clean and maybe stay out of trouble."

He looked at Ash's badge and then at his face. "What trouble could I get into in Indianapolis? I've been in prison if you didn't know."

"Have you had any contact with anyone in Indianapolis in the past couple of weeks?"

"My lawyer won't return my calls."

"How about anybody else?" asked Ash, leaning back in his chair. "Maybe an old business partner, maybe someone you made documents for."

He shook his head. "I've been out of that life since I went to prison. I'm making amends."

Ash nodded and removed his notebook from his pocket. "The woman who prosecuted your case offered you a pretty good deal. Fines and probation in exchange for testimony. I've seen a lot of people brought to trial, and not many would turn down a deal like that. Why did you?"

He blinked a few times. "I rejected it on the advice of my counsel."

Ash shook his head. "No, you didn't. You were caught dead to rights. Your lawyer wouldn't advise you to reject that deal."

He leaned back and adjusted his arms, apparently getting a little more comfortable. "If you don't believe me, I don't know what to tell you."

"How about you start by being honest. Your cellmate

was. He said you talk too much for your own good. How do you know Marvin Spencer?"

Ross sat forward. "Whatever that son of a bitch told you is a lie."

"Which son of a bitch are you referring to?" asked Ash. "Your cellmate or Spencer? I've talked to them both. I want to hear your story."

Ross shook his head and licked his lips, not answering immediately. "I know Spence, all right? I haven't talked to him in a long time."

"I know," said Ash. "He doesn't want to take your calls anymore."

"What'd he tell you?"

Ash shrugged. "A little bit of this, a little bit of that. He told me about the girls you made IDs for. Was sex with them part of your payment, or did you do that on your own?"

Ross narrowed his eyes. "I don't know what Spence has told you, but I never touched anybody. I thought he was just smuggling girls in."

"And you didn't ask."

"I made new identities for people. That's why I'm here. I didn't ask my clients why they needed my help."

Ash nodded and pretended to write something down.

"Why didn't you take the plea deal Susan Mercer offered you?"

Ross didn't say anything, but his face had turned red. The question made him nervous; Ash would have to come back to it.

"How'd you get Rita Morehouse to let you call him?" asked Ash.

"Leave Rita alone."

Ross's tone had shifted into a throaty growl. He almost sounded protective.

"Why do you care about Rita? She's just a prison guard, and she's not even going to be that anymore. Hell, she's probably going to be behind bars. Maybe you guys can become pen pals or something."

"She didn't know who I was calling. Leave her alone."

Ash had definitely stumbled on something. Ross cared about her.

"I'd like to leave her alone, but I can't. I don't even know how much damage you've caused."

"I didn't cause any damage. Spence didn't call me back. And even if he had, it wouldn't have hurt anybody."

"What'd you want from him?"

Ross looked past Ash's shoulder and licked his lips.

"He puts money in my commissary account every month, but he was late. I wanted to find out what the holdup was."

"Is that why you didn't testify against him and the rest of his partners? They promised you money?" Ross didn't respond. "If you want me to help Rita, you've got to help me. I'll talk to the prosecutor on her behalf. She's up for some serious charges."

"What charges? She hasn't done anything."

"That's not my call," said Ash. "I can guarantee you, though, that without help she'll go to jail for a long time. It's called accomplice liability. She'll go to jail for every crime you committed."

Ross seemed to weigh that for a moment before coming to a decision.

"They offered me four hundred grand. A hundred large for each year until I'm up for parole."

"And they'd give you some spending money while you were in prison."

"That was the deal."

Ash nodded. "Okay, we're getting somewhere. Do you know the name Palmer?" Ross shook his head. "How about Ann?"

"Oh, yeah," he said. "I've met Ann. She's the one who paid me."

"Did you ever go to that bed-and-breakfast of hers?"

"No. I always met her somewhere else."

"Where?"

Ross leaned forward. "If I tell you, you'll talk to the prosecutor about Rita?"

"I'll do everything I can for her. You have my promise. I think she made a mistake, but I don't think she's a bad person."

Ross thought that through before nodding. "It was a house in Avon. In one of those new subdivisions, the kind where every house looks alike."

"You'll have to be a little more specific than that," said Ash.

Ross sighed exasperatedly. "The neighborhood was called Rabbit Run. I remember because I thought it was a stupid name. The house was on the third cul-de-sac on the left side after the entrance. It had a big stone deer on the front lawn. Good enough?"

It didn't sound like a great place to lie low with seven girls, but it was a lead. Maybe he'd get lucky.

"If it pans out, yeah," said Ash. "If you're lying to me and wasting my time, I'm going to come down hard on you."

"What about Rita?"

"Let me worry about Rita. I told you that I'd do what I can for her, and I will."

Ross seemed to accept that because he didn't say anything else. Ash pounded on the door for the guard, who led the prisoner back to his cell and allowed Addison and Terrance inside. Ash filled them in on his conversation. Terrance seemed a little disappointed that Ash didn't have further titillating details about the relationship between Rita and Ross, but he'd get over it. Addison said he'd look into things and get in touch with Ash again if they found anything that seemed pertinent to his case, leaving Ash free to pursue his lead.

He got his firearm and left the prison almost two hours after arriving. The sun baked the surrounding fields, causing visible fissures to form in the earth. Ash opened his car to let it air out and called Susan Mercer again. He didn't talk to her long, but he told her that Ross had cooperated, but only on condition that Ash would try to help out Rita Morehouse. Susan said she'd call the local prosecutor and put in a good word; that ought to be enough.

22

Ash's phone rang about ten minutes after he left the prison. Arid fields full of stunted corn and soybean plants surrounded him. Having seen enough car accidents involving distracted drivers to know how dangerous it was to do otherwise, he pulled off on the side of the road, but kept the windows closed and the air conditioning cranked. Even through his cruiser's filters, the air felt gritty in his mouth. Bits of dirt carried by the breeze pelted his car.

He glanced at his cell phone before picking up and groaned after seeing the time.

"Hey, Mike," said Ash. "I missed my meeting. Sorry."

"Really? You missed our meeting?" he said. "It's funny you say that because I was just sitting with Chief Reddington and Charity Lewis from the prosecutor's office and Kristen Estrada—I asked the union to send your lawyer down, by the way—and I couldn't figure out what was wrong. We had a great conversation about how our department can better utilize its resources, but I couldn't help but feel we were missing something. Now I know. You weren't there for debriefing. Thanks for telling me. I wouldn't have figured that out."

Ash hadn't heard Bowers use sarcasm before, so he didn't know what to make of it.

"You sound perturbed," said Ash.

"Perturbed?" asked Bowers. "What is that? Some word they teach you to use in law school? I'm pissed off, Ash. I fought to have you kept on this case. Everybody else wanted you gone. By not showing up, you made me look like I couldn't do my job, and worse, you wasted everyone's time."

"I apologize. I've been working on the Elliots' case, and I lost track of time. It wasn't intentional."

"And you didn't have a phone with you at the time?"

"I was visiting a prisoner at the Pendleton Correctional Facility. He was caught trying to call Marvin Spencer eight times over the past few days. I didn't think to call you."

Bowers swore. "Did you at least find anything useful?"

"A house in Avon potentially linked to the people who ran the Dandelion Inn. They might have taken the girls there."

"It's not even in our jurisdiction. We'll have to call the locals."

"I will, but I'm going to drive by first and see if I can even find the place. I didn't get an address, just the name of the neighborhood and a description of the house."

"That's not liaison work."

"It is if you consider how pissed off our partners would be if I start giving them leads that don't go anywhere."

"Fine," said Bowers after a moment's pause. "Check out the house. If it looks promising, make a call." He cleared his throat. "We're not done talking about the meeting you missed, though. A gangbanger skips a court date, and we issue a warrant for his arrest. You missed a meeting, so you're going to get the same treatment. I'm going to write a letter of reprimand and stick it in your personnel file."

"It was an oversight, Mike. I got wrapped up in some interviews. It wasn't malicious."

"I don't care. It was unprofessional. You're paid to do a job, and part of that job is to give statements when required."

Unfortunately, Ash agreed with Bowers. He took a deep breath.

"It was a mistake. I admit that, and I—"

Bowers interrupted before Ash could finish the apology. "Stop before you say anything else. You made a mistake. Thank you for admitting it. Don't do it again."

"I won't." Ash paused. "Did Chief Reddington say anything?"

"He wanted to know why I defend an officer who can't be bothered to show up for a simple meeting. I'm starting to wonder that myself."

"It won't happen again."

"If it does, I'm done with you. We'll set up another appointment shortly."

Bowers hung up before Ash could say anything else. He gripped his steering wheel hard. A letter of reprimand might not hurt him directly, but it did make him feel like an asshole. Worse, he knew he deserved it.

Ash pulled back into traffic a few minutes later. The afternoon had quickly worn into early evening during his visit to the prison, leaving the sun low on the horizon. He flipped the visor down and scowled. Under normal circumstances, he would have sent uniformed officers to cruise by the house in Avon, but with such a nebulous description of its location, he didn't even know if it actually existed. He needed to check things out himself before wasting someone else's time.

He settled into the slow lane for the drive, watching as cars on both sides of the road suddenly braked whenever his car came into view. Courtesy may have been a lost art on the area's overcrowded roadways whenever he drove a civilian vehicle, but it amused him to see it found once again when he drove his department-issued cruiser. By the time he reached the outskirts of Indianapolis, rush hour had begun in earnest and traffic had slowed to roughly a quarter of its usual speed. At least they could still move; a lot of times, they couldn't even do that.

It took Ash almost an hour to cross Indianapolis and reach Avon on the city's west side. By that time, traffic had thinned considerably, allowing him to make good time into the community. Like a lot of small towns in the area, the community of Avon had existed for well over a hundred years, but the town had been incorporated only since the midnineties. It had a decent grocery store, a strong public school system, and relatively low taxes for the services offered. During the housing boom, developers saw the potential and built neighborhoods of inexpensive tract homes in the middle of every cornfield they could buy. Unfortunately, the families who bought those homes couldn't always afford them. At its height, there had been several hundred home foreclosures a month in a county with just under a hundred and fifty thousand residents. The housing market still had yet to recover, leaving neighborhoods full of vacant and abandoned homes. Of course, the same could be said for nearly every town in America.

Ash didn't know Avon well, so he used a map on his cell

phone to find Rabbit Run, the subdivision the prisoner in Pendleton told him about. As expected, the homes inside it appeared uniform and gargantuan, a common theme of homes mass-produced during the housing bubble. Ash had several colleagues with large families who had bought into similar developments only to find that their new home came with construction so shoddy it started falling apart within weeks of completion.

Ash followed the prisoner's directions until he found a two-story, siding-clad home with a gabled roof. The sod in the front lawn had been improperly laid, leaving dead streaks like spaces on a checkerboard, and the flowers had been left to wilt and die in the summer heat. A late-model Chevy with rusting wheel wells had been parked on the street between his target home and the one beside it, while a Hispanic man with thin graying hair watered his lawn next door with a garden hose. Judging from the stone deer on the front lawn, he had found the correct home.

Ash parked in his target's driveway, stepped out of his car, and swept the area with his eyes. He heard kids playing somewhere distant and smelled manure, presumably from the neighbor's immaculate flowerbeds. In order to convince a judge that they had enough probable cause to issue a search warrant, they'd need more than just the word of an inmate. They'd need corroboration, which the neighbor might be able to give. Ash waved and started across the lawn toward the Hispanic man.

"Can I talk to you for a minute, sir?"

Before the man could answer, Ash heard a door being slammed from behind his targeted house. The Hispanic man flinched and Ash took one step forward and then another before vaulting into a sprint. A figure streaked toward him from the home's rear yard, his shoulder down. Ash tried to brace himself but found little traction on the grass and dirt. The runner barreled into Ash's stomach. He didn't carry a lot of weight on him, but his momentum sent Ash sprawling backward, knocking the wind out of him. The runner meanwhile ricocheted across the Hispanic man's yard, his arms flailing to catch his balance.

Ash rolled onto his stomach and gritted his teeth before pushing up, forcing air back into his lungs. His ribs felt bruised, and his breath came back slowly in gasps. The neighbor ran toward his porch and then heaved hard on his hose so it rose a few inches over his yard. The man who had run from the house paid so much attention to Ash that he didn't even see it until it entangled his feet. He crashed onto his face, and Ash sprinted toward him, his lungs and chest hurting. If he had a Taser, he would have just shot him right there and taken him down safely and easily. With only a firearm, a particularly lethal one at that, Ash's options were limited.

Before the runner could push up and take off, Ash grabbed his wrist and yanked it across his back while putting his knee in the back of the suspect's head, forcing the man's cheek into the dirt. He tried to push up with his free arm, so Ash cranked the suspect's wrist upward at an angle contrary to the shoulder's design. If the suspect kept fighting, he'd rip his joint out of socket and potentially do some significant, permanent damage.

"I don't want to hurt you," said Ash. "Stay down."

He stopped trying to press up, but he squirmed and

writhed on the ground. Ash released some of the tension on his arm and reached to his belt for a pair of handcuffs. As soon as Ash shifted his weight, the suspect tried to push up again and then started screaming when Ash responded by cranking on his arm.

"If you keep fighting me, you will get hurt. Stay down."

Apparently having learned his lesson, the runner stayed down this time and let Ash put the handcuffs on his wrist. Once he had the runner's arms secured, Ash stood him up and patted him down for weapons—finding a switch-blade—before sitting him in the backseat of his cruiser. He got his first good look at him then. The runner had thin, willowy arms, hollow cheeks, and bones that seemed ready to protrude from skin as thin and light as white tissue paper. His eyes darted from one object to another, never linger-ing long enough to focus. Ash glanced at the inside crook of his elbow. Red and purple track marks ran the length of his arms where the veins had collapsed, probably from intrave-nous drug use.

"Was anyone else in the house with you?"

He shook his head, but that didn't matter. Someone needed to look anyway.

"Good. Stay put."

He started to protest that he hadn't done anything wrong, but Ash tuned him out and shut the door. Rather than leave him to cook in the heat, Ash opened the windows on both front doors, allowing some air in and his prisoner's curses out. The neighborhood children might learn a few new words, but it'd keep the department from being sued. He called the local sheriff's department and requested that they send officers and an ambulance out. The dispatcher estimated that she could have deputies out there in ten minutes, but an ambulance would take a little longer. Ash felt okay with that; he had called the ambulance as a precaution more than anything else.

He waved toward the Hispanic neighbor and walked to the edge of the lawn. "Thank you for your help with the hose."

He nodded toward the house. "I'm glad he's gone. He gave me a bad feeling. I didn't like my grandkids around him."

"Does he stay here often?"

The Hispanic man shrugged. "Three nights out of five. I don't know where he went the other two."

"Was he alone, or would other people stay, too?"

"For the past week, he's been alone. Before that, a lot of girls went through there."

Ash nodded; the neighbors at the Dandelion Inn probably thought the same thing.

"How about men?"

He shook his head. "Almost never. He was the only one who ever stayed the night."

Amina said she lived in an apartment in Chicago with a number of other girls when the traffickers first brought her to the U.S. Maybe they used the Avon home for the same purposes.

"Would you mind repeating this to a detective later?"

He nodded, so Ash handed him a business card and asked him to stick around for a few minutes until local officers arrived. The neighbor went back to watering his lawn, giving Ash a moment to consider his options. He wanted to walk through the house and see what was in there, but it'd be stupid to go in without backup. He waited beside his car for about ten minutes.

The first two squad cars came from the Avon Police Department. Ash didn't even know they had a department, but their officers seemed to know what to do. Two men waited by the home's rear entrance through which Ash's runner had emerged while the other two went through the front door to perform a safety search. Almost as soon as they went in, one of the officers ran out to call for an ambulance, claiming he had found a girl. Ash jogged to the front porch but stopped before going through the door so he wouldn't surprise the officer already inside.

"I'm Detective Rashid from IMPD, and I'm coming in."

"Get an ambulance. We're in the bedroom upstairs."

"It's on its way," said Ash, stepping across the home's threshold into a two-story entryway. A light oak stairway wound upward to a second-story landing, while rooms branched left, right, and straight ahead. The drywall above the front door had already begun to crack and Ash could see water damage on the ceiling near a skylight. The finishes throughout appeared utilitarian and plain, and the interior smelled musty.

Ash took the stairs two at a time until he reached the carpeted landing. A hallway spanned the length of the second floor and had several empty bedrooms jutting off. He jogged toward the bedroom at the end of the hall from which he had heard the officer shout earlier. The master bedroom occupied the entire space above the garage and had a vaulted ceiling with two skylights, an en suite bathroom, and a large, open closet. A king-sized bed—the only furniture Ash had seen in the house—occupied most of one wall, and a girl wearing only a pair of black panties occupied the bed. She didn't move even when the Avon police officer felt her neck for a pulse.

"Is she breathing?" asked Ash.

"Barely," he said. "We're going to need that ambulance quickly. I think she's OD'd on something."

Ash walked toward the bed, noticing a syringe and burned spoon on the floor. He wouldn't be able to tell until forensic technicians ran some tests, but the girl and her boyfriend had probably been mainlining heroin. As he stepped closer to the bed, he felt his stomach contort. He recognized the girl as soon as he saw her face. She had been in the Dandelion Inn.

"Damn."

* * *

Officers from several agencies, including the FBI, descended on the house in short order. Separate ambulances took the runner Ash had chased down and the girl from the Dandelion Inn to the hospital for evaluation and treatment. He wanted to talk to them both about Kara and Daniel Elliot, but the FBI would get first crack, and even then only after their doctors cleared them. Ash stood by his cruiser, watching and trying to stay out of everyone's way. Eventually, an FBI agent asked him how he found the place, information that Ash relayed as quickly as he could.

Truth be told, aside from the initial report he had given to the FBI and Avon police officers, no one at the scene needed a liaison officer from Indianapolis. Detectives from the Hendricks County Sheriff's Department secured a search warrant, and the FBI's forensic technicians moved through the house bagging potential evidence. No one mentioned the murder of Kate or Daniel Elliot, nor did Ash think they'd find anything pertaining to the Elliots' murder there. He had already done everything his job required by sharing the information he had; staying around merely wasted his limited time and he had better things to do. Nathan Ross, the counterfeiter at Pendleton, had told him the truth about the house. He needed to use that while he still could.

He got back in his car. Marvin Spencer, the bouncer at the Dandelion Inn, had been moved from the Hancock County jail to the Marion County jail in downtown Indianapolis to facilitate communication and future interrogations. Ash called a deputy he knew who worked for the Marion County Sheriff's Department, the agency that ran the jail, and asked him to set up a meeting with Spencer and his lawyer in half an hour. That gave Ash just enough time to drive across town, park, and get through security.

Spencer and his lawyer sat conversing in the interrogation room when Ash arrived. Spencer wore a jail-issued pair of orange pants and a white T-shirt. Ash didn't recognize his lawyer, but he knew the type. He wore a black pinstripe suit, a bright red tie, and matte black leather shoes. No expression crossed his face once Ash walked into the room, but he did lean back, his arms crossed.

"I sincerely hope you're here to inform us that you will be dropping all charges against my client."

Ash closed the heavy steel door behind him, locking them into the room. The jail deputies had given them one of the nicer interrogation rooms in the building. Thin gray carpet covered the walls and floor, reducing echoes, while a vent high overhead pumped in copious amounts of cool air. Ash couldn't see any surveillance equipment, but they might have had something hidden. Unlike many rooms in the jail, it didn't smell like body odor, either. That was a plus. He pulled out a folding chair from the table in the center of the floor and sat down before looking at the lawyer and smiling.

"It's very nice to meet you. I understand that you drove all the way down from Chicago. I assume you're licensed to practice in Indiana as well as Illinois."

The lawyer tilted his head to the side. He hadn't introduced himself, but Ash assumed he had a pretentious name. Rutherford Amadeus Johnson III. Or at least something like that.

"Of course I'm licensed in Indiana."

Ash put up his hands defensively. "You don't have to get snappy. I'm just trying to save your client a headache later on," he said. "I'm here to help."

Rutherford scoffed. "Any offer you're about to extend to us had better be accompanied by a signed letter from the U.S. Attorney's Office."

Ash waved him off. "I'm not authorized to make any offer," he said. "I'm just here to talk."

Rutherford clenched his jaw hard enough that muscles beneath his cheeks flexed outward. He stood and put his hand on Spencer's arm.

"Then you're wasting our time."

"I don't think I am," said Ash, looking at Spencer. "Nathan Ross says hello."

Spencer glared. "Whatever Ross told you is bull."

"Everything Ross told me has panned out so far. I'm

starting to believe him. He told me a couple of things about you, too, and I think we should clear them up."

Ross hadn't actually told Ash much about anything, but Spencer didn't need to know that. As long as he didn't compel a confession, Ash could lie to him all day with impunity.

"Get up, Marvin," said Rutherford, physically trying to pull his client out of his chair. Spencer's arms were so large that it looked like a child trying to pull an adult away from the dinner table. Spencer shrugged his lawyer's hand away and stood up on his own. He leaned forward and rested against the table, causing it to groan under his weight.

"Ross is a liar."

"Don't say anything else," said Rutherford. He looked at Ash. "And don't waste our time like this again, Sergeant."

Ash pushed his chair back. "Don't blame me when you get screwed at trial," he said. "I came here to help you. I did my part."

"What are you talking about?" asked Spencer.

Rutherford exhaled loudly. "Stop speaking, Marvin."

Ash glanced from one to the other before finally settling on Marvin. "Who's paying your legal bills?"

Rutherford turned his glare on Ash. "That's out of line, Sergeant. We're done. Call for the guard."

Ash didn't take his eyes from Marvin. "I'm just watching out for you. I like my boss and all, but if my ass were on the line, I think I'd want to hire a lawyer myself. That way, I know who he's actually working for."

Marvin's eyes flicked from Ash to his lawyer and back. "What'd Ross tell you?"

"For starters, he told me about the house in Avon."

Rutherford ignored his client for a moment and knocked

on the door for the guard. He looked over his shoulder. "Don't say a word, Marvin."

"I'll say whatever I want to and listen to whoever I want to."

"Sergeant Rashid is paid to lie to you. We gain nothing by talking to him."

"I get the same feeling about you," said Marvin.

Rutherford took a step toward the center of the room. He partially turned so his back faced Ash.

"Marvin, we can talk about this in private. I took an oath to put your interests ahead of anyone else's, and I'm not lying to you now. We shouldn't talk to him. Trust me."

"That's what you've been telling me all along, and I'm still in here and you're still out there. I think I'm going to start trusting myself."

Marvin's friends had taken seven girls from the hospital, at least one of whom—the girl from the Avon house—had a high probability of being dead already. Purposefully driving a wedge between an attorney and his client skirted on being unethical, but Marvin's victims didn't have time for Ash to worry about right and wrong.

"We found a girl at the house in Avon," said Ash. He nodded toward Rutherford. "You think this guy's going to protect you against her once she gets on the stand? It's time to get in front of this and start talking."

"Don't say anything," said Rutherford. "He's trying to turn us against each other."

"I'm not dying to save Lukas's ass," said Marvin. Ash hadn't heard Lukas's name before, but he tried not to let his surprise show. "It's time to start looking for a deal. You can start making some calls, or you can get the hell out of here."

Rutherford pointed toward Ash. "He's just a cop. He can't do anything on his own."

Marvin looked at Ash.

He shrugged. "I can't make a deal, but I know the people who can. Right now, they're visiting Nathan Ross at Pendleton and talking to some whacked-out asshole we just picked up in Avon. Whoever talks first walks home a winner. If you tell me who Lukas is and where he might be, that winner could be you."

Rutherford sighed and looked at Ash. "If we're going to make a deal, I want it in writing from the U.S. Attorney's Office. And we want transactional immunity."

"You want complete immunity from all crimes?" asked Ash, narrowing his gaze. "If you're shouting out things that you know aren't going to happen, why not ask for world peace while you're at it?"

"That's our price," said Rutherford. "Take it or leave it."

Ash shook his head. "I've got at least one girl still in the hospital who said two employees at the Dandelion Inn drugged and raped her. I'm guessing she'll point the figure at Marvin here, and I'm guessing more girls will step forward. No one's going to walk. Give me a realistic request and I'll take it to my superiors."

"What's realistic?" asked Marvin.

Ash doubted Marvin had just asked for a definition, so he had to think for a moment.

"If you give us good intel, I bet I could convince the prosecutors to let you plea to the rapes. You'll get life without the possibility of parole. We might even be able to send you to the facility of your choice."

"And what if I don't do the deal?"

Ash shrugged again. "We're still building a case against you, but we've already got quite a few bodies. If we can tie you to any of them, I'm willing to bet the good people of Indiana will sentence you to death."

"That doesn't sound like much of a deal," said Marvin. "You've got to do better than that."

"You want me to be honest?" asked Ash. "Or are you looking for a lie that will make you feel better?"

"Honest."

"If you go to trial for trafficking and raping multiple girls, it's going to make the papers. Let's say you beat most of the charges and get a couple of years for criminal confinement. The inmates in your future facility will know exactly who you are and exactly what you've done. They don't take kindly to rapists in jail. My guess is that you'll last a year or two before someone murders you. Jail is a dangerous place. The guards can't protect everybody twenty-four hours a day. In your case, I don't think they'd want to."

"And if I make a deal, that won't happen?"

"Protective custody can be part of your deal. You'll have to work on that with your lawyer and the prosecutor."

Marvin took a deep breath. "I don't like either option."

Ash tilted his head to the side. "You give up enough information, you might be able to get something better than that. I don't know. You've got to give me something right now, though, before I even begin to consider taking your request outside this room."

"What do you want?" asked Rutherford.

"I believe we already established what I want. If Marvin tells me about Lukas, we might be able to work something out. Who is he?"

"He's more valuable than we're willing to give up without a written guarantee of a deal," said Rutherford. "Try again."

"Palmer. Who is he?"

Marvin looked at his lawyer. Rutherford nodded.

"His name is Alistair Hines," said Marvin. "The FBI should know who he is."

"Why would they know him?" asked Ash.

"Give me a good enough deal, and I'll tell you."

Marvin had caught on quickly. Ash nodded and wrote the name down.

"I'll call Special Agent Havelock and run the name by him. I'll also call Susan Mercer, Marion County's prosecutor, and tell her you're looking for a deal. She and the U.S. attorney will work things out. You should probably keep your lawyer, too. He's not completely full of it."

"Thank you for your endorsement," said Rutherford. "Now if you'll excuse us, I'd like to talk to my client alone."

"Good luck. I bet you guys have a lot to talk about."

23

As soon as Ash got outside, he called Susan Mercer to tell her that Spencer had cooperated and was looking to make a deal. The legal wrangling would get complicated quickly because Spencer had likely committed crimes at both the state and federal level, which meant any deals struck would have to satisfy both the federal and state courts. Susan and the other lawyers would get it done, but Ash felt grateful to stay out of it. He didn't need those kinds of problems.

With that call made, Ash walked to the parking lot in which he had left his cruiser and called Special Agent Havelock.

"What have you got, Sergeant?"

"I might have Palmer's name. Alistair Hines. Is that familiar?"

Havelock paused for a moment. "Not that I can recall. Should I know him?"

"I got the name from Marvin Spencer, the guy Hancock County picked up at the Dandelion Inn. He said the FBI would know the name. What do you think that means?"

"Nothing probably. He's trying to make himself sound important."

"So he's not some famous undercover agent who went rogue? Because that would make this case sound like a cheesy direct-to-video movie."

Havelock made a noise that came somewhere between a chuckle and a deep breath.

"I guarantee he's not a rogue agent. Contrary to what the movies portray, it's very, very rare to see one of our agents go bad. I'll look into it and see what we've got."

"Thank you," said Ash. "Did your teams find anything interesting at that house in Avon?"

"I'm at the office, but they're still working the scene. I got a call earlier that said they found some cots in the basement just like they found at the Dandelion Inn."

"How many girls did these people have?"

Ash said it under his breath, so he didn't know if Havelock heard him or not.

"Traffickers bring fifteen to seventeen thousand people into the United States each year. It's as prevalent as homicide."

Ash swore without realizing it. "We average almost a hundred homicides a year. Is that how many girls we're looking for?"

"Probably not. Some cities get more than their fair share, while medium-sized cities like Indianapolis get a little less. It's everywhere, though."

Ash swallowed. "If you find anything on Hines, let me know."

"Will do."

Havelock hung up. Seventeen thousand people a year, enough bodies to fill a midsized college campus. The things people did to each other made him think sometimes the world would be better if humanity never existed. Eventually, he took out his cell phone and called his wife.

"Hey, hon. I'm on my way home. Can you do me a favor and make sure the doors are locked before I get there?"

* * *

Ash drove home and had evening prayer with his wife and then dinner. Kaden went to bed shortly after they ate, but Megan stayed up for another hour. They played a board game, but Ash's mind kept slipping back to his case. As he sat in the living room with his wife and daughter, seventeen thousand families somewhere in the world were without their daughters, their sons, their mothers, their fathers. He couldn't think about that.

After half an hour of playing, Ash slipped away from the living room and went to the kitchen to make some calls to the other detectives on the team. Neither Detective Doran nor Detective Smith had been able to find a safe deposit box registered to the Elliots or their company. Ash filled them in on what he had found and then used Hannah's aging laptop to write a memo that would go out to the department heads about the investigation. It made him feel useful, and that, in turn, kept him from thinking about what happened to the girls in the Dandelion Inn.

Ash and Hannah tucked Megan into bed shortly afterward, and he went into the backyard. Insects chirped around him, and he could smell a faint whiff of burned charcoal and lighter fluid from a neighbor's barbecue grill. The leaves on nearby trees swayed in a warm, evening breeze. Ash sat on the hammock he had strewn between two cedar posts of the pergola over his patio. Hannah joined him a few minutes later.

"You okay?" she asked.

"It's been a long day."

"Are you thinking about having a drink?"

He hesitated before answering.

"I'd be lying if I said no."

She nodded but didn't say anything for a few minutes.

"We can talk about it if you want."

"How about we talk about your day instead?"

They talked for maybe fifteen more minutes before they both lay back on the hammock and stared at the sky. Neither of them said anything, but for the first time that day, he felt normal. It was nice.

*   *   *

It still felt like the middle of the night when Ash's alarm rang the next morning. He rolled over and found his wife's half of the bed empty. Hannah liked mornings; Ash didn't know how she did it. He kicked off the covers and threw some water on his face in the bathroom before throwing a robe over his pajamas. The sun would rise in another half hour. Ash normally looked forward to Ramadan every year. It helped him focus on his family and his faith, the two things he cherished most in the world. This year had been difficult, though. Every day felt longer than the one previous, and every day came with new burdens for his already overburdened self to carry. Maybe today would be better.

When he walked into the kitchen, Megan immediately scooted her chair from beneath the table and ran toward him with her arms extended. Ash knelt down and caught her in a hug that lifted her from her feet.

"Good morning, honey," he said, smiling.

"Hi, Bob," she said. "*Ummi* said you needed a hug."

"I always need a hug," he said. He kissed her forehead and put her down so she could finish her breakfast. She joined her mother at the breakfast table. Ash mouthed, *Thank you* and then picked up Kaden. The morning went as well as he could have asked for. They had *suhoor* and then dawn prayer, followed by a few minutes watching cartoons in the living room. By the time he left at half after seven, he felt better than he had since starting his case a few days earlier.

When he arrived at work, Ash went to the conference room and immediately started making phone calls. The Tippecanoe County coroner's office had conducted an autopsy of Rebecca Cook late the night before. The gunshot wound killed her, but a deputy coroner found bruises all over her body; residue from tape along her mouth, wrists, and ankles; skin cells from beneath her fingertips; and hairline fractures in her knuckles. An acid phosphatase test for seminal fluid reacted positively on swabs taken from various parts of her body. She had been assaulted, but Rebecca fought with everything she had before dying.

Ash took a couple of breaths and sat back before thanking the coroner for his time and hanging up. When his initial revulsion passed a minute or two later, he called Captain Bowers with the news. Someone would need to talk to Rebecca's family, and since the case kept Ash glued to his phone, Bowers said he'd track down the department's nondenominational chaplain and go over with him that morning before the news hit the papers.

Ash wished him luck before hanging up the phone. He thought they needed it. He tried calling Agent Havelock last to ask about Alistair Hines, the name Marvin Spencer had given him last night, but the phone rang four times before going to voice mail. Ash left a message asking for a return call but didn't expect to receive one anytime soon. If Havelock had become too busy to answer his phone first thing in the morning, he'd probably be too busy for a while.

With the current state of the investigation in mind, Ash needed to start thinking about how to move forward. One course of action stuck out more than any others, though; they still had two parties to the case that, as far as he knew, no one had talked to yet. The man and woman who had been picked up at the trafficker's home in Avon. Ash called Captain Bowers for the second time that morning.

"Mike, you got a number for anybody in the Hendricks County Sheriff's Department?"

"I know the chief deputy. Why?"

"I can't get in touch with Agent Havelock, and I want to find out where they took the man and woman from the house in Avon yesterday."

"Indiana University Hospital. Havelock told me last night. No one's going to be able to talk to them anytime soon, though. The girl is in a coma. They're watching her and hoping she pulls through. The guy is going through withdrawal pretty bad."

"They know what he was on?"

"Heroin. He was a real winner."

"Is he physically able to talk?"

"I guess. From what I hear, he mostly just screams a lot."

"I'm going to visit anyway and see if I can have a conversation with him."

"If you want to waste your time, go right ahead. I won't stop you."

"I appreciate and value your words of encouragement, Mike. I truly do."

Bowers grunted before hanging up. Opiate withdrawal hurt like hell, and it might make someone want to die, but it alone wouldn't kill somebody. Ash thought he could use that. He used his cell phone to find the grocery store nearest the hospital and drove over. He purchased a bag of the darkest brown sugar he could find, cling wrap, rubber bands, and a package of metal spoons. When he got to his car again, Ash broke open the bag of sugar and poured a couple of grams into the cling wrap. He then used the rubber band to close it up. He did that two more times and then laid the bags on his seat to gauge his results. It looked close enough to brown street heroin that it could fool Ash at a glance, and he saw bags of it once or twice a month. It ought to look close enough to the real thing to fool a user hurting for a shot. He also grabbed a spoon from the package he purchased and put it in his pocket.

He slipped his packages inside his jacket and drove to the hospital and felt a sense of déjà vu as he walked through the front doors. About eight months ago, he had driven himself to that hospital in the middle of the night after a car accident. Before he could explain what had happened to him and why he had driven there, a pair of security guards saw him reaching into his jacket and tackled him, thinking he meant to grab the firearm clearly visible against his chest. In fact, he had been reaching for his ID. It hadn't been a fun trip.

He kept his head low as he walked into the lobby, half-expecting to see burly men in blue careen around the security desk and pin him to the ground. That didn't happen, thankfully. Men and women, both hospital staff and not, walked around him without saying a word. Even in the public space where few patients strode, the building smelled like antiseptic. The porcelain tile floors gleamed and the oak receptionist's desk appeared large and imposing in front of him. Ash waited in line and then showed his badge to the first available receptionist. As soon as she saw that, she called the hospital's chief of security, a heavyset older man, who escorted Ash to the small section of the hospital where they held inmates needing medical care.

Neither he nor the security chief said anything until they reached the inmate's private room at the end of a long hallway. Thin carpet muffled sounds around them. The white walls appeared sterile and clean. The prisoner's door had been propped open, and Ash thought he could hear panting from inside.

"I'm going to need to talk to him alone for a few minutes," said Ash. "Is it okay if I close the door?"

"As long as you're in there, I don't see why not," said the security chief. "He's secured to his bed, so he shouldn't be a problem."

"Good. Thank you."

Ash waited for the security chief to walk partway down the hallway before going inside the room. The stark white walls and gray carpet continued inside. A thin man in a hospital gown lay on the bed, a grimace on his face. Brown leather straps on both wrists and ankles immobilized him and kept him from ripping the IV needle out of his arm. Machinery monitored his heart rate. Ash closed the door behind him and partially opened the blinds covering the room's only window, allowing in sunlight. The prisoner recoiled.

"Get out. I'm not talking."

Ash ignored him and picked up the medical history report from the receptacle built into his bed. Francis Hayes. He probably went by Frank. The attending physician had declined to put him on methadone maintenance treatment, one of the standard treatments to help heroin users detox, after learning that Frank had abused it in the past. A nurse noted on his chart that he had marked muscle cramping and diarrhea overnight, so, under the supervision of a physician, she gave him over-the-counter drugs to relieve those symptoms.

Ash put the chart back on the bed and pulled a rolling stool to a stop near the bed.

"You go by Frank or Francis?"

He clenched his teeth. "Fuck you."

"You and your buddies must read from the same script because Marvin Spencer told me the same thing."

"Fuck Spence."

"At least that's new," said Ash, nodding. "How'd you meet that girl we found you with?" Frank clenched his jaw and closed his eyes but didn't answer. "I get the feeling something is bothering you."

"It fucking hurts, man. They won't give me anything."

"That's because you broke into a methadone clinic the last time doctors tried to help you. Don't worry, though, because this time, you'll be in prison. It's much harder to break into their clinic. That should keep you on the straight and narrow."

Frank tried to sit up, but the restraints held him down. "What do you want?"

"I'm here to talk. Where'd you get the girl we found you with?"

"She's my girlfriend."

"No, she's not," said Ash. "Where'd you find her?"

He didn't say anything.

"She's in a coma. If she dies, I'm pretty sure you're not going to like the next needle put in your arm. You talk to me now, we might be able to work something out."

"Leave me alone."

Bubbles of spittle formed at the edges of his mouth. Ash wheeled the stand and table containing Frank's IV bag closer to the bed and reached into his pocket. Frank's eyes opened wide when he saw Ash put one of the packets of sugar on the table. The collapsed veins in Frank's arms stood out bright and red against his skin as he strained to grab the bags.

"What is that, man?"

"I think you know what it is," said Ash. "And it's yours if you talk to me."

Frank coughed violently. "You're lying."

"No lie," said Ash. He reached into his pocket and pulled out a second packet as well as the spoon. "It's yours if you talk to me."

"Where'd you get it?"

Ash scowled. "I'm a cop, moron. Where do you think I got it?"

Frank shook his head and struggled to sit up straighter. "It's not real. You're trying to trick me."

"It's real, and it's right there," said Ash. "We picked up four bricks of this from some kid driving from Los Angeles to Baltimore. Our lab said it was pretty good."

"Give it to me. I need it."

Ash pulled the third bag out of his pocket and started to give it to Frank, but then pulled his hand back and looked at the bag.

"I think you ought to give me something first. Don't you?"

"What do you want?"

"Tell me where you got the girl."

"My boss gave her to me."

"Who's your boss?" Frank started shaking his head. Ash stood, walked to a white cabinet on the far side of the room, and started rummaging through its drawers. He found what he wanted in the third and pulled out a disposable syringe. Frank's breathing increased in tempo. "Is Lukas your boss?"

Frank nodded. "Yeah."

Ash walked to the IV stand and lay the syringe beside the bags of sugar. "What's his last name?"

"Fleischer. It means 'butcher' in German. That's how he introduces himself. Lukas the Butcher. He thinks it makes him sound scary."

"I don't know. Bill the Butcher sounds scary. I'd even say Bart the Butcher sounds scary. Lukas the Butcher doesn't have the same ring to it."

Frank's eyes never left the bags of brown sugar. "You going to give me that stuff now?"

"Nah," said Ash, shaking his head. "We're just starting. I'll tell you what, though. I'm going to go get a lighter for you so you can get started soon."

"Fine, whatever. Just hurry."

Ash said he'd do his best before grabbing the bags of sugar and slipping into the hallway. He called Captain Bowers and told him that they needed to look for someone named Lukas Fleischer. He didn't have a spelling on the name, so they'd have to look at multiple variations. If they were lucky, the Bureau would have something on him. When he went back inside, Frank had resumed shaking. Ash waited beside his bed without saying anything until that passed.

"Thank you for waiting for me. Assuming you're ready, let's get back to my questions."

"Where's the lighter, man?"

Ash furrowed his brow as if he didn't know what Frank meant. Then he tapped his forehead and rolled his eyes.

"I feel like an idiot," said Ash. "I went to the bathroom and totally forgot. Don't worry, though. I'll get it. You said Lukas was your boss. What'd you do for him?"

"I drove a van." Ash waited for him to elaborate on that, but he didn't say anything else.

"I see. You wasted gasoline for him. Did you do that for any special reason?"

"I picked up girls for him and then moved them wherever they needed to go."

Ash nodded and jotted a couple of notes.

"So you actually interacted with him?"

"What the hell does that mean?"

"You saw Lukas. He gave you orders."

He nodded. "Yeah. I used to meet him at a bar."

"A bar in Indianapolis?"

"No, Chicago. It was in Bridgeport, my old neighborhood."

Frank seemed to finally understand that Ash wanted more than just one-word answers.

"Good," said Ash. "What's he look like?"

"What do you care?"

"Just in case I happen to go to a bar in Bridgeport and see him," said Ash. "I'm a nice guy. I like saying hello to people."

"He's got white hair and gray teeth. What else do you want to know?"

"Is he old?"

"I said he's got white hair, didn't I?"

"Fair enough," said Ash. "Where'd you pick up the girls, and where'd you take them?"

Frank kicked his legs against the bed and shook. "Come on, man. I need some stuff."

"All good things come to those who wait," said Ash. "Where did you get the girls, and where did you take them?"

"All over," he said. "I picked them up at O'Hare and either took them to an old house in Englewood, or I'd drive them to that house in Indianapolis."

"You mean the house we found you in?" asked Ash. Frank nodded, his eyes closed tightly. "How many girls would you say you've picked up at the airport?"

"I don't know. I didn't keep track."

"Just guess."

"Fifty or a hundred. They sort of blend together. Haven't I said enough?"

"You've said plenty," said Ash. "Are those the only two places you took girls?"

Frank didn't respond. He coughed hard enough that

Ash considered calling a physician to check him out. According to the monitor beside his bed, his heart rate remained steady, though, so Ash simply let him catch his breath.

"Do you want me to call a nurse? She might give you some water."

"Water isn't what I need."

"I know, and we're almost there. Did you take girls anywhere but those two places?"

He closed his eyes tight. "Some big house out in the sticks east of Indianapolis and a farm near Louisville."

Ash wrote that down. They hadn't found the farm yet. The girls might have been there.

"Where is this farm?"

"It's off Sixty-Four. Just some rinky-dink town."

"Describe it."

Ash managed to coax enough detail out of him that he had a fair idea of the farm's location. He ought to be able to find it.

"When did you last go to this farm?"

"Yesterday morning."

Ash almost stopped breathing. "And you took girls with you?"

Frank nodded. "Seven, but Lukas let me keep one. Somebody else brought in a few others. He gave me some stuff, too, as a thank-you. I gave some to Maya, but I didn't get to take any."

If Ash had to guess, that "stuff" had been designed to kill them both and eliminate witnesses who could identify Lukas in court.

"Maya was the girl you were with, right?" asked Ash.

Frank nodded and gritted his teeth. "How many men work for Lukas?"

"A lot. I don't know."

"Does the name Palmer mean anything to you?" asked Ash. Frank shook his head. "How about Alistair Hines?"

"He and Lukas know each other. He came in to clean up this mess," said Frank. "I never met him. Come on, man. Just give me the stuff now."

"Sure," said Ash, reaching into his pocket. He put the packets on the heart rate monitor. "They're brown sugar. Maybe the nurse can put them in your coffee."

"What are you talking about?"

"I'm not going to give an addict drugs. Are you kidding me? Who do you think I am?"

Frank thrashed against his restraints. The monitor beside his bed started emitting a high-pitched tone, signaling a dangerous rise in his heart rate. Ash took a step back from the bed and grabbed the sugar packets. Two male nurses ran into the room in short order.

"What happened?"

"We were just talking, and he started freaking out. I don't know."

"I'll kill you, fucker," said Frank. "I'll fucking gut you."

One of the nurses injected something into Frank's IV line. Almost instantly, his face and voice slackened, and he stopped fighting. His eyes stayed open, though.

"I hope that was non-narcotic," said Ash.

The nurse with the syringe nodded. "It's just a mild sedative. He'll be fine."

For a mild sedative, it worked remarkably well.

"He's in some pretty intense pain," said Ash. "Is there anything you can give him?"

"We tried giving him a time-release pain capsule, but he chewed it to get high."

Ash normally felt sympathy for drug addicts. They made mistakes, but he knew how powerless addiction could make someone feel. He had a hard time feeling anything at all for a man who admitted trafficking in young girls and accepting one as chattel for a job, though. The world would be a better place without him. If the girl he took—Maya he called her—died, maybe the court system would make that happen. On his way out of the room, Ash made a short prayer that it wouldn't come to that.

24

K iev, Ukraine, 1971. It looked like a party or family re-
union. Well-dressed men and women congregated around
tables on a concrete slab beside a quartet of apartment buildings. Most of the women wore simple, long dresses and scarves
over their heads to keep their hair from becoming disarrayed in
the wind, while the men wore long-sleeved wool shirts and
black or brown slacks. Almost all of them looked at each other
fondly and laughed at each other's jokes and remarks.

The image stood in stark contrast to the propaganda Kostya
had seen on television. The west proclaimed the Soviet Union
a dystopian wasteland where lines to buy bread or other
basic necessities stretched for blocks, where men and women
dressed in dull uniformity, where secret police officers trolled
the streets, looking for dissidents. Soviet propaganda, on the
other hand, depicted the empire as a utopia where people had
ample leisure time, children could play, and everyone had
enough to eat. The reality lay somewhere in between, as it
oftentimes does.

Kostya hadn't been to the Ukraine since being shipped to
a gulag and later joining the Red Army. His military service
hadn't been by choice, but it had worked out for him. His superiors recognized his abilities, allowing him to become a junior

officer. When he left the army a year ago, he left as a captain, a very high rank for someone not formally a member of the Communist Party. He had a wife, a young family. He could have lived out the rest of his life in relative ease. He had little interest in being another cog in the center of a giant bureaucracy, though, and he had even less interest in joining the Party and hoping for something greater. He had promises to keep.

"Are you ready?" asked Kostya, glancing to his left. At nineteen years old, the man beside him, his new brother-in-law, still had several years of military service left. He may not become an officer, but he'd do well for himself and his much older wife, Kostya's sister. He had the temperament of a soldier. Even though Kostya had only known him for two years, he trusted him, something he couldn't say about many people.

"He deserves to be in prison," said Lev.

"He will be," said Kostya. "At least for a few days."

Kostya walked forward. The apartment buildings around them, like the streets and sidewalks, had been constructed of dull, reinforced concrete, causing the otherwise bright day to feel almost gloomy. Children laughed and played somewhere distant, and he could hear the clattering of an old car engine on the street. Kostya straightened the lapels of his suit. He doubted Vladimir would recognize his face, but he'd know what the suit signified. Very few men other than Party leaders could afford a suit like that. Kostya refused to join the Party, but he had found ways to earn a comfortable living despite that. Lev's simple, olive-green uniform would complete the image.

The family gathered around the table stopped speaking as they approached. Kostya looked over his shoulder and found his brother-in-law staring at Vladimir, unblinking. Had those eyes been directed at him, Kostya would have been driven into silence, too.

"I'm truly sorry to interrupt what appears to be a happy family," said Kostya, smiling. Several of the family members closest to him relaxed. Kostya looked at Vladimir. His shoulders no longer had the square, muscular shape Kostya remembered, nor did his eyes hold the same strength. Vladimir looked away, like an animal wishing to avoid a confrontation. "My friend and I would like to briefly abscond Vladimir. He's an old friend."

"How do you know my husband?"

The woman who spoke had broad shoulders and a flat face. She could have lost thirty pounds and still been slightly overweight. Kostya smiled but felt uneasy around her. Growing up on a collectivized farm that sent most of its production hundreds of miles away to Moscow, he had waited in line for hours to buy potatoes, and hours more in a separate line for bread or milk. It was a part of life. Few average Soviet citizens had the chance to become overweight because few had the time to wait in that many lines. He doubted Vladimir's wife had to wait in too many lines. Despite his transgressions and changes in the government, her husband was still an important man. Kostya counted on that.

"Your husband was one of the MGB officers who most influenced my own career choices," said Kostya, reaching into his pocket for an ID card that identified him as a former army captain. He held it up and smiled. "I've told so many stories about Vladimir that my brother-in-law demanded I introduce him."

Vladimir's wife looked at Kostya's ID before sitting straighter and putting her hand on Vladimir's shoulder, urging him to stand. Kostya wondered if she knew about her husband's activities while he had worked for the MGB. Probably not.

CHRIS CULVER

"I'm sure my husband will be most pleased to meet your brother-in-law, Comrade Captain."

Vladimir slowly stood up and looked at his wife. "We'll be back. Stay here."

Kostya held out his arm, gesturing for Vladimir to precede him from the courtyard. The day felt warmer and brighter out of the shade cast by the buildings. Trees along the streets swayed in the breeze, but Kostya paid them little mind, instead focusing on the man in front of him, the man who had assaulted his aunt and allowed others to do the same to his sister. For many years he had plotted to shoot him in the back when no one could see, but he realized now that wouldn't do. Eight years in the GRU, the main intelligence directorate of the general staff, had taught him the virtue of patience when punishing others.

"I remember you," said Vladimir. "You're Myra's nephew."

"I'm glad to have made an impression," said Kostya, looking around. Residents of the nearby apartments had planted flowers in wooden boxes hung on balconies and windows, granting a bit of bright color to an otherwise dull building.

"How is your aunt Myra?"

"Dead," said Kostya. "Breast cancer."

"I'm very sorry."

"No, you're not," said Kostya. "You used her like she was a toilet and then discarded her when you were done."

"I did no such thing. Our relationship was complicated. You were a boy. You didn't understand."

"I wasn't as young as you think."

"Perhaps not," said Vladimir, staring straight ahead. "I presume you came to my home for a reason."

"This isn't your home. This is your sister's apartment. It's

318

her birthday. You have a much larger apartment several miles away."

Vladimir stopped walking and looked at Kostya and then Lev as if for the first time.

"What do you two want?"

"An apology."

Vladimir squared his shoulders to Kostya and straightened. "I'm not a man to trifle with, boy."

"Neither am I," said Kostya. "You sent me to the same gulag you sent my uncle Piotr. That was a mistake."

"I did my job. That's all."

"You worked for a tyrant and had my uncle executed so you could fuck my aunt without worry."

Vladimir turned and headed back toward his sister's apartment.

"Never come back here again," he said. "I still have some sway with my former colleagues. They will arrest you."

"If you do, you'll find that your former colleagues don't have the power they once did. My colleagues, on the other hand, are at your house right now."

Vladimir stopped and looked over his shoulder. "Don't lie to me."

"I'm not. Go home and find out on your own."

He looked at Kostya from his feet to his forehead.

"Are you trying to scare me? It's not working. Let the past stay in the past and leave me be."

Kostya shook his head. "You could order me around when I was a child, but not anymore. Right now, you have KGB officers in your house, men I know. They will find stolen letters to Party leaders, diplomatic cables, maps showing troop deployments, documents discussing troop levels, tactics, and morale.

They'll even find an English-language typewriter. I used every favor I accrued in my years of service to acquire them."

"You'll have to do better than make up stories to intimidate me. Leave."

Vladimir turned toward the apartment again and started walking. Kostya grabbed his arm by his shirtsleeve and pulled hard. Vladimir cocked his arm back to hit him, but Lev caught the old man's arm and pinned it behind his back before he could.

"You will go to prison for this," Vladimir snarled at them. "Army careers or not. I'm a member of the Party. You can't touch me."

Kostya shook his head. "As soon as you go home, you'll be arrested. After that, you will be taken to Lubyanka Square in Moscow where you will be questioned and tortured. When you pass out from the pain, they will inject you with adrenaline so they can start over again. That's all that will happen."

Vladimir squirmed in Lev's grip and sneered. "If you're confident of these things, why tell me?"

"Because I can. When they strip you naked and tear out your fingernails, know that I ordered the evidence against you to be placed in your apartment. When they burn you with cigarettes, know that I'm watching. And when they force your face into a pile of your own filth at the end of your miserable life, know that it will be my sister's husband who pulls the trigger. You did this to yourself, and you made me who I am, Comrade Orlesky. I will never forgive you for that."

* * *

Chicago felt ten degrees cooler than Indianapolis, but that didn't make it comfortable. The wind whipped through the row houses and buildings around him, carrying the scent of cinnamon and clove from a nearby bakery. When Kostya first came to the United States, the Ukrainian Village had been a neighborhood for Eastern Europeans wanting to maintain a common identity and culture, but as time progressed, many of those immigrants assimilated into the greater American culture and left the area. Now the neighborhood had more yuppies in restored Victorian row houses than Ukrainians and more sushi restaurants than Orthodox churches. Some people called that progress; Kostya had his doubts.

"Vitali still lives here?" asked Lev, looking toward the window in front of a Southwestern restaurant. Kostya and Lev had parked on the street in the center of a dense commercial district. Unlike the Loop or other major business centers in the city, few of the buildings in the Ukrainian Village reached over four stories. Kostya looked around him. From his vantage point, he could see Vitali's bakery, several restaurants, and an art gallery on street level. Cars jammed the roads and pedestrians crowded the sidewalk. The noon sun stood high overhead. Lunch break.

"I haven't talked to him in several years, but hopefully."

"I hope he's as smart as you remember."

"Me too."

Kostya had met Vitali Kozlov almost forty years ago in Tel Aviv, Israel. They had both been young men then, both eager and hungry to put their mark on the world outside Soviet borders. In Vitali's case, his sojourn abroad hadn't been entirely by choice. He grew up in a Soviet orphanage and was sent to a gulag for hooliganism at eighteen. At twenty, his Soviet jailers, in a cost-saving measure, handed him a passport that labeled him Jewish and sent him to Israel. Eventually, he immigrated to the United States and settled in Chicago. When Vitali became an information broker, Kostya didn't know or care as long as he could use him.

Kostya walked to Vitali's bakery and pulled open a heavy glass door. The scent of cinnamon became stronger, as did smells of yeast and sourdough. Baked sweet goods filled display windows and racks behind the counter displayed loaves of bread. Several people waited in line for service, but Kostya ignored them and flagged down a young female cashier with dyed blond hair and brown roots, drawing annoyed glances from some of the other patrons.

"I'm looking for Vitali Kozlov. Is he in?"

The cashier looked at Kostya for a moment, but then quickly looked away. "Let me get my manager."

The cashier wiped her hands on her apron and then left the register, drawing still more annoyed glances. Kostya took a breath and leaned against the counter, ignoring those around him. When the cashier came back, a man who could have been her older brother stood beside her. He had brown hair with just a hint of red, a pinched face, and a few freckles on his cheeks. The cashier went back to ringing up customers, but the manager leaned forward and lowered his voice.

"Do you have an appointment with Mr. Kozlov?"

Kostya shook his head. "He's an old friend," he said, turning to Lev. The big man produced a bottle from behind his back and handed it to Kostya. "Tell him I've brought his favorite scotch."

Kostya handed the bottle to the manager and eyed him as he walked off.

"That's an odd way to treat your friends," said Lev. "You might as well have pissed in a bottle."

The flicker of a smile sprang to Kostya's lips, but it disappeared before anyone but Lev could see it.

"Vitali will know what it means."

"I hope so."

They waited for about five minutes before the manager returned. Behind him stood a man with thin lips, glasses, and shoulders stooped with age. He smiled broadly when he saw Kostya and held up the bottle.

"The last time I drank this, I was sitting in a bar in Brighton Beach and my girlfriend had just left me for a football player."

"You met your wife that night."

"I did," he said, chuckling and looking at the label. "She bought me a drink and warned me that not even homeless people would drink this excrement. Where'd you find it?"

"I had to call around."

"Come back to my office," said Vitali, gesturing for Lev and Kostya to step behind the counter. The customers remaining in the shop parted for them as they walked past the display counters and to the rear of the bakery. Flour dusted the countertops and floor, while loaves of bread and sweets cooled on racks beneath an exhaust fan. Men and women in white smocks and hairnets hustled from one counter to the other, carrying racks of unbaked bread, sacks of flower, or containers of yeast.

"Aside from hand mixers, we try not to use much machinery anymore," said Vitali as they passed two men kneading bread. "Our customers like to know that our goods are handmade. We charge more for them that way.

You should tell Michael out front to give you some poppy seed rolls on your way out. We made them special this morning for a wedding reception, but nobody picked them up."

"We will," said Kostya, watching the men and women around him work. Vitali had a thriving business, and no one stood idle. Kostya wondered if the men and women who worked there knew their boss's primary profession. "Can we talk in private?"

"Of course," said Vitali, gesturing toward a white door with a brass OFFICE sign screwed into the wood. Vitali opened the door with a key and stepped in first, gesturing for the two men to follow. The interior felt cramped, but cozy. It had room for a desk, two chairs, and a bookshelf containing cookbooks in various languages. Vitali sat first and put the bottle of scotch on the desk. "It's been a long time, Kostya. I didn't know that I'd see you again."

"It's been too long," said Kostya. "Unfortunately, I have little time to reminisce. I'm here because I need help, and you are the only person I know who can give it. A man murdered my daughter and her husband."

Vitali blinked and leaned back.

"In Chicago?"

"In Indianapolis," said Kostya. "I have reason to believe the man who ordered her murder lives here."

"I'm sorry for your loss. Do you have a name?"

"Just a first name. Lukas. He traffics young women."

Vitali ran a hand across his chin and sighed audibly. "And how did your daughter know him?"

"Does it matter?" asked Kostya, raising his eyebrows.

"To me it does," said Vitali. "If you said your daughter was missing, I'd help you without question. I haven't seen you for fifteen years, though, and suddenly you drop into my office looking for a very dangerous man. I want to know how you became involved with him. I don't work with those who peddle the lives of others."

"He murdered my daughter and her husband because my son-in-law took a girl from him in order to send her home. My family has nothing to do with his business besides having a desire to dismantle it."

Vitali nodded, his eyes absent. "You're sure the name was Lukas?"

"Positive."

Vitali's Adam's apple moved as he swallowed, considering the request. "He calls himself the Butcher and thinks he's more important than he is. He pays off the right people, though, so he's allowed to operate with little interference from law enforcement or others."

"Do you know where he lives?"

Vitali shook his head. "No, but I might be able to find out."

"Please do. Cost is no concern," said Kostya. "And please be discreet. I want him alive and well so I can greet him properly."

25

A sh left the hospital and immediately drove to the police department. If Frank had delivered girls to the farm near Louisville yesterday, they needed to find them fast before Lukas's men moved them again. Before he could do that, though, he needed to nail down the farm's location. He commandeered an empty desk in the homicide squad and pushed aside a pair of empty diet soda cans before opening a Web browser on the computer and navigating to Google Maps.

Frank described Cecil, Indiana, the town he drove the girls to, as a rinky-dink town off I-64 near Louisville, Kentucky. Ash zoomed the satellite image as far as it would go so he could see the different buildings and streets. According to the town's Wikipedia page, Cecil had just over a hundred residents and had been founded in the late nineteenth century by a farmer named Dublin Cecil. Ash didn't generally consider Wikipedia to be a reliable source—the world had better fact-checkers than high school kids with computers—but nothing he saw on the map or in pictures conflicted with the information. A town that small almost certainly didn't have its own police force, making it quite a good place to hide out.

Ash switched the map to a street view. In addition to its database of satellite imagery, Google had sent cars with panoramic cameras attached to their roofs throughout the country. Those cameras had created a database of still images that allowed a computer user to see the countryside as if he had driven through it himself and taken pictures. Frank navigated via landmarks rather than street names, so the directions he had given Ash consisted of vague directional indications and descriptions of various buildings. Even that didn't make things very difficult, though; the town only had three streets.

Ash guided the map past the town's only gas station and a small community bank before coming to Cecil's only four-way stop. He hung a left as Frank said and then he took the third right past a white, clapboard bungalow proudly hanging a pair of confederate flags out front. Had Ash actually seen that in person, he probably would have started whistling "Dueling Banjos."

Frank's instructions became even more vague at that point. He hadn't known the address of the farm, but he said it lay just past a large curve in the road and overlooked a creek. Ash followed the map for perhaps a mile up the road and found two locations that could have matched that description. One looked like a simple house with a red barn in the yard. It fit the description Frank had given him well. The other spot looked similar from the road. Ash could see the gray asphalt roof of the farmhouse through the trees and a white barn to its left. He couldn't say with any certainty if Frank had been talking about either one, which meant he couldn't get a warrant based on that information alone. They needed to find something else.

Ash logged out of the computer and called Captain Bowers on his cell phone.

"Mike. I've got a possible location on Alistair Hines and the girls taken from the hospital last night."

"Where?"

"Southern Indiana," said Ash. "A little town about ten miles north of the Ohio River."

Bowers took a breath. "How sure are you about this?"

"I can't say. The guy I picked up from the house in Avon told me he drove the girls there yesterday."

"It's out of our jurisdiction. We'll have to bring in the state police and the Bureau on this. He tell you anything else?"

"Nothing pertinent."

Bowers paused for another second. "Okay. We'll follow up. On its own, I doubt the word of a convict will be enough for a warrant. We might be able to convince a judge to sign one anyway if we tell him about the girls, though."

Ash coughed, clearing his throat. "Even if I was certain about this place, I may have stretched some rules getting the location. It's not going to hold up in court."

Bowers muttered something inaudible. "You didn't do anything to your suspect that's going to get the department sued, did you?"

"I dangled some novel motivation in his face to get him to speak. Nothing illegal, I just don't think a judge would appreciate it."

Bowers seemed to consider for a moment before speaking. "Havelock called me about half an hour ago to set up a meeting," he said. "We'll tell him about the house and see how he wants to handle it. Maybe he can claim Hines is a domestic terrorist or something and get a warrant based on that."

"You really think that'll fly?"

"No, but we don't have a lot of options."

Unfortunately, Ash couldn't come up with a better idea. "When's Havelock want to meet?"

"In about twenty minutes, so get your stuff together and meet me out front. I'll drive."

"See you in a few."

Ash hung up the phone. He didn't have anything to get together, so he went by the bathroom and threw some water on his face to wake himself up. He also got a drink, breaking the fast early. With everything else going on, he had enough to worry about and didn't need to add dehydration to the list. Ash met Bowers's Honda Accord in front of the building about two minutes later, and they sped off.

The FBI had a new, state-of-the-art emergency operations center in Castleton on the city's northeast side. Ash had only been to the facility at its dedication about a year ago, but he had left feeling impressed by the federal government's ability to spend money on frivolous things. Marble floors in the entryway and expansive, manicured lawns may not have reduced the crime rate or decreased terrorism, but they sure looked nice. Of course, after spending forty million dollars, the government better get something that looked nice.

Bowers took the interstate for most of the trip and got off about a mile from their destination. The FBI field office had been built in a large section of an ever-expanding office park. A tall, black fence surrounded the complex, clearly separating it from the surrounding buildings. Bowers hung a right on a nondescript road and stopped at a brick guardhouse with smoked glass windows. Thick, steel pedestals protruded four feet or so from the roadway, blocking the entrance and guaranteeing that not even a Humvee could pass without the guard's say.

"We're here to see Kevin Havelock," said Bowers, thrusting his badge out the window. The guard, a fit, middle-aged man in a navy blue uniform, nodded and then went back into his guardhouse, but he didn't retract the pedestals.

After about five minutes, Ash crossed his arms. "Think he's forgotten we're here?"

"Doubtful," said Bowers, drumming his fingers on the steering wheel. "Last time I was here, the guard just waved me through. This is planned."

"And were you informed of this plan?"

"No," said Bowers, waving him off as the guard emerged from his house. He pointed up the road from which they had just turned.

"Agent Havelock is getting a cup of coffee at Hardee's right now," said the guard. "He asked me to tell you guys to meet him there."

Bowers stared at the guard for a moment. "Hardee's?" he asked.

"Yes, sir. You passed it on your way in."

Bowers paused for a moment. "Can you open the gate so I can turn around in your lot?"

"No, sir. Please back up. If you'd like, I can direct you."

Ash started to say something about Havelock's professionalism, but Bowers held up a hand, shushing him.

"No need for your help," said Bowers. "Do I need to sign anything to say I was here?"

The guard shook his head. "No, sir."

"That's what I thought," said Bowers. He closed his window and slipped his car into reverse.

"Well, that was a waste of time," said Ash.

Bowers shook his head. "If we went in, we'd have to sign in as guests. Havelock doesn't want our visit on the record."

"Why wouldn't he want to meet us on the record?"

"You'll have to ask him."

"At Hardee's."

"Yeah, at Hardee's."

Ash paused for a moment. "Does Hardee's even have coffee?"

"Does it matter?"

Ash shrugged. "I'm just saying. It seems like there are better places to go for coffee. If I wanted a two-pound cheeseburger with enough bacon on it to give a horse a coronary, sure I'd go to Hardee's. Coffee, though? I think I'd probably go elsewhere."

Bowers reversed the vehicle until arriving at the main road outside the FBI's complex.

"Are you done?" he asked.

"I think so."

They drove the rest of the way to the restaurant in silence. Unlike the FBI's building, Hardee's sat at the intersection of two major roads, both of which had cars backed up from one stoplight to the next, oftentimes blocking the intersections. Horns honked intermittently, and the stink of exhaust hung heavily in the air. Bowers parked on the edge of the restaurant's lot beside a black Chevy Suburban with dark tinted windows. As soon as their car pulled to a stop, Havelock stepped out of the SUV and motioned for Ash to roll down his window.

"Sorry about all the cloak-and-dagger," said Havelock. "We needed to talk off campus."

"Somehow, I get the feeling you say that often," said Ash. "Admit it. You use that line to pick up women."

He glanced at Ash. "I'm happily married, Detective," he said. "More to the point, I've got news on Alistair Hines and Lukas Fleischer."

"And for some reason, you couldn't share this in your office?" asked Bowers.

"Correct," said Havelock. He turned toward his car and grabbed a manila envelope before nodding toward a pair of empty tables outside the restaurant. "Let's have a seat."

Ash reluctantly opened his door and stepped out of the vehicle. Cracks striated the asphalt parking lot, and the sound of car engines, horns, and the occasional stereo reverberated against the nearby building. Before sitting down at the plastic outdoor table in front of the restaurant, Ash brushed grass off the seat so it wouldn't stain his pants. Havelock did likewise.

"What have you got?" asked Bowers.

"We'll start with Fleischer," said Havelock, opening his folder. He handed Ash and Bowers two photocopied rap sheets, most of the information on which had been written in French. Havelock or someone else at the Bureau had stamped INTERPOL—CONFIDENTIAL at the top of each page. The mug shot in the upper right corner drew Ash's eyes. Fleischer was probably in his fifties and had hair like steel wool and a nose that screamed for attention. No facial hair, but Ash could see a tattoo on his neck.

"Do you have an English translation?" he asked.

"Afraid not," said Havelock. "And I'm going to need these back, so don't get too attached to them."

"Can you give us the gist?" asked Bowers, dropping his copy on the table. Havelock tapped Fleischer's picture on Bowers's now discarded paper.

"Lukas Heinrich Fleischer. Born in Berlin, 1958. His father was a physician, his mother a seamstress. Normal childhood for the area, joined the National People's Army at seventeen and served five years as a logistics officer. Interpol had little information about his military service, leading them to believe he had an unimpressive career. Postmilitary service, things get a little murky. He disappeared for a while, and to this day no one knows where he went. He showed up again in 1982 selling Soviet arms to two different groups fighting in Lebanon's civil war."

"How'd he end up in the U.S.?" asked Ash.

"He kept friendly ties with a number of influential people. After the Berlin Wall fell in late eighty-nine, his friends helped him immigrate."

Ash nodded. "And I assume he didn't mention he was an arms dealer on his visa application."

Havelock didn't even crack a smile. "Without having seen his application, I'd say that's a fair guess."

"Let's fast-forward some," said Bowers. "How'd he go from arms dealer in Lebanon to trafficker in Indiana?"

Havelock took a deep breath. "Interpol thinks he had supply problems. He lacked the personal connections to arms manufacturers or military quartermasters that would have allowed him to become a major player, so when he couldn't supply what his clients needed, they went elsewhere. Trafficking young women across a border isn't that much different than smuggling illegal weapons. He went where he could make money."

"Word on the street is that people call him the Butcher," said Ash. "I assume he's never smuggled bacon."

Havelock furrowed his brow.

"I...I don't think so. We don't have anything on nicknames," said Havelock. "Who told you that?"

"A friend of a friend. You know how that is."

Havelock opened his mouth to say something, but Bowers interrupted him.

"What sort of assets does he have? Tactical and political, I mean."

"Limited. This isn't a James Bond film."

Bowers smiled but allowed little humor into his face. "If we pick him up, will a politician in Washington call your boss and tell you to let him go? That's what I want to know."

Havelock hesitated for a moment. "We consider him a relatively minor player, but he does have connections. There's a fair chance that the Department of Justice will want to deal with him." Bowers and Ash both started to protest, but Havelock spoke over them. "He will see the interior of a prison. You have my guarantee."

Ash crossed his arms. "That fills me with confidence."

"Like it or not, that's how things are done in the real world, Detective," said Havelock. "Sometimes you've got to give a little to get a lot."

"I'm not so sure the girls he kidnapped and brought to brothels in the U.S. would appreciate that."

Havelock narrowed his eyes, forcing them to become as

sharp as serpent's teeth. "You want to put Fleischer in the ground. I get that. He deserves it. In a perfect world, I'd loan you a shovel. In our world, though, he'll get a deal so we can prevent more people from being hurt. I don't like it any more than you do, so can you please tone down your self-righteousness, Detective?"

"This isn't self-righteousness. It's common sense," said Ash. "You let someone like Fleischer go, you're just going to arrest him in another five years for committing the same offense. The whole cycle repeats. You want a better world, grow a pair and put him in jail for the rest of his life."

Havelock crossed his arms. "And what would you do about his accomplices? Let them go? We make deals so we can build cases."

"If you were better at your job, that wouldn't be a problem."

Havelock took a deep breath and started to say something, but Bowers coughed loudly, interrupting him.

"I didn't come here to hear you two bicker," he said. "Truce, all right? You two can throw down later if you want, but right now, let's focus on the job." He looked at Havelock and then at Ash. Both men nodded, and Bowers returned his attention to Havelock. "Do you know where Fleischer lives?"

Havelock took another couple of breaths before looking at Bowers. "He's got an apartment in Miami and a house in Chicago. I put both under surveillance, but we haven't seen him yet."

"So you'll pick him up when you can," said Bowers. Havelock nodded. "How about Alistair Hines?"

Havelock laced his fingers together over his folder and

leaned forward. "We need to talk about Hines. He could be a problem for us."

"What kind of problem?" asked Bowers, crossing his arms.

"The kind I might need to bring Washington in on."

"Who is he?" asked Bowers.

"First of all, I should note that Marvin Spencer didn't lie to you," said Havelock, producing two images from the folder. "Hines *is* involved with the case."

The FBI agent slid the images toward Ash and Bowers. The first image depicted a young man with a thin, angular face and brown hair. He stared straight at the camera, nary a smile on his lips. He wore a beige beret with an eagle crossed by a sword. Clearly, Hines was a military man, or had been at one point. The second photo showed the same man but older. His brown hair had streaks of gray, and the angles on his face had rounded somewhat with age. In the second photo, he wore a suit and tie. Ash recognized the hallway the picture had been taken from immediately, having walked in it to talk to Amina.

"Who is he?" asked Ash.

"Alistair Hines is his real name," said Havelock. "Born in the East Midlands, just outside of Leicester, England, in seventy-one. Joined the British Army at nineteen and then became a Special Air Service operator at twenty-three. He left the military at thirty-two with a wife and two daughters. A drunk driver killed the wife and daughters in 2004, after which Hines joined an American private security company with contracts in Iraq. While there, his unit came under fire from insurgents hiding under cover near a mosque. His unit returned fire, killing the gunmen as well as eight civilians. As the unit commander, his company blamed him for the incident and fired him. He went freelance after that."

Ash looked up from the pictures. "You've got better information on Hines than Fleischer."

Havelock nodded. "The records are better kept."

"He doesn't sound like a murderer, much less a rapist," said Bowers.

"People change," said Havelock.

"How'd he get mixed up with Fleischer?" asked Ash.

"I presume the same way he gets other clients. He has a reputation to live up to."

"And what is that reputation?" asked Bowers.

"He finds people and brings them home."

"In this case, he murdered at least three people," said Ash. "I'd say he's failing to live up to his reputation."

Havelock shook his head. "I think he's living up to it well. Think back to the Elliots' Mercedes. We found blood and gunshot residue on the backseat. Our lab has since matched that blood to a sample provided to us by the British Army. I think Fleischer hired Hines to bring him Kara and Daniel. While doing that, Daniel Elliot shot Hines, and in response, Hines shot them both."

Ash had thought something similar earlier, but didn't say anything.

"So in your scenario, Hines abducted Rebecca because he needed a driver?" asked Bowers.

"And because she identified herself as a nurse. He was shot and needed help. Lafayette detectives found surgical equipment, sponges, and bandages at the barn up north. I think Rebecca sewed him up and administered an antibiotic called cephalexin. A vet's office up there reported a break-in and theft of medicine, so they might have gotten it there. Fleischer's men could have assaulted Rebecca while he recovered. Hines may or may not be involved with that. I think she was just in the wrong place at the wrong time."

"Then what's he doing now?" asked Ash.

Havelock shrugged. "I don't know."

"What's his connection to the Bureau?" asked Bowers.

"That's where things get tricky. After Detective Rashid mentioned Alistair Hines, I looked him up in every database I have access to. Couldn't find a thing." He looked at Ash. "I wanted you off my back, so I called a colleague in D.C. He filled me in on the details."

"Why didn't you have access to it?" asked Bowers.

"Because it's an executive-level, read-only file on a mainframe computer in Quantico, Virginia. You've got to be a deputy director or above to see it."

"Any particular reason for that?" asked Ash.

"Because we've hired him."

Bowers swore under his breath and looked away, but Ash continued staring.

"You lied to me," said Ash. "You said he's not an agent."

"And he's not," said Havelock. "We hired him as a consultant in Algeria."

"Why?" asked Bowers.

"In 2008, two local staffers at the U.S. mission in Algiers got into a fight, and one of them ended up stabbing and killing the other. Wasn't a tough case; they were fighting about a girl. We sent two agents to consult with the Diplomatic Security Service and local authorities. They watched some interviews and closed the case. No big deal. On their last night, our agents went out with two embassy staffers and got separated. A couple of hours later, when our agents didn't show up at the embassy, DSS tried to track them down. No go, though. The local police weren't helpful, so we reached out to other governments and asked for assistance. The French have significant intelligence assets in the region and suggested we hire help. They gave us Hines. He got our people back, and we didn't ask questions."

The story might have made a fine spy novel, but it didn't explain why the Bureau buried it. Ash squinted.

"How'd you pay Hines?"

Havelock hesitated, but then swallowed and licked his lips. "We made him a deal. Since he was a private contractor with the U.S. government, the Department of Justice could have prosecuted him in federal court for the shootings in Iraq. We agreed not to if he found our people."

Ash nodded. "I can see why you're so enthusiastic about making deals with criminals. Sounds like they work out well for everybody."

If Havelock's eyes had been daggers, Ash would have been dead before he finished speaking. "I had nothing to do with Alistair Hines or any deals made with him, and I'd appreciate it if you could keep that in mind. I think you also see why we have to act delicately. I've risked my job even telling you this. The Bureau is interested in finding him quickly and quietly before things get out of hand. We will provide whatever tactical and support units are required to end this as soon as we find him."

"Hines has put three bodies in the morgue already," said Ash. "Things are already out of hand."

"And if we don't find him soon, it will be worse."

Ash wanted to remind him that Hines wouldn't be free to kill anyone had the Department of Justice not made a deal with him earlier, but Bowers cleared his throat before he could.

"Thank you for the meeting. As far as I'm concerned, Hines is yours. If we find anything on him, you'll be my first call."

Havelock took his gaze from Ash, his face and posture softening. He nodded toward Bowers. "Thank you, Captain." He looked at Ash. "It's good to have a partner who understands the complexity of what we do." Ash bit his tongue to avoid saying anything further. Havelock gathered his papers. "I will keep your department in the loop as much as possible. This will be your bust as much as it will be ours."

"I'd appreciate that," said Bowers. Havelock nodded at both men before tucking his folder under his arm and heading back to his SUV. Ash waited until his car left the parking lot to speak.

"You didn't tell him that we had a lead on Hines."

"I noticed you didn't, either," said Bowers.

Ash nodded and watched as the FBI agent's SUV barreled up the road toward the field office. "I'm not interested in making a deal with this guy. I want Hines in prison until he drops dead."

Bowers nodded. "Then we've got some work to do."

26

When they got back in Bowers's car, neither man spoke for about half the drive. Eventually, Ash couldn't hold the question in anymore.

"Why didn't you tell Havelock about the farm?"

Bowers pulled their car to a stop as a traffic light shifted to red. They were on Fall Creek Parkway with the eponymous waterway behind a tree line to their left and a historic residential neighborhood to their right. Cars queued from one stoplight to the next.

"I trust him, if that's what you're asking," said Bowers. "I can't say that for his superiors, though, especially during an election year. If they're afraid of being subpoenaed by Congress for what they did with Hines, they're going to be more interested in covering their asses than building a case. I'd rather not let a bunch of political appointees screw this up."

Ash nodded. "What do you want to do?"

"We'll work with the state police and take him on our own. With Indiana's human trafficking laws, Hines and his crew will get thirty years each per victim."

That sounded about right. After Indianapolis won the bid to host the 2012 Super Bowl, the state legislature, in a rare fit of common sense, realized that the deluge of visitors would bring with them a darker side, including drugs and sex workers. In the four years between the announcement and the event, Indiana passed some of the harshest penalties in the country for human trafficking, making the punishment for the sexual trafficking of a minor equivalent to murder.

"We're going to need a warrant. How do you plan to get that?"

Bowers glanced at him and then returned his attention to the road as the light turned green.

"You went to law school, so you're going to have to figure it out. There's got to be something we can use."

Ash thought for a moment, and then shook his head. "We can't get a warrant with what we've got. If we creep by the house, we might find exigent circumstances that would allow a warrantless search."

"Not going to happen, cowboy. If we go down there, we need to go down in force. Hines is too dangerous. He's put enough bodies in the ground. Find me something."

Ash sighed. "I'll see what I can do."

"You take care of that, and I'll take care of tactical arrangements with the state police."

"Sounds fine."

Bowers finished the drive to their station without saying another word. As soon as he got back to the homicide unit's floor, Ash sat at the same desk he had commandeered earlier and allowed gravity and the floor's slight lean to spin his chair. Maybe he could tie one of the farms to Kara and Daniel Elliot or the Dandelion Inn somehow. If he could do that, he might be able to convince a judge that law enforcement had cause to search it for evidence of crimes committed elsewhere. It was a stretch, but they would have to rely on stretches.

He logged into his computer and then opened a Web browser. Every county in the state had property taxes, and a lot of them now had property tax information available online. Ash doubted either farm had been registered to Evil, Inc., but he might get lucky. He logged on to the Hancock County assessors website and found a link with real estate property tax information for Cecil, Indiana. The first farm he found belonged to Doug and Loretta Brown, and from what Ash could tell, it had been in their family for as long as records were available. Ash wrote the names down before moving on.

The second home belonged to a company called Equine Express Farms, LLC, and they owed the local county just under twelve grand in back property taxes. That information wouldn't help him get a warrant, but it did indicate that its owners might have been desperate for money. Ash pushed his chair back from the desk and rubbed sleep out of his eyes before looking up the non-emergency number of the Hancock County Sheriff's Department. The phone rang four times before a woman with a slight Southern drawl picked up.

"Hi, this is Detective Sergeant Ash Rashid with the Indianapolis Metropolitan Police Department. Can you put me in touch with the shift supervisor tonight?"

"Sure thing. I'll get Jerry."

Ash thought the dispatcher would actually put him on hold. Instead, it sounded as if she put the phone down and shouted until a new voice came on the phone. Very high-tech system they had down there in Hancock County.

"Yeah, this is Jerry Friedlander. I'm the deputy sheriff. Tanya says you need to talk to somebody, so what can I do for you?"

"I've heard a rumor that a murder suspect I'm looking for is in your area, and I wanted to ask you about two locations."

"Shoot." Ash shuffled through his notes until he found the address of the first farmhouse he had looked up. Jerry clucked his tongue for a few minutes. "I've known Doug and Loretta for going on fifty years, and they're good folk. Wouldn't hurt nobody."

"And I'm assuming neither of them has a record," said Ash.

"You're assuming right," said Jerry. "Cecil is a small town, so I know who the troublemakers are. Doug and Loretta ain't them."

Ash jotted a note down. "Good. That's what I wanted to hear," he said. He asked about his second address, and Jerry remained quiet for a moment.

"That one I could see being a problem. We've had some calls about strange smells coming from that place. I walked around with the owner one day, but I couldn't find anything. Wouldn't let me in the barn, though. I suspect they might be cooking something, but I can't prove that."

Ash nodded to himself. Hancock County had one of the lowest population densities of any county in the state, so meth cookers probably did find the area attractive.

"If I can get a warrant, I think I'll be visiting them tonight with some state troopers. I'll keep your department informed," he said. "You think Doug and Loretta would talk to me if I called?"

"I bet they would. Just tell them I gave you their number." Jerry rattled off a phone number, which Ash wrote down. "If you get a warrant up there in Indianapolis, are you sure that's going to work down here?"

"Yeah, as long as we stay in Indiana."

"Huh," said Jerry. "We don't do too many search warrants down here, so I didn't know that. Well, I guess you need anything else, you just let me know."

"Will do. Thank you," said Ash. He hung up the phone and then called the number Jerry had given him. The phone rang several times before a woman's scratchy voice answered and said hello.

"Evening. This is Detective Ash Rashid with the Indianapolis Metropolitan Police Department. Jerry Friedlander from the sheriff's department gave me your number. Do you have a minute to talk?"

She gasped. "Is it Jennifer? Is she okay?"

"I'm sure she is, ma'am," said Ash. "Nothing's wrong. I'm calling to ask some questions about one of your neighbors."

The woman, presumably Loretta, paused.

"Oh. I'll get my husband."

Ash started to tell her that he'd rather talk to them both individually, but she put down the phone with an audible clank. The man who got on the phone next had a soft, low voice that could have belonged to a lounge singer.

"This is Doug Brown."

Ash introduced himself again and explained why he had called. Doug seemed a little more comfortable on the phone than his wife and answered questions readily. He and Loretta had lived on their farm for nearly twenty years, having inherited it from her father. He worked as the plant engineer at a nearby factory, while Loretta had retired from the local school system a year earlier. To hear Doug tell it, he knew the personal history of everyone and every place in town. Ash got the feeling that he liked talking a lot.

"I'm calling about a farm up the street from you owned by a company called Equine Express Farms. You know it?"

"I used to pass it every day going to work. Used to be a nice place. Sixty years ago, I had a paternal uncle who used to work as a farmhand for the family that owned it. Their grandkids sold the place a couple of years back. Don't know what happened to them since."

Ash wanted to tell him to focus on the present, but he didn't think that would help the conversation much.

"You said it used to be a nice place. So it's not anymore?"

"Well, everything around here used to be nice. I mean this is pretty country. We've got trees that are older than the state of Indiana, we got streams, we got hills. You should see this place when the leaves change color. Tourists pack the roads so thick you need a bicycle to get around."

"I'm sure it's very pretty. Can you tell me about the farm?"

He sighed. "There ain't much to tell, tell you the truth. Used to be owned by a family named McIntosh, like the apple. Nice folk. Took my paternal uncle in when he got out of the army after Korea."

Ash rubbed his eyes. "Why is the farm not nice *today*?"

"Well, the owners, of course," said Doug, sounding perturbed. "They shot my dog with a BB gun. Had to have surgery to get it removed."

"Is that the only reason why you think it's not a nice place?"

"Hell, no," he said. "They're weird. They shot my dog, too."

Ash had to force himself to avoid sighing. It sounded like Doug had issues with his memory. Ash might be able to get some information out of him, but no one could use him on a warrant application.

"Why are they weird?"

"They just are. I don't know. I went over there to set them straight about my dog. 'Fore I get there, some guy comes out to the road with a hunting rifle over his shoulder and stops me. First of all, his face doesn't even look like it's seen a washcloth in years. Second, what's he doing trying to scare me away with a rifle?"

"Did you call the sheriff about them?"

"'Course I did. Jerry went out and talked to them. I don't know if they got the message or not, but Jerry told me to keep my eyes open. If I see anything else, I should give him a call."

"*Did* you see anything else?"

"I sure did," said Doug. "Smelled things, too, like real sharp smells. I went over there to see what was going on. I got to their driveway this time before somebody stopped me. I don't know what they're doing in there, but they put fabric all over the windows in the house, so you can't see out, and they put up signs everywhere warning people to stay away. Only time I ever see the people who work there is when they go smoke by the road. "

Ash could see why the sheriff wanted the place under observation. It sounded like a meth cookhouse. The cookers probably had to go by the road to smoke so they wouldn't cause an explosion.

"Do they have a lot of guests?"

"Yes, sir, they do. Almost always after it gets dark. Sometimes four, maybe five cars come by in one night."

"And how about their garbage?" he asked. "Do they have a lot of garbage?"

"You sure you haven't been over there? We get garbage picked up twice a month, and they've got so much, it just about fills the truck. Fifteen, twenty bags sometimes. They got so much garbage, I caught them putting it with mine once."

"Did you get a look at whatever they were throwing away?"

"Sure," said Doug. "That was the weird thing. It was all empty cans of automobile starter fluid."

If Doug had been a police officer, that would have been enough for a warrant. Starter fluid was usually somewhere between forty and sixty percent ether, one of the chemical precursors required for one production method of methamphetamine. Meth cookers bought it by the case, sprayed it out of the can, and then separated the ether from the rest of the ingredients. Ash even knew a couple of auto part stores that had started putting it in racks behind the counter and limiting the number of canisters they'd sell to individuals. Eventually, it'd probably be regulated like Sudafed.

"Okay," said Ash. "You've helped me a lot, so thank you for talking to me tonight. I'm going to start looking into things, and hopefully I'll be able to get those people out of your neighborhood."

"They shot my dog. Did I tell you that?"

"I'll make a note of it," said Ash.

"If you find that BB gun, can you shoot the big one with the tattoos in the ass like he shot my dog?"

Big one with the tattoos. That could have been Marvin Spencer.

"I'll see what I can do."

"I'd appreciate that."

Ash thanked him again before hanging up. He jotted down a couple of quick thoughts. He considered calling Bowers with the news, but he needed to verify something first. He searched through his phone's call history and dialed the sheriff's office again and asked to speak with Jerry.

"Did you talk to Doug and Loretta?" he asked.

"I did," said Ash. "Does Doug have problems with his memory?"

Jerry grunted. "You noticed, huh?"

"It wasn't hard."

"Yeah, well, he's a smart man. He just forgets things now and again."

"I asked him about the farm up the street from him, and he told me a couple of things that make me think you've got a meth lab on your hands."

Jerry sighed. "You're probably right. When I walked through it last, I didn't find anything I could get a warrant with, and we don't have the manpower to stake the place out."

"Doug mentioned they had a lot of garbage. He also said they put bags of empty starter fluid canisters in with his trash. You find anything like that at the house?"

Jerry paused for a moment. "Yeah. I walked through about two weeks ago. Found, I don't know, five or six cans beside their barn. I asked one of the guys there, and he said he liked fixing cars."

"Did you smell anything?"

"Are you asking if I think it smelled like a meth lab?" asked Jerry. "Because if I smelled chemicals, I would have gotten a warrant and we wouldn't be having this conversation. I know how to do my job. We're not just a bunch of hicks around here."

"I know that," said Ash. "I just have to cover all my bases. It's nothing personal."

"Yeah. If you need anything else, you can just leave a message. I'll be sure to return your call."

"Tha—"

Jerry hung up before Ash could finish speaking. Ash looked at his own phone and scowled before flipping through his address book. Hopefully he wouldn't have to talk to Jerry again because Ash doubted he'd be up for doing him too many favors. As soon as he found it, he hit the CALL button on Bowers's entry and waited for him to pick up.

"I've got a lieutenant colonel with the state police on hold," said Bowers. "What have you got?"

"One of the houses we're looking at is probably a meth lab. We might have enough to get a warrant. I want to show a picture of it to Frank Hayes and see if he recognizes it."

"I'll take care of that. You call the prosecutor's office and start working on the warrant."

"I'm on it."

Ash hung up the phone with Bowers and went to work, writing two different probable cause statements. The first included just the information he received from Jerry as well as some background information, but the second included a potential ID of the location by Frank. Ash had quite a bit of confidence in the second statement; the first, though, they'd have to find a sympathetic judge to get signed. He called Susan Mercer next. They didn't speak for very long, but she agreed to put her weight behind whatever they came up with. Hines and his entire crew had committed crimes that broke both state and federal law, so she also agreed to fight to keep the case in Indianapolis if the FBI tried to intervene post arrest. Both were helpful.

Ash called Bowers again.

"Susan's a go. She'd prefer if we get an ID of the house from Frank Hayes, but she's willing to try to get a warrant without it."

"We'll have to go without it," said Bowers. "Hayes went nuts, so the hospital sedated him for his own safety. They gave him something to clear his body of opioids, and they're going to keep him under until he's clean."

Ash winced but tried not to let his disappointment enter his voice.

"Susan will run the warrant application by a judge and said she'd fax it to us when she can."

"Then we're as ready as we'll ever be. We'll drive down together, so meet me out front. Get ready to work."

27

By the time he got outside, darkness had fully descended upon the city. Rain caught the headlights of passing cars, splashing and glistening on the blacktop like quicksilver mirrors. Ash's stomach rumbled as he smelled the sharp scent of oregano, basil, and bread wafting from a pizza place up the street. In the excitement of putting his warrant together, he had missed dusk prayer and dinner. God could probably forgive the former, but Ash's stomach wouldn't forgive the latter without consequences. He didn't have time to stop for a meal anywhere, so he went back inside and bought a soda and the last two cold turkey sandwiches available in a vending machine in the building's basement. His meager dinner wouldn't tide him over for long, but it was better than nothing.

Bowers came down within a minute and suggested that they take Ash's marked cruiser. The community relations' vehicle would do little to strike fear in the hearts of the men they hoped to arrest, but its lights and siren would allow them to make better time on the interstate. Ash agreed, and they headed out. About twenty miles south of town, he pulled off at a gas station where he filled up his tank and bought a package of peanut butter crackers and a cup of double-caffeinated coffee. He didn't plan on doing any heavy lifting tonight, so the crackers combined with what he had earlier ought to tide him over.

When he got back to the car, Bowers was on the phone. He gave Ash a thumbs-up, which, considering the circumstances, could have meant the state police picked up Alistair Hines walking beside the highway, an anonymous do-gooder rescued their trafficking victims on his own accord, or Bowers saved a boatload of money on his car insurance. Ash leaned against his cruiser, feeling the warm engine beneath him and listening to the consistent, dull roar from the interstate as he waited.

Bowers hung up shortly after Ash's arrival.

"Mercer got the warrant," he said. "She faxed it to ISP's district headquarters in Sellersburg. We'll meet our team there."

"Did she say who signed it?"

"Thurman."

That explained it. Judge Thurman had been a prosecuting attorney before joining the bench, and he signed a lot of warrants other judges would have rejected. Susan likely didn't even have to beg.

"Then let's go," he said, yawning.

"You going to be able to stay awake for the drive?"

"I'm fine," said Ash. "Just a little tired."

"Did you eat anything today?"

"Breakfast and a couple of sandwiches of questionable provenance from the vending machine at work."

"If you pass out while driving, I'm going to be pissed."

"If I do, just elbow me or something. I'm sure I'll wake up."

"That's not funny."

"It wasn't meant to be," said Ash, climbing into his car. Bowers grumbled something but then followed suit. They drove the remaining forty-five minutes to Sellersburg in silence, the lights on top of their car and the occasional blast from its siren clearing the path ahead of them.

The state police post was just a mile or two off the interstate and faced a Mexican restaurant. Ash parked at the end of a long line of police cars and stepped out, his feet sinking in the gravel lot. He could hear music and see kids playing volleyball on the front lot of the Baptist church up the street. Ash adjusted his sport coat and clipped his badge to his belt.

"Let's get this over with. I want Hines rotting in a cell as soon as possible."

"You're not the only one," said Bowers, already walking toward the building. The post's interior walls had been painted an off-white that had dulled over the years, while a thin navy blue carpet muffled his footsteps. The air held the fetid odor of mildew. Aside from arrestees, few members of the public went into the post, so it lacked an area for the reception of guests. Instead, a dozen uniformed officers milled about an open room crammed with desks, talking to each other in subdued voices. Bowers cleared his throat, getting the attention of the nearest officer, a young man with straight black hair. He directed them to the office of the lieutenant in charge of the post.

The next hour went quickly with the state police doing most of the work. The lieutenant colonel Bowers had talked to earlier came in and read through Susan's warrant while the post lieutenant briefed the officers who would be involved in the raid on tactics and locations. Since Ash and

Bowers were from Indianapolis and since their department's insurance broker would be less than pleased if they became involved in a raid almost a hundred miles outside their jurisdiction, they'd stay well away from the house and watch as everyone else worked.

Consequently, Ash tuned out the tactical briefing and focused on the men and women in the room. Every officer there knew the consequences of screwing up. Somebody— a partner, a victim, a neighbor minding his own business— might not make it through the night. As their lieutenant spoke, the seriousness of the situation descended upon them and choked away any traces of merriment.

After the briefing, Ash called Hannah to tell her what was going on. She wished him luck and suggested that he try to avoid being shot if at all possible. He told her he would and that he loved her before hanging up. At the appointed time, Ash, along with another Islamic officer, had evening prayer in an empty conference room. That stilled his mind and allowed him to think clearly. He and Bowers wouldn't be anywhere near the actual raid, but a nervous pit wore at his gut nonetheless. The men and women assigned to that station had gone through a state-certified police academy, but Ash didn't know them. He didn't know what they could do, how experienced they were, what sort of temperaments they had. Sending strangers after a man who had already killed at least three people felt wrong.

At a quarter after eleven, the team got together for final assignments before heading out. Ash and Bowers left at the tail end of a six-vehicle convoy. They took the interstate at first, but then simultaneously exited at a small, two-gas-station town. Their target house lay ten miles distant, but the only road to it writhed through fields, cow pastures, and woods. It'd be a slow trek.

Ash had followed that route on his computer, but actually driving it made him feel as if he were on a roller coaster. Maybe his small dinner was good for something after all. Aside from sodium safety lamps on barns and farmhouses, the moon alone, peeking through wisps of clouds, lit the night. He cracked open his window. The scent of damp earth with an undertone of rot and manure filled the car. The temperature had dropped probably twenty degrees from the time they left Indianapolis, making the air feel comfortable on his skin. Had he been at home, it would have been a great night to sleep outside on his hammock.

"These guys sure know how to pick them," said Bowers, staring as they passed the charred remnants of what had been a single-story home. Weeds covered the clapboard to the windows, while scorch marks rose to the remains of the collapsed roof. Neat rows of cars lined the front lawn. In the city, scavengers would have picked the area clean of metal within a night. In the country, though, nature had been allowed to take its revenge upon the blight, slowly rotting it into dust.

"Remote, low-population density, low law enforcement presence. It's a good spot for a meth lab. And out here, they're only going to blow themselves up if something goes wrong. Downright considerate of them if you ask me."

"Except us," said Bowers. "If something goes wrong, they blow us up, too."

"There is that," said Ash. He paused for effect. "At least we'd go out with a bang."

Bowers didn't crack a smile. "How long have you been sitting on that line?"

Ash shrugged. "Longer than I'd like to admit."

Bowers grunted, plunging the vehicle into silence again.

They drove for twenty more minutes before Ash started recognizing landmarks. Cecil lay in the south-central portion of Hancock County and had so few residents that it barely registered as a dot on the GPS in his cruiser. A vehicle at the head of the convoy turned onto a smaller side road about a mile outside of town. Those officers would park at an intersection west of their target farm in case someone managed to escape in a vehicle. Bowers and Ash would do the same thing on the east side of the farm. If the other officers did their jobs well, neither would be needed.

He slowed to a stop at the town's only four-way intersection and hung a left, almost immediately passing a ramshackle bungalow with black shutters and a wheelchair ramp leading to the front door. A pair of confederate flags waved in a light breeze on poles in the front yard. Ash had seen pictures of the area online, but being there in person felt almost surreal.

"How far out is this place?" asked Bowers.

"Not too much farther."

Ash followed the cruiser in front of him for another mile or two, passing Doug and Loretta Brown's ranch home and farm, before finding a small inlet between a thicket of woods and a cornfield. Doug—or whichever local farmer owned it—probably used it as a path to get his tractor to and from the worksite. While the state police officers pushed on, Ash backed his car into the inlet and then drove forward, leaving his vehicle perpendicular to the road and blocking access from either direction.

As soon as Ash put his car into park, Bowers checked the two-way radio he had been given at the state police post in Sellersburg and got out of the car. Ash followed suit and leaned against his door, facing the direction of their targeted farm. Trees followed the asphalt around a curve, blocking his view of the farm. Not that he would have had much chance to see anything two miles up a winding road.

"They tell you when they planned to hit the house?" asked Ash.

Bowers held up his radio. "No, but somebody's supposed to call."

Ash nodded and settled in. A dog barked somewhere distant, and if the wind blew right, he thought he could hear car engines, presumably from the state police officers. The constant white noise of the creek up ahead covered everything else.

"I think I've got a candy bar in the car if you want half," he said. Bowers declined, so Ash sat down on the driver's seat and leaned over so he could root through his glove box. Eight months ago, he wouldn't have done that with another officer within sight because eight months ago, he had carried a pint of bourbon inside, beneath paperwork. Now it held chocolate-covered granola bars that had melted and hardened dozens of times over, turning each into a sticky, gummy mess. They still tasted good, so Ash didn't mind. He tore a package open and then perked his ears up as he heard something rumble distantly.

"Are they moving?" he asked, sticking his head out of the car.

Bowers leaned forward and held his hand to his forehead as if he were trying to blot out the sun. "They didn't say anything, but it sounds like it."

Ash squeezed the bottom of the candy bar's packaging, forcing enough of the granola up that he could have a mouthful. He and Bowers turned at the same time, watching a pair of bright headlights filter through rows of corn.

"Probably just a farmer coming home," said Bowers. "Get a flashlight. We'll have to turn him around."

Ash had already started toward his trunk when the headlights extinguished. Judging by the sound, though, the truck kept moving. The noise from the engine decreased, and then Ash heard brakes squeal. The truck's engine then spooled up again after that, rumbling the ground even a couple hundred yards away.

"I'm not from the country, so is there any reason why a farmer would turn his lights off at night aside from an attempt to hide?" asked Ash.

"I don't know," said Bowers, picking up his radio. "You got a shotgun in your trunk?" Ash nodded. "Get it. We're going for a walk."

While Bowers radioed the state police, Ash walked to his trunk and grabbed the weapon and a box of shells before joining Bowers by the front of the vehicle.

"What'd they say?" asked Ash.

"Warned us not to shoot any cows. They take that seriously around here."

"They're not going to send anybody?"

Bowers shook his head. "The lieutenant said farmers around here work at night sometimes so they don't stress their livestock during the heat of the day."

"How far out are our boys?"

"Five minutes on these roads."

Ash nodded and took a breath. "Let's hope it's just a farmer."

Bowers nodded before starting to walk down the road. Ash followed a few steps behind, cradling his firearm. Both men wore Windbreakers with the word POLICE splashed across the back in bright yellow letters, so they should be identifiable as law enforcement officers from a distance. Ash didn't know if that would make the local farmers more or less likely to shoot them. The Browns' farm lay maybe two hundred yards up the road, but the trees cast a moat of blackness around it so thick Ash could barely see through it. He took a breath and stepped off the road and onto the grass, muffling his footsteps. It had just been a truck, but it left a bad feeling in his gut.

A line of evergreen trees with boughs that ran from the tree's crown to the ground separated the Browns' farm from the road, blocking Ash's view inside. He could hear talking, though, and the sound of feet crunching on gravel. Someone had turned the truck's engine off. Bowers, crouched low, walked toward the evergreen trees and then pushed between two of them, quickly becoming enmeshed in the gray-green branches. Ash did likewise. The tree's foliage stopped at the tips of its branches, creating a sort of cocoon inside of which they could comfortably peer at the Browns' farm unseen. It smelled sticky, like sap.

A light atop the Browns' barn illuminated a concrete parking pad. Ash squinted as his eyes adjusted to the light. The noise that drew their attention originally had come from a yellow rental truck that had backed up the steep driveway. Its nose pointed toward the exit, while its rear pointed toward a pair of open barn doors. There must have been fifteen people in the space of a couple of parking spots. Young women in sweatpants and loose tops lined up behind the truck while four men ambled about, casting sideways glances at their surroundings. One leaned against the side of the truck and smoked a cigarette maybe thirty feet from them. Like the last time Ash had seen him, he wore a pair of jeans and a polo shirt, this time in red.

It was one of the men who had dumped him at the barn near Lafayette. Before consciously willing his legs to move, Ash knelt and crooked his left leg in front of him, creating a steady platform on which he could aim. He raised the shotgun to his shoulder, felt one bone click against another, felt the slight give of the trigger. Thirty feet away, there'd be nothing left of his target but a stain on the side of a moving van. Something within him, a voice out of some dark crevice of his soul, screamed at him to do it. He swallowed that desire back and licked his lips, his hands starting to feel the weight of the weapon.

"That's one of the guys who took me to Rebecca's body," whispered Ash. "We got a warrant for the wrong farm."

Bowers glanced at him and then nodded before taking a couple of steps back. Ash heard him whisper into the radio. Red Shirt took a drag on his cigarette and blew the smoke toward the truck's cabin. Ash couldn't see a firearm on him, but he assumed he had something within reach. If they had to start shooting, he'd be the first target. With him down, Ash and Bowers could use the truck as concealment from the rest.

Ash turned his attention next to the concrete pad. He

counted twelve young women, but he couldn't recognize faces at that distance. None of the girls said anything; they simply huddled together like animals heading to the slaughterhouse. Ash considered the scene and scratched his chin, trying to form a plan. One stray bullet, and another girl would die. He had seen enough of that, which meant they needed to separate the men from the girls. If he had to guess, the traffickers would do that for them by putting the girls onto the truck. Once that happened, the state police could lay a spike strip on the road and shred the truck's tires before it even left the driveway. With so little light penetrating the woods, the men in the truck wouldn't even know what had happened until a dozen firearms pointed at their chests. It wasn't ideal, but the plan could work.

Bowers crept beside him again and leaned close to him. "Backup is on the way. We wait, we watch, and we report any changes."

"How long?"

"Five to ten. The men were in place around the other farm. They've got to get back."

Ash nodded and took a breath. About a minute after Bowers placed the call to the state police, a fifth man emerged from the barn. He had black hair streaked with silver and, despite the time of night, sunglasses on top of his head. He looked like a skunk. He threw a cigarette on the ground with one hand and slipped a phone into his pocket with the other.

"The old man just got hit in Chicago. We move now."

Red Shirt stood straighter and walked onto the parking pad about fifteen feet from their hiding spot. Ash held his breath.

"He was arrested?"

"No. He caught eighteen bullets in an alley," said the skunk, already jogging toward the truck. He undid the latch on the rear door with a clank and threw it open. "We've got to move."

"You sure it was him?" asked Red Shirt, walking toward the others.

"Pretty sure," said the skunk. He used a handle to climb onto the bed of the truck before waving toward the girls. "Let's move, ladies."

None of the girls took a step, but that might have been because none of them spoke English. The skunk reached behind him, pulled a semiautomatic from a holster at his belt, and chambered a round. Ash adjusted his aim on his new target. A shotgun was usually a close-quarters weapon, but Ash had loaded his with rifled slugs, which increased the accuracy to a reasonable distance. Several of the girls nearest the skunk flinched. Red Shirt threw down his cigarette and started herding the girls toward the rear of the truck while the skunk pulled them inside. The other three men strolled about the yard as if nothing were going on.

Bowers started lifting his radio but stopped before saying anything as one of the girls looked directly at them. She wore a pair of light blue hospital scrubs with a pink drawstring. Her auburn hair had been pulled away from her face and put into a ponytail. If Ash had to guess, she was in her late teens.

"Turn away," whispered Ash. "Turn away and do as they say."

As if hearing him, she turned her attention toward the girl in front of her. Unfortunately, she also shuffled to her right, toward them. Ash held his breath and shook his head, silently willing her to get into the truck. Separated from the men, they might be able to get her. If she bolted toward them...Ash didn't want to think about it. Bowers reached into his jacket and withdrew his firearm. He held it low against the ground and slid the receiver back, chambering a round. His lips were straight and his body rigid.

The girl looked over her shoulder at them again, and Ash felt his stomach drop. He shook his head, hoping she could see it.

"Don't do it," he whispered. "Stay where you are."

Ash heard Bowers's feet shift as he readjusted his position into a shooter's stance. Their backup was still a few minutes out. She needed to wait. The girl licked her lips and shivered before taking another step toward them. The skunk and his men didn't seem to notice her as they forced other girls into the truck.

"Not now, honey," whispered Ash. "Take a step back."

Five shells. That's all Ash had. He didn't know what kind of firearm Bowers had, but it wouldn't carry more than fifteen rounds. With five men who might possibly shoot at them, that didn't leave them much room to miss. He felt his throat tighten.

Turn away and get in the truck.

In his mind, Ash pleaded with the redhead over and over, but to no avail. She took another step toward them and then another until she finally slipped into a run.

The skunk reacted immediately and pointed his firearm at an Asian girl at the head of the line while looking at the thug nearest the tree line.

"Bring her back. Seems someone needs to learn a lesson about consequences."

Red Shirt nodded and started jogging, but not before the redhead reached Ash and Bowers. Ash lowered his firearm and motioned her forward as her face passed the first row of branches. Her eyes were wide, pleading. Bowers kept one hand on his gun but scooted her toward the other side of the tree line with his other. Ash did likewise, hoping she understood. Neither man could turn his head to find out, though, because they had another visitor jogging straight toward them.

"Whoa," said Red Shirt, immediately upon stepping through the trees. He held up his hands and straightened his back. His Adam's apple bobbed as he swallowed. Ash pointed the shotgun at his chest.

"Put your hands on top of your head and back up," said Ash.

Red Shirt paused and looked from Bowers and then back to Ash before putting his hands on top of his head. He took halting steps back, emerging from the trees. Ash followed, the barrel of his shotgun a foot or two out of Red Shirt's reach. The safety light from the barn seemed brighter out of the trees. Ash had a clean shot on the skunk, elevated as he was on the back of the truck, but the other three men stood on the far side of the parking pad, a crowd of increasingly listless young women blocking the path. If someone started shooting, it would get ugly fast.

Ash took a hand off his shotgun and started waving the girls down. An Asian girl in front hesitated and then knelt. Several others followed quickly.

"What the hell is this?" asked the skunk.

"Drop your weapons and put your hands on top of your heads," said Bowers, not taking his eyes from Red Shirt's. "A dozen police officers are in the woods behind me."

The skunk stayed still for a moment. Ash held his breath, silently praying they'd believe Bowers's bluff. The stalemate lasted only a moment, though, before the skunk raised his weapon and fired twice. Ash squeezed the trigger on his shotgun, feeling the heavy weapon jerk against his shoulder like a jackhammer. A one-ounce led slug hit the skunk in the chest, blowing a hole the size of a grapefruit clear through him. Bowers stumbled back and fell to a knee, clutching his chest and shoulder. The girls immediately started screaming, their heads down as they huddled in the middle of the concrete.

Red Shirt turned and reached behind him. Ash chambered another round and fired a second time as Red Shirt raised his weapon. He went down hard, most of his chest a confused mass of red. Ash whirled and faced the remaining three men.

"Drop your weapons!" screamed Ash. "Now!"

Two complied by throwing down their firearms, but the third, the man closest to the truck's cabin, ran for it. Ash started to give chase but then stopped and looked at Captain Bowers. His vest caught both rounds the skunk shot at him, but even that could cause serious injury. The girls wailed. Bowers waved in the general direction of the truck.

"Go."

Ash didn't need further prodding. He ran after the thug and careened around the side of the truck in time to see the front door being opened. He didn't hear the truck's engine, but he saw it start to roll forward, slowly at first, then speeding up. The thug had probably just put it in neutral, knowing it would roll down the hill. Ash dug his toes into the ground and sprinted. By the time he reached the cabin, the truck was moving too quickly for him to run beside. Ash tried grabbing a handhold beside the door, but the thug inside kicked his chest and shoulder hard, knocking him back. Ash slipped and fell, facedown, his weapon clattering against the gravel. He barely got his arm away before the truck's rear tires would have run over it.

Ash tried pushing up, but his shoulder couldn't support his weight. He flopped down, helpless, as the truck's engine started with a dull roar and the thug closed his door. By the time the vehicle reached the end of the driveway, it had probably hit forty miles an hour. In a car, that might have been doable, even on those curvy back roads. A moving truck at those speeds on those roads might as well have been a bowling ball. As Ash watched, it slammed into a pair of trees at the end of the driveway with a crack and a thump and moved no more.

Ash stayed still for a moment, trying to catch his breath. Eventually, he rolled onto his back and sat up. In an hour or two, he might be screaming with pain, but for the moment, he had so much adrenaline flowing through him that he didn't feel a thing. He looked up the hill. Captain Bowers still held the two remaining men at gunpoint, his face a mask of pain.

"You okay?" asked Ash.

"I think I broke some ribs," he said, grimacing. "You?"

"I'm breathing."

Bowers nodded toward the truck at the foot of the driveway. "Find out if that asshole is alive."

Ash nodded and headed down the driveway. As he neared the truck, the smell of diesel became almost over-powering. The truck must have ruptured its fuel tank on impact, which meant they'd have to get a fire crew out there soon. Cracks striated the windshield and blood painted the interior like stained glass. Ash pulled open the door and watched as the driver, the second of the two men who had taken him to Rebecca's body in Lafayette, tumbled out.

"You should have worn your seat belt."

28

Ash and Bowers stayed at the farm in Cecil for the next hour. Both men answered questions, but mostly they sat around and watched while detectives from the state police worked the scene. They took Doug and Loretta Brown in for questioning, but neither seemed to have any idea what was going on. They claimed to have rented their barn and back pasture out to a nice couple who wouldn't cause trouble. It would have been nice if they had mentioned that on the phone when he called earlier. They'd be questioned, and based on what came out, the local county prosecutor would decide what to do with them.

Intermixed with the girls from the Dandelion Inn, they found a number of girls who had come from other locations, including the home in Avon. Among them they found Faria, Amina's younger sister. At fifteen years old, she had already seen and experienced some of the worst atrocities one human being could do to another. No amount of therapy could help her undo that, but God willing, she and her sister would be okay. God willing, everyone would be okay.

The ambulances started arriving half an hour after the raid. Those girls under the age of eighteen were taken to a children's hospital in Louisville, Kentucky, for evaluation, while those over eighteen were taken to a hospital for adults. They'd be assigned social workers who could figure out what to do next. Faria didn't speak English, but Ash gave her a note on which he had written his contact information. He'd call the hospital as well to make sure she was okay. After the girls were shipped off, he sent a text message to his wife to let her know that he and Mike Bowers had survived with relatively minor injuries. She sent a message back almost immediately to let him know that she loved him. She must have been waiting up for him.

At about one in the morning, a state police officer drove Bowers and Ash to a hospital for evaluation. The ER physician had an X-ray taken of Ash's shoulder and found that his collarbone had been fractured, presumably when the thug in the truck kicked him. The physician set it into place and put Ash into a sling that forced his shoulders back. Bowers had two broken ribs. His vest probably saved his life.

While waiting for a physician to check out Bowers, Ash sent a text message to Leena Tahir, telling her they had safely rescued Faria. She could tell Amina the news at dawn prayer. Meanwhile, he'd look into having Faria transferred to Indianapolis when he could so the two girls could see each other again. What would happen to them afterward was anyone's guess. The tribal regions in Pakistan were brutal and backward. A girl who had sex outside marriage—whether or not she consented to it—was considered by many to be a black mark on the family. Even if their family took Amina and Faria in again, the local tribal elders might pressure their father to kill them as a way to reclaim the family honor. Islam taught that all innocents—man, woman, child, believer, unbeliever—were equal and that to murder someone was as bad as murdering all of humanity. Unfortunately, some people seemed to forget that.

Bowers stayed overnight in the hospital near Louisville because he hurt too much to move, but a state trooper drove Ash back to Indianapolis at about three in the morning. Before leaving, an ER physician gave Ash a painkiller that blurred the entire drive home into a narcotic-induced fog. He didn't even remember getting out of the car and climbing into bed when they made it home. He did remember seeing his wife, though, and somehow that made his night easier.

Ash slept straight through *suhoor* and dawn prayer the next day and woke only after his daughter jumped on the end of the bed at around nine. A pink ribbon held her black hair away from her face, a gap-toothed grin on her lips. Two of her primary teeth had begun wiggling a few days earlier, another sign that she was growing up.

"I lost a tooth last night."

"I see," said Ash, sitting upright. "Did you show *Ummi?*" When Megan nodded, her entire body moved. "Did she tell you what it means?"

She nodded with her entire body again. "I'll put it under my pillow, and the tooth fairy will come and get it."

"Oh, I'm sorry," said Ash. "She didn't tell you the bad part. Now that you've started losing your teeth, you have to get a job."

She shook her head no just as enthusiastically as she had nodded. "No, I don't. You won't make me get a job."

Ash put his hands on his chest and shook his head. "I'm sorry, but I don't make the rules. You're going to have to get a job. Have you ever worked a backhoe or crane before? I hear heavy machinery operators are in demand."

Megan narrowed her eyes. "I don't believe you."

Ash shrugged. "When the tooth fairy asks to see the stub from your last paycheck, don't say I didn't warn you."

Megan looked at him and then to the door and then back at him. "I'm going to talk to *Ummi*."

"How about you give me a hug first."

She scampered up the bed and threw her arms around Ash's neck, jostling his injured shoulder. Despite the pain, it felt nice to hug her again. When she left the room, he stretched, showered, and then dressed. The brace the physician had given him to hold his shoulders back kept him from carrying a gun, but that wouldn't be a problem for the foreseeable future. No one would hand him a firearm until the department's psychiatrist cleared him, a task that might take a while with his baggage.

Ash met his wife and kids in the kitchen. His shoulder prevented him from picking up Kaden, but it didn't stop him from playing with him. They stacked up blocks together and then laughed when Kaden knocked them over. At around eleven, play stopped when Special Agent Kevin Havelock knocked on the front door. He wore jeans, a white polo shirt with the FBI's logo on the breast, and a pair of mirrored aviator sunglasses. Must have been off duty.

"Detective Rashid," he said, extending his hand to shake before wincing and then pulling it back. "Sorry. I heard about your injury."

"That's all right," said Ash. "I'll recover. What can I do for you?"

"I hope you don't mind me coming by. I got your address from Chief Reddington."

Ash leaned against the door frame and then gasped and stood straighter when pain ripped through the top of his rib cage. That wasn't the smartest thing he'd done that day.

"No, I don't mind," said Ash, once he caught his breath again. "What do you need?"

"Just a conversation," said Havelock. "Off the record."

Ash breathed out of his nose for a moment before turning his head and shouting over his shoulder, "Hey, Hannah. I'm going to talk to a guy in the backyard."

"Okay. Thank you."

Ash stepped forward and started to close the door behind him, but Havelock didn't move. He tilted his head to the side.

"Aren't we going to the backyard?" he asked, nodding toward the house.

"We'll go around. Hannah wears the hijab, and she doesn't like men seeing her without it."

"Oh. I didn't know you were a Muslim."

Ash shrugged and started toward the driveway. "The Imam at my mosque told me the same thing last year." Havelock followed him through the gate in his cedar fence. No matter how many times Ash saw his backyard, he still felt lucky to have it. At over one acre, it felt like a park in the middle of the city. It even had an old oak tree that swayed in the warm, morning breeze. Ash crossed the lawn to his bluestone patio and took a seat at a teak table and chair set beneath his cedar pergola. Havelock did likewise.

"You have a nice yard."

"Did you not see it on the surveillance video your agents shot eight months ago?"

Havelock looked at him for a moment and then shook his head. "We focused on Konstantin Bukoholov, not your yard. Our agents stayed in a van on the street."

"What do you want?"

"How'd you know to find that farm last night?"

Ash leaned back in his chair. "I asked Frank Hayes, the junkie I picked up in Avon. He told me he had driven a van full of girls there the day before. You should consider talking to people. I bet you'd be amazed at what you can learn."

"I do talk to people. I talked to you yesterday, and you didn't share that information with us."

"I wasn't sure we had the same objective. I wanted to put Hines in jail. You wanted to quell a controversy before it happened."

"Is there anything else you're not sharing with us?"

Ash leaned forward and rested his elbows on the table. "Like what?"

"Fleischer's dead. We found his body in an alley in Chicago. He was shot eighteen times."

Ash shrugged. "Eighteen shots will do it. I wish we brought him in ourselves, but I won't shed too many tears over his death."

Havelock stared at him, apparently waiting for him to say something else. Ash crossed his arms. The motion aggravated his shoulder but no more so than leaving his arm hanging against his side.

"We can work together, Detective," said Havelock. "We don't have to be adversaries."

Ash raised his eyebrows. "You took video of an informant visiting my house. Then, instead of asking me about it, you showed it to my commanding officer as evidence of some sort of conspiracy. That sounds adversarial to me."

"I wanted to know if I could trust you."

"I've spent a long time as a law enforcement officer. I think I've earned some trust."

Havelock broke off eye contact and sighed. "Do you think Bukoholov murdered Fleischer?"

"Yeah, but he wouldn't see it as murder. He'd see it as justice. Depending on how well his lawyer argued it, a jury might agree."

"How about you?"

Ash shrugged. "Fleischer trafficked in young women and killed people for a living."

"That didn't answer my question."

Ash looked off to the old oak tree that shaded his yard. "Why are you really here, Agent Havelock?"

"Alistair Hines disappeared last night. We found out this morning that he's on a plane heading to Moscow. We don't have an extradition treaty with Russia. How does that make you feel?"

Ash chuckled. "How does that make me feel? What, are you a psychiatrist now?"

"I'm just curious to see how you'd react. We'll try to get him back, but the Russians will want something in return. I don't know if the Department of State will be willing to pay their price."

"He murdered three people. They can't just ignore him."

"He's done more than murder three people. We've heard from some of our international partners that he and Fleischer might have been partners. Hines acquires and transports the girls, Fleischer exploits them."

"Okay, problem solved," said Ash, shrugging. "He's probably committed crimes in Russia. They'll pick him up."

Havelock shook his head. "Wealthy men don't spend time in Russian prisons unless they've pissed off the Kremlin."

Ash started to sputter that no government could be that obtuse, but then he caught himself. He narrowed his eyebrows. "Why are you telling me this?"

"This is your case, at least in part. I told you that I'd keep you informed, and I am. It's over. The bad guy got away."

IMPD had a homicide clearance rate of somewhere between seventy and eighty percent, meaning they managed to arrest a suspect in the vast majority of the cases they investigated. No department got everybody, though. He always wished they could do better, but inevitably, cases went unsolved. That had bothered him at first, but over time he realized he couldn't do anything about it. Ash took a deep breath.

"What happens now?" he asked.

Havelock shrugged. "We wait and hope for a miracle."

"And Hines keeps working."

"Eventually," said Havelock. He shrugged. "Probably quickly. We've disrupted his operations for now, but he'll pick up the pieces."

"We'll send out bulletins to other law enforcement agencies," said Ash. "IMPD will keep an eye out."

"I'd rather deal with the disease than treat the symptoms. Unfortunately, I don't know anybody who has pull with the Russian government. Do you?"

Ash started to shake his head, but then stopped himself. "What are you asking me?"

"Until he's sitting in an American prison or dead, Alistair Hines is a problem. I'm asking if you know anyone who could take care of that."

"Are you asking if I know someone who could go there and pick him up?"

Havelock shrugged. "Or do whatever. Hypothetically, if you knew someone like that, we wouldn't need to know the details. Hell, we wouldn't want to know the details. We would just want Hines taken off the streets. Permanently."

"Someone like Konstantin Bukoholov?" Havelock shrugged but didn't say anything. Ash broke off eye contact and blinked. "What kind of range do the Bureau's wireless transmitters have?"

Havelock cocked his head to the side. "Why are you asking?"

"I'm wondering where the surveillance van is."

Havelock shook his head. "There is no surveillance van."

"You're too smart to play stupid. You want me to tell Bukoholov that Alistair Hines, the man who murdered his daughter, is sitting in a Russian prison. As soon as Bukoholov gets on a plane, you'll arrest us both for conspiracy to commit murder."

"That's preposterous."

"It might also be entrapment," said Ash.

Havelock stood. "I'm going to leave before either of us says something regrettable."

"You want a tip for the future?" asked Ash. Havelock started toward the gate. "If you really wanted Bukoholov to murder Hines, you would have held a press conference and

377

mentioned that he flew to Moscow. Bukoholov would have taken care of the rest. You came to me for a reason, and it wasn't very difficult to see through."

Havelock stopped at the gate before leaving. "Get your affairs in order, Detective."

"Get out of my yard."

Havelock turned and left. Ash listened until he heard a car start up before going to his cruiser to get the prepaid cell phone he had used earlier to talk to Bukoholov. He dialed the same number Bukoholov had called him from earlier and waited for the old man to pick up.

"Special Agent Kevin Havelock just told me what you did in Chicago."

Bukoholov inhaled deeply. "The view from the Skydeck on the Willis Tower is breathtaking."

"Yeah, I'm sure it is," said Ash. "He told me about Fleischer. Eighteen shots, huh? That's overkill, don't you think?"

Bukoholov coughed. "I heard about his death on the news. I feel for his family. They said it was a mugging that went wrong."

"Muggers don't reload when they finish a magazine. Eighteen shots is a message. Who'd you leave it for?"

"I think you're mistaken about my trip. My daughter and her husband passed away, and I needed a break. I took my brother-in-law and my nephews to Chicago for a Cubs game. We saw the sights, toured the city, ate deep-dish pizza. In fact, we were at the game when the news said Fleischer was shot."

"Who'd the Cubs play?"

"The Cardinals. I kept the ticket stubs because they had

a coupon for a free sandwich on the back." Bukoholov paused. "Have you checked your mail today? I sent you something."

"No, I haven't checked it," said Ash, standing and walking toward his gate. "I received your last package, though. I think you might have saved some lives. I didn't know you had that in you."

"I'm a humanitarian."

"Sure," said Ash. He walked out of his yard and to the mailbox at the front of his house. "I'm getting my mail now." He grabbed that morning's mail and flipped through catalogs and bills until he came to a stark-white envelope without a return address. He flipped it over and tore it open, exposing a photocopy of a lined piece of paper. Someone had written names, addresses, and phone numbers on it as well as shorthand notes that Ash couldn't decipher. Most of the names were unfamiliar, but one stood out. Leonard Wilson, the only man currently in the race for Marion County prosecutor. "What is this?"

"I've heard it's a page from the black book of the young woman who ran the Dandelion Inn."

"What happened to that young woman? As far as I know, we haven't found her."

"Women like that know how to make themselves unavailable quickly," said Bukoholov.

"What do you expect me to do with this?" asked Ash.

"I don't expect you to do anything. I simply thought you might like to see it."

Ash looked at the page again. "What does 'YTB' and 'CGR' mean? It's in the notes section beside Leonard Wilson's name."

Bukoholov paused. "I'm not an expert, mind you, but I believe that means 'younger the better' and 'can get rough.'"

Ash swore under his breath. "And after the election this fall, this guy's going to be the top law enforcement official in the county. That's wonderful. You should be proud."

"You forget your own part. Without you and your unorthodox investigation into Thomas Rahal, this election would have turned out very differently. He couldn't have beaten Susan Mercer."

"I didn't intend for her to drop out of the race."

"I'm sure you didn't," said Bukoholov. "But knowing what you do, would you have acted differently?"

"And allow Thomas Rahal be sent to death row for a crime he didn't do?"

"Yes."

Ash took a breath. "That's beside the point."

"No, my friend, that is the point. I set you down a path you would have taken anyway. Leonard Wilson's future position is as much your responsibility as it is mine. You can whine like a petulant child about him, or you can do something. He offered you a position in his administration. I can think of no better way of keeping him in check than to watch him."

"I can think of at least one better way. Give me the black book you took from the Dandelion Inn, and I'll send him to jail."

Bukoholov clicked his tongue. "I'm afraid that's not possible. I merely have a photocopy of a single page. Someone sent it to me anonymously. You should keep it, though. When you take the job, you can show it to him. It will make him amenable to your needs."

"I'm not going to become you. I'll tell you what, though. I bet I can find a judge willing to sign a search warrant for your house based on what you sent me."

"If you do, can you wait a few days? I'm out of town, and I'd like to be there for the search. I'm very particular about how my possessions are handled."

"Where are you?" asked Ash.

"Moscow. An old friend of mine left Indianapolis without saying good-bye. I tracked him down so I could wish him well."

"Is your old friend Alistair Hines?"

"As much as I enjoy talking to you, I really must go," said Bukoholov. "Consider Leonard Wilson's job offer. He needs someone to keep his moral compass straight."

Bukoholov hung up the phone. Ash stared at the swing set he had built for Megan a couple of years ago. As a police officer, he couldn't condone Alistair Hines's murder, but as a father, he'd sleep just a little better at night knowing he was dead. Whether that made him a bad person, Ash didn't know, but if that was the price to keep the people he cared about safe, he'd gladly pay it.

The rest of the day went smoothly and quickly. In between reading stories, playing on the swing set with his kids, and napping, at least one reporter from every major television station and newspaper in town called. Ash spoke to a few of them off the record, but hung up on Kristen Tanaka as soon as he saw her name on the caller ID. At about four, the phone rang once more. Not wanting to wake his kids, he took his cell phone through the house, meeting his wife in the kitchen on the way.

"You're quite popular today," she said.

"I'm popular every day," said Ash. "I try to leave my fans at work, though. I don't want to get a big head."

"Right," said Hannah, putting her hand flat on his chest. "Answer the phone."

Ash did as she suggested and answered right before the phone would have gone to voice mail. He recognized Mike Bowers's voice almost immediately.

"Hey, how you feeling?" asked Ash.

"Better now that I've slept overnight," said Bowers quickly. "We should talk. Can you meet me somewhere?"

"I don't know if I can drive with my shoulder. Can we just talk on the phone?"

Bowers hesitated and took a deep breath. "Sure. I just spoke to Dan Reddington. He said Agent Havelock filed a formal complaint against you this afternoon."

Ash scoffed. "He filed a complaint because he doesn't have enough to file charges."

Bowers paused. "That's an awfully cavalier attitude."

Ash looked at Hannah and mouthed that he'd be a minute before slipping through the back door to the yard. "It's the truth. Havelock came by my place this morning and tried to get me involved in a conspiracy to murder Alistair Hines. Is he telling you that I agreed to it?"

"No," said Bowers. "He said you gave Frank Hayes drugs so he'd talk to you."

Ash startled and then closed his eyes. "Well, that's just complete bull."

"Frank Hayes mostly backs up the story."

"He's lying," said Ash.

Bowers sighed. "Give it a rest, okay? Hospital surveillance video shows you going into Hayes's room, so we know you were there. What's more, there's now an open IA investigation into your affiliation with a drug dealer operating out of a mailing center in Carmel. If you didn't give Hayes drugs, how'd you get him to talk?"

"The complaint with IA, that was filed by Tim Smith, right?"

"I didn't ask."

"It's retaliation for turning Eddie Alvarez in."

"Whatever, Ash. How'd you get Hayes to talk?"

"I didn't hurt him. I didn't threaten him. I didn't give him drugs. I didn't do anything wrong."

"At least we've got agreement about the drugs. Hayes says you took them away before he could use them. You know what he did show me, though? The spoon and syringe you left in the room."

Ash winced. "I can explain that."

"I don't want an explanation. I vouched for you on this case. I put my ass on the line for you when Chief Reddington wanted to pull you off."

Ash's legs felt weak, forcing him to sit down. "I showed Hayes dark brown sugar and told him it was heroin. I never gave him drugs."

"Is that supposed to make me feel better?" asked Bowers. "Jesus, Ash. I don't even know what to tell you."

"I got Hayes to talk. What's more important? Following proper procedures or saving someone's life?"

Bowers swore under his breath. "Do you have any idea what happens if this story gets out? Every convict you've put in jail suddenly has grounds to appeal his sentence."

"Weighed against the lives of twelve young women, I'd say we still came out on top."

"How about weighed against your job?"

"I did what was necessary to save people's lives. If that means losing my job, maybe it's not a job worth having."

Bowers didn't say anything for a long couple of seconds. "I want your letter of resignation."

Ash closed his eyes and held them shut, sure that he had misheard. "Say that again."

"I want a letter of resignation on my desk by tomorrow morning."

"I was speaking rhetorically. My job is worth having."

"You've got two very serious complaints against you, and both of them look like they have merit. You're a liability our department can't afford. If you don't give me a letter of resignation, Chief Reddington will seek to have you fired. Can I count on you to come through with that?"

"No, this is ridiculous. If you think it's justified, demote me or suspend me. I won't fight that. But you can't fire me, not over this."

"We *can* fire you. Allowing you to quit is a gift. Take it."

Ash started to sputter something, but then caught himself. "Neither of those charges have any merit whatsoever."

"When can I expect your letter of resignation?"

Ash had never thought his life would turn out as it did. As a child, his mother had drilled into his head the importance of education, that he should become a doctor or a professor, a member of the learned, professional class. In the end, he did, becoming an attorney. Before that, though, he took an oath of office and became a police officer. At the time, he saw it simply as a steady job with decent pay and benefits. As the years passed, it became more than that, though; it became who he was. He put the world right, or at least tried his best to do so. As far as Ash was concerned, it was the highest calling a man could have; he refused to turn his back on that.

"You won't be receiving it."

"Excuse me?"

"You heard me. I'm not going to resign."

"Before you make this decision, think about your family. You're a lawyer with extensive law enforcement experience. If you quit now, this will go away quietly and every criminal defense firm in town will pound on your door. When we fire you, your reputation will take a hit you can't afford. I'm trying to look out for you."

"I appreciate that, but I didn't do anything wrong. I'm not going to quit and say I did."

Bowers didn't respond for a five count. "And you've made up your mind?"

"I think so."

Bowers sighed. "Then effective immediately, I'm putting you on suspension pending formal internal and criminal investigations into your conduct. I'll get the paperwork in the mail within twenty-four hours."

"Is that it?"

Bowers paused. "You're a decent, moral man. Get a lawyer."

"I will. Thank you."

Ash hung up the phone and ran his fingers through his hair. He didn't go inside immediately. Instead, he stayed on the porch. Hannah must have seen him put down the phone because she came out a few minutes later.

"Everything okay? You look pale."

Ash looked at his wife and then at the table before drawing a breath. "I've got to go into work."

"I didn't think you'd have to go back to work for a while."

"There's just something I have to do. I'll be back in a little while."

Hannah put a hand on his chest, stopping him from walking away. "Don't shut me out. What's wrong?"

Ash had so many answers to that question he didn't know where to begin.

"I'm in trouble."

"What kind of trouble?"

"I didn't know there were multiple kinds."

Hannah blinked. "Don't start with that. What happened?"

Ash broke eye contact with her. "I did my job to the best of my abilities."

"Are they going to fire you?"

"They're going to try."

Hannah nodded as if she had expected that. "My nursing license expired a couple of months ago, but I can renew it. I might be able to get my old job back. We'll survive."

"Yeah, we'll be okay. I need to go in and fill out some paperwork."

"Okay," said Hannah. "But come home as soon as you can. We need to talk. We'll figure this out together as a family."

"I love you."

"I love you, too."

Ash kissed her before leaving the house. Instead of taking his cruiser, he drove his wife's aging Volkswagen downtown. He didn't go to his usual place—it'd be too full of cops, people he knew—and instead went to a sports bar a couple of blocks from his station. The chattering of the after-work crowd and the smoke from their cigarettes enveloped him, welcoming him like a long-lost friend. He pulled a stool from the bar and sat before motioning to the bartender.

"Shot of bourbon and a beer. Whatever you have on draft is fine."

"You've got it."

Ash watched the bartender splash the liquor into a glass. His hands shook when he picked it up. They shook even more when he put it to his lips. For years, alcohol had been his constant companion, a friend who simultaneously comforted and robbed his life of meaning. He forced his hand back to the bar and stared at the glass. He was an alcoholic. He couldn't explain the hold alcohol had over him any more than he could deny its influence. He imagined the hurt, the disappointment he'd see on Hannah's face if he stumbled through the door. She deserved better than to have a husband who could barely walk in a straight line, and his kids deserved a father who didn't smell like liquor when they gave him a hug at night.

"Something wrong?" asked the bartender. Ash looked at him and then blinked, forcing his mind to work through the question.

"No. Everything's fine," said Ash, standing. He took a twenty from his wallet and laid it on the bar. "But I've got to go home. My wife and I have a lot to talk about."

ACKNOWLEDGMENTS

Beyond the act of writing, it always surprises me to see how much work actually goes into publishing a book. I owe more people thanks than I can possibly list in this short space, but I would like to thank a few by name. Robert Gottlieb, the best literary agent in the business, and the staff at Trident Media Group: thank you for believing in my work. Mitch Hoffman, the editor without whose suggestions this book would likely suck, and everyone else at Grand Central Publishing: thank you for everything you've done. My family, especially my wife: thank you for putting up with me. And most of all to my readers, without whose superior taste I would be unemployed: thank you.

ABOUT THE AUTHOR

Chris Culver is the *New York Times* bestselling author of the Ash Rashid series of mysteries. After graduate school, Chris taught courses in ethics and comparative religion at a small liberal arts university in southern Arkansas. Between classes, he wrote *The Abbey*, which spent sixteen weeks on the *New York Times* bestsellers list and introduced the world to Detective Ash Rashid.

Chris has been a storyteller since he was a kid, but he decided to write crime fiction after picking up a dog-eared, coffee-stained paperback of Mickey Spillane's *I, the Jury* in a library book sale. Many years later, his wife, despite considerable effort, still can't stop him from bringing more orphan books home. The two of them, along with more houseplants than any normal family needs, reside near St. Louis, where Chris is hard at work on his next novel.

Ash Rashid wants out of the police department.
The last thing he needs is to become embroiled
in a new homicide investigation.

But everything changes when the mother of
one of his daughter's friends is murdered...

Please see the next page for an excerpt from

THE OUTSIDER

1

There were two armed men in his backyard when Detective
Ash Rashid came home from work, and neither looked
happy to see him. The first man was an inch or two under six feet
tall and had a slight build and a wisp of a goatee on his chin. He
sneered as soon as Ash came into view, clearly trying to look men-
acing but just as clearly failing. He centered his weight on his heels,
which meant it would take him at least a second and a half to remove his weapon from his shoulder holster and pivot into a
shooter's stance. He would have been dead twice over by the time
that happened. He wasn't a threat.

The man's partner, though, was a different story. Ash didn't
know his name, but in his internal monologue, he called him the
Hulk. They had run into each other about a year earlier, after Ash
shot the man's son in the chest and shoulder during an investigation. His son lived, but the Hulk didn't seem to be the forgiving
sort. He stood at least six-five and had to be pushing three hundred
pounds. Someone that big could take a lot of damage before going
down, and Ash doubted his department-issue, forty-caliber Glock
would cut it.

He slid his hand from the firearm inside his jacket to his side
and closed the gate to his cedar fence before stepping deeper into
the yard. As soon as he did, he spotted the real threat. Konstantin
Bukoholov. The skin on Bukoholov's neck was loose and jaun-
diced, and fresh liver spots marked his hands. His eyes were as Ash

remembered them, though: cold and unfeeling. The old man had tipped him off to a drug-smuggling ring operating out of a night-club in one of the city's suburbs a year ago. Ash investigated and ended up bringing down one of the largest drug suppliers in the re-gion; in the process, he unwittingly eliminated one of Bukoholov's biggest competitors and likely doubled the old man's market share. Why Bukoholov sat in his backyard now, Ash didn't know.

He crossed the lawn, eyeing the guards. Bukoholov sat at Ash's teak outdoor table under a cedar pergola. The table had been set with three coffee mugs, all of which held a thick, black liquid. Bukoholov stood as he approached and held his hand out as if he wanted to shake. Ash ignored it.

"What are you doing here?"

Bukoholov gestured at the chair opposite him. "I'm enjoying your wife's very interesting coffee. Please sit. We have business to discuss."

Very interesting was one way of describing Hannah's coffee. It was so black and acidic it could have doubled as drain cleaner. If Hannah had made Bukoholov and his men coffee, she must be okay.

He nodded toward the Hulk. "Tell the goon squad to go back to your car. Call it a good faith gesture."

Bukoholov barked an order, and the two men slipped through the gate, exiting the yard. Ash pulled out a chair and sat down.

"You look good, Detective Rashid."

Ash leaned back and crossed his arms. "What do you want?"

Bukoholov took a sip of coffee but dropped the cup as a fit of coughing wracked his body. Hannah's coffee had a tendency to do that to the unprepared. Ash remained silent as Bukoholov regained his composure and ability to speak.

He stared at his spilled drink. "Excuse me. Your wife's coffee is quite strong."

"Yes, it is. I'll ask you again, though. What do you want?"

Bukoholov tilted his head to the side and shrugged. He managed to appear almost grandfatherly.

"It's always business with you, Detective. You should learn how to make small talk. We haven't seen each other in almost a year, and yet you dive right into business. How is a friend supposed to react to that?"

"We're not friends. We worked on a project once, and I've regretted it ever since. That project is now over, as is this conversation. Get out of my yard."

Bukoholov held up his hands in a placating gesture. He closed his eyes. "Just give me a moment," he said. "I want to talk to you about a job. You need to hear what I have to say."

Ash leaned forward. His eyes felt dry, and he wanted to blink, but he forced them to stay open. A shiver traveled up his spine as a late-fall breeze sent leaves skittering across the blue stone patio.

"I've already got a job, Mr. Bukoholov. A good one."

At least he had been truthful about part of that statement. Ash was the highest ranking sworn officer assigned to the investigative unit of Indianapolis's prosecutor's office. In most units, Ash's status as detective sergeant would make him a supervisory officer with privileges and responsibilities in accord with his rank. His actual unit was so small and specialized, though, that rank rarely mattered; everyone simply did whatever the prosecuting attorneys needed. It was a good job, usually. The pay was steady, and the work was interesting and varied. But with an election coming up, things were changing, and not for the better.

"This is a special sort of job. At four this afternoon, there was a car accident about two miles from here. A woman was killed. Did you see it on the news yet?"

Ash shook his head.

"It was a hit-and-run," Bukoholov continued. "The woman who was hit died on the way to the hospital."

"We'll pray for her family," said Ash, glancing at his gate. "If that's all you came to tell me, you can leave now."

"The woman's name was Cassandra Johnson. She had a daughter named Lisa. I believe you know them both."

Ash blinked several times, sure that he had misheard him.

"Cassandra and Lisa Johnson?"

"I believe that's what I said."

Ash felt as if he had just been slapped in the face. Lisa was his daughter's best friend. They rode the same bus; they played T-ball together; they had sleepovers. They were together so often in the summer that it felt as if he had a third kid; Lisa even called him Uncle Ash. Hannah and Cassandra, while perhaps not as close as their daughters, talked regularly and went to the same all-women's yoga class. Bukoholov stared at him knowingly.

"Is Lisa okay?"

"I'm sure she's fine."

Ash inhaled deep enough that he could feel his chest rise. Indianapolis wasn't generally big enough to have organized crime like Chicago or New York; instead, it had loosely affiliated gangs, most of which came and went after their leaders killed each other in disputes over women or turf. Bukoholov was the closest thing the city had to a real crime boss, and he wouldn't risk being in a detective's backyard without damn good reason.

"Why are you really here?"

Bukoholov smiled. "I have only the best of intentions, I assure you."

"Bullshit. Get out of my yard."

Instead of leaving, Bukoholov reached into his jacket. Instinctively, Ash reached into his own and pulled out his firearm. He rested it on the table, a finger hovering over the trigger guard.

"Carefully reconsider your next move," said Ash. "I want to see your hands right now."

Bukoholov did as he was told and pulled his arm back, exposing a brick of hundred-dollar bills in his hand. He dropped the money onto the table and pulled his hands back slowly, showing his palms as if he had nothing to hide.

"For any expenses you may come across in your investigation."

Ash knew detectives in the narcotics squad who could look at a bundle of money and estimate its value to within a couple hundred bucks without batting an eye. Stacks of cash were just another part of their world. Ash didn't live in that world, though. He crossed his arms, trying not to stare.

"Take your money and get out of my yard."

Bukoholov stared at him for a moment, but then broke eye contact and sighed audibly. "I'm sorry we couldn't come to an arrangement," he said, pushing himself upright. "I'm sure someone will eventually discover what happened to her."

"Get your money and get out of my yard."

Bukoholov waved him off before turning to leave. "Put it in your kids' college savings accounts. You need it more than me."

Ash followed him out of the yard with his eyes before taking out his cell phone. He didn't trust Bukoholov, but the old man didn't make a habit of lying to him. Something was going on. He searched through his contact list for Cassandra Johnson's cell number. Her phone rang six times before going to voice mail.

"Hi, Cassandra, this is Ash Rashid. When you get this message, can you call me back either on my cell phone or at the house? Nothing is wrong, but it's important that you contact Hannah or me as soon as you can. I'd really appreciate it."

As soon as Ash finished that call, he called Cassandra's home number and left a similar message when no one picked up. It was probably a waste of everyone's time, but he also called IMPD's dispatcher and asked if there had been any accidents near Cassandra's home. The dispatcher hadn't heard of any, but Ash requested she send a squad car by Cassandra's house for a resident safety check anyway. No one would go in the house without cause, but officers would knock on the door and peer in a few windows to see if they could find anything untoward inside. Hopefully Cassandra and Lisa went out somewhere and left her cell phone at home.

With his immediate concerns quelled somewhat, Ash picked up the money from the table. Fifty one-hundred-dollar bills. As much as his family needed it, he'd sooner beg than accept a gift from Bukoholov; his money was dirty no matter how many times he washed it. He holstered his firearm before slipping the bundle of money into the inside pocket of his sport coat. If nothing else, the food bank at his mosque would have a nice donation.

Inside the house, Hannah stood at the sink with a cast-iron skillet in one hand and a green sponge in the other. She smiled at him as he walked through the door, a loose pink scarf covering her hair and neck. Its religious implications aside, Hannah said wearing the hijab around men other than Ash or her father made her feel comfortable in her own skin. She didn't have to worry about strange men hitting on her or staring at her. That was worth well more than a yard or two of silk.

"Look what I drew, *Baba*."

Ash mouthed hello to his wife before sitting across from his daughter at their breakfast table. As far as he could tell, Megan had drawn an abstract.

"That's a beautiful drawing," he said. "When you're done, we'll hang it on the fridge."

"It's our house," she said.

Now that he knew what it was, Ash saw the resemblance. Megan had drawn a series of brown squares with amorphous green shapes in front. Much like their actual home, Megan's roof sloped unnaturally to one side and her bushes had branches that veered off in every direction. He kissed her forehead and told her that her drawing was very realistic before walking toward his wife at the sink.

"You want me to take over?" he asked, nodding toward a pile of dirty dishes.

"No, I'll finish," said Hannah. "Are those men outside coming back?"

"No."

"Good," she said, pulling the scarf from her head. Her straight black hair was pulled back into a lopsided bun, exposing the nape of her neck. "Who were they?"

Ash didn't say anything for a moment as he considered his response. He never liked lying to his wife, and not just because it was a sin. She put up with him, she loved him, and she stayed with him, despite his faults. She deserved the truth; it was as simple as that. At the same time, he didn't want to upset her without cause. Bukoholov, as bad as he was, would never hurt a cop's family. The attention wouldn't be good for business. On balance, it seemed that a white lie in this situation was the best approach.

"It was a couple of guys from work. They wanted to ask me about a case."

Hannah nodded and stared out the window as if she were watching the conversation replay itself. "And what did that man hand you?"

Ash coughed and shifted on his feet. "Some money, but it's not for us. I'm going to give it to charity."

Hannah dropped her sponge and set down the dish she had been scrubbing. She put her hands on the edge of the sink and leaned forward, keeping her gaze riveted on the window. "Why couldn't he donate the money himself?"

On a lot of levels, Ash understood her trepidation. Hannah may not have known Bukoholov, but she still carried the scars—both literal and figurative—from the last job Ash had done for him. He leaned in, catching a whiff of the rose oil she had put on earlier that day.

"When was the last time you talked to Cassandra?"

"Yesterday, I think. Her car's in the shop, so she asked me to pick her up for yoga tonight at the YMCA. You didn't answer my question."

Ash nodded toward the back patio. "That man just told me Cassandra may have been in a car accident. Before you get worried, I called my dispatcher, and she didn't have any records of it. I also tried to call Cassandra but couldn't get in touch with her. Our guest wants me to look into things. The money was a bribe."

Hannah looked confused. "Why would he tell you Cassandra was in an accident if she wasn't?"

"I don't know, but I plan to find out."

"Maybe we should go by her house right now and see."

"I already sent a squad car," said Ash. "If they find anything, they'll give me a call."

"Did he say anything about Lisa?"

"He said she's probably fine. I'm concerned that Cassandra's not answering her phone, though. Would she leave her cell at home if she was on a date?"

Hannah's voice faltered. "I...I don't know," she said. "She's not seeing anyone, though. I think she would have told me if she had a date. I live vicariously through her."

"Okay," said Ash, feeling his worry start to build. "Could you make me a sandwich? I'm going to go back into work and see what I can find out."

"Sure," she said, nodding. "Can you check on Kaden while I do that?"

"Of course," he said. "And I'm sure everything's okay with Cassandra. I'm just going to follow up."

"Yeah. Okay."

Ash squeezed his wife's shoulder before walking to his son's nursery. Kaden slept in his crib, his arms raised above his head victoriously as if he had just kicked the game-winning field goal in the Super Bowl. His skin was light brown, and his brown eyes sparkled whenever he smiled. He was a good baby, and he seemed to like his father. At least he had stopped peeing on him whenever he changed his diaper.

Since Kaden was asleep, Ash stayed outside the room, watching. After finding out that Hannah was pregnant with a boy, Ash had converted his old home office into a nursery by replacing the dingy carpet with oak hardwood and painting the walls a cheery, pastel yellow. Hannah had then drawn bumblebees near the ceiling. Islamic tradition was to sacrifice a pair of animals and have a party for friends and family when a boy is born. Since Ash was reasonably sure his neighbors would object if he slaughtered a pair of sheep on the front lawn, he and Hannah had instead donated money to Heifer International. Heifer used the money to purchase bees for poor families in Africa; Ash thought the décor fitting.

He watched his son for another minute before joining his wife and daughter in the kitchen again. It was time for *salat al-Maghrib*, dusk prayer, but nobody made a move to grab their prayer mats from the living room. Ash's mind was focused on his conversation with Bukoholov. At any given time, half a dozen government agencies had open investigations on the old man, and he still managed to conduct his business with relative impunity. He didn't get that power by nosing into other people's business, and he didn't act without thinking first. He expected to get something from his trip to the Rashid household. What, though, Ash didn't know, and that left him unsettled.

As soon as Hannah handed him a sandwich, he kissed her and hugged his daughter good-bye for the evening. In general, traffic accidents were handled by uniformed patrol officers from the various precinct houses around town, but hit-and-runs that ended in death or grave injury went straight to the homicide squad. Ash had spent six years in Homicide, so he knew a good number of the detectives assigned to the unit; hopefully someone would talk to him. He ate his sandwich on the drive but stayed in his car for a moment upon parking and called the dispatcher for an update on the safety check he had requested for Cassandra's place. A pair of officers had swung by the house, but no one answered the door. Unfortunately, without signs of forced entry or other problems, that was all they could do. He'd go by later to see if he could find anything himself, but in the meantime, he'd try another angle.

Ash left the car and went to the homicide squad's floor. As he should have expected at that time in the evening, the office was deserted. He took a few tentative steps inside and weaved his way around desks and stacks of cardboard file boxes, hoping to find someone but knowing he probably wouldn't.

When his suspicions came true, Ash took the elevator to the lobby and walked to the watch sergeant's desk. IMPD's headquarters had been built when public buildings were a source of community pride. Its white marble floors and granite walls had seen more than their share of abuse, but it was hard to deny the craftsmanship of the ornate crown moldings and perfectly straight joints on the floor. For all its aesthetic appeal, though, it was hardly adequate for a modern police department. Deep cracks in the granite walls ran from the floor to the ceiling, and the entire first floor smelled like laundry that had sat soaking in a washing machine for several nights. Ash didn't envy the officers who spent considerable amounts of time there.

He coughed, getting the attention of both the sergeant behind the front desk and a couple who were sitting and holding hands in the lobby. Ash didn't recognize him, but the sergeant looked to be in his late fifties or early sixties. Police work was taxing, both mentally and physically, so a lot of officers hoped to retire by that age. About a decade ago, that was a real possibility for a lot of people. But now that the world's economy was in an extended and seemingly never-ending slump, more and more officers kept plugging away until they were pushed out the door at sixty-five. At least those guys would have a pension and Social Security to fall back on; the way the economy was going, Ash and his family wouldn't even have that.

He leaned against the counter. "You got a minute?"

"If it's important."

Ash removed the badge from his belt and held it up. "It is important. I'm Detective Sergeant Ashraf Rashid, and I'm an investigator with the prosecutor's office. I've got a couple of questions that you might be able to help me with."

The sergeant slowly closed the magazine he had been reading before lacing his fingers together and leaning forward so he was only about a foot from Ash's face. Ash glanced at his nametag. Robert Doyle.

"And for what reason are you gracing me with your presence, Detective Rashid?"

It smelled as if the sergeant had eaten something with garlic for dinner. Ash forced himself to smile and took a quick step back, glad for the fresh air. "Have you heard anything about a woman named Cassandra Johnson tonight?" he asked, clipping his badge to his belt. "She may be a hit-and-run victim on the north side."

Doyle broke eye contact and picked his magazine back up. "If she was a hit-and-run, patrol has it."

"Someone told me she died at the scene, so Homicide might have it. I'm trying to find out what happened. Cassandra is a family friend."

Doyle stared back with a pair of dull, expressionless eyes. "Since someone told you about her, why don't you talk to him and stop wasting my time?"

Doyle was evidently quite a charmer. Had Megan been so charming, he would have called her Miss Grumpy Pants and made her sit on the naughty chair until her attitude improved. He doubted Doyle would respond well to the same sort of treatment.

"I did consider it, but I haven't had the opportunity yet. When'd your shift start?"

Doyle stared at him a moment, unblinking. Eventually, he must have figured out that Ash wasn't going to leave because he sighed and closed his eyes.

"Six. Anything else?"

"If there had been a call at four, would you have heard about it?"

"It depends."

Ash waited for Doyle to continue. He didn't.

"On?"

"Any number of things. Look, Detective, I don't know anybody named Cassandra Johnson. We didn't get a call about her, and I didn't hear about a hit-and-run. I don't have any clue what you're talking about, and I've got things to do." He opened his magazine again. "So unless there's anything else?"

Ash held up his hands in front of him, palms toward the desk. "That's it. Thanks for all your help."

"Anytime."

The sergeant had buried his face in his magazine. Doyle must have been on a complex case; *Sports Illustrated* didn't often make it into investigations. The lobby had room for twenty or thirty people, but it didn't feel very welcoming. He walked through the front doors and exited onto the street. The night was cold, and the street was wet from a downpour earlier that evening. Thursdays weren't big nights downtown, so the area was empty save the occasional passing car.

Ash buttoned his jacket and rubbed his arms for warmth, considering his options. There were two or three bars within walking distance, and chances were high that at least one would be quiet enough for him to make a couple of calls from. He considered going but decided against it. Even a quiet bar would be more distraction than he needed. Besides, he had been trying to stay out of bars after someone from his mosque spotted him walking into one about a month ago. That had been difficult to talk his way out of. Islam forbids the consumption of alcohol; unfortunately, drinking was one of the few activities that allowed Ash to sleep soundly at night and forget about the things he saw at work.

He stepped into the glow of a nearby streetlight and thumbed through his cell phone's directory until he found the entry for IMPD's dispatcher. News sometimes took a while to trickle through a bureaucracy, so if Cassandra had been in an accident, it was possible that Doyle just hadn't heard about it. The first officer on the scene might have even skipped the regular channels and called the homicide squad directly. Patrol officers weren't supposed to do that, and it screwed up normally clear lines of communication, but it did occasionally happen.

The dispatcher picked up after two rings and transferred Ash's call to the watch sergeant at the Northeastern Precinct house. Unfortunately, she knew as little as Sergeant Doyle. In the off chance the calls had gone through them, he called the two precincts bordering the Northeastern Precinct as well but got the same story both times. Nobody had heard of Cassandra.

Ash paced under the light, considering his next move. Bukoholov might have lied to him about the accident, but Ash couldn't figure out what he would get out of that. Moreover, despite having fewer moral scruples than most of the men and woman on Indiana's death row, Bukoholov hadn't ever lied to Ash before. Something else was going on, and he needed to find out what. He dialed the gangster's number and waited through two rings for him to pick up. Ash spoke before Bukoholov could.

"I just asked around, and nobody's heard of Cassandra Johnson. Tell me what you know."

Bukoholov paused. "I'm fairly old and I know a lot of things, so that may take a while."

"Cute. Tell me what you know about Cassandra Johnson."

"I've already told you everything you need to know."

"No, you haven't. No one has heard about the accident, and I can't find Cassandra. You know more than you're telling me. Where is she?"

"By this point, I would presume she's at the morgue."

"No, she's not. If she was killed in a hit-and-run, my department would know about it and they would have told me."

"I assure you, Detective, the accident did occur, and Ms. Johnson is, unfortunately, deceased. If you're half the investigator I think you are, you'll find out why. Just follow the evidence."

Bukoholov may have been a criminal, but he had his finger on the city's pulse better than anyone alive. When something in town was rotten, he knew it even if he wasn't always willing to share his information.

"What's really going on here?"

"You need to find out on your own. It will be better that way."

"Better for who?"

"You'll find out that, too."

"Okay," said Ash, hoping his growing frustration didn't seep into his voice. "If you're not going to tell me anything else, tell me this. If I keep going, what am I going to step into?"

Bukoholov chuckled. "You wouldn't believe me if I told you. If you're still stuck in a couple of days, give me a call. Otherwise, rely on your instincts and you'll do fine."

The Russian hung up before Ash could say anything else. Rely on your instincts. Follow the evidence. It wasn't the most helpful advice he had ever received.

Ash paced the empty sidewalk, thinking. If Cassandra were dead, her body would still be around. Finding that would answer some of his questions. More pressing than that, though, Lisa would still be around. He needed to make sure someone was taking care of her. He thumbed through his phone's contact list until he found the home telephone number of Julie Sims, the assistant director of Marion County's Department of Child Services.

The phone rang twice before she picked up.

"Julie, this is Ash Rashid. I need a favor. I've heard rumors that a family friend has been in a car accident, and I want to find out if you guys have her daughter."

Julie rattled what sounded like a drawer full of silverware.

"I'm at home. Did you call the information line?"

"Why would I need to call the information line when I've got good friends like you?"

Julie grunted. Good friends do that sort of thing when they're asked for favors.

"I guess my date with Ben and Jerry can wait, then. I'll see if she's in the system. What's her name?"

"Lisa Johnson. She's Megan's best friend."

"Give me five minutes."

Ash slipped his phone back into his pocket after hanging up. It was cold, but he was so lost in thought that he barely felt it. Julie called back within two minutes. A uniformed patrol officer had brought Lisa in a few hours ago, but Child Services hadn't placed her with a family yet. She agreed to a meeting if Ash met her downtown; he didn't need to think before saying yes.

As soon as he hung up, he glanced at his watch. It was a little before eight, and Julie would take at least twenty minutes to drive into town. For the second time that night, he considered going to a bar, and for the second time, practical concerns overruled his desire. He couldn't show up to the Child Services office with liquor on his breath. Instead, he went by a diner and grabbed a cup of scorched coffee and a slice of cherry pie. Neither improved his mood, but at least they distracted him for a while.

At the appointed time, he met Lisa and Julie in the Child Services office. Lisa brightened when she saw him, and he forced himself to smile in response. If her mom was dead, she evidently hadn't been told. Lisa had dark hair and dark brown skin. She had been Megan's best friend since the day they met almost three years ago. Now they spent more time in the principal's office than any other kids in school. They were both good girls at heart, just too rambunctious for their own good. Megan got that from him, and if he was any guide, they'd grow out of it.

"Hi, Uncle Ash."

"Hi, sweetheart. I'm going to talk to Miss Sims, but I'll be right back, okay?"

Lisa nodded, so Julie led her to a nearby playroom with a two-way mirror for observation. Once the door was shut, Ash slouched against the wall and put his hands in his pockets, one eye on Lisa and one eye on Julie.

"You guys have a file on her yet?"

Julie nodded and opened the tabbed manila folder she was holding.

"An officer brought her in at approximately six this evening. She's six years old and weighs fifty-three pounds. We don't have her medical records yet, but we ran her through Riley Children's Hospital. The attending physician said she looked healthy and couldn't find any signs of abuse or malnutrition. Lisa said she's not on any medication, but we'll check to make sure."

Ash nodded. It was nice to hear that she was healthy, but the rest was background information he already knew.

"What do you have on her mom?"

Julie's lips moved as she scanned the form. "My information says she died in a car accident, but IMPD had her house on a regular rotation. She was thirty-two years old at the time of her death, and according to our files, she had a history of mental illness. I have a report from a patrol officer requesting we send somebody by the house to check on things because he suspected Cassandra was manic and posed a threat to her daughter. I don't think we had time to follow up yet."

Ash narrowed his eyes and dropped his chin. "Are you sure you have the right file?"

Julie nodded.

"Unfortunately, yes. It looks like Lisa's mom hit the trifecta. Drug use, mania, and probable prostitution while her daughter was at school. If we had the manpower, we would have pulled her out of the house months ago."

Ash straightened and crossed his arms. "How old is this information?"

Julie skimmed the file and then shook her head before looking at him again. "There's no date listed."

"Something's not right," said Ash, turning his attention to Lisa again. "Cassandra was a good mother. She wasn't a drug user, and she sure as hell wasn't a prostitute. You might want to double-check to see that you have the right file." He paused. "Has anyone told Lisa what's going on?"

"Not yet."

Ash considered his options. Lisa was surrounded by strangers and probably scared out of her mind. It wasn't just unfair; it was cruel. He didn't know what the county's policy was in that situation, but he knew what it felt like to be scared and alone. He looked at Julie.

"Give me five minutes. I'm going to tell her what's going on. I'll be right back."

"Hold on just a second," said Julie, putting her hand on his chest. "We have a counselor on staff who will talk to her in the morning. That's how we do things when a parent isn't around."

"And by *counselor* you mean a stranger, right?"

"By *counselor* I mean someone with the training to deal with a traumatized child."

"With all due respect, Julie, I've known Lisa for almost half her life. She calls me Uncle Ash and my wife Aunt Hannah. She doesn't need to talk to a stranger with a degree in psychology; she needs someone who will give her a hug and tell her that everything will be okay."

"And what happens if everything isn't okay? We need to prepare her for what's going to happen next in her life. Besides, we haven't even talked to her father yet. Don't you think he might want to tell his daughter what happened?"

"He's serving a life sentence in the Wabash Valley Correctional

Facility for killing an off-duty police officer at a nightclub. After losing his last appeal, your department petitioned for and won termination of his parental rights. I was Lisa's advocate during the hearing. She's never met him, and God willing, she never will. If that's not in your file, it should be."

"I forgot you were a lawyer," she said, taking a step back and flipping through the contents of her folder. When she looked up again, her gaze wasn't quite as sharp. As much as he cared about Lisa, though, Julie was probably right. It wasn't his place to tell her that her mom had just died. That should come from a real family member.

"Lisa has a grandma on the West Coast. She flies in whenever she can afford the airfare. If anyone should tell Lisa about her mom, I think it should be her," said Ash. "They're a close family, so she'll probably be the one who gets custody anyway."

Julie stared at Lisa through the two-way mirror. "Where on the West Coast is she?"

"Seattle. I'll fly her in if I have to."

Julie's nostrils flared. "That should be fine. We can let her do it."

It may not have been what Ash wanted, but it was still a victory of sorts. He breathed a little easier.

"Do you have housing lined up for her for the next few days yet?"

"We'll put her in a girls' home until her grandma arrives."

"How about you let me take her home?" Julie started to protest immediately, but Ash spoke over her. "Hannah and I are registered foster parents, so we're already in your system. We take kids on an emergency basis, and this sounds like an emergency."

At first, Ash thought Julie would fight, but she gave in. While she filled out the paperwork, he called his wife to arrange things at home. Hannah didn't even miss a beat in offering to put Lisa up for as long as needed. Ash went into the playroom and told Lisa that she would be staying with Megan for a few days. Since Lisa didn't know about her mom, she thought it was a rare Thursday-night sleepover at a friend's house. It almost broke Ash's heart to see how excited she was. After twenty minutes of paperwork, he buckled her into the back of his cruiser and drove home. Megan met them at the door, and the girls immediately ran to the living room where Hannah had set up a cartoon about a princess and a frog. The girls would probably fall asleep in the middle, but it would keep them occupied until they did. Hannah stayed in the kitchen.

"What happened?"

Hannah had been able to hold back most of her emotion when Megan and Lisa were around, but her eyes were growing red now.

"I don't know yet. I still don't have any confirmation of anything, so I'm going to go back to work and see what else I can find out."

The girls giggled loud enough that he could hear them all the way from the back door.

"Come back as soon as you can."

"I will."

Ash kissed her before stepping out. Rather than drive to his office, he drove to Cassandra and Lisa's house. The windows were dark, and the front door was locked. He knocked hard and rang the doorbell, but as expected, no one answered. He was alone but for the crickets. On his way back to the car, he pulled out his cell phone and found the number for the coroner's office. That's when he got his first break; the morgue didn't have a Cassandra Johnson, but they did have a Jane Doe who matched her description. The victim of a purported hit-and-run, she had significant trauma to her chest, shoulders, and head. It fit the story Bukoholov and Julie Sims had told him.

He drove over. The coroner's office was housed in a two-story brick building south of downtown near the White River. As soon as he went inside, Ash covered his nose. No matter how many deaths he investigated, he could never get used to the smell. Dr. Hector Rodriguez met him in the lobby and gave Ash a moment to throw on a surgical smock before leading him to the refrigerated vault where the bodies were stored.

Ash could see the outline of a petite woman's body beneath a sheet on an exam table at the far end of the room. As soon as Dr. Rodriguez pulled the sheet from her face, Ash recognized Cassandra. The blood had already begun pooling beneath her, leaving her face pale, but it was definitely her. According to Indiana law, only an immediate family member could provide an official visual identification, but Dr. Rodriguez wrote Cassandra's name down anyway as a provisional ID.

Cassandra's mother or sister would have to come in and do the official identification later. On television, that was a relatively easy process. A victim's spouse or immediate family member would stand at a window while a technician pulled back a sheet covering the deceased person's face. On TV, a simple nod of the head sufficed. In real life, it was harder, more invasive than that. Cassandra's mother would have to give details. She'd have to identify tattoos, scars, birthmarks, and other unique marks that Cassandra might have had. She'd have to stick around the morgue for a while and possibly identify her clothing as well as fill out copious amounts of paperwork. It was a lot more than a casual glance, and it caused a lot more pain than anyone deserved.

When he got back to his car, Ash stayed in the parking lot and allowed the reality of the situation to set in. Cassandra and Lisa were as close to his family as they could be without being related. This was going to be hard. Instead of driving home immediately, he put the car in gear and drove until he found an open liquor store. Practical concerns didn't hamper him anymore, so he bought a pint of bourbon and drove to a small city park about a mile from his house. He started with a small sip, but that turned into a mouthful and then a second in short order. After that, he rested the bottle in his lap and closed his eyes, praying that the world would be different when he opened them but knowing it wouldn't.

Ten minutes after parking, he screwed the cap back on the bottle and drove home. The girls were in pajamas now, but they were still up and watching TV. Hannah had her arm around both of them. Ash must have been wearing his emotions because she closed her eyes and inhaled deeply as soon as she saw him.

"Hi, *Baba*," said Megan, looking at him for the first time since he came in. "You look funny."

"I'm tired, honey," he said. "It's late."

"Why don't you girls brush your teeth?" said Hannah. "It's time to get ready for bed."

Lisa and Megan dutifully slipped off the pullout sofa and made their way to the bathroom in the hallway. Hannah stared at him, her eyes growing glassy.

"She's gone?"

Ash swallowed and nodded. "Yeah."

She inhaled deeply as a tear slid down her face.

"We're out of toothpaste, *Ummi*."

Hannah stayed seated for a moment, but she eventually got up to help the girls. Ash took the opportunity to slip into his bedroom's en suite bathroom to brush his teeth and cover the smell of bourbon on his breath. When he finished, Hannah was in the bedroom, crying softly. Ash didn't say anything, but he held her and she cried on his shoulder until the girls went back to the living room.

Hannah went to bed a little after midnight, but Ash stayed up. For some reason, Megan and Lisa both liked professional wrestling and were watching a match with rapt attention when he got back to the living room. Thankfully, they weren't boys or they'd be reenacting everything the wrestlers did; as it was, Ash had his hands full telling them not to repeat the more inappropriate phrases the wrestlers used. He probably should have turned it off, but he didn't have the heart. Lisa had enough rough days ahead of her; she deserved another carefree night with a friend.